A Matter of Loyalty

For Ray – Kerry

A Matter of Loyalty

SANDRA HOWARD

with every good love

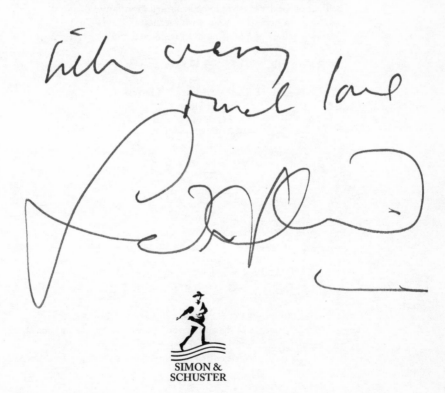

SIMON &
SCHUSTER

London · New York · Sydney · Toronto

A CBS COMPANY

First published in Great Britain by Simon & Schuster UK Ltd, 2009
A CBS COMPANY

Copyright © Sandra Howard, 2009

1 3 5 7 9 10 8 6 4 2

Simon & Schuster UK Ltd
1st Floor
222 Gray's Inn Road
London WC1X 8HB

www.simonsays.co.uk

Simon & Schuster Australia
Sydney

A CIP catalogue record for this book
is available from the British Library

Hardback ISBN: 978-1-84737-234-5
Trade paperback ISBN: 978-1-84737-235-2

Typeset in Garamond by M Rules
Printed in the UK by CPI Mackays, Chatham ME5 8TD

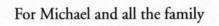

For Michael and all the family

Acknowledgements

My thanks, first and foremost, must go to James Davenport for his fount of eclectic knowledge in all matters technical, nautical and geographical that has been such a wonderful boon. Enormous thanks, too, to Naweed Khan for his humour, patience and kindness in dealing so good-naturedly with my many nosy queries, and also to Sayeeda Warsi for sparing precious time to help.

And no lesser thanks to Alan Judd and Steve Delabecque for their illuminating insights into the ways and mores of surveillance and counterterrorism, and also to Elizabeth Buchanan, and to Steve Hare. A special thank you to John Entwistle for invaluable help in guiding me around Kendal and the Lakes, to John Wolfe for his sage medical expertise, to nurse Wendy, far more warmly responsive than the nurse in my story, and to Jonathan Holborow for answering persistent questions about editorship with unfailing good humour.

I am grateful to Adrian Lee at Life Works, who explained the clinical programmes and science-based therapies they offer to help people with an alcohol addiction. Their facility near Woking is a caring, compassionate place to begin the long journey to recovery.

I would like to thank Ed Husain for writing *The Islamist* and Shiv Malik for his readably informative, in-depth articles that have, along with others, done much to shape my thinking.

Without my stout-hearted agent, Michael Sissons, and inspirational editor, Suzanne Baboneau, who sees all the potholes and steers me round them, I would be lost. I can never say a big enough thank you. Nor to Michael, Sholto, Nick and Larissa for their constant, loving, supportive help – whatever they've had to put up with.

Once did I breathe another's breath . . . And in my mistress move . . . Once I was not mine own at all . . . and then I was in love . . .

anon.

. . . In thy face I see, The map of honour, truth, and loyalty:

William Shakespeare (*Henry VI Part II*)

A Matter of Loyalty

CHAPTER 1

A gale was blowing. The last tenacious leaves were being torn from the copper beech and maples in the garden, from the horse chestnuts in the lane, the cherry trees over the yew hedge in the church car park. Leaves everywhere, floating, whirling past the kitchen window. They made Victoria think for a moment of a wartime sky filled with parachuting soldiers and she felt almost tearful. But the house was comfortingly snug and warm.

It was in the village of Ferndale, near Southampton. A small mellowed 1830s house that would have creaked and let in draughts had William not modernized and insulated it, extended and stretched it outwards and upwards to its rafters. Just as cars revealed much about their owners, Plumstead House spoke eloquently of his passion for space and light.

She had married him knowing his innermost thoughts and feelings, but not his living habits. Two people in the public eye, she, a government minister and Member of Parliament for Southampton East, he, editor of *The Post,* a national newspaper; they'd hardly met more than a dozen times in the nine long months of their love affair. It had been a constant media cat and mouse game before everything was explosively blown apart. Then had come the immense emotional upheaval, the private pain of finally extricating themselves from other loyalties.

Two years on, with all her new responsibilities, life was quite frightening but William was in it now, happily, tenderly, sparringly, combatively – in it full time.

He looked up from the Sunday newspapers. 'You're deep in thought. What is it?'

'Oh, nothing much; you, the gale. I know you won't be going into the office for high-sided vehicle dramas and upended trees, but there is all this stuff about Peter Barnes in the papers . . . It isn't going anywhere, he'll stay Foreign Secretary, he and the PM are intertwined. Can't you be more original and stay above it all?'

'The paper can handle fallen trees.' William grinned, making clear that while he wasn't going into the office he had every intention of zapping Peter Barnes – who deserved all he got, the disloyal shit – in thick black headlines in tomorrow's *Post*.

There was always a government Cassius, Victoria thought, feeling as irritated by the Foreign Secretary as if with an itchy rash. He took out his fury with *The Post* on her.

William seldom went into the office on Sundays now. He had done so quite often during his first marriage and it was hard not to feel a little smug about his changed routine. Strange to think he'd edited the paper for just on a decade; that was quite a landmark achievement, a triumph even, in the fast-moving dog-eating-dog media world.

She thought about his lunch on Friday with his South African proprietor, Oscar Bluemont. There had been a venture capitalist along whom Oscar was keen to impress and William had suddenly found himself elevated to editor-in-chief. 'First I'd heard of it,' he said dryly. 'You'd think he'd have got round to sharing that with me.'

His proprietor was an eccentric with a keen business head, a cool couple of billion, a svelte blonde wife and several ex-ones, too. Victoria was fond of him. He was a quirky little gnome-like character who pranced about on spindly legs like a puppet and he had a definite soft spot for her. He had been loyally supportive all through the painful publicity over the affair – when William was making news instead of reporting it. But then he hadn't wanted to lose a first-rate editor.

Oscar had just won a bidding war for a failing Sunday newspaper, *The Dispatch*, and she hoped William's new title didn't mean he'd be overseeing that as well. He already did a weekly current-affairs programme on television, *The Firing Line*, on top of editing *The Post*. It was more than enough.

'Is Oscar going to do something to mark your ten years?' she asked, knowing how much the proprietor loved lavish parties. 'He's here all this month, isn't he, till December?'

'Don't! He's talked of nothing else. I've insisted any sort of bash has to be at the office, though, and kept internal and contained or he'd ask a thousand or so of his closest chums along and ensure it was in every diary column – and all saying it's been ten years too long already.' William grinned and went back to his paper.

He was concentrating intently on an article and it reminded her of first meeting him only three years ago, a tall, dishevelled editor with a fearsome reputation whose arresting stare had been entirely focused on her. It had thrown her completely off course. He'd been forty-eight then and looked his age; his face deeply grooved, the careless unhealthy newspaper hours carved deep. He seemed no older now, though; he had taken all the knocks and professional strain and done all the hard living going.

It was time to get on. Breakfast needed clearing and nothing would be further from William's mind. He wasn't domesticated or a first-class cook like her ex-husband Barney, but there was a load to be shared – and never more so than now.

Three months of being Home Secretary and it didn't get any easier. There were policemen in the garden. They had installed two huts, one with high-tech equipment and another for resting up. Being guarded night and day, weekends as well, was a huge hideous intrusion, but she had to accept the need. A Special Branch detective was with her at all times when she was out and about. It was as much for the safety of others, they said: if she was a target then everyone round her was at risk as well.

With privacy in such short supply Sundays were to be treasured. On Saturdays she was busy with her constituency surgery and William was often off to collect his two just-teenage girls. He returned them on Sunday nights, on the way to London, trailing back for the long hours of the working week.

He had left Ursula, his wife of twenty years, walked out on his three children, Tom, Emma and Jessie. Victoria had felt consumed with guilt while never quite seeing herself as the other woman. Her feelings for William had been too powerful and deep. She had fought against them, broken off all contact, yet all the while been waiting, hoping, willing him to leave.

Who could say now, she thought with wry relief, that it had been so wrong? Ursula was living with Julian, a writer and antiquarian bookseller, whom she seemed to love with a far greater passion than anything she'd felt for William – for all the bitter hurt and accusations.

There was even Martha too, now, their wonderful pink peaceable baby with a solemn steady gaze who was adored by all.

Ursula was forty-five, three years older than Victoria, yet she was the one with a new child. It seemed rough justice – although Victoria knew that was an unjust thought even as it came to her.

Having a miscarriage, losing William's baby in the thick of their affair, had gouged so great a hole in her that nothing could fill it. No warm earth of passing time, no grass had grown over. Victoria carried her loss, she wore it like a baby-sling. It had been late in the pregnancy, the sex already determined, a boy. She thought of him being sucked out of her in all that warm wet blood, the tourniquet-like contractions. The lasting pain, though, had been emotional. At a stage when it had seemed too much to hope that William would leave Ursula, the baby had felt a part of him and uniquely theirs.

Her only other child, Nattie, had been sixteen at the time. Nattie had known about the affair, the pregnancy, the particular stresses with her father, Barney, and coped with it all. Nattie was a golden doted-on daughter and beautiful; everyone said so. Her face was open, gentle, smiling, trusting; men were a constant worry. Long fine hair, fair like her father's – Victoria's was dark – and wide amber eyes that glowed.

She was good friends with William's son, Tom, who was in his early twenties. They often came to Hampshire on the same weekend. Julian's 18-year-old son, James – who lived with his father now, together with Ursula and the girls – came too, occasionally. James's childhood had been in Africa; his mother was a Ugandan doctor whom Julian had always supported but never married. She had let her son come to England while doing his A-levels and he'd just got into Cambridge.

They were all in each other's slipstreams now, Victoria thought. Her life, like a fast flowing river, had hit rocks and thrashed about, but miraculously found its smooth new path. An unhappy marriage, Nattie her only child, and suddenly there were five offspring around at times, all variously connected and getting on fine. The constituency house had certainly needed to be stretched.

The roads were quite traffic-free on that filthy night, driving back to London. They talked little. Travelling with a police driver and a detective made it hard, but on the flipside it put pay to any marital eruptions and full-throated rows.

Rodney was on duty. Victoria liked him the best of the 'tecs, as they were called, the three detectives on the protection team. He was good-looking in a Kevin Spacey sort of a way and never tried too hard to be unobtrusive. Asked to join in a conversation he was always cheerfully forthright in his views.

A story running in all the Sunday papers about a trouble-making Islamist cleric got William going and he broke into the subdued atmosphere of the car. 'They use religion like a web, like flypaper, these fundamentalists,' he declared. 'Luring in susceptible students, distorting their faith. It's serious. We'll be demanding this guy's removal in the paper tomorrow and getting plenty of support, you can be sure.' Victoria shot him an impatient look; that stance could only make life harder and add to her workload.

'And they can always beat the system,' Rodney chipped in airily. 'They stand on their soapboxes stirring it up, seeking the destruction of the very country that gives them the freedoms they enjoy. They'd wipe out democracy, yet we're not allowed to infringe their so-called rights,' he finished, letting slip a very non-PC sneer.

Victoria fought back, feeling got at. 'But isn't that as it should be? We fought wars for freedom of speech; millions gave their lives. You've got extremists, sure, but don't forget the silent peaceful majority, Rodney; a lot more sympathizing Muslims might become militant if we start clamping down. It's a delicate balance.'

William, the police, they all wanted a tough-talking Home Secretary, but they should know by now she was no softy. After all those painful decisions taken in her last job at Health, all the bad press . . . They could give her a little credit for that.

A policeman was on guard as usual at their South London house, standing patiently in the paved front garden, half-hidden by two huge sentry-like camellia bushes. He was at the bottom of the front steps – still with the original Georgian black and white tiles that Victoria loved – that led up to the wide Oxford-blue front door.

They had bought the house in squatters' condition when William was still supporting Ursula. Polish builders and double-glazing had transformed it. On a busy main road, but shielded by a front garden wall and trellis, the house itself had symmetry, space and light. It was close to Parliament and *The Post* too, located in its tall tower, tight to the river on the South Bank. William's twelfth-floor office had a sensational view.

Rodney said his goodnights and the two armoured cars drove off, one of them the usual backup car. Victoria had work to finish and William set about making tea for the policeman on duty.

He would take up the morning's first editions then, always delivered to the door, and read in bed till she came upstairs. Climbing in beside him she would lift away the papers, lean across to turn off his light. He would intercept her hand and pull her on top of him, talking of love. He knew her needs, knew when to hurt, bite, scratch, pull, when to be gentle. He'd once said she had incredibly sensitive nipples and she had queried how he was such an authority on the subject and the extent of his research.

If he rolled her over, as he mostly did, he'd stretch out for the light so that neither had to do it later. It was a comfortingly physical end-of-weekend routine.

At something like five the next morning she felt William's toe. It brushed her calf, a cautious exploratory touch, and she sleepily took his outstretched hand.

'Did I wake you?'

Victoria considered that. 'No, it's okay.' She was already half-awake, thinking of the week ahead, one marathon after another, fraught meetings, questions in Parliament, even a state banquet at Buckingham Palace.

She turned and looked at William in the semi-dark. The clocks had only just gone back and despite the heavy cream curtains, the lifting sky outside was giving a hint and promise of morning. 'It's a bit rough,' she said, yawning, 'when a state banquet at the Palace is about my only chance of seeing you all week.'

'We were asked to a royal film premiere too, on Wednesday – the Countess of Wessex is going.' William squeezed her hand. 'It's the new Kidman film—'

'Same night? I suppose the Royals don't all have to show up at every banquet.'

'Are you deliberately missing the Kidman point? I've always wanted to meet her. A temp had accepted for us without a call to your office. I despair.' William paused a moment. 'How awake are you? Can I talk?'

'Sure.' She wondered what was coming.

'We're breeding terrorists, MI5 can only scratch the surface. I've just taken on an impressive young Muslim reporter – his stuff's sensitive and sharp, but twats like George are so suspicious they think he could be an activist mole. That's typical fucking George, but, from the tip-offs we get, the stories I could print, it's bad out there. People resent communities turning in on themselves. It's a grim scene.'

'British born, your new reporter?'

'Yes. Leeds, I think. I like him, Ahmed Khan. He's going places. He'll be editing *The Post* one of these days.'

'George is right to be cautious,' she said, thinking of the insidious infiltration of the universities, the turning of those bright young minds.

'George? Right? Give us a break.' William never let up on his poor deputy. 'I'm getting up,' he whispered, squeezing her hand again. 'It's thinking time. And you need some more sleep.'

She had an hour or so more in bed and dressing for the office felt much readier for the day ahead. Fit for department cock-ups, jealous colleagues, media snares – all the invisible wires that would be strung across her path through the week.

'Morning, Minister – good weekend?'

'Wonderfully quiet! And you, Tony?' Victoria asked, coming in through the outer office on the way to her own. 'Yours too, I hope?'

Her principal private secretary smiled. He was competent, pleasant, dutifully hardworking, though no match for Marty who'd filled that role in her very first job in government, three years ago, as Minister of Housing and Planning at DEFRA.

Victoria still had feelings of awe, walking into her vast ballroom

of an office. With its red slub sofa and chairs, oval mahogany conference table and cheering paintings the trappings were impressive
enough, but it was really a strategic war room where she fought her
corner and life-affecting decisions could be made.

The morning newspapers were all laid out and *The Post*'s predictable headline, 'Sack The Man!' brought a small smile. Peter
Barnes, the 'Snake-in-the-grass Foreign Secretary', was accused of
openly briefing against Number Ten and, in *The Post*'s eyes, should
be shown the door.

No chance, Victoria thought. The Prime Minister was a believer
in the better-inside-the-tent principle, he wasn't having any Cassiuses
on the backbenches hurtling killer-darts. She wished he would sack
Barnes. The Foreign Secretary was out to get her and knew his way
round Westminster, all the subtlest ways of doing her down.

They were late for the state banquet. Victoria's long white gloves had
gone missing, her fake diamond necklace wouldn't do up and she
couldn't wear her favourite dress because of an archaic code about
not wearing black in front of the Queen. And William wasn't even
home.

He came panting upstairs then and said all the right things about
her second-best burgundy dress. 'Can't we skip the whole thing and
be ill?' he grinned, wasting precious minutes kissing her. She waggled
her watch arm and tried to hurry him up with the whole fiddly rigmarole of dressing in white tie.

William succeeded with her necklace clasp, she gave up the hunt
for the gloves and they shot out of the house. Rodney had the car
doors standing open and the two heavy vehicles sped away. Over
Lambeth Bridge, down Horseferry Road, along Grosvenor Gardens:

Victoria was aware of a discreet rear blue light being on and suspected it was professional pride. It mattered, getting them there on time.

They swept in through the imposing Palace gates – no searching of her police-driven government car – and drew up at a more leisurely pace alongside the red-carpeted stone entrance steps under cover of the drive-in porch.

Hurrying up the palatial Grand Staircase past handsome ornate portraits of George III and Queen Charlotte, she whispered they were the last King and Queen of America; it was impossible, in that rarefied atmosphere, not to speak in a hush.

Footmen directed them along wide passages into the Picture Gallery where the paintings were by Rembrandt, Van Dyck, Rubens, Vermeer. The hundred and fifty or so guests were gathered there for drinks. A scattering of tiaras shimmered and more white-gloved footmen were circulating with trays. She and William took flutes of champagne and turned to speak to whoever was nearest, and in that long length of elegant hall it happened to be the Foreign Secretary, Peter Barnes.

His smile was sophisticated and easy. 'Short of copy this week, I see, William. Although a bit rich, don't you think, calling our excellent Prime Minister wet.' He was alluding slickly to *The Post*'s continued personal attacks while twisting the slant.

'On the contrary,' William said, smiling just as smoothly. 'These are important matters that have to be aired.' Victoria imagined the recharging of Barnes's vitriolic feelings and inwardly sighed.

A senior Palace dignitary touched her arm. The banquet was in honour of the Chinese President and as Foreign and Home Secretaries, she and Barnes, along with their spouses, were being invited into the Music Room to meet the royal party.

A military string band, the Welsh Guards, was playing in the Minstrel's Gallery as they joined the other guests in the State Ballroom. The long tables were sumptuously bedecked with gold plate and immense silver-gilt epergne centrepieces piled with pyramids of fruit. The flowers were spectacular, vast arrangements of deep-red velvety roses set in branching foliage of golds and browns.

They had been seated well apart. William stayed with her for a moment as they stood waiting for the royal party, chatting to the Chinese diplomat she would be next to.

'Better get to my place now,' William said, touching her arm.

As he turned to go Victoria saw him feel in his trouser pocket for a vibrating mobile. It shouldn't have been on; a couple of people gave very sniffy looks as he took it out. The paper would only call in an emergency, she thought, stiffening, imagining some new Home Office horror, before being distracted and filled with alarm by the sight of a white-faced official hurrying towards her.

They moved to a corner where they could talk more privately. 'There's been a bomb explosion in the West End, Minister,' he whispered, his face panic-stricken. He looked helpless without precedent or protocol. 'Eleven dead, I'm afraid. You may, um, want to leave now . . .?'

Eleven people dead . . . her stomach was lurching. There was a strange ringing sensation in her head. The scale of the injured didn't bear thinking about. It was her duty, her responsibility, to keep the public safe from terrorist bombs and she had failed.

'You'll explain?' Victoria said to the agonized official, outwardly calm as she looked round urgently for the nearest exit. Then, grabbing her bag from the table, she and William made a conspicuous dash, aware of the rustling disapproval, everyone's eyes following their path. The murmurings about bad form would be very short-lived.

The bomb had exploded in Leicester Square, in the cinema entrance where the royal premiere was taking place, right by the barriers with the pressed-up crowds.

Where were Nattie, Tom, James? Any one of them could have been out in the West End. Had they wandered by to glimpse the stars arriving for a premiere? Oh, God.

William had his mobile clamped to his ear and was relaying all he was being told. 'Seems the Countess was only seconds away. The film stars were all up on the first floor, though, waiting in the receiving line. They're in shock, but okay. It was the people at the barriers, photographers, police, and the suicide bomber, of course.'

Victoria was soon on her own mobile, listening as her Permanent Secretary, Sir Adam Childs, methodically, unflappably, gave her the same sickening details.

'Just leaving the Palace now, Adam,' she said breathlessly. 'I must get home quickly and change – you'll keep in constant touch?' They could have been just arriving at that cinema themselves. Had their names been on an acceptance list? William's office had said they were coming at first.

They called Nattie and Tom who were fine. James was, too.

In the car Victoria found it hard to speak for the lump in her throat. She pulled herself together and, turning to William, said flatly, 'I'm doing the television statement, the PM's leaving it to me. I'll need to get to a studio fast.'

'You'll have time, you'll be fine,' he assured, trying to give comfort.

The feeling of gagging stayed with her as she worked out what to say: inadequate words, but the only ones. She had a terror of crumpling weakly in front of the cameras, although the adrenaline was ripping through her like wildfire.

William, who was brilliant at expressing things, knew better than to offer help. He was staring out of the window, thinking professionally she could tell. It still gave her a start when he suddenly turned and started to quiz Rodney.

'Suicide bomber for definite, do we know? The cinema will have been searched, won't it, with a royal coming? The dogs brought in, full-blown security?'

'Yes, all of that,' Rodney replied, 'and our chaps will have been scrutinizing the crowd. It's more difficult in the colder weather with all the anoraks and bulky clothes. Seems the guy was wearing a bomb vest. That's new here. The 7/7 and 21/7 bombers' explosives were packed in rucksacks, peroxide-based stuff. With a vest it has to be a much smaller volume, far more sophisticated—' He dried up then, probably remembering William's role as editor and the need for more restraint.

Images swirled in her mind, looming and receding like a fairground hall of horrors, distorted and obscene – only these were real: flying bodies, severed limbs. Victoria could hear the pulverizing sound of the explosion, the screams. She thought of the unsuspecting happy crowd; parents and loved ones glued to their televisions at home.

The royal car had been so close. The bomber seemed to have panicked and hurled himself at the barrier, instantly flinging his own and the lives of ten others away. And the toll was sure to rise. His exploding bomb vest had showered lethally detonated shrapnel everywhere, like omni-directional shotgun fire, like the blasting of a mine.

The attacker's personal details were likely to be known soon; suicide bombers seldom bothered to strip themselves of all clues to their identity since they were going to die anyway. But who had masterminded the whole plan? That would be harder to uncover.

Keeping the country safe from terrorists, Victoria thought, was her job, the task she'd been given. Protecting ordinary decent people, guarding the nation's borders. 'We're breeding terrorists,' William had said. The threat was constant, in cities and quiet provincial streets, in attitudes and prejudice. She had done her utmost and more, but it hadn't been enough.

CHAPTER 2

Ahmed had heard the blast. It sounded shatteringly loud coming across the river as he walked along the South Bank path to take the tube from Waterloo. The bus went closer to his Brixton flat, but one stop on the train to Kennington was quicker in spite of a walk each end.

He'd immediately thought of a bomb, the reverberating sound, a faintly cordite burning smell wafting across the Thames – or had he imagined the fumes? It had stopped him in his tracks. He'd stood still a moment, picturing a possible scene of devastation, and considered going back to the office. It could have been a blast from some demolition work. It had seemed better just to get on home and catch the news.

Now, hurrying down backstreets from the station, he felt more certain than ever it had been a bomb. There was a sense of hush in the streets; few people around. Everyone was probably indoors watching telly.

Imagining the horror of a bomb, and what it would mean, caused a sudden eruption of seething rage. It subsided and dissipated and Ahmed was left feeling limply despairing, bleak with frustration at the futility of it all.

Weariness too, at the thought of people's hostility; they would be sharp with suspicion, eyeing any bag or briefcase of his and edging slightly away. He sighed and, reaching his street, felt relieved when the Turkish guys in the corner kebab house gave him an unconcerned wave.

Ahmed slotted in his key to Number 12, Enders Street, a short cul-de-sac of Edwardian terraced houses where he lived. The '2' of the house number was hanging upturned, dangling on one nail; he or Jake, his flatmate, was going to have to fix it, as no one in either of the other flats would.

Certainly not the old pensioner on the ground floor, a sour old fart at the best of times who swore like a redtop hack and always had the back of an arm to his streaming nose. Nor the middle-aged woman with two cats on the first floor; Ahmed carried up bags of litter for her. She had a sort of dry puffiness to her face that made him think she wasn't well.

He and Jake had the two top floors. He had to keep pinching himself: a job at the BBC and now *The Post*, a fantastic flat – with his upstairs bedroom that was light and bright with good dormer windows. The bathroom was practically en suite. He paid a bit more rent for the better room, but it was worth it twice over.

Jake's room was like a railway carriage, half of it lost to the kitchen. He was an architecture student, permanently broke, who went home to his parents in Oxford most weekends and seemed to manage happily enough in his cramped space with a divided window.

Ahmed heaved at the front door that would keep sticking, slammed it shut and sprinted up the narrow stairs. There was a dank mustiness to the hall. The red and cream striped wallpaper was stained, lifting off the walls, and the ill-fitting strip of patterned carpet smelled tiresomely of cabbage, age-old grease, beer-spills and embedded food.

Walking into their spare, white-painted flat gave a lift every time; it made him feel ten feet tall. No Jake around. Ahmed grabbed the television remote before anything else, impatient to know about the bomb.

He stared at the set. The scene was horrific. The cordoned-off area: all the shattered glass, hanging beams, jagged brickwork – the poignantly blackened remains of a rolled-out red carpet. A gleaming cinema entrance reduced to a yawning gaping hole. Ahmed felt renewed anger. Did they really think that carnage and havoc was the way to achieve their ends? His fury subsided again into a flat sad despair, empty feelings of inadequacy that were draining, shrivelling; his heart felt wrung out, limp as a twisted chicken's neck.

Pulling up a chair, he concentrated on the television news. A young Muslim girl whose hijab was covered in blood was being interviewed and assuring a reporter she was fine. 'It's just a few cuts. I was right at the back – lucky. The force of the bomb threw us so hard against each other, though, and I actually heard a man's leg crack—' She turned away then, keeping her head low, obviously too overcome to go on.

A man who'd been on the far side of the square tried to describe the blast. 'It was mind-blowing, a ten-times thunder crack, then it was like everything was in slow motion, even the flying debris. There was an awful delayed reaction before the screams – and a terrible smell, not sort of like fireworks, really evil, with thick dust that was suffocating. The cries were heartrending and they won't go away; it's like they're downloaded, clamped to my ears.'

Three photographers were among the dead as was a group of young girls who'd been hard up to the barrier. They must have queued for hours. The cinema manager had been killed, waiting to greet the Countess, and two policemen and a security guard. Over fifty taken to hospital, it was thought: five on the critical list.

An elderly doorman was interviewed. 'It was like watching film footage from the war, scenes of the Café Royal. When I think of the foyer all shining and spruced up, the red carpet rolled out—' He began shaking his head mournfully.

The cameras cut to a studio, to the Home Secretary who was about to make a statement. Ahmed sat forward, tense, trying to anticipate what she might say.

She walked to a chair, a slim graceful figure in a dark grey suit, and looked straight to camera. Was her lower lip trembling – would she handle it? He thought of all the publicity about her, good and bad, crude and admiring. In his two years with BBC News – doing an internship then formally hired – Victoria Osborne had been right in the thick of things, politically and personally, constantly in the eye of some storm. And now, as Home Secretary, she was all over *The Post* almost daily.

New on the paper, Ahmed lived in fear of his editor's legendary wrath. He couldn't, though, help but admire the man. Osborne was a tiger, a powerhouse. There was no tougher operator in the business and it seemed weird, almost unbelievable, to think he was married to this woman who could tell him so much, but almost certainly never did. He never held back with attacks on her in *The Post* either, he was always having a go, sounding off about the latest hair-raising Home Office drama.

Ahmed had minded decisions she'd taken at Health, but watching her now, he felt strangely affected; her emotion was so evident, genuine and deep. She looked . . . too vulnerable, he thought, too beautiful, even. It was odd, being aware of her looks suddenly, seeing her afresh as she sat facing the camera, stiff and upright, brushing at a fall of soft-looking brown hair.

He listened keenly as she began speaking.

'Those who are responsible for this appalling atrocity must know they will gain nothing as a consequence . . .' Her clear voice, the steely control, came as a slight surprise. She seemed to be looking straight at him; Ahmed shifted uncomfortably. 'The British people will always remain steadfast, strong in their resolve . . .' I'm a British person, he thought, a Muslim one too. 'Strong in their determination to retain cherished values, our precious way of life. Our thoughts and prayers are with the families . . .'

The Home Secretary spoke in heartfelt tones, about the tragic loss of life, the unstinting work of the emergency services. When she hesitated a moment and the tremble to her lip crept back he found himself willing her not to falter, but she kept control. 'We will do everything we humanly can to bring those responsible swiftly to justice, let there be no doubt about that.' Powerful closing words, he thought.

The cameras returned to the devastated site. Ahmed sat thinking about the suicide bomber, a sad programmed pawn in a deadly political chess game, a used dispensable human being. It would end in stalemate, the real plotters never found.

He was busy trying to unravel his emotions when his mobile rang.

'You're wanted upstairs, summons from the editor. Better leg it back here and fast, young man.' It was his boss the news editor, Desmond Wallis – sounding as though he was still in the office. Three hundred odd staff on the paper, Ahmed thought, all thrusting and hungry with ambition every one of them.

'Sure, I'm out the door,' he said, springing up on to his feet as he spoke.

He was still in his brown leather jacket and grabbing his Leeds United scarf – football was big in his life – he wound it round his neck and made for the door.

Jake was coming in, clutching a brown paper carrier of food. Ahmed eyed a French loaf sticking out. 'Got to go, the bomb. Can I have a bit of that?'

He snapped off half the loaf without waiting for an answer. Jake glared. 'Suppose that loaf was for a candle-lit supper for this fantastic chick who's about to arrive?'

'She's not, no chance. And if she were she'd be sympathetic to a starving friend. See you, man – don't wait up.'

A taxi was passing and Ahmed flagged it, a clear case for expenses. He wouldn't have dared in his first weeks, but had soon wised up. He could imagine why the editor wanted to see him. That summons had come right after the Home Secretary's statement and Osborne would have been watching his wife. It must have sparked the idea of hearing his point of view, getting a Muslim slant. It was inevitable. Still wearying, though. Ahmed longed, just sometimes, not to be a token ethnic, interminably put in a box and typecast.

'Come in, come in.' The tone was peremptory and Ahmed's knuckles hadn't even brushed the door. It was a millimetre ajar. He pushed cautiously and went in, hesitating, staying just inside the door. His editor was standing in front of the television keeping his eyes fixed on the screen.

Osborne looked up suddenly. 'Good you could get back in, come on over and sit down.' He went to some tubular-armed chairs grouped round a table by the window, took one facing the view and gestured to another.

Ahmed hadn't been in the editor's office before. It was large and modern except for a huge traditional leather-topped desk, and entirely dominated by the spectacular view. All London was out there, its bright lights winking in the recently bombed blackness like stars in a Christmas fairy grotto. Hard to believe that right at its heart was a hollowed-out cinema where hearts, limbs, lives had been lost.

Conscious of having glanced away, Ahmed turned back quickly and looked at his editor with anxious eyes. He was feeling tense and expectant.

Osborne nodded at the television set. 'What's in your head when you see those scenes? What do you feel?'

'Anger,' Ahmed said, without a second's thought.

'British anger, Muslim anger?'

'British anger and Muslim shame.'

'Why the separation? You were born here, don't you feel British through and through?'

'Yes,' Ahmed replied, drawing out the word, 'I do, but I know too many Muslims who have latent sympathies and want to close ranks – not just the politically active, but quiet quiescent people too, who work on buses and in hospitals and shops.'

'You grew up in Leeds. Why didn't you become a suicide bomber?'

'That doesn't deserve an answer,' he snapped back, hotly resentful, instantly certain he must have just blown his job.

Osborne had been fixing him with a half-aggressive stare; his face suddenly broke out in a warm and appreciative grin. 'Tell me about your family,' he said, swiftly changing tack.

'Loving, reasonably devout, they don't approve of me doing journalism and having non-Muslim friends. I share a flat with someone I met through the BBC. I'd known him a year and been sharing for months before I discovered he was Jewish. I could never tell my parents that!'

What was he doing, pouring out his whole bloody life story? Ahmed looked down at his hands. He had shed his jacket and scarf, dropped them off at his desk, and was in a suit, although he didn't wear one every day. 'If you want me to write an angry condemnatory piece as a Muslim,' he said, feeling he might as well burn his boats and battle on, 'it would kill my street-cred stone-dead – certainly in Leeds where I come from. But if I could go there and talk around, try to make sense of what's going on, how the activists are winning—'

'That's what you want to do?'

'The longer I'm on the paper, the more chance I have of being mistrusted, but I do know my way round certain parts of Leeds. I grew up in Harehills, which is a deprived corner of the city with a tight Muslim community, very like Beeston where the leader of the 7/7 bombers came from. I moved away, went to Manchester University, not Leeds, but I go home to see my family quite regularly and I've been picking up some disturbing signs.'

The editor was staring. Ahmed took a breath and went on. 'Our kitchen at home is always full of my mother's gossiping friends. I come across people I was at school with and hear things . . . I do know the troublemakers among them. It would be a long shot, of course, discovering anything useful, but I feel a real need to do something to help prevent another attack. This is my country,' he finished, smiling weakly.

'So if I sent you up to Leeds,' Osborne said, 'what sort of pieces would you file? No bylines obviously, but surely these people all know you're a reporter?'

'True. Most do. I'd have to win trust. I could write about the closed-rank atmosphere on the streets, though, without passing judgement; that would just about be accepted either way. Those who know I work on *The Post* would certainly think anything with a local slant came from me. No one's going to speak out, of course,' Ahmed went on. 'Muslims feel that's disloyal, dishonourable. There's a lot of underlying sympathy for the cause.'

'You mean the spread of Islam, Sharia law being imposed far and wide?'

'Yes. Islamic domination. The militants want a new caliphate, a worldwide Muslim state long-term.'

Osborne kept on staring; it was disquieting. 'Nothing new or specific to Leeds in what you're suggesting,' he said. 'I don't need to send you for that. What else?'

'Militant extremists are out in the open, but not the criminal plotters, the terrorists. I am worried about one or two people I know. If I could just, well, sniff around, I do believe there might be useful things I could find out—'

Osborne looked sceptical. 'You sure? MI5 aren't idling around with their feet up on desks. There are plenty of cells under surveillance.'

'That didn't stop tonight's bomb—' It just came out and Ahmed carried on in a rush fearing he might have overstepped the mark again. 'I could write about other things too, something on honour killings for instance, working up a relationship with one or two girls under threat – as long as any story could be held up till I was back in London. I'd need to avoid my cover being blown while I'm there.'

'Are Muslim communities in general as disturbed about honour killings as you or me?'

'It's not talked about, just accepted as something that goes on. People don't come forward and some can be quietly supportive.'

'You mean they actually approve?' Osborne looked unusually shocked – as though, if true, that was beyond sane thinking and normal understanding.

'In certain circles there will be people who do,' Ahmed answered. 'Any differences are of degree. It's tribal, the Baradari system transported here. A girl going with an outsider, even if he's Muslim, say an Iraqi or Arab, brings shame.'

'Explain the Baradari system.'

'My parents are Pashtuns, but many of Leeds' Muslims are Mirpuris from poor villages in conservative Pakistani-controlled parts of Kashmir. Out there the system helps the community; they stick together supporting and policing each other, but here, with social security and British justice, there's no need. People still cling to a tight code, though; they think tribally, are socially insular and fight against integration. It's a matter of honour above all, which, in terrorist terms, plays into the fundamentalists' hands. They find it quite easy to radicalize and twist impressionable minds.'

Ahmed had Osborne's full attention and carried on. 'Islamic militants have a more relaxed attitude over honour killings than these tightly knit communities, which may surprise you. They make no tribal distinctions, they're about the spread of Islamism worldwide, after all. As long as a girl's lover is Muslim, that's fine. They would condone an honour killing, of course, where the lover was a *Kafir* – that's a derogatory term like wog – Hindu or Jew.

'It goes on more than the media and the outside world would

ever believe,' Ahmed added. 'Girls are sent home to Pakistan, Afghanistan, not seen again—'

Osborne rose. 'Okay. I'll send you to Leeds for a couple of weeks. Talk around. File some background stuff and get something on honour killings too, a personal desperate heart-tugging story. You'll need a good reason to be hanging around there; think up a decent line. Copy direct to me. I'll tell Desmond what's happening.'

Ahmed stood up hurriedly, wondering how his boss was going to take it.

Going to his desk, Osborne threw back as an afterthought, 'Oh yes, and get back here, Friday week. There's some kind of boozy do for me that night. Ten years of yelling at this useless shower.' He sat down and gave an unexpected smile. 'You should show up for that – always good being seen around the place.' He picked up the first edition that was on his desk and said crisply, 'First copy in two days,' then began reading, immediately absorbed. It was a dismissal.

'Will do,' Ahmed said, in a general way, making for the door. 'And thanks!'

He glanced back before going out, unnerved when Osborne's head shot up and they had a meeting of eyes. 'I'm putting trust in you, Ahmed,' he said searchingly. 'I want loyalty.'

He'd get it, Ahmed thought, racing back to his desk, his mind in turmoil. He made a call to his parents and checked train times. It wouldn't be easy, hanging around in Leeds, taking up with old school contacts. What the hell could his line be? And what about freedom of movement? Living at home was going to be stifling.

He took the bus back to the flat, his adrenaline coming in waves. It wasn't about his career, pulling off a coup – although that wouldn't hurt – it was simply a gut need to try to redress some tiny fraction of balance. Osborne's compelling demand for loyalty was making him feel all the more fired up. Somehow he had to earn that trust; something had to give, to break.

It was almost midnight. Jake was still at it, wearily arching his neck up and down. His laptop was on his knee and filled-to-bursting ring binders beside him on the sofa. Architecture students, he said, worked harder than Scrooge's clerk.

The television was on. 'Death toll's twelve now,' Jake said, 'two more expected to cop it. They say it could have been worse if the bomber hadn't thrown himself clear.'

Ahmed unwound his white and blue scarf and flopped into a fold-up director's chair. 'I've been in with the editor. He's sending me up to Leeds. Back Friday week for a do at the office, but only overnight, I think.'

'To do the bomb?' Jake queried. 'That's a bugger. I wanted you to come for the weekend. I need help with Mum and Dad, money-help, or it'll be a slow death from starvation. They're cotton-wool wrapped out there in academia, they haven't got a clue.'

'You'll sort it,' Ahmed said, his feelings of camaraderie as warmly enveloping as a fleecy lined coat. It was those solemn grey eyes in that long face, the close-cut brown hair: Jake's generous expressive mouth that flashed into a sudden grin. He was just on six foot and had a couple of inches on Ahmed. Crooked teeth – Jake's parents had no more clue about braces and orthodontists than of their son's financial plight – but that was all part of the charm.

They'd first hit it off at a party where Ahmed had been feeling a spare wanker and Jake had put himself out for him. It was typically sensitive, picking up that a small group of boozing Oxford graduates hadn't been easy ground. The BBC guy who'd invited Ahmed along had quickly made a determined play for a girl and forgotten about him.

The idea of sharing a flat together had been Jake's. He was living in Clapham with other boozing friends of his, finding it impossible to study and having an awkward journey to the Bartlett, his architecture college on Euston Road.

Ahmed had been stuck out in Dagenham, lodging with a cousin of his mother's. Moving into the Brixton flat had felt like swapping the jailhouse for the Ritz.

His parents had found the idea of their son sharing with a Christian – as they'd assumed – distressing beyond belief. The snob factor had kicked in, though; Ahmed had laid it on about Oxford, Jake's parents being dons, and their beautiful Georgian home. He was always made welcome and regretted missing a weekend with them.

Staying there once, he'd discovered that his good friend and flatmate, Jake Wright, was Jewish. Having the run of the house one afternoon – Jake and his parents had gone to a christening, a fellow don's new baby – Ahmed had opened a door on to a study and been about to close it when he noticed a row of gilt-lettered titles in Hebrew in a wall of bookshelves. A little more snooping and the facts became clear.

His immediate reaction had been a sense of alienation and letdown; Jake not telling him had felt like an infidelity. Had it seemed irrelevant? Had he just not thought about it? But then would Jake really have had a clue about a Muslim upbringing in a closed community whose ways and traditions bred deep suspicion if not outright hatred of Jews?

The friendship had stood the test and pulled aside that iron curtain of drummed-in prejudice and mistrust. The two of them were intelligent, like-minded; they got on. He'd become that day, Ahmed thought, a more rounded civilized human being.

It was late. He thought about his mission and being stuck in Leeds and it all seemed suddenly crazy and doomed. Shit, whatever had he taken on?

In his home community many believed 9/11 had been a conspiracy, all part of the West's battle against Islam. Bush and Blair were thought to have plotted the 7/7 bombings; it had been a set-up, they'd had the most to gain. Was that just an ignorant closing of ranks, and more or less harmless? What about the political activists behind the façade, the infiltrators spreading hate, indoctrinating minds?

Ahmed felt exhausted and brought down. Jeanette came into his thoughts for a moment, now that he was going away. It was over, yet he was still feeling sore.

They had been fellow researchers at the BBC. He'd taken things pretty slowly, although when she talked about her deep feelings for him they'd become involved. It had been hurtful, discovering that she'd been talking bullshit, that Catholic Jeanette played the field. What a joke, what a phoney.

At least he hadn't been messing around with any pure Muslim sisters, Ahmed thought bitterly. The Harehills crowd he was about to take up with would approve. Fucking around with *Kafirs* was fine, you just didn't do it with your own kind.

Lifting himself out of the chair he yawned widely and smiled at Jake. 'Might not see you in the morning, I'm off early. You'll keep an eye for Mrs Green and her cats? Oh, and if an architect knows what a screwdriver's for you might even fix that hanging 2 on the front door. Think of all the luscious talent you could be pulling in while the flat's all yours.'

CHAPTER 3

Victoria was in her office, skimming the morning papers in an edgy mood. Tony came in and she looked up impatiently. 'They will say it with such authority, Tony. They don't *know* Wednesday's bomb was just a foretaste, that the "big one", chemical, nuclear, whatever, is on the way – unless they know a whole lot more than I do. There'll be a depressing new spate of attacks on Asians now, whether or not they're Muslim.' She stared crossly as Tony reached her desk, a fair man whose bland pleasant face was looking more than a little discomfited.

'The Assistant Commissioner is on his way up,' he said soothingly. 'They have the bomber's full profile now, a complete picture. We'll be right up to date. And Sir Quentin is, in fact, coming after all.' Tony's smile acknowledged the many changes of plan.

Sir Quentin Clayton was Director General of MI5. Victoria had known his two immediate predecessors and held them in high regard. Her tiny hard-to-pinpoint reservations about Quentin were illogical, simply bad chemistry, she thought. It was unreasonable and irrelevant that she didn't appreciate his studied silver-haired charm and elegant, almost lackadaisical style, the slight hint of the self-congratulatory about him. The fault was within her.

She couldn't help wondering whether he ever allowed anything to touch his heart. He was trained not to let in feelings, she told herself; it was the wiser way. Quentin's job involved quiet detached evaluation, calm assessment of critical intelligence. Hers was the more up-front role – and the public face.

Luke Andrews, the Assistant Commissioner, arriving to brief her, was a more approachable, likeable man. Head of the Anti-Terrorist Squad, solid and reliable, he would cover all the bases, she thought. But did he or Quentin really have a truly original mind, that unique intuition and vision so desperately needed? Someone had to see through the fog of misinformation, the blizzard of false leads, and anticipate a terrorist plotter's next move. Everything depended on it.

Andrews was a towering presence walking in. Victoria stood up to greet him, her smile masking a sense of impotence. His face was impassive; they were no further on. Tony followed in, Bridget Morley too, who was on the Home Office Board with the daunting title of Director General, Crime, Police and Counterterrorism.

They pulled chairs up to Victoria's vast desk and rested coffee cups on it carefully. A call had come through from Quentin's office, he was running a little late, and while they waited Andrews groused about all the rumours in the press.

She couldn't blame him. *The Post* was as bad as the rest; she and William had fought about it, but he would never reveal his sources, only say darkly that 'someone wanted it known'.

'They will play on the public's fears,' Andrews complained. 'All this talk of dirty bombs is hard to deny categorically. We can give out the suicide bomber's details in a media conference now, though, and see they have a few hard facts.'

Victoria remembered past police conferences, information given on seized bomb-making equipment, DNA, chemical analysis, hand-writing comparisons – all the forensic disciplines. Convictions had *sometimes* followed.

She was keenly anxious to get going. The moment Quentin arrived and was seated, she turned to Andrews. 'Tell me all you know, Luke. Start with the suicide bomber and bomb vest.'

Luke Andrews spread his hands, turning to half-glance over his shoulder as if checking for eavesdroppers, then spoke directly to her. 'Kamran Yousuf was British born and a former heroin addict, Home Secretary. Aged twenty-one and a recent recruit, we think. His aunt is in considerable shock, but has been quite forthcoming.

'He went off the rails when his parents were killed in a plane crash, got into drugs – was eventually kicked out of a flat he shared with others. The aunt is understandably at pains to say he's innocent, a young man cruelly manipulated while he was down. She hadn't, however, seen him in recent weeks and nor had any of his old uni-versity friends.'

'Where did the plane crash happen? When were his parents killed?'

'In Pakistan, a couple of years back; they'd been on an internal flight visiting family. Yousuf went out to identify the bodies, stayed on a while then right after he returned, dropped out of his studies.'

'Where was he born?'

'Birmingham. But he'd been living in London since leaving school, doing a BSc in biosciences at the University of Westminster. His aunt said he was showing promise and receiving high praise, before the tragedy unhinged him – the drugs, too, presumably. He'd done petty crime to feed his habit, she admitted, and we've learned from an ex-flatmate that he'd resorted to some street prostitution as well. He became scarecrow-thin, but that would be the effect of the heroin, which is a powerful appetite suppressant.'

Victoria fidgeted, irritated at being told what she perfectly well knew. She didn't need time-wasting extraneous detail. 'The spiral downwards was rapid and dramatic,' Andrews continued, seeming quite impervious to her pique. 'After his return from Pakistan it appears Yousuf had started attacking the British way, cursing and denouncing the West. It's all of a piece,' he finished, a little complacently, sitting back.

A bright young student one minute, a crushed desperate loner the next, bitter and emaciated, on drugs, and doing incalculable harm. Victoria felt emotional. 'But you say he was a *former* addict,' she confirmed, 'so we must assume he'd found some sort of salvation and strength through prayer. He would have been encouraged to see his life as worthless, told the true path to redemption was by waging violent jihad – finally persuaded to blow up as many innocent people as possible and his own body to bits along the way.'

It came out too passionately. She was seeing girls as young as Nattie out having fun in London's West End, their whole futures stretching gloriously ahead. The shrapnel had severed an arm of one girl and blown a hole the size of a grapefruit in the head of another.

Andrews was looking somewhat ill at ease. He replied cautiously, 'Yes, the casualties were horribly grim. Kamran Yousuf would no doubt have been told to un-learn the brand of Islam of his parents, to live off the state, since all monies belong to Allah anyway, and prepare for glory. That the message from Muhammad was to terrorize the West who rape and kill innocent Muslims—' He dried up. Victoria was making very plain, despite her own outburst, her need to get on and keep to the point.

She switched her gaze. 'Quentin, what have you got to tell me?'

Sitting forward, preparing to say his piece, Quentin's expression bordered on the supercilious; it certainly conveyed his view that too much emotion was being aired.

'Home Secretary,' he began, 'I'm afraid that Kamran Yousuf's not come to our notice at any time. He wasn't under surveillance. We've no idea who was controlling him, although he was extremely unlikely to have been acting alone. None of the cells we're currently observing seems to have any connection with him. I'm sorry to say we're completely in the dark. We'll be going back over all those people we've looked at in the past and thought no real threat. Doing all we can.' He managed, even as he gave that woeful assessment, an honest catalogue of non-progress, to allow a shadow of superiority to float across his cultured-looking face.

'I do understand,' Victoria conceded neutrally. Turning back to Andrews, she asked, 'And the bomb vest, Luke? Could you explain about the explosives, what, in your opinion, there is to be learned and if it gives any leads.'

'The use of bomb vests is new here, Home Secretary. It was concentrated in Israel and the Palestinian territories and of course spread to Iraq too, as extremists began operating there.' Andrews paused to scratch at the side of his eye, then sat back up to his full commanding height. With close-cropped, greying hair he had the look of an American colonel.

'We think the vest implies foreign involvement and a bomb-maker was brought over from the Middle East, the West Bank or Gaza. It contained TNT, probably stolen from an explosives store at a quarry. It's easier to access here in the UK and very stable – unlike the home-made TATP they use in the Palestinian territories. That's terrible

stuff; handlers lose their lives. They call it the Mother of Satan,'
Andrews said with a half-smile. 'They've had to resort to it, though,
since all the crackdowns on smuggling TNT.'

'The vests look a bit like those orange over-the-head life jackets
you see airline staff using in safety demonstrations – if you can imagine one in dark grey with several slim TNT-filled cylinders fitted in
upper and lower layers and wires attached. The grey surround is the
fragmentation jacket that produces the shrapnel and does all the
lethal damage. Wearing that, Yousuf became a sort of deadly self-
flung body grenade.

'TNT is detonated by an initiating explosive, lead azide in this
case. Lead azide is highly sensitive, usually handled and stored under-
water in insulated rubber containers, and a whitish powder in usable
form. A capsule of it would have been placed in each tube. The sec-
ondary, TNT, charges were detonated by the pressure wave from
those first initiating capsules. A loaded vest can weigh up to twenty
kilos,' Andrews added.

'Our view is that the string-puller, whoever he is, must have
imported a bomb-maker to construct the device. We've had no
reports of stolen explosives, however; either someone doesn't want to
admit anything's gone or it hasn't even been missed. As you would
expect, Home Secretary, we're doing everything we possibly can to
track down the source.'

There seemed little more to be said. Victoria asked questions, but
felt the walls of impasse closing in. MI5 and the police would pick
dry the blasted bones of a desperate bomber, strive for any breakthrough, but learn nothing. That was too defeatist. Forensic evidence
and discoveries about the theft of TNT might yet yield vital information. There was always hope.

Goodbyes were said, light asides made in an attempt to brighten the no-progress gloom, then Victoria rushed down to her waiting car. Her next meeting was routine, at the Cabinet Office to discuss a proposal from the Transport Secretary.

It was in the way. Her mind was on Kamran Yousuf. He came with her in the car; he loomed in front of her eyes. The only recent photograph of him was as a first-year student. He'd been a good-looking boy, she thought, almost a man, like William's son, Tom, on the brink of a future full of achievements, marriage, fatherhood.

His face transmogrified in her mind, it grew gaunt, became bearded. She saw him in his cadaverous decline, a wretched used human being, so thin that a bulky bomb vest would have been easy to conceal. He'd been wearing a Puffa jacket with most of the stuffing removed.

'Life can be tough, Home Secretary,' Rodney suggested, turning round from the front seat of the car. Was her lowness so very transparent?

'Just thinking of all that's wrong in the world,' she replied.

CHAPTER 4

Nattie was coming home. She wanted to be at William's party to celebrate his ten years as editor; she and her stepfather had been close from the start. The party was that night and she was due home by lunchtime. Victoria felt starved of quality time with her daughter and was longing to see her. As she dressed that Friday morning, the anticipation was soaking in like the warmth of a tingling hot bath. William's son, Tom, would be at the party too, the family together for the weekend. She couldn't wait.

The Friday night had been carefully chosen. All the staff would be in the building with a Saturday paper to bring out. They could sleep it off next day with no Sunday edition. Victoria had rescheduled her constituency work so there was no need to pack up work, clothes, containers of leftovers, and be in Southampton by nine. A long weekend in London made a rare enjoyable change.

Except that Tony, her principal private secretary, was appreciating it too, and had grabbed the Friday for Home Office business. He'd arranged an official visit to the Border and Immigration Agency at Heathrow. It looked set to be heavy-duty and meant she couldn't be there when Nattie arrived.

Victoria left her a note, belted her new camel coat with an irritable tug and set off for Heathrow with Rodney and Tony. She was feeling resentful. Her job was desperately important; work-intensive, drama-prone, thrilling, exciting, but there did come a time . . . the idea of long weekends and normal living seemed whimsical, a distant memory.

Nattie was at Durham University, reading English, but managed occasional weekends at home. Victoria never stopped worrying about her: the boyfriend she really came to see, her safety – even about her being at William's party. Ever since being elected an MP she'd been trying to keep Nattie clear of the media's clutches. Taking her to *The Post* that night felt like swimming past the red flag, ignoring all the warnings of strong currents and sharks.

Nattie had wanted to come, though. William would make sure nothing was written about her and Nattie was mature and sensible enough, surely, at nineteen, to avoid the nosy questions of prying reporters, eager to chat her up.

Victoria also worried slightly that the Home Secretary being there might put a dampener on things, like the head-teacher at a school disco – although William had set her straight on that. She could be the Pope himself, he'd said pithily, and they'd be too blind drunk to notice. He seemed more concerned about all the embarrassing trade secrets his drink-soaked staff might let slip.

He was scathing about *The Post*'s managers who'd insisted the party had to be in the atrium foyer, not up on the office floors with their stunning view. It was typical of the pettifogging pygmies to imagine champagne would be showering into every computer. How could he bring out a halfway decent paper, William had snorted, which made them the money they were so tight-fisted with, if that was their attitude? They were carbuncles, parasite hirelings who should be working for the Inland Revenue.

The party lay ahead. First came the Heathrow visit. Sitting beside Tony in the back of the car, Victoria was uncommunicative, slightly suspicious – after Luke Andrews's remark about the bomb-maker probably being from the Middle East – of the Border and Immigration Agency she was on her way to see. Had someone slipped the net and got into the country illegally?

She couldn't start blaming the Agency. No terrorist plotter would risk a dodgy passport; these were clever criminals who knew better than to bring anyone in with the scent of explosives on his hands. Nothing could have been untoward.

The Agency's Chief Executive showed her round the various departments; she met staff – experts at spotting the most brilliant of passport forgeries – and had measures such as iris recognition explained, saw interviews being conducted in booths. The waiting suspects were tense and drained, their slightest easing of position, faintest twitch of an eyebrow or facial muscle seeming as nuanced as the Chinese language. Was it just their nerves? Victoria thought more humbly that the staff had an impossibly difficult responsible task.

The Chief Executive was explaining something highly technical and detailed and he was taking his time. She was suddenly wild with impatience, aching to be home with Nattie.

It was Nattie's boyfriend, Shelby, who was the great worry. Victoria's long-term hope for her daughter was another friend called Hugo – which meant it was bound never to happen.

Hugo had adored Nattie ever since they met in their mid-teens, despite her chill unresponsiveness at the time. It had been just after a terrible first sexual experience with a boy from school; Hugo had sensed the rawness, given her oceans of space and they had eventually got together – but then Shelby came on the scene.

The Chief Executive was still talking. Victoria flicked a look at her watch – which made her think of the elegant one Hugo had given Nattie. It looked so fitting on her slim wrist. At least she was still wearing it.

Tony, ever the dutiful official, noticed the glance. Rodney had, too. He began edging forward from his discreet detective's position a few paces behind and soon he and Tony, in a highly polished fluid operation like the perfect passing of a relay-race baton, were smoothly speeding up her departure. They had her out of the door and into the car in no time. She smiled up her final thanks and good-byes to the Chief Executive through impregnable glass.

It was a dark November day. The car felt too solidly protecting and armour-plated, too remote from the outside world. She stared out of the window as it sped up the M4; the sky seemed to be sagging, the low-hung clouds heavy as an aircraft undercarriage.

Could she talk to Nattie about Shelby? He had glamour and sex appeal in spades with that thick thatch of gleaming black hair, but there was something not quite right about him, a hidden fault line, too disguised to define.

He over-egged the charm, Victoria thought, the times he came to the house in his all-black gear, always sucking up to his girlfriend's ministerial mother.

So he'd ducked out of Durham and was doing not very much – was that such a crime? He did seem awash with money. Was it all handouts from his impresario father? Tom, who knew her particular concerns, had tried to be reassuring. As far as he could tell, he said, Shelby wasn't into snorting cocaine. That still left a large open field of other sins.

Eight o'clock. Victoria and Nattie were dressed and ready for the party. William had come home so they could go together and was upstairs having a shower. Tom was meeting them there. He was through art college and doing any job at all – presently helping put on a big exhibition of young artists' work, including some of his own.

Nattie was miles away, deep in thought, as they waited in the kitchen. It was at the back of the house and overlooked their small London garden. William nurtured it in summer, but now it was winter-bare with moss on the paving. Nattie was dressed much as for going to the pub with friends: layered T-shirts, a very mini black skirt; opaque black tights. She had added a partyish touch, though, of a broad silvery sash slung low round her slim young hips.

She looked up, suddenly conscious of being studied. 'Mum, that's a worried smile! It's Shelby, isn't it? Can't you relax a bit more? You do show your feelings.'

Victoria tried to unworry her smile. 'I obviously shouldn't be saying this, but he is, well, rather flash.'

'Sure – don't I know it. That's not really the point, though. With the little he shows up to see me it would be mad to think I mean anything much. It's just that when he is around . . . he does sort of make me want to go on putting up with it.'

The gleam of a tear crept in and she wiped at her eyes with an impatient back of hand. Victoria felt anguished. But Nattie would make her own mistakes, it was the way it had to be.

'Sorry, you lot,' William called, coming downstairs. 'Come on then, let's get this crazy show on the road.' Leaving the house, he had an arm round both of them. 'Don't feel you have to stay,' he said almost shyly. 'Just for Oscar's speech if you can bear it, then I'd bugger off fast. Guess I'll have to hang on till the bitter end.'

Rodney came up the front path to meet them. 'Hello Nattie,' he said with a freely given look of admiration. 'And *very* good it is to see you, too!'

It was no distance to *The Post* in the car. William's abashed attitude to the celebration of his ten years was a whole new side to him, Victoria realized, as the three of them sat silently in the back. He couldn't admit to pride, but he'd made the paper what it was and the party meant a lot. She felt a sense of rightness.

Tom caught up with them as they reached the security turnstiles. He had his father's grin, same colouring, height and loose-limbed way of wrapping himself into chairs, same gestures. But Tom had none of his father's determined aggressive drive; he was a dreamer, in love with art and with Maudie. She'd been Nattie's best friend at school and they kept in touch. Tom helped with that. William longed for Tom to be more proactive, yet he was intensely loving, deeply proud of his son's talent.

There was a ridiculous amount of balloons saying 'Ten Years!', human statues, people on stilts, flame-throwers, bunny girls. *The Post*'s proprietor certainly knew how to made a splash. Oscar was hovering, beaming – hopping about on those spindly legs of his in a way that made him a near comic character, but he had a big heart as Victoria knew. She and William had been recipients.

Oscar advanced on Nattie with a whoop and scooped up both her hands. 'You're a beauty, a stunner – why haven't we seen you before? Where have they been hiding you?'

Nattie smiled coyly, pink with embarrassment, but Oscar's attention span was nil: he had already swung focus. 'What's with these
bombers then, Victoria? You gonna sort it? Tough job you got there.'
He switched again, making airy backward circles with his hand, as
though to illustrate points distant. 'Bella couldn't make it, she's some
place like Monaco, I think. I lose track.'

His willowy blonde fifth wife would have looked as out of place
as a hoodie at a choral concert in that atrium hall. The drinking must
have started right after lunch.

Oscar spied a girl with a Pre-Raphaelite mane of ginger hair arriving; she was in fishnets, a shiny red skirt and tottering on six-inch
heels. 'Hey,' he called, 'you need looking after!' He had his host's
duty to perform.

Beverly Leander, *The Post*'s diminutive auburn-haired fashion
editor, took his place and was all over Nattie like an excitable dog.
'We must do a fashion feature! You're a natural – didn't anyone ever
tell you that?' Bev took a deep swig from a beer bottle.

'I'm at Uni,' Nattie answered shyly, looking tempted. 'Be a bit difficult, really—'

'Less of the hard sell, I think, Bev,' William said with authority,
taking a hand.

She gave him a confident eye, clearly not one to be cowed,
downed her beer and moved on.

'Quite a hit you're making, Nattie!' William teased, not noticing
when Tom left them and bravely approached the paper's art critic, his
shoulders hunched, visibly stiff with embarrassment. Victoria kept
glancing anxiously his way.

She enjoyed seeing the transformation, Tom's loosening limbs and
ease of manner, as he and the pallid critic – whose energetic black

hair seemed at odds with his effete air of entitlement – became locked in some deeply passionate discussion.

William was smiling at Nattie; he knew her mother's concerns. 'Now, there's a reporter I want you to meet, Nats, and be nice to. And you, darling – I talked about him, remember, Ahmed Khan? The good stuff he's doing, how bright he is.'

William led the way, Rodney discreetly following. Victoria could see the young reporter through the crush; he was talking to Jim Wimple, *The Post's* political editor. Ahmed Khan stood out, she thought; he had a kind of lithe energy about him, clean-shaven good looks and an obvious intelligence that would take him far. William, who never suffered fools, or anyone else for that matter, certainly considered he had star quality.

Ahmed was gesticulating animatedly and asking demanding questions as far as she could see: Jim was looking mildly on the defensive. Why? Why should a very junior reporter be interrogating the paper's chief political editor? Ahmed wasn't drinking either . . . God, she thought, that was getting paranoid: too much time spent with spooks and the police, too much politicking. He was a quick-thinking young man having a normal peppy argument.

Jim had been distracted elsewhere by the time they pushed through the packed hall and up a couple of steps to the raised level. Ahmed was alone, looking round.

'How're you doing, Ahmed?' William said. 'Liked the stuff from Leeds: atmospheric, got things across. Week go well? I want to hear about it,' he muttered, before making introductions. 'This is my wife, Victoria, and my stepdaughter, Nattie.'

Victoria shook hands. 'I've been hearing good things about you.' She smiled.

'Surely not! It is a great privilege to meet you, Mrs Osborne.' She was amused to see that, for all his apparent awe and natural shyness at being introduced to the Home Secretary, his eyes were travelling to Nattie. Although turning her way, he suddenly became quite tongue-tied and seemed unable even to say hello.

Nattie took over and helped him out. 'Is my stepfather as fearsomely impossible to work for as they say? Why don't we go over there, where it's quieter and you can tell me the honest truth.'

CHAPTER 5

Nattie led Ahmed down two steps to the lower part of the atrium; it was high and arching, with glass walls and a display of bold structural greenery marking the divide.

'I thought you needed rescuing,' she said smiling, leaning against a low wall containing the plants and resting her glass on the soil.

Ahmed could only stare. He could hear his mother saying, 'Cat got your tongue?' She had an embarrassing way of trying to use English idioms. Nattie was smiling patiently. He had to say something. Not what he was thinking – that she was the most beautiful creature he'd ever set eyes on, ever to walk the earth. That wouldn't do.

She'd give up on him any minute. 'I'm very glad you did,' he said, finally getting something out and returning the smile. 'No disrespect to your mother, of course! But I'm sure you don't really want to be here talking to me.'

'You're quite shy for a reporter.' She gave a teasing half-laugh. The sound she made, that almost-laugh, felt intimate; he wanted to take hold of her wrists and pull her gently closer. 'What about my step-father then?' she asked, getting back to her starting point. 'Is he as bad as they say? You haven't answered the question.'

'No, reporters never do, they do all the asking. There's plenty I'd like to ask you.'

'Like—?' She touched his sleeve in another teasing gesture.

'Like—' He glanced at the hand she was taking away. 'Did someone close to you give you that watch?' Shit, what was he saying – just the sort of jerkish inquisitive obvious question to irritate her. 'I just meant, well, some special friend.' He smiled apologetically, feeling filled with despair at only making it worse.

She looked at him quizzically. 'You're not really shy at all. Yes, it was from a boyfriend, if that's what you mean. Shall we leave it there?'

She had sounded firm, but not cold, he thought, and even implied it was in the past. There must be a queue of others, though, damn their eyes.

He wanted to ask more questions and bury the bad start. 'Do you have your own protection,' he carried on quickly, 'a minder of your own, like the one over there with your mother? He's keeping well back. I imagined her having at least a pair of heavies, not just one discreet guy in a suit.' In jeans and a shirt himself, Ahmed was still conscious of the touch of Nattie's light hand; he imagined it lingering on his arm and longed to reach down and hold it tight.

She was laughing at the idea of a minder. 'God no, not me! I'm a free agent, I couldn't stand it, I can't think of anything worse. My mother thought she might be a drag, coming with Rodney tonight; she didn't want to slow things down. Rodney's good fun, though, and he's not into people getting stoned, stuff like that, he just has to look out for Mum. The other detectives are good, too, Charles and Rob. They sort of rotate.'

Ahmed stared, slightly surprised at the use of first names. She was talking easily, being friendly, not stiffly trying to be nice. He relaxed more and lightened his face into a grin. 'Next question! Are you working, at university, living at home? You don't mind this quizzing? I'd hate you to feel put-upon and go away—' His blood ran faster, he was sounding such a tool.

'No, I don't mind – but that was three questions in one! I'm second year at Durham, living out this year, in a little house with two girls. It's cool. I get home when I can, though, on weekends like this as well as the holidays.'

Her mother was looking their way and he dreaded his time running out. She was with Jim, the political editor, and had been having what seemed a serious talk. Ahmed had been keeping her in his sights. He'd taken on Jim himself, just before Osborne came over with Nattie. Jim had been slagging off the Home Secretary, as it happened, calling her useless and wet. There needed to be a good strong bruiser in that job, he said.

Ahmed had demanded examples of wetness and got none. He'd minded Jim's right-wing views and superior tone. Odd guy, Jim. He seemed politically out of step with Osborne, yet stayed the course; he was given plenty of slack rope.

There was a lot of noise. Waiters were struggling to get round with trays of luxury finger food, lobster tails, oysters, mini-steaks and little bowls of chips. The champagne was flowing faster than a high-pressure hose.

Nattie was describing her college and having to shout, but Ahmed felt grateful for the scrum, the pushing and shoving that was pinning him in closer to her. He joked about the paper's more colourful characters, told her about Jake and the flat.

'I'd never seen *The Post*'s proprietor before tonight,' Ahmed went on. 'He's, um, weird looking – like from a different time. Certainly knows how to throw money around!'

'When he gave the wedding reception for Mum and William there were whole fruit-bowls full of caviar. And the cake was like a min-ister's red box, pretty kitsch!'

Journalists never missed much, even drunk as kites. His cosy talk to Nattie was being noticed; two leader-writers were staring and the deputy editor was looking crossly suspicious. Interfering fucking hack, Ahmed thought, shifting his position to be more out of view.

He felt desperate to get further with Nattie. 'I'm in Leeds for a few weeks,' he said. 'Your stepfather's sent me, I'm back here just for tonight. Could we have tea sometime, do you think? I can easily come to Durham—' He tried to keep the tension from showing; his whole world hung on her reply.

'Why Leeds? Does *The Post* have offices up there or something? I didn't know that.'

'No, he just wants pieces on the Muslim mood. It's where I grew up so I know my way round.'

'Hardly near Durham, a long way to come for a cup of tea!' She wasn't ruling it out, he thought, smiling hopefully. Nattie smiled, too. 'Tell me more about you,' she said. 'My turn to ask things.'

Her smile was unbelievable. Ahmed thought he'd tell her his entire life story seven times over if she would just keep looking at him like that. By some miracle she did seem comfortable with him, and wasn't casting round for an easy exit route.

'Did you go to Leeds University as well?' she queried.

'No, Manchester, which was good, I made new friends. And got stuck into the student paper and the university TV channel. It was

cool. I was news anchor, cameraman, lighting, dogsbody – it got me
an internship with BBC News in the research section and they later
gave me a job. I was there two years. Then I met a journalist on *The
Post* and—'

A heavy sweaty hand landed on his shoulder. Ahmed sank under
its weight, inwardly swearing as long a string of curses as the man in
the Brixton downstairs flat.

Desmond Wallis, his boss, was leering at Nattie, still keeping his
heavy-handed grasp of Ahmed's shoulder like a caricature of a plod-
ding fat cop. Des could get the fuck out of it, the turdy drunken
creep, Ahmed thought bitterly, desperate for Nattie's phone number
or email address.

'Is this man molesting you?' Desmond was wheezing slightly, tipping his drink at an angle like an up-ended boat.

'Not at all,' Nattie answered coolly, but with a sweet polite smile.
'We were having a very interesting talk.'

Osborne was coming over. 'I think your stepfather might want
you,' Ahmed muttered, since her back was turned. She glanced
round and Desmond, too, looked that way, straightening out of his
flab-bellied slouch at the sight of *The Post*'s editor-in-chief. His path
was being impeded; people were intercepting him, wanting a say, and
Des – who might even just have picked up what a spare prick he was
being – went to join in.

'Can I have a mobile number or email,' Ahmed whispered, 'if you
really don't mind me coming sometime. Just a cup of tea.'

She gave him her email address. He found a scrap of paper in
a pocket and scribbled it down, but it made him feel low, his
stomach tight and cold. She seemed to be keeping him at arm's
length.

Then Nattie's face shone with another glorious smile. 'Durham's lovely,' she said, 'I know cool places for tea. Be nice.'

Oscar Bluemont was making a speech and was in full flow. 'This editor of yours has chalked up a number of firsts,' he was saying, bouncing on the balls of his feet. Ahmed kept his eye on Nattie, standing over with her mother; there was a young man with them too, who had to be Osborne's son. 'The first editor with his own television show,' the proprietor carried on, 'the first of mine to last ten years, the first to be married to a Home Secretary . . .' He paused, a moment, for effect. 'The pillow talk must be interesting – the spooks will be bugging them soon . . .' There was a lot of drunken laughter. Ahmed stared on at Nattie.

He kept it up, all through Osborne's speech, in response, which was funny and particularly moving.

He had never seen a girl whose face held such glowing grace, whose eyes were so richly iridescent amber, whose mouth was so free with its subtly teasing smile.

Without that touch of humour about her lips her face would be almost too pure. As it was her character shone through. She would have warm strong emotions, plenty of depth and fire he felt sure.

The doors revolved her away, out of sight, out of the building. Her mother's detective seeing them into the car blocked his last glimpse. Rodney seemed a funny name for a minder, but then would you ever give their names much thought at all?

Ahmed kept his eyes on the doors. He debated ducking out to go back to the flat and send Nattie an email. It would be counter-productive, though, embarrassingly soon. Better to check out trains to Durham and hire-cars first. And he should hang out at the party a while longer, take the advice of being seen around.

'You're not drinking, Ahmed?' He jumped. Osborne was right beside him, sipping from a glass of champagne. He'd been seeing off his wife and Nattie; Ahmed hadn't noticed him coming back in – or anything else going on for that matter. Osborne was looking at him rather intently. He must have noticed his new junior reporter's eyes constantly on Nattie; nothing ever passed him by.

'I'm going easy on the drink,' Ahmed answered. 'Off early back to Leeds again tomorrow, and it might turn out quite important. Your speech was really great,' he carried on, 'especially about how you feel it's like a shot of brandy, just walking into the building, what it does to you. The hairs were standing up on the back of my neck! And I was thinking of all you'd put in—'

He knew it must sound lickspittly, but watching Nattie all the while, seeing how fond she seemed of her stepfather, he had been genuinely moved by Osborne's words. 'Sorry,' he said sheepishly, 'I'm probably talking out of turn.'

'Too damn right you are, what a load of fucking balls! But since you're not blotto I do want an update on Leeds.' Osborne, who had in fact looked less than irate at the earnest praise, deposited his glass and strode towards one of the small tables dotted around the walls.

They were covered with burgundy cloths, piled high with party detritus, lipstick-rimmed smeary glasses, dirty plates and congealing food. Osborne soon had a waiter sweeping one clear, smoothing it down – bringing a bottle of vintage Moet and two glasses. Osborne poured champagne into both and took up his own. 'Well then, what's going on? Give me the scene.'

Ahmed picked up the other glass, feeling in need of being fortified.

'My parents live in the Harehills area of Leeds as I said, and the house is just off the Roundhay Road, which is usefully close to the mosque. My father's despaired of ever getting me to come to prayers; he always routinely asks, though, and looked quite shocked when I actually agreed to go the Friday I was back.'

His father hadn't imagined he was being disingenuous. Ahmed had hated not being straight with him and could still hear himself saying, 'Okay, Pops, you win, you've twisted my arm,' and he took a sip of champagne, feeling guilty.

'Parts of Harehills are okay,' he carried on, conscious of Osborne's watchful eyes. 'There are Labour and Conservative clubs, shopping parades, a Law Centre, but it's mostly dirty, rundown, deprived – and very Muslim. Talk to any young Asian hanging around and you'll get the sense of how implacably in on itself the community is, and full of hate. There's such a build-up of hostility; the youths call a white person a *gora* and watch DVDs the radicals leave lying round in the mosques with just that aim in mind. Anti-Semitism is rampant. There are no sanctions against petty crime and if a Muslim gets arrested it's as likely to spark a riot.'

'What reason did you give for being back?'

'I told my parents I had to write a series of pieces on the Muslim mood, reactions to the bomb, and they've read the couple that have appeared. I also said London was getting to me, that I was owed some holiday and needed time out.'

'Who else did you say this to? Who have you made contact with?' Osborne was alert, demanding as ever.

'Three people I was at school with. I haven't really kept up with them, but their families see mine, we all know each other, it's that sort of community. One of them has been causing his parents secret distress. They needed to let it out, I think. I heard them talking in low mutters last time I was home. When they left, my father was subdued. I sensed he was depressed and disturbed by what he'd heard.

'It's been on my mind ever since. I'd been feeling an itch, a reporter's need to dig a little, even before the Leicester Square bomb, you see,' Ahmed tried to explain. 'But that really crystallized things and made me all the keener to suss out the mood, discover what's what. It almost feels like a race against time.'

Osborne was silent, giving no clue, and he ploughed on. 'This person's called Yazid and he's a graduate; he was at Leeds University, works for the council now. He thinks he's smarter than God, but is actually quite thick. There's a lot of hate in him and he's a stirrer, a show-off, forever hanging out at the university spreading anti-West crap. Yazid does love lording it and being Mr Big. Or at least – and this is the strong impression I formed this week – being at the beck of someone who really is.'

His editor still said nothing and Ahmed continued. 'Yazid couldn't help letting slip, in a nose-tapping sort of a way, that he was having a visitor this weekend. It was very private stuff, he murmured, as though he shouldn't have been breathing a word.'

'Tell me about the other two,' Osborne chipped in.

'They stick around with Yazid – he sort of runs the show. One's called Khalid, a gentle gullible kid who does deliveries for a takeaway. He's deeply religious. The other guy, Iqbal, is a tougher nut. He uses religion like a box of tools; it helps him dodge the system and claim every benefit going; he doesn't insure his car, does jobs for cash, that kind of thing, and justifies it all in the name of Allah.

'Yazid imagines himself in charge, that's clear, and I suspect he kicked himself slightly, for bragging about the weekend visitor. He seemed edgy, scared I might turn up at his flat unannounced or something. But I had been laying it on about being in sympathy with the cause, anything to avoid being seen as a despised Westernized traitor – and possibly quite successfully since Yazid felt lulled enough to drop those hints.' Ahmed smiled. 'Anyone a quarter cleverer, though, might have questioned my sincerity.'

'How did you make the first approach?' Osborne said.

He was tuned into every last detail – even at a party in his honour, even just after making an emotional speech. But people had been killed in Leicester Square, innocent lives lost. That came before any celebration.

'I didn't have to. They made the early running – at the mosque when I went that time with my father. They came over to find me after Maghb, that's the fourth prayer. It was more out of suspicion, frankly, than any attempt to be friendly. I'd already spotted them eyeing me. My father had too, and he talked forcefully, later on at home, about their heads being plum full of stupid dangerous ideas, the summer camps they'd been to – that's those military-style shockers with calls to jihad. He blames the radical politicized clerics whom he thinks need locking up.

'Anyway,' Ahmed continued, 'these three, who knew me well enough, seemed so warily suspicious that I decided it was all about my job. They know I'm on the paper. I talked about London being a sick place full of unbelievers and said I was actually thinking of jacking it all in. They ended up asking me back for coffee at Yazid's flat. I spat on the ground on the way there, keeping it up till the last.

'I've been making my number with them all week. Then just this morning, when I mentioned coming to London today, possibly to resign my job – saying how hard it was, that I might just take more holiday before deciding – they exchanged discreet looks. When I talked about seeing them at the weekend Yazid, the puffed-up creep, said darkly, for the benefit of the others, that it might be *difficult.*'

Ahmed looked at his editor. 'I am worried. I would really appreciate the chance to keep at it and try to discover pressure points, influences. Something seems not right . . . Although I know I'm almost certainly reading too much into it,' he added cautiously.

He felt unable to explain fully his genuine fear that they were potential candidates who could conceivably become drawn, like helpless floundering fishes, into the strong-mesh net of highly organized, terrorist crime.

Yazid hardly seemed helpless, far too cocky, yet he was susceptible, malleable – useful to someone who needed a local pair of eyes and ears. Was that completely crazy? To start suspecting guys he knew, on his own home doorstep, was as bad as all the people who eyed him on the tube, convinced of a bomb in his briefcase.

Osborne was staring, chewing on his thumb. 'You really think this is more than just disaffected young men sounding off?'

'What can I say. It's just a sixth, well, sixteenth sense more like, a smell of adrenaline in the air. Khalid has that kind of back-of-the-eye look of private internal fear. He's young and simple with a profound religious belief: he always goes to dawn prayers. I had the feeling he's deep-down scared; he seemed relieved, grateful I was on the scene, as though he was craving support in some sort of undefined way.'

Despite his penetrating stare, Ahmed thought Osborne was just sizing up the situation. 'Right,' he snapped briskly. 'I think it's all a bit far-fetched, but I hear you. Here's what you do. If you're right and there really is something fishy going on, this Yazid or any overlord would want to check out your story about ditching the job. The paper could back that up, but I suspect any mischief-makers might quite fancy a lead into *The Post*. They're getting a lot more savvy about PR and the Internet.

'You've already told them you're holding off a minute; say as well, you're likely to jack in the job all the same. Leave a question mark hanging.'

'I take my cue from them in other words?'

'Yep. You get a month on this, right? Two more weeks. Tell anyone on the paper who asks that half is unpaid holiday. Keeps the peace.' Ahmed nodded, taking the point. 'And I want you working on the honour killings situation too,' Osborne said. 'That preys on my mind. Do it on the quiet or however you want; show some concern, whatever. Try to find a girl living in fear; talk to her.

'Money? You'll need a float. I'll see some is paid into your account. Keep careful records, you know what they're like. Oh, and Ahmed – better make your peace with Desmond. He's not a bad sort, just needs a stroke-up now and then.'

Osborne drained his glass and stood up, 'I want regular reports. And keep your fucking wits about you. Could get messy.' He gave a brief nod and walked off.

Ahmed picked up the almost-full bottle of vintage champagne; Desmond would appreciate it. Holding it by its neck, swinging it slowly back and forth as though contemplating hurling it, his thoughts were immediately back on Nattie. Osborne hadn't been sharp about that; surely he'd have said something if it had really bugged him? Probably just assumed it was a non-starter. Nattie was at university, after all – or maybe there was some great boyfriend on the scene who her stepfather knew about.

The thought plunged Ahmed into despondency. Shit, what a time he was in for, having got so instantly obsessed. It was certain to go nowhere, what the hell was he thinking about? It was hopeless.

He hung loose a while, then, having psyched himself up, went to seek out Desmond. 'Looks like I'm to be sticking it out in Leeds a couple of weeks longer,' he said ruefully. 'The Special One has spoken. Sorry, Des, but he's got the bit between his teeth about the Muslim scene. Hope I'm not letting you down.' He brought up the bottle and waved it. 'Top-up?'

It was well shaken and fizzed splashily into Desmond's held-out glass. The old hack focused on Ahmed who smiled back benignly. He could imagine the news editor's none-too-sweet thoughts on a cocky young upstart who was supposed to report directly to him.

Desmond took a deep swig then broke out into an unexpected great chortle. It practically doubled him over. 'That's what you get if you fuck around with the Home Secretary's darling little daughter, young man. You end up doing bleeding time in Leeds.'

CHAPTER 6

Ahmed often felt uncomfortable, taking the tube after midnight and walking down the backstreets on his way home. It was easy to start thinking about racist gangs and have moments of morbid melancholy, imagining his own end, his photograph splashed in the papers. He could picture old ladies clucking and saying what a shame it was and a good-looking lad, too – for a Paki.

He took a taxi back after the *Post* party. Not out of nerves, the staff had all been told they could, and anyway his mind was too filled with his extreme impatience to see Nattie again, even just for tea, and the tension-packed weekend that lay ahead.

Jake was still up, yawning over the usual pile of overflowing ring binders. 'Hi, I thought that taxi might be you. All right for some.' He grinned. 'Okay party? What's new?'

'What's new,' Ahmed said, slinging off his leather jacket and flinging himself down on the sofa with a beam as wide as his spread arms, 'what's new is . . . I've met a girl. I'm in love. It's official. Why aren't you in Oxford?'

'Going tomorrow – well today, now. Like who?'

'Ah, well that's kind of tricky, the big problem.'

'Why? She's married, a nun – a chaste Muslim?'

'None of the above. She's the editor's stepdaughter.'

Jake made the connection and gave another grin. 'You'd better watch it or her ma will be having us bugged . . .' He hesitated for a moment with an anxious face as if weighing up whether to relay a thought. 'I, um, met a guy last week who seemed to be quite in with the Home Secretary's daughter. He was a prick; probably just shooting a line—'

'Who was he? Where did you meet him?' Ahmed could feel the knots tightening. Amazing how instantly you could crash out of a fanciful dream. He stared at his flatmate, feeling cruelly deflated.

'You really are quite serious, then?' Jake mumbled, looking awkward. When Ahmed continued to stare, needing answers, he went on, 'He's a guy called Shelby Tait. I met him at my friend Jane's – he was round seeing a boy she shares with. He dropped out of uni, she said, and always acts loaded; her other flatmate thinks he deals. That figures – I wouldn't have trusted him with my grandmother's toe-clippings. He did go on about this girl being the Home Sec's daughter, but maybe there was kind of an extra kick in it for him if he's into dealing.' Jake's long face was sombre. 'Better you know, isn't it? I mean—'

'Sure, sure,' Ahmed said impatiently. 'I have only just met her. She's at Durham. I'd even been thinking of going there, it's not that far from Leeds. I'm up north for rather longer now; work and a bit of duty time with the parents – remember me to yours, by the way.' He stood up. 'Night then, got another early start. I'll be in touch.'

'Cheer up, pal, for God's sake,' Jake urged, snapping his books shut. 'Sounds like she's in need of rescuing and you're just the man.'

The train rolled out of Peterborough and thundered on north through the flat winter landscape. It was a barren picture out of the window, as though a poor artist had painted the clouds too leadenly and left out shafts of glinting, enlivening light.

'I thought you needed rescuing,' Nattie had said with that golden smile. Ahmed couldn't get her out of his thoughts. It had been all about being polite and nice to an ethnic reporter; she'd been drawing back, only giving her email, keeping it contained.

Shelby sounded a low-down piece of dirt – couldn't she see through a shit like that? There must be some attraction. Jake hadn't, after all, mentioned looks or charm. Ahmed rubbed his eyes, tired and depressed, just managing to cling on to a thimbleful of hope, though, remembering Nattie's warm glow.

He turned his mind, cast his eye at his watch. It was ten in the morning. Might as well make the call to Yazid, no point in hanging about. His weekend visitor had been getting into Leeds Friday evening, according to Khalid. If anything were really going on, Ahmed thought, fishing for his mobile, any visiting superior would be twitchy about a reporter on a national newspaper turning up and keen to check him out. He had a strong hunch Yazid would ask him round to his flat again.

He brought up Yazid's number and whisked a look round the carriage. It was fairly full, but no one was paying attention and he wouldn't say anything to cause a stir.

Ahmed was at a table seat, opposite a girl with scraped-back fair hair and a silver nose stud. She'd been staring at him. He thought her quite pretty apart from a droopy turn of mouth like a line saying 'sad' on a stick drawing. She had shed her herringbone coat, leaving it bunched round her middle, and was wearing a front-buttoning grey T-shirt with plenty on view.

He smiled across, thinking a newly met girl on a train might be something to talk about to Yazid and co., if, just suppose, he made progress with Nattie and went more than once to Durham. If anything was really afoot, the last thing he'd want was for a friendship with the Home Secretary's daughter to become known. He gave another little smile of contact to the girl, one of apology at making a mobile call, and clicked the green button.

'Who's this?' Yazid answered guardedly.

'Ahmed. Just getting back into Leeds and wondered if you're around this weekend. Be good to see—'

'Oh yes, Ahmed,' Yazid broke in, affecting to sound casual, 'I've got visitors here and we were talking about you last night, funnily enough. You should come and meet them. Come for food – about two, okay? My uncle has the kebab house on Copter Road; he's good to me! And Aunty Noor is baking her famous roghni naan.'

'Try and keep me away,' Ahmed said lightly. 'I could never have enough of your auntie's cooking!' He thought that was overdoing it. 'I'll come round then,' he added, giving a slight yawn, which was probably heard, but possibly no bad thing. 'See you.'

He sat thinking. He would need facts at his fingertips, quotes from British Islamist troublemakers like Anjem Choudary who was always making a noise in the press and urging Muslims not to co-operate with the police. And a few anti-Semitic slurs, sentiments like 'monkeys and pigs', the British media being 'Zionist-controlled' and television magnates 'of the Tribe of Judah'. He must praise the suicide bomber for being 'shaheed', a martyr, and 'fulfilling his duty to Allah'. It was going to take iron nerves, Ahmed knew. He had to sound believable and pitch it right.

'Penny for them?' the girl said, causing him to snap back fast.

He grinned. 'Cost a lot more than that. You on the way home? Visiting?'

'My nan lives in Leeds.'

'She'll be glad to see you, I'm sure.' The train was arriving. He felt relieved, blackly depressed about Shelby – in no mood for chatting up. Giving a friendly nod, he stuffed hardly-read newspapers into his small rucksack and rose.

'They're going great now, aren't they, back in the Premier League!' She was picking up on his blue and white Leeds scarf, pushing for more contact.

'Yeah. It's an away day, though. Next Saturday should be good. Take care.' He smiled, getting ready to run. Then, bundling off the train and out of the station, he just made a bus that took him to seedy rundown Harehills, home of his childhood years.

Of course he loved his parents, but, walking in, he felt swamped with a weary stifling sense of confinement. The house, a small post-war semi with an ugly flat front window, was in a lone street of semis near the huge green-domed mosque.

All the surrounding streets were terraced: short, steep and for-bidding, swept through with filthy litter: streets where sunlight seldom managed to penetrate and yellowish moss was about the only thing to grow. The terraced houses were dirty dark-red brick with tall front steps, hazardous for toddlers and old bones. In a nearby row of shops the Kareem Immigration Services, Specialists in Asylum Law, nestled between the Harar restaurant and the Shaan pharmacy and there were vast incongruous advertising hoardings backing on to the mosque.

Ahmed found the glaring ethnicity of his parents' front room – whose gaudy carpet with its thundering horses and desert scene hit you right between the eyes – newly depressing. A black-glass-framed picture, one his parents had always clung to, was bordered with the ninety-nine names for Allah worked in gold. Al-Hakam, the Judge, Al-Wahhab, the Bestower, Al-Malik, the King . . . Ahmed thought of devout Muslims murmuring every name as they counted their thirty-three beads three times.

'Hi Mum, hi Pops,' he called, shaking himself out of the grudging mood.

'That you back, Ahmed? You got an early train.'

He kissed his mother. 'Must get going on the laptop, something urgent.' Escaping upstairs, he knew his brusqueness had hurt and went back down to give her a proper hug.

It was going to drive him mad, living at home. He'd called to say he wouldn't need feeding, wouldn't be in their hair – hardly in his father's, of course, whose head was as light-brown and smooth as a shiny acorn. Ahmed dreaded the loss of his own. He felt a swell of emotion for his small dear father who went to the mosque most evenings and never missed a Friday. That was when the older generation sat around drinking tea and made it a social occasion.

His hometown had been Peshawar, an ancient city close to the Afghanistan border that Ahmed hoped to visit one day. His father had studied at the University of Lahore, done some civil engineering, come to Britain, worked in the mills, progressed to cabdriver, gone home briefly for an arranged marriage and returned with his bride.

Ahmed's mother was from a village near Ghorghushti, the northernmost town in the Attock region. Girls in the rural villages had a very basic education, all the more so in his mother's day; forty years on she still spoke heavily accented English and hung on to old ways.

His father's English was faultless; he was qualified, intelligent, but still driving a cab. If only he could have made the leap into a job more suited to his capabilities.

Ahmed's two older sisters were married, living locally and often round with a toddler for their mother to mind. He had five little nephews and nieces who would be under his feet the whole time. Where else could he stay, though? The mosque was unlikely to rent him a room. Student accommodation? Swinging that would be hard.

It was a problem for later, he thought, as he went online. He checked his email first, holding off composing one to Nattie. It made sense to wait. Better if she found it when she was back in Durham and knew the shape of her week.

Yazid's flat was above a launderette owned by one of his many relations. Ahmed walked there slowly, thinking of his father's obvious deep bitterness over the spread of radical Islamist views. Yazid's parents blamed a charismatic speaker at one of the summer camps apparently; in Ahmed's father's eyes, however, they were weak and wrong to have had even a shaky reconciliation. He considered Yazid a disgrace and thought he and his friends were abusing the prophets, in league with the devil. He had understandable suspicions about his own son's behaviour too, the sudden newfound interest in prayer and the mosque, the company he was keeping.

His father had chosen to let off steam about it just when Ahmed had been hurrying to leave for London and the *Post* party. He'd come home for lunch and over the meal had let rip, nearly making Ahmed miss his train.

Pushing away his plate, his father said forcefully, 'I hope you're not going to write about Yazid's views and his friends'. Don't you go speaking out, we'd be ostracized. You just remember brotherhood unity, son. This community sticks together.'

'It's not like that, Pops. I'm only doing research, it won't appear in the paper.' Ahmed had strongly resented being made to feel like a recalcitrant teenager.

His father's eyes, angry and disbelieving, latched on to his son. 'Wasting that good brain of yours. Why couldn't you have studied law and got a proper job, a profession. Newspapers, pah! They're for soggy chips. All your highfalutin ideas and airs: it's that boy in your flat. And now you come back here, putting your head above the parapet and making trouble – think where your loyalties lie. You leave Yazid and the like to their warped minds and keep your peace.' His small hands had set up a tremble of rage; they gripped the table to gain control.

'You have to trust me, Pops. It's serious, I'm really worried about the way things are. I won't do anything to bring dishonour.' How could uncovering dangerous extremism ever do that, he thought, in deep frustration.

He turned the corner. The launderette was at the end of the street.

Why did he feel quite so certain something was going on? In the previous ten days of spending time with the trio, all their propaganda about Islam and the evils of the West had been comparatively superficial. They'd praised a Hezbollah DVD – whose PR was better than most, Ahmed knew – and intimated owning others showing beheadings and suicide attacks. If it came to watching that sort of terrifyingly morbid pornography, Ahmed thought, there was a real chance he might throw up.

He'd inquired after school acquaintances, girls; they'd had plenty of more general chat. Yazid and Iqbal had presented a moralizing front; they didn't mess with the sisters, sure, but Ahmed knew they drank in private and had sex with Western girls. Khalid was different, pious and pure with his big gentle smile. That was one of the worries: his smile was absent now, he was unhappy and withdrawn.

What confused Ahmed most were the missing surges of fiery extremist zeal, the reflected gleam of some great speaker's spell-casting passion – wouldn't true converts and disciples find it hard to hide their messianic fervour? Either he was driving the wrong way up a one-way street, he thought, or the group were well schooled, trained not to draw that sort of attention.

He rang the bell at the side door, glancing in through the launderette window at a row of glum-faced singles staring at their tumbling smalls in the machines. Yazid came down to let him in. Seldom seen out of the dreary dark suits he wore for the council, today he was in Hilfiger denim.

Where did he get the money for designer labels? The radicals knew the appeal; the kids they were after needed role models, something better than the dead-end prospects they assumed they faced. Religion didn't really come into it.

'Hi there, come on up,' Yazid said with positive warmth. Even a mite of respect, Ahmed thought, quite a contrast to his early aggressiveness.

Yazid was tallish with short springing-backwards hair; a long low curving hairline gave it a rather monk-like, pudding-bowl look. He went ahead upstairs and into the front room of the flat. The rumble of machines from the launderette filtered up through the floorboards. There were chairs with wooden arms, beanbags, a low table and four people standing around.

Yazid introduced the strangers. 'You must meet Fahad,' he said with enough awe in his voice to suggest the man was royalty.

'And I've brought along a friend,' Fahad smiled, comfortable in the role. 'This is Haroon. We needed to chat; always difficult, living in different parts. I'm Cumbria way; he's Halifax. I was brought up there too, then got into Cambridge, did a bit of travelling, moved on.'

'I'm living away too,' Ahmed said easily, 'but this is home and it's good being back.' Fahad and Haroon were about ten years older, light years more senior and sophisticated than Yazid and his friends. What were they doing, spending time together? 'Actually, London was getting to me,' he went on. 'I've been feeling three-quarters detached at work, even, well, a bit lonely, I guess.'

Keeping marginally still attached seemed politic at that point. Ahmed could sense that Fahad, with his obvious high intelligence, was making sharp assessments.

'You share a flat, though, didn't I hear?' Fahad queried. Who from? Had they been checking him out already? No, that was fanciful. His parents knew, Ahmed thought. They must have just happened to mention it to Yazid's, who'd passed it on.

'Yes, and I quite like my flatmate,' Ahmed answered, 'but he's not a soulmate. It's hard to explain. I've been feeling a real need to get out. It was a number of things, odd influences, a particular conversation with my editor.'

He met Fahad's eye while absorbing his well-cut grey flannels and mauve-stripe suitably casual shirt: the short, neatly trimmed hair. He was a broad-shouldered man with a thick neck, slightly squat and square in build. It was his emollient cultured tone of voice that marked him apart, Ahmed thought, knowing that he, too, was in the spotlit arc of Fahad's studying gaze. The interest cut both ways.

'We should have a chat about it sometime,' Fahad said, as Yazid was opening foil bags and letting out a meaty aroma. 'I'd like to hear more.'

The meal was imminent. Through in a passage-width kitchen Iqbal was to be seen piling naan bread and tossing salad. He worked in a café nights, and by day used his lovingly tended, uninsured Ford Focus as a mini-cab. *Kafir* capitalism was unsupportable, he'd said with a wink, going along to draw his dole.

Fahad was expecting some response. Ahmed said evenly. 'Yep, be good to talk about it all, I'd appreciate that. You're only here for the weekend?'

'Sure. Just touching base with these chaps.' Fahad gave Yazid a friendly shove. 'They came on one of the summer camps I organize – lectures, prayers, football, physical training, that sort of stuff. It's good for the brothers to have a break from all the Islamophobia – being socked shit the whole time.'

'How do people get to hear about the camps?' Ahmed asked, anxious to keep his interest sounding mild. 'Do you advertise, have a website?'

'It's mainly word of mouth. Yazid invited Iqbal and Khalid. We operate through an Internet forum too, invitation only. That's recently launched and going well.'

Haroon had come to sit on a sofa arm and listen in. He seemed in almost comically inverse proportion to Fahad. His hollow face was more bony-looking for a beard; he was thin as a string bean. Yet he had a naturally easy manner, like a party animal, a good mixer. Ahmed thought he would do well in a non-Muslim environment despite the black beard.

'And the camps help spread the word,' he remarked approvingly, responding to Fahad before bravely branching out. 'Just after I arrived in London a few years back,' he said smiling, 'I went to a big protest outside Westminster Cathedral.' He was lying and hurried on, hoping he'd mugged up enough to get by. 'The Pope had said violence had no place in spreading faith, you remember, and even tried to suggest that was a command of God in the Koran.'

'What made you go?' Fahad looked at him keenly. 'Did you feel that strongly?'

'I was working at the BBC. It felt good to be among friends.'

'Anjem Choudary has spoken up about that, hasn't he?' Ahmed felt Fahad was setting tests.

'Yes,' he answered, 'and I've heard him give reporters an impressively hard time! Saying in effect that for any insults to Islam and Muhammad there were certain deserving actions ... Choudary talked of "the divine call of jihad". The Koran does, after all, say, "Strike with your wealth, hands and tongue".' He stared at Fahad, trying to mask his nerves.

Fahad maintained eye contact. 'Anjem was once asked on the BBC why he wouldn't condemn the killing of innocent people.'

'I heard that interview. He had a good answer, I thought. "At the end of the day, when we say 'innocent people' we mean 'Muslims'." And he got across too, that non-Muslims haven't accepted Islam, which is a crime against God.'

'Grub up,' Yazid broke in awkwardly. It was a welcome intervention, as Ahmed was running out of quotes. He got up to help move chairs and beanbags, hoping he'd sown a seed or two and that Fahad might consider him on side enough to be worth pursuing.

The afternoon was spent in a fuggy haze, the atmosphere as thick with smoke as a political backroom – which it pretty much was. They had endless cups of coffee with their cigarettes. Iqbal and

Khalid drank tea. Ahmed, who had been trying and almost succeeding in licking smoking, gratefully lit up. He savoured every drag, letting it out through his nostrils in long slow breaths, fancying it was sharpening his mind, dispelling any weariness. An iron will was going to be needed not to slide backwards and undo months of good work.

He tried to concentrate, but Nattie was on his mind. Disconnected thoughts: she was unlikely to smoke, sure to disapprove. Shit, how was he going to get it into his thick stupid head that the mildest come-on at a party meant less than nothing? Even warm smiles over a cup of tea, should it ever happen, would mean little more. Accepting another fag, he thought that if Shelby Tait were the tool that Jake made out, then the physical appeal must be strong.

Tiredness was setting in; he feared making silly slips and being wrong-footed. Khalid finally broke things up, saying it was time for prayers – to Ahmed's relief. He took the opportunity, saying he should really check in at home, given he was just back from London and also, which was true, he was seeing a few of the brothers later on, old school contacts.

'Did I hear you've decided to give up your job at *The Post*?' Fahad asked, picking up on the mention of London. 'That's quite a dramatic step. I'm interested in why – what you began saying earlier about your editor. You free tomorrow? Shall we have a chat round noon?'

'If you can spare the time,' Ahmed said, with a throb and burn of adrenaline like circulation returning to numb limbs. 'I'd be grateful for some advice.'

He left the flat almost immediately, feeling exhilarated. Things could be hotting up. Then a wave of dread depression doused him down. If he had stumbled so quickly and easily on to something as serious as he feared, did that mean cells were proliferating? Were there similar little gangs of potential terrorists in communities everywhere? Or was it simply happenstance, discovering this group? Were they simply Islamic sympathizers and nothing more?

CHAPTER 7

Ahmed set out just before noon the next day to go back to Yazid's flat. He felt nervous, unprepared for his chat with the mysterious Fahad.

After leaving them the previous evening he'd spent hours in a smelly stuffy café, trying to pick up the threads with old school contemporaries. They were a rebellious lot, frighteningly full of conspiracy theories, feeling failed by the state, stuck in dead-end jobs in their tight little locality, imagining futures as thrilling as a mud-spattered walk in the rain.

He had needed to tune into their wavelength, listen and glean clues, sense the mood of the moment. Osborne wanted a story on honour killings as well which, since it involved trying to unravel dark family secrets, would be a difficult, delicate business.

It had seemed an amazing coincidence at first that all the talk had been about a girl at risk of her life. But it happened; perhaps it wasn't so surprising. She'd been badly beaten up by her father for an affair with a Hindu doctor, it seemed, but had escaped and hadn't been seen since. The gossiping crowd in the café had swapped meaningful glances. If the father found her, the looks implied, that would be the end of her.

Ahmed had spent all morning trying any way he could think of
to reach the girl; he'd failed dismally, for all his training and skills.
Her name was Leena, she was a student at Leeds University, but no
one there had been forthcoming. His calls to refuges, Women's Aid,
domestic violence helplines had been met with wire-topped suspicion and total lack of success; he was Muslim, male, a reporter.

He knew that telling the police would achieve nothing except get
him personally involved, which would be no help to Leena and undo
all his groundwork so far.

Poor wretched girl, he thought, as the launderette and Yazid's flat
came into view. Even in some safe house or refuge and more closely
guarded than an American president, she was at risk: such things had
a habit of getting out.

His morning's efforts had left no time for more mugging up in
advance of his meeting with Fahad. Ringing the bell for the door
beside the launderette, Ahmed was in despair of his ability to make
progress in any direction – although his adrenaline shot up like a
high temperature when Fahad himself came downstairs to let him in.

'Only me here,' he said, going ahead. 'Yazid's taken Haroon to
meet a few students. I was making some tea.' Inside the flat he
poured them both a cup, took his to one of the chairs with wooden
arms and lit up.

The cigarette packet on the table was pushed his way. Ahmed sat
down opposite his host, sipped tea and struggled not to give in.

Fahad blew out smoke. 'So tell me . . . Why exactly do you want
to give up your job? What are you thinking of doing instead?'

'I haven't finally decided. I'm considering a PhD. I did journalism
with criminology at Manchester so possibly something to do with
crime. I've saved a bit and could take out a student loan.'

'But why are you so suddenly turned off journalism? I'm curious. You've progressed fast by all accounts.' Whose accounts? How did he know so much?

'Have I?' Ahmed sneered, hoping his thoughts were well masked. 'I'm a minion, a first-rung gofer, a Paki, a token ethnic reporter. I write up robbed corner shops,' he exaggerated sarcastically, 'muggings. You think I'll progress at the rate of my *Kafir* peers?' He attempted to curl his lip and let his eyes glaze over with hate – a look he'd been carefully rehearsing in front of a mirror for days.

'Who's your immediate boss? Is he the problem – you don't get on?'

It seemed a neatly slipped-in question. Ahmed wondered whether someone, at Fahad's behest, would soon be calling Des in the office, casually checking, in some neat way, on whether he really had talked about giving up his job.

'Don't start me on the subject of Desmond Wallis!' he snorted, draining his cup and setting it down vigorously. 'Des is an oaf, a tool, a spluttering drunk, a porn-mag wanker.'

May Des forgive him, he thought, feeling a sudden spark of fondness for the old hack. A warning email would need to be sent fast, carefully worded – just in case anyone should call. Fahad would know Des could easily have been primed, of course, but the story still had to stand up.

'I've never been to Pakistan either,' Ahmed went on. 'I'd thought of spending a little time there before getting stuck into studying again.'

'For what it's worth,' Fahad said pleasantly, with an avuncular gaze, 'I'd advise you to hang on to that job for a while. Your mood of disenchantment may pass. You might get promotion, and you know, working on a newspaper . . . there are ways you could be helpful to the cause.'

Ahmed tried to achieve a look of slow dawning. 'That's quite some advice,' he smiled. 'It's taken me months to feel brave enough, sure enough to think of taking this step. My boss has picked up the vibes. He did suggest taking some unpaid holiday before making any rash decision. That's given me pause – it might suggest I'm rated in some paltry way.'

'Of course they rate you. You're clever and they need a Muslim view – as well as being seen to be PC.' Fahad got to his feet. 'I should be off soon. Fancy a ten-minute stroll? Wouldn't mind stretching my legs.'

'Sure – just need a quick slash.'

The door of the john opened outwards. Ahmed pulled it slowly to, keeping his eye firmly trained on the hair-thin line of visibility, just in case. He saw Fahad take out his mobile. Leaving the door not quite closed, straining round over his shoulder, peeing without checking aim – better an audible sound of piss – Ahmed could still just peer through the crack and keep Fahad pinpointed. He saw him opening up the back of his mobile. Why? Was he swapping SIM cards? To avoid being traced?

Ahmed waited a second, flushed then pushed on the door. He'd needed a minute to collect himself, hadn't expected to gather intelligence. But was it really any help?

Fahad unhooked a velvet-collared greenish overcoat, Ahmed put on his leather jacket. They wandered up the street to a small needle-ridden amenity park. A couple of drunks were slumped on benches, a few swearing youths were kicking a ball.

'I'm interested in the conversation you had with your editor,' Fahad said.

'It was just after the Leicester Square bomb,' Ahmed answered. 'He called me in and asked me what I felt inside, British or Muslim.'

'And?'

'I said I felt both. But deep down I knew the answer.'

Fahad stroked his chin. Then his mobile rang. 'Sorry, I must take this call,' he said, fishing under his coat and walking a little away to be out of earshot. He was brief – quickly alongside again and returning the phone to an inner pocket.

He turned to Ahmed and gave a relaxed smile. 'We should meet again. It'll be a while before I'm back this way. Would a visit to the Lakes be of interest at all? I need to get out from under at times, too! You could use Iqbal's car; I'll organize that. Give me your number and I'll call.'

The ground was suddenly feeling very boggy. What the hell was he wading into? 'Keep your fucking wits about you,' Osborne had said. 'Could get messy.'

Ahmed turned up his collar against the persistent drizzle and set off home. As he was passing the library a voice hailed him. 'Hey, Ahmed!'

He looked back. Khalid was speeding his pace to catch up and they fell in step. He was a strong young lad, lifting and carrying, biking round deliveries: soft-eyed, clean-shaven, wearing today a cheap-fabric blue and grey anorak and black trousers, old enough to have a sheen. They were of similar height, although at barely twenty Khalid had only just stopped growing.

'Glad you're back, brother,' he said with a shy glance. 'You've come from seeing Fahad?' His quick smile had a questioning 'How was it?' about the eyes, but before Ahmed could answer an unreceptive cloud had sailed in to replace the smile. Khalid's face made clear that had been a blip. No questions, no answers, must have been drummed in like learning tables, like praise for Chairman Mao.

'I'm meeting Fahad again soon,' Ahmed said. 'He's going to call and make plans.'

Khalid looked dubious. They walked on. Ahmed could feel the kid's misery, his obvious yearning to offload. 'You going to the game, Saturday?' he tried.

'If only!'

'I'm sure I can fix a ticket, my sister's in-laws have an in.'

Khalid's face became one big smile again, as of old. Would his defences weaken in time? But how much time, Ahmed wondered tensely, did he actually have?

Ahmed went up to his room immediately after supper that night, well aware of his father and mother exchanging glances. He composed his email to Nattie.

> I so much enjoyed meeting you at Friday's party and hope we can have that cup of tea. Have you got a spare half-hour this week – like Tuesday or Wednesday? Or any day if that's no good. I'd love the chance to see you again. It would mean a lot.

He stared at it long and hard, changed 'love' to 'like', deleted the last sentence and added his mobile number. He signed it 'Ahmed'. No surname, he thought, it was quite restrained enough already.

It wasn't original or witty. Did that matter? Leaving it unsent, he carefully thought out an email to Des explaining the need for cover over the chucked-job story. He pinged that one off instantly, deleting it from 'Sent Items' too, as a precaution. Mindful of his editor's peremptory demand to be called with regular reports, he thought it made sense to contact Osborne as well, in the morning.

Ahmed lay on his bed and thought about Nattie: her face, her golden smile, her way of standing with a foot out to the side, slightly bent-kneed. She was quite tall, conscious of it perhaps? Less tall than him, though: he was glad to have the edge.

He began imagining her body and, hard and aroused, undid his trousers. After a few strokes the mechanical act was a turn-off; he wanted to see her, not be lying on his bed pathetically wanking. He got up abruptly and sent the email after reading it over one last time. Then he wrote up his diary in shorthand, a discipline for a distantly planned novel, and prepared for bed.

He'd been meaning to read Osborne's book, *Press Liberties*, which had been published a while back. Ahmed picked it up, hoping it might be dull and dated enough to help send him to sleep.

CHAPTER 8

Nattie's train was just coming into Durham. The house she shared with Sam and Milly was in the Viaduct, no distance from the station, but her mother had insisted she take a cab. It was cold and dark, late on a Sunday night, and Nattie felt quite relieved about it now.

William had run her to King's Cross, given her taxi money and a big hug goodbye. They got on so well, Nattie felt they had a real bond. It could have been very different, though, when you thought of the affair and all its baggage, her father's miserable faltering state. But the marriage break-up had been inevitable.

She'd felt close to William right from the start, first meeting him in a hospital side-room, waiting while her mother was operated on to stop a life-threatening haemorrhage of blood on the brain. She'd been Housing Minister then, hit on the head by a stone when a riot started up at a controversial development site.

Nattie's father, Barney, had been close by. Her mother's condition had been critical. William had rushed to her side with the media chasing, the affair suddenly exposed. He'd had no thought for his own circumstances or career and Nattie had known from the start that he truly cared.

The train was slowing; yet another announcement being gabbled out in a voice that sounded like clacking knitting needles. Reaching down her bag from the rack, refusing help from an annoying man, she thought of her father. They'd had lunch just that very day.

Blood ran deep, her love for Barney did too, but he'd brought it all on himself. He was so much his own worst enemy. Even marriage to a nice young fellow solicitor seemed to be off. Nattie could imagine why. Her father had no control and could be violent occasionally, although always desperately contrite afterwards. He was back living with Dick, his ghastly golfing mate, in Dick's cavernous Holland Park flat.

Barney had looked really rough at lunch, his hands shaking badly. Shouldn't he go to some alcoholics' place and get dried out? Her mother was the only one to persuade him, Nattie knew, but she was working crazy hours and William would get so uptight. He and Barney still couldn't be in the same room together.

Standing by the train door poised to get out, Nattie thought resentfully of her father going on about Shelby at lunch. He never left off. Pity they'd ever met.

'How's that dago boyfriend of yours, then?' His grin had been maddening.

'Shelby's English, Dad, just dark-haired. And he's not mine, I don't see him that much, hardly at all.' Only once in a while when he chooses, she thought bitterly, while trying to avoid eye contact with the man who'd leaped up to help with her bag.

William knew not to ask about boyfriends. He'd said once to tell him if she ever needed help, he'd always treat it in confidence, and left it at that.

Nattie thought about her mother's twitchiness all weekend. It was the bomb, but to start feeling personally responsible was just mad.

It had been because of Shelby, too. The low mood Nattie was fighting crept back as inevitably as the wash of a night tide. She felt a deep sense of anticlimax and let-down over Ahmed; she had been so sure he would get in touch. No email, though. She'd just checked. It never did to assume things, she thought, however wonderful and keen he'd been at the party. And, anyway, wasn't it all about needing a morale booster, self-protection, a diversion from Shelby? He was the real cause of her depressed mood.

Standing her up again on Saturday night – and at the last minute. She'd been all psyched up, dressed and ready. How could he be such a knob? He'd needed to see a man, Shelby said; it was work, good money, hard to turn it down. That was his shit explanation.

Her best friend, Maudie, had tried to set her straight, but she was a more confident person. Nattie felt worried for Tom, who must sense there were other attractions in his girlfriend's life; she'd been having a very good time away at uni.

Maudie had said she should stop being so *there* for Shelby, which hardly took a degree in rocket science. But Maudie had no clue, had never been drenched by his deluge of charm; it drowned out good sound sense, it was as addictive as the whisky bottle was to Barney.

Shelby had called that morning, sheepish and contrite, sounding like a little boy in need of his mother. He'd begged her to stay over. 'What's a day or two matter? I need you a whole lot more than dinky provincial Durham. Stay in London a couple more nights – please!'

Nattie had only found the will not to do that, to leave to go back Sunday as planned, because of feeling buoyed up by meeting Ahmed. She'd been so certain he would get in touch. And he couldn't even be bothered to email. Oh, shit.

The train shuddered to a standstill and she climbed down. The irritatingly attentive man, who was wearing a gold ring, tried to help with her bag. 'No, it's all right, really – not heavy.' She smiled briefly, clinging to it, and looked straight ahead.

On the short cab-ride to Hawthorn Terrace Ahmed was on her mind. Her mother never let up, saying you couldn't trust the press, there was always an ulterior motive. Ahmed hadn't been like that. He was different. And it was a bit rich of her mother, she thought crossly, who had only gone and married one of the toughest pressmen around. That was an irony and a half.

Her lowness pressed like a plank across her shoulders; she'd really liked Ahmed and felt comfortable with him, not strained. It all sucked. She just wanted to get indoors, back in her little house, maybe hang out with Sam and Milly, but really needing to be on her own and in bed.

Monday morning's lecture was boring, boring – why ever had she chosen a module on Chaucer? Nattie had overslept, been late, couldn't concentrate and couldn't wait to get through it. She stayed around town then, hanging out with a crowd of students at their favourite café, Brown Sugar, and finally went home quite late in the afternoon.

It was a relief to be first in. The house in Hawthorn Terrace had no hall, not even an internal porch; you walked straight into the living room with the staircase off it. The kitchen was through to the back with a Formica table against the wall and a back door out to a manky little yard.

Sam and Milly's rooms were on the first floor. Nattie's was the sloped-ceiling attic room; she regularly hit her head getting in and out of bed. All three girls fought over a draughty, cracked-lino half-landing bathroom.

She made a mug of tea, took it upstairs and sat at her desk taking reviving sips as her laptop warmed up. Her depression still hung heavy. Shelby hadn't called again, not even a text.

She brought up her emails: none from Shelby – but there was one from Ahmed.

Opening it, Nattie's heart felt tense. It seemed restrained and cautious, but warm, too. 'I so much enjoyed meeting you . . . hope we can have that cup of tea. Have you got a spare half-hour . . . like Tuesday or Wednesday?' Unlike Shelby Ahmed had followed through. His mobile number was there; she felt tempted to call, but matched his restraint and emailed.

> Say Wednesday for our cup of tea! Will you get the train? Call me and we can fix when and where to meet. Nattie.

She gave her own mobile number with a small qualm, so conditioned not to hand it out to the press. It would be all right, she thought. William was Ahmed's editor, after all.

The front door slammed. 'Hi, whoever it is,' she yelled downstairs. 'That you, Sam?' She felt full of bounce suddenly, shaking off all the damp feelings of lowness like a dog coming in from the rain.

'Both here,' Sam yelled back. 'We're opening some vino, come on down.'

Nattie sipped wine and looked over the glass at her two girl-friends. Milly, so serene, fair and rounded, often on diets, but never boring about it, and Sam who was the opposite, pointy-elbowed and angular, though in an attractive sharp-featured way. She was good fun, super-bright, always working out some amazing money-making wheeze for the future. Sam played up an estuary accent, loved to shock and never turned down the chance to bitch or slag someone off. But she was direct, you knew where you were with her.

'I had a nice time at the *Post* party, amazingly enough,' Nattie said, feeling a need to prepare the ground. 'I even met this quite nice bloke. He's coming over from Leeds for tea.'

'That's keen,' Sam said. 'A reporter? Has he got a byline? Do we know his name?'

'Ahmed.' His surname came to her thinking of the email address. 'Ahmed Khan.'

'What else!' Sam laughed. That grated. She saw it had, though, and said quickly, 'I wasn't having a go, it's only just there are an awful lot of Khans.'

Nattie made a forgiving face and sipped her wine.

Her mobile rang. She dug in her jeans pocket and answered casually. Ahmed's voice took her by surprise. With a noisy scraping-back of her chair, Nattie went hurriedly to stand by the glass-panelled back door in the kitchen. It was raining, large drops were clattering down on the rubbish bin outside.

'Thanks for the email,' Ahmed was saying. 'I'll come by train and I've printed off a map so I can easily find my way. You just say when and where.'

'There's a tearoom, the Georgian Townhouse – but I'll come to the station,' Nattie said spontaneously when it would have been better holding back. 'I live very close. Say about two? I can show you round, we can have a walk or whatever, then have tea.'

'I'll call with a train time. I, um, don't suppose Tuesday's as good as Wednesday?'

There was nothing she couldn't miss. 'If it suits you better,' Nattie said quite coolly, feeling it was typical of her, so readily agreeing as well as offering to meet him.

'Well, yes, really . . . That's great, wonderful! I'll get back about the train.'

She clicked off and stared out at the spattering rain for a moment before going back.

'From the look of you,' Milly said, 'he must be cool, a real keeper. When do we get to meet him?'

'It's not like that,' Nattie grinned, desperate not to be drawn. It had been hurtful thinking Ahmed hadn't been much interested, but now . . . 'He's okay,' she said dismissively, enjoying her private thrill, 'sort of easy. It's like, well, anything to give up Shelby. Do you know, he stood me up again Saturday, the knob. I'm such a loser, couldn't even tell him to go and put it elsewhere.'

'They're all fuckers and arseholes,' Sam said. 'We might as well just stay home and get stoned.'

Ahmed's train was on time. Hurrying over the viaduct bridge, Nattie saw him come out of the station and look round anxiously. She thought he had a good face. Strong brows and wonderfully warm eyes – and there was a warmth to his expression too, like someone with a sense of fun who was also thoughtful and humane. His hair was cut short, straight and glossy, as jet-black as Shelby's. He was in a brown leather jacket and jeans.

He waved and hurried over. 'Hi! It's good to see you.' He gave her hand a quick touch.

She smiled. 'Okay journey? Must have taken ages!'

Ahmed was staring, just like at the party. He shook his head. 'It was easy, just a change at York.'

'I thought we might walk a bit,' Nattie said, feeling in the role of host and reassuringly flattered by his gaze. 'Perhaps take in the Cathedral.' She was forgetting there could be sensitivities and added clumsily, 'If that's not a problem or anything?'

'No, I love looking at beautiful churches. There's so much I want to see.'

'It's massive, Norman, very sturdy and unfussy with huge chevron-patterned pillars – lovely and quite sort of butch! And I do remember being told once,' she said, pleased at the thought, 'that there's some Islamic influence: the rib vaults in the choir. It was through the Crusaders. So there's a link. And also there's the most beautiful bridge you ever saw, near the Cathedral, Prebends Bridge. It's eighteenth century—' Nattie dried up then, thinking she was wittering on too much.

They were walking down a narrow street of old townhouses that were well kept, the woodwork freshly painted; she felt proud of the city. Ahmed was taking it all in, but mostly turning to look at her. He gave a sidelong glance down at her hand, she noticed, as though half-wanting to take it. She half-wished he would.

After the Cathedral she touched his arm. 'Now come and see Prebends Bridge. It's just down South Bailey. I love it, the old stone, the special little inset places for looking out, they're like tiny theatre-boxes, or balconies – very popular with people proposing, I'm told!'

'It's mystical,' Ahmed said, as they stood together in one of them, gazing downstream. 'Beautiful. The river's so peaceful and serene. I wish I felt as calm.'

'Why don't you?'

He turned to smile. 'I'm standing too close to you.'

Pleased, but uncertain how to react to that, she said hurriedly,

'There's a Walter Scott poem engraved at the end of the bridge. It's about the Cathedral. Come and see!' She resisted taking his arm, although it had felt an instinctive thing to do.

He read out the lines, rather movingly, she thought.

> 'Grey Towers of Durham,
> yet well I love thy mixed and massive piles,
> half church of God, half castle 'gainst the Scot,
> and long to roam these venerable aisles,
> with records stored of deeds long since forgot.'

They began walking back through the town and on up Crossgate to the Georgian Townhouse, the place she thought best for tea.

'Thanks,' he said with a light squeeze of her arm, 'for Prebends Bridge, for being with me.'

'It was good; I enjoyed it.' They went into the teashop. 'The pancakes are the thing here,' Nattie said smiling, happily conscious of enjoying herself.

She was glad to get in the warmth; it had begun to drizzle. They sat on a bench-seat together, narrow, but comfy with cushions. There was no one else there that wet winter weekday although it might easily have been full of students.

Ahmed was looking round. 'That's a cool mural, like a French provincial kitchen.' There were cats painted in, pots and pans, books, foxes and pheasants. 'And I saw there's a B&B next door too,' he said, half to himself. 'It would be a perfect place to stay.' Nattie studied the menu-card thinking that had been provocative; she didn't want him pushing it. Or was she just reading too much into his words?

Her hand was up on the table and he rested his fingers lightly on its back. 'Have I said something? Can't you give me your smile? I need it right now.'

She couldn't help her face lighting up; she laughed at herself for doing it and he did, too. He could sense the slightest change of her mood, she thought.

A waitress came to take their order. 'I only want tea, but you should have the famous pancakes,' Nattie pressed. 'And the hot chocolate's really good.'

He ordered two pots of tea. 'I can't not have tea, it was sort of the whole point! Well, actually,' he hesitated a second then grinned, 'not true. Tea doesn't come into it. You do, your amazing smile.' He touched her hand again. 'Can I ask things? You won't think I'm just being a reporter?'

Nattie was basking, enjoying being stared at, loving the attention after having slight nerves that it might turn out to be a difficult draggy afternoon. A flirty little chat at a party was one thing, but it could have got heavy and awkward. You couldn't trust reporters, after all . . . 'Go on then,' she grinned. 'Ask me things.'

'When you didn't try to put me off coming, was that mostly about feeling you should be polite? Like, well, your stepfather did bring you over to meet me, probably saying be nice to me, I expect. Did you feel, well, good about it when we were talking?'

Ahmed was holding her eyes, his face unsmiling. She stared back feeling slightly caught out, but wanted to be honest and take it seriously. 'I don't know. Possibly there was a bit of that, sort of subconsciously. But I forgot to think about it – if I had done at all. I certainly wasn't thinking anything like that in the Cathedral. You're you, I enjoyed talking to you at the party, I like you.'

'Like's an awful word.'

'So's awful . . . Don't push it!'

'But is "liking" enough to let me come back and take you out?'

Nattie didn't answer. Her heart was thudding loudly. She wanted him to, but it would go places and what about Shelby? Two-timing wasn't her thing.

'There's someone else?' She looked down. 'I do know about him,' Ahmed went on. 'My flatmate's met him and said he talked about you.' Talking was about it, she thought bitterly, no good to her at all. How much more was she going to take from Shelby?

'It's a bit of an on-off thing,' she muttered, still with her head bent. Ahmed lifted her face. She gave him her eyes and said suddenly, just thinking of it, 'Why don't you come over for supper, Saturday? We're cooking, having a few in.' She had talked about the house and Sam and Milly, on the way to the Cathedral. Her insides were fluttering, his hand had felt so gentle lifting her face. She imagined it bringing her closer for a kiss.

'It's nothing special, just a few friends,' she said, then added, remembering Ahmed was twenty-four, 'There's a mature student coming too, who's twenty-eight.'

'I'd like that very much,' he said. The tea had arrived; it was poured, getting cold. She sipped from her cup. 'I'm in Cumbria during the day,' Ahmed carried on. 'I've got to meet someone who wants to walk in the Lakes – so as not to be overheard, I think. I don't trust him. I'm going by car, though, so I'll have wheels.'

'Will you be safe?' He seemed surprised, alarmed even, at the question and she went on to explain. 'You see, I, um, asked William if you were writing a series on Leeds or something. It seemed odd really, you being there for so long.'

'What did he say?' Ahmed looked amused, intrigued.

'That you were sniffing out terrorists. I took that as a joke. William plays things so close. He and Mum are both as bad, secretive as spies about work. But it wasn't a joke then?'

'Half a one, he was exaggerating. I'll be fine – just hard to know my timing.'

'Come whenever.' She smiled. 'I should get back, now. I'm way late with an essay on the Brontës.'

He asked for the bill and she went to the ladies. Staring into the mirror, putting on lip-gloss, Nattie thought supper with friends was a good solution, nothing to feel guilty about – however she was feeling inside. Anyway, how could she be disloyal to Shelby?

Ahmed helped her on with her navy reefer coat, a reject of Tom's. 'Can I walk you home?' he said. 'I'll know where to come then, on Saturday.'

'Thanks. It's not far.' She flashed him another smile as they went out.

'Pity.'

They set off and he reached for her hand. 'Does this count as molesting, do you think?'

'Definitely. You know it does.'

He smiled and lifted her hand to his cheek. Bringing it down, he entwined fingers. 'It's going to be a long week.'

'I hope you'll like Sam and Milly. Sam's a bit spiky, she'll try and shock you.'

'Not easy.'

'She'll say something awful, racist even, just to see how you react.' Nattie smiled. 'But she's okay underneath. Cool looks, you'll fancy her.'

'I'm very focused right now.' He brought up their linked hands and kissed hers. They were walking in a narrow residential lane and two youths ahead of them were watching their progress. One was swinging a beer bottle. Nattie felt a small coil of fear.

'They'll roll that or throw it to trip me up,' Ahmed muttered. 'I'm sorry, we can't really turn back.' He tried to let go her hand, but she held on tight wanting to stay connected. Almost level with the boys, the bottle came hurtling. Ahmed sidestepped it and it crashed into the kerb.

'Mother-fucker,' one of them sneered. 'Get your filthy Paki hands off, stick to your own brown shit.' He spat. Nattie felt the spray and resisted wiping at her face.

The other boy was sniggering, chanting out, 'Paki, Paki, Paki.'

They got past. The first one yelled after them, 'We'll get you, fucker.' A jagged piece of brown beer-bottle glass came singing their way and shattered beside them.

'We should go straight and report them,' Nattie said furiously. 'I feel so ashamed. They should be locked up.'

'There speaks the Home Secretary's daughter! It's pointless. I feel dreadful, exposing you to that – it was holding your hand. I shouldn't have been, it's kind of a red rag. You should have protection, given your mother's job; you would do in other countries.'

'Don't be funny. Think of having Rodney with us all afternoon.' They both giggled at that and she leaned into Ahmed's side. 'This is my street,' she said, as they rounded a corner. 'We're the one with the green door.'

She fished in a pocket for her key and looked up. He traced round her face. 'We won't be able to talk, Saturday, and there's so much I want to say and ask . . . Would you come for a drive on Sunday? I'll stay up here overnight.'

'I don't know.' She felt panic rising, far more so than walking towards the thugs. Ahmed was here, wanting to see her, Shelby wasn't. But he might appear any time. He did things like that, turned up with huge armfuls of red roses, champagne, quantities of scent. He'd sweep her off to a snob restaurant. It was easy to feel over-whelmed, showered and feted, even though money and presents weren't the point.

Ahmed brushed over her lips with his fingers. He put his mouth to hers, the lightest kiss, but her lips began to tingle. The sensation left her feeling torn in two and, strangely, with a sense of loneliness.

'I'll call. You won't mind?' His eyes were so warm. She stared back with a knot in her stomach, feelings of physical need, then turned away and slotted her key in the door.

'No, it's cool,' she said, smiling back over her shoulder. 'You'll be okay, going for the train? The station's only five minutes: two lefts and over the viaduct bridge.'

She went indoors with a thundering heart and ran upstairs to her sloping attic room not knowing whether to keep up a Cheshire-cat smile or fling herself down on the bed and have a good long tension-releasing cry.

CHAPTER 9

It was Saturday. Ahmed had got through the three days since seeing Nattie, although he wasn't quite sure how. She'd filled his every waking thought. He had called, they'd talked, emailed, had long interesting discussions with texted afterthoughts; it had felt like they were laying the base bricks of a real relationship.

Dangerous imagining that, he thought, driving across-country to the Lakes. He couldn't wait to be going on to Durham, to be through the gruelling nerve-racking meeting with Fahad that afternoon. It felt pivotal, make or break. Ahmed was sure he was about to discover how trusted he was, if at all. How dangerous Fahad was.

And Osborne had called the day before, tellingly, making it seem more certain than ever that something seriously scary was going on. Someone had phoned in, Osborne said, which he thought – and Ahmed did too – had been a clever snooping inquiry about whether Ahmed had genuinely talked in the office of giving up his job.

Des had taken the call – from a girl who seemed panicky about not keeping a date with Ahmed, saying she'd lost his mobile number and hadn't a second now, just boarding a plane, but could they tell him she'd ring in a couple of weeks.

'Desmond gave her the line,' Osborne said, 'told her, in his own chosen words, you were mucking them about, being given too much rope by half in his humble opinion and might be permanently "not at your desk" by then.

'Could it have been a genuine call?' Osborne had added, almost as an afterthought. Ahmed said there was no one who could fit. A girl on a train might conceivably have been chasing, but she hadn't even taken his name.

It had to be Fahad's doing, the idea of a girl, the lengths taken. Driving to meet him, Ahmed shivered, fear of the unknown niggling his gut.

He tried to assess what little he did know. Fahad had let slip he'd been to a top university; he thought himself clever and wanted it known – sign of a slight inferiority complex? Given the sim card, the walk outdoors, he certainly covered his tracks; was that out of shifti-ness or simply some weird complex, an obsessive need to stay shadowy? One thing was clear. Fahad was no low-level incompetent; he paid immense attention to detail. Ahmed felt up against a serious player.

He was minutes away from Kendal, close to where they were to meet, and driving a hired car, not Iqbal's. Using that as Fahad had suggested had seemed like a bad idea. It wouldn't have pleased Iqbal – and he was going on to Durham, after all, staying at the B&B next to where he and Nattie had tea. He certainly didn't want Nattie in Iqbal's car.

Driving round with raw nerves, Ahmed was calmed by the charm of Kendal, the 'auld grey town', as he'd heard it called – although he thought that sounded too austere. The dove-grey of the huddled limestone buildings was soft in the pale sunlight and even the impos-ing town hall had a downy, hazy hue.

The town was buzzing, alive, its coffee shops filled with young locals, shoppers; there were plenty of tourists even at this time of year. There was a distant line of low lavender-blue hills like an autumnal stage-set backdrop and the River Kent's old stone bridges had settled charm.

But none touched Prebends Bridge. Ahmed thought of standing beside Nattie at one of its viewing points; he'd been feeling more than just physical nearness. She hadn't minded all his calls and had returned them, gladly helped their understanding to develop. He felt desperate to see her again, to cement the intimacy. And alone, not with half-stoned students hanging around – and no fucking Shelby, either, looking over his shoulder like a ghoul.

There was a reason for the detour into Kendal. Fahad, who seemed a rather unlikely seasoned fell-walker, had been firm about the need for walking boots. Ahmed also wanted to buy Nattie something, but after the lousy traffic time was short.

He thought of her call that morning; full of concern, insisting he buy Kendal Mint Cake to keep up his energy levels. It had felt natural telling her about a meeting with a man he didn't trust, comforting really, but he couldn't possibly let Nattie get involved.

This meeting wouldn't be about recruiting him to the Ramblers' Association. Every taut nerve in his body told him the stakes were high – that Fahad on a roll could cost lives.

In keeping with his need to stay shadowy Fahad had given no phone number. He'd made only a single call himself, saying he'd be in contact nearer the time in case Ahmed was lost.

Losing the car was more of a problem at that moment and, seeing an approachable-looking man in tweeds coming towards him, Ahmed stopped to ask where to park.

'Best place is the Westmorland Shopping Centre. And for the boots, K Village in Stricklandgate. It used to be Clarks Factory Shop – but that perhaps won't mean much to you.' Ahmed resented being presumed a foreigner and it came as a pleasant surprise when that was sensitively picked up. 'But then everyone knows about Clarks shoes,' the man added kindly.

'And where would I buy Kendal Mint Cake?'

'Anywhere. The 1675 Chocolate House is near where you'll be and quite famous.'

Ahmed thanked him warmly. He was soon in the shoe shop having his foot eased into a stiff-sided lace-up by a gnarled white-haired assistant, who lectured him rather tediously about the need for even experienced walkers to take maps and a compass.

'I'm hardly climbing Everest,' Ahmed said with a smile.

It didn't go down well. The elderly salesman yanked hard on the laces. 'Don't know why I bother,' he grumbled. 'It would actually help us, you know, to let you guys get stuck out there when the mists close in.' He sat back on his heels. 'Our mountain rescue team was just turned down for a lottery grant because they hadn't rescued enough ethnics and asylum seekers. Life and death matters should be colour-blind, so our MP said. Bloody political correct-ness.'

'I agree with that,' Ahmed said, grinning. 'The paper I work on ran the story, actually, but getting lost to help the cause is asking a little much, I'm afraid.'

The old boy grunted. 'You'll have it boggy out there after the rain. Watch how you go. These fit fine. You take them to the till – there's a tin right there for our fund.'

Back outside, walking as stiffly in his sturdy new shoes as someone with piles, Ahmed hoped he wouldn't have need of the fundless mountain rescue team to bail him out with Fahad.

Could Fahad really be involved in some ghastly plot? Were Yazid, Khalid and Iqbal being used as pawns? Thinking of simple religious Khalid tugged on the strings; to be snooping in this undercover way was to be breaking the brotherly code. Was Khalid's faith being manipulated and politicized? Was he planning to be a human bomb, to die in the cause? That seemed so melodramatic, yet Ahmed still felt an almost unbearable weight of responsibility.

And if Fahad really were a terrorist would Osborne stay supportive and loyal? Ahmed could imagine becoming an outcast, rejected on every side. That paled into insignificance, though, if his worst fears proved to be true.

It was ten to one, forty minutes till the meeting. Fahad had seemed anxious about the fading light – just how far was he planning to walk? Ahmed tried to calm his nerves thinking of Nattie; he hoped he could find something to take her.

Flowers felt too obvious, and embarrassing with others around. He went into a small second-hand bookshop, cobwebby and Dickensian, with a tinkling bell: a place to shed cares, he thought.

He resisted a Walter de la Mare anthology of love poems and settled on a slim book about the Lakeland poets, mainly Wordsworth and Coleridge – a book he would have liked himself. Finding the 1675 Chocolate House then, quaint and bow-fronted, on an upper level above a cobbled street, he bought a quantity of slabs of Mint Cake. He thought about Nattie describing her stepfather's passion for chocolate, how much ground they had covered in the week.

The Windermere road rose steeply uphill out of the town. When his mobile sounded suddenly Ahmed braked too sharply and his stomach reeled.

'Are you lost yet?' Fahad inquired, slightly patronizingly.

'No, but I could still use some further instructions!'

Fahad's directions were as lengthy and detailed as any zealous scoutmaster's. Taking them down in shorthand, Ahmed felt exhausted before walking a step. He'd had no time to grab a sandwich and, setting off again, broke into a steadying bar of Mint Cake. It brought an instant energy rush. He burned to see Nattie.

He found the Gateway roundabout, took the A591 and after three miles turned off to Staveley. 'Park in Mill Yard,' Fahad had instructed, 'then turn left, left again by St Margaret's Tower and cross over the River Kent on a footbridge.'

So far so good; the river was noisily invigorating, surging, pounding as fiercely as Ahmed's chest. Walking upstream, he could see the backs of old mill buildings and there was a weir too, with what looked like the salmon pass he'd heard talk of in the car park. A couple of naturalists had discussed it with great excitement.

He found the public bridleway with a lovely outlook over open countryside, then the farm with the footpath running through. It was all exactly as Fahad said.

An uphill walled track came next. Ahmed could hear the thundering river way below. Finally he began his descent to the appointed meeting place, a small stone bridge over a stream. It was twenty-eight minutes past one, not bad going.

Fahad was waiting, drawing on a cigarette. He was in a zip-up black fleece, gloves and a grey wool scarf. His walking boots looked properly worn in; either he walked for pleasure – or perhaps regularly conducted remote meetings that required exacting orienteering challenges as an early test.

'You made it. And on time.' Fahad looked approving. Stubbing out his cigarette he felt in his rucksack and handed over a water bottle. 'We should be able to get in three hours or so before the light goes.'

Ahmed stuffed the bottle into a pocket of the old green anorak he'd found at his parents' house. 'They said in Kendal it'll be boggy with all the rain,' he ventured, as they set off uphill. That seemed to deserve no reply.

He'd rejected the idea of bringing a hidden recording machine. As they walked on, climbing more steeply, reaching quiet pasture, taking a series of narrow tracks, he began to wonder fancifully whether Fahad was 'walking out' the length of a tape. They were talking only in generalities, politics, the persecution of Muslims.

Sport even. Fahad asked after his football team.

'It's great, Leeds being back in the Premier League,' Ahmed said. 'I've stuck with them through thick and thin.' He grimaced. 'We're at home today and it's a key match – but, of course, walking is a lot healthier!' He attempted a grin.

'Your editor's into football too, isn't he? I remember he was in Milan for a match when his affair first came to light.' Fahad stopped, stuffed his gloves in a pocket, swigged some water, wiped his mouth and lit up. Ahmed refused a cigarette.

'I find it amazing,' Fahad went on, letting out smoke, 'that now they're married and she's Home Secretary, she goes with him to football games. It's degrading for a woman holding high office.' He was watchful, with narrowed eyes, expecting some responsive comment.

Ahmed was uncertain how to reply. 'You'd find few football fans agreeing with that,' he laughed. 'And she is supposed to be genuinely keen. She supports her constituency team, Southampton – they're also back in the Premier League. They're playing Liverpool soon, that's Osborne's team. It's a home game for her, definitely one she'll try to go to. It'll be a marital shoot-out!'

Giving a diffident grin he went on, 'Politically, of course, it's good for her, being seen at matches, brownie points in it, the television cameras on her. Spineless, self-serving lot,' he added, more watchful of his role. 'She's in the directors' box, featherbedded, her minders on hand.' He could have revealed their names, he thought wryly, feeling a powerful tug of need.

'Yes, I know about that match,' Fahad said, surprising him. 'I saw something about it in the papers – describing it as a marital battle royal.'

Was there nothing that passed him by? They walked on. A dis-lodging rock made Ahmed's heart stop. He thought of those narrowed eyes – surely something must happen soon?

Two women were approaching. With severe faces and practical clothes, they looked like stereotypical magistrates. Nodding, giving faintly suspicious glances, they carried on in the opposite direction.

The tracks had become as boggy as predicted. After a brief uplift-ing view of mountaintops they were in the shadow of conifers. The sky had clouded, a chill wind creeping in. Ahmed picked his way through the squelch with aching legs, keeping braced. He was determined not to let down his guard.

Fahad showed no signs of tiring. When they came to a clearing where anyone could be seen approaching, he stopped. 'I didn't bring you here to talk football,' he said.

'I know that.' Ahmed felt his adrenaline flare like a struck match.

Fahad stared with hardened eyes. 'I wouldn't like to think you'd betray us. You do know what happens to brothers who can't be trusted?' His tone was menacing.

'Of course,' Ahmed answered flatly, suppressing dangerous anger at the threat. Fear was tight-coiled in his gut; he hoped it wouldn't rear up like a snake and be his undoing. He had to keep hold of his cool.

'There's a project I'm handling,' Fahad went on, 'brothers and sisters prepared to give their lives in the name of Allah. Do you want to be involved?'

'Obviously, if I can – you mean through the paper?' Ahmed felt rigid. He tried hard to think of how he might respond in genuine circumstances. Tension was natural, to be expected. Odd if he showed none at all.

'Yes. The spreading of information is always helpful. It's just possible Yazid's flat is being watched and you've been seen, but that shouldn't affect anything.'

Ahmed felt fresh shivers. Without Osborne's backup, he thought, it could be tough proving his innocence. 'You really think the flat might be?'

'Always a chance. However, Yazid is little involved.'

'And the information you want placed?' Ahmed held his breath.

'Petrol tankers are very good at exploding – all by themselves, an initiating device is hardly needed. Think of one driven straight at a service station in a busy town, a residential street, anywhere with space for an accelerating spurt.'

The destructive force of petrol-tanker explosions didn't bear thinking about. Hard to believe, though, that this was truthful information, given all the intensive training, preparation and money that would have been involved, so much at stake. Fahad certainly wouldn't have ruled out the chance of Ahmed being a mole.

'Tanker drivers rest up, they don't all lock their cabs. Drivers can be "replaced", the disposal of bodies is no problem with explosions about to happen,' Fahad commented, taking it further. His single-minded ruthlessness shone out for a second, like the flash of a wild animal's eyes in the forest. Ahmed felt sickened.

'But surely tanker drivers would be drilled, vetted to the skies, given extra warnings, if a story like this appeared in the press?' He tried to look excited and awed.

'Exactly. We want the authorities looking the wrong way, resources stretched.'

'And the reason for that—?' Ahmed assumed the object was to have a freer run for another, still more devastating plot.

Fahad said nothing. He stubbed out a cigarette and set off down the track.

'I am with you, brother,' Ahmed tried again, walking abreast, struggling to keep his breathing even.

Fahad stopped walking, eyed him and looked up at the dusky sky. 'It's getting late. We'll be starting the descent quite soon. I'll point you to a track that takes you to the A592 and from there it's only a few hundred yards to the village where you parked.'

He was lighting up again. Ahmed waited.

'You can't be much involved at this late stage,' Fahad said, blowing out smoke, watching with his narrowed eyes. 'It's taken months, years, of careful planning.'

'But what's going to happen? Can you at least tell me that?'

'There are privately owned aircraft whose pilots are sympathetic to the cause. Whether it's planes or helicopters . . . It is a proven route.'

Ahmed kept on staring. It was impossible to know what, if any of it, could be true. Were they both decoy stories? Was there another plot altogether? Fahad was bent on causing mayhem and panic. Could he even, just possibly, have chosen to trust him?

What motivated the man? Power? Political intrigue – deep religious belief? Born here, a top education. But even the most civilized native Britons had turned traitors in their time.

He was waiting, with watchful eyes, returning the stare. Some response was needed. 'It's so simple,' Ahmed stumbled out, 'awesome! I need a cigarette.'

Fahad held out the packet. He clearly thought his own plan awesome, too. 'The fine timing, tying up dates, perfecting each link in the chain . . . it's mammoth,' he muttered, with cold, pleased conceit. 'You'll see what you can do at *The Post*.'

Ahmed nodded. 'You're asking quite a lot, of course,' he said calculatedly. 'I mean when the story is found to be false, after, um, a successful operation, I'd be suspected of planting it – interviewed, probably sacked, certainly hauled up in front of MI5. But then to think of those martyrs giving their lives, it does kind of fall into perspective.' He chucked down his cigarette. 'I'll do what I can. You can trust me.'

Fahad looked up at the darkening sky. 'You'd better go. I'll stay a few minutes more. I love the solitude out here.'

The car was a haven. Ahmed sat back in the driver's seat feeling in a cold sweat of nervous exhaustion. His thighs were trembling.

He wanted to be well away before phoning Osborne to offload and gathered himself enough to set off. Two hours of driving lay ahead. A hot bath and change of clothes were going to be a long time coming, he thought, relieved to have a room booked.

The call to Osborne was urgent and he began looking for a lay-by. Would his editor dismiss it all as little people talking big? Ahmed felt unsure how much of it to believe himself.

He wasn't hungry, but it seemed sensible to eat. Finishing off the bar of Kendal Mint Cake made him feel close to Nattie and better, more revived. After the call, he decided, he could give himself over to indulgent fantasies – what, in his dreams, might possibly happen later that night.

Nattie was bound to ask about the afternoon. It would be tempting to share it all, the agony of what to believe, what to do. To tell someone who wouldn't talk or leak – except possibly to the only safe source, her Home Secretary mother.

It would be even harder not to share it, too, if they ever became intimate. Would they? He was eaten up with need, but determined not to hurry Nattie, to push and shatter his chances.

Finding a lay-by Ahmed brought up Osborne's number and peered out of the car windows with instinctive caution. It was already dark, the lights of parked-up lorries all he could see. He took a moment to ease his sore feet out of the muddy boots and thick socks – with difficulty in the driver's seat – then, with his cool pliable Nikes back on, he felt better prepared. It wasn't easy, a call to *The Post*'s editor-in-chief on a Saturday evening out of hours.

'You can talk. It's private – I'm at home having tea and fruit cake in front of the fire,' Osborne said, sounding unexpectedly human.

All right for some, Ahmed thought, feeling chilled to the bone. He breathed in and set about explaining everything, succinctly, but with occasional stray thoughts and asides such as Fahad's apparent love of the Lakes. It seemed to sit oddly with someone bent on destroying the ways and laws of the land.

'So how do you read it all?' Osborne said thoughtfully, after a long pause.

'I'm sure Fahad's far too sharp really to trust me. And it's hard to believe he was giving actual details of an existing plot. He'd know we'd think that, of course, but he probably feels it useful if false trails have been laid. Then again there's always the slim chance he does trust me. I'm certain something is being planned, whether petrol-tanker bombs or not. The real terror is what, when, where it might happen.'

'Hmm. I think you'd better get yourself down here fast, like tonight. We need to talk.'

Fuck. Osborne couldn't do that to him, he just couldn't, Ahmed thought. It was a knife to his heart, the disappointment acute. 'Um, well, I couldn't actually be there till around midnight. Would it be all right if it's early tomorrow morning? It's just that, well, I was seeing someone tonight . . . I needed to hire a car, I can drive straight on to London. Of course, if it makes a real difference—'

'In my office by noon, then,' Osborne barked, in his authoritative tone. 'And be alert.'

Back on the road Ahmed wondered what Osborne would think if he knew the someone was Nattie. He drove on, still tense about Fahad, but elated anticipation of seeing her was catching hold, flames of it curling round his cold tired limbs. He tried not to burn himself out with longing and took care not to speed. He dreaded being stopped, a puncture, a crash – anything going wrong.

Six-thirty. In an hour's time he should be checked into the B&B and having the hot bath he was craving. Nattie had texted, anxious to know all was well; it would be when he saw her smile was his reply.

'Come as soon as you can,' she'd urged on an earlier call. 'We'll be cooking, you can watch!' Her voice had held such invitation. He imagined the three girls, all so different, knocking up food, knocking back wine. How was he going to be alone with Nattie? Osborne had just deprived him of Sunday, his one precious chance.

His mobile rang. It came as a shock and played into a telepathic sense that his reprieve with Osborne might be short-lived. His mobile slipped to the floor and pulling hurriedly on to the hard shoulder he saw it had been Nattie and she'd left no message. He felt the ground opening up under his feet.

Calling back, his mobile grasped tight, he asked breathlessly, 'Are you all right? Anything happened?'

'I was in a panic when you didn't pick up. I can't be long—'

'What do you mean, can't be long?' He waited, silent, tense, his pulse racing.

'It's difficult, this . . .' she hesitated. 'You see Shelby's suddenly turned up – on the doorstep, half an hour ago and he won't go. I've told him I've got a friend coming, that he can't do that, just turn up, but he only kept grinning and saying he'd be a date for Milly or Sam. I couldn't handle it, so I muttered about needing something from the corner shop and shot out. I'm calling you in the street . . .'

'Yeh, well, I get the picture. Some other time, maybe.' He was bitter, gutted, so demoralized that his heart felt frozen, bloodless. 'Have a nice night,' he said sardonically.

'No, Ahmed, don't go – it's not like that. You don't understand. I need you. He's the one who's got to get the picture. I can't physically push him out of the house, and the girls are keeping out of it. But I don't want him here. I know that now.'

'You're asking me to come and be a lemon – is that it?'

'No, to come here and help and be with me.'

'You have to sort out your feelings for Shelby,' he said, so bleakly hurt as to keep up his sarcastic tone. 'No one else can.'

'I'm asking you, Ahmed. I need you here; don't let me down. And tell me nothing awful happened this afternoon, that you're really all right?'

'I'm okay.'

'You will still come?'

How could he not? He felt impelled. And he had no reference points for the way he was feeling; it was new ground. He wanted the feel of her soft lips and to see again the look in her eyes that had suggested the moment had been shared.

'If you really want me to,' he muttered. Then he forgot about holding back, about feelings of pride and, dropping all his defences, said passionately, 'I couldn't not come; you mean everything. I couldn't turn and go, not now.'

CHAPTER 10

Nattie hurried down Hawthorn Terrace. Her heart was thudding in her chest. She had expected Ahmed's first reaction, not his sudden raw emotional outburst. That had thrown her completely.

It was also covering her in guilt. After being keyed up and impatient to see him, and now feeling it all the more intensely, she couldn't bear to think of the crucial little lie tucked into what she'd just been saying.

She *had* been angry with Shelby for just turning up, *had* told him about Ahmed coming, Shelby *had* made cracks about dating Sam or Milly, but he *hadn't* refused to leave. Nattie hadn't asked him to. They were still in a kind of flaky relationship after all and there were live loose ends. He'd arrived with armfuls of roses . . .

The evening filled her with dread. Shelby would think Ahmed no more than a casual friend and be free with his looks and kisses – and he would certainly want to get it together the moment Ahmed had gone. If only she'd been stronger and made things clearer to Shelby. But he'd been all over her . . . The girls had been around . . .

Now, after hearing Ahmed's passionate outburst, everything felt different. It was suddenly clear, the blinding clarity of a tropical sun, how much she needed to see him – and that the last person she wanted to end up alone with that night was Shelby.

It was over, finally, definitely. Nattie felt determined, however hard it was, to break it off with Shelby. Her spirits had dived when he'd turned up on the doorstep.

He had to know right away exactly how things stood. That mattered; it was vital. Ahmed cared, she was sure of that now – and sure of her own feelings, they'd been growing all week. She smiled. Ahmed had said she alone could sort herself out, but he had just done it for her, shown the way like a bright torch. She could walk down that lit path and see Shelby for what he was, admit to herself at last something she'd really known all along.

She was still smiling, slotting in her key, thinking of her mother trying to caution her about Shelby. Then, opening the door, he was right there, arms held wide and a full-on charmer's grin all over his face. It took her by surprise. She was stiff in his arms as he gave her a hug, and looking over his shoulder her heart plummeted at the sight of all the champagne bottles arrayed. He'd arrived with a whole case as well as the roses – without even knowing people were coming for supper.

'That you back, Nats?' Sam called from the kitchen. 'You were doing the meat sauce, remember, before you shot off out the door.'

'She'll be right there,' Shelby called, keeping her held and about to kiss her.

Nattie pulled away sharply and it was his turn to be surprised. As he brought her head back, she saw a flare of anger flash on to his face then, quickly, a teasing smile.

'You really are cross with me, aren't you?' He let his fingers trail her cheek. 'Sorry for fucking you about and not calling. It's been a sticky week, I had a lot of business deals on the go. I shouldn't have just showed up, all keen to see you . . . You went out to call your date just now, didn't you? You put him off?'

Standing clear of him, Nattie stayed calm – although feeling newly immune, not quite trusting herself. Her secret fear had been never getting out from under, being casually pushed about like a cat with a mouse or plaything. Now she feared Shelby's claws.

'Yes, I was calling a friend,' she replied evenly, staring. 'His name's Ahmed Khan. I told him you'd pitched up unexpectedly, but I want him to come this evening. That's how it is.'

Sam was coming out of the kitchen. 'Bit greedy,' she said, 'two blokes in a night. I don't mind being the understudy. Want to take me clubbing later, Shelby? Any more of that nice bubbly?' She turned over an empty glass and waggled it.

She was making it all the easier for Shelby to stick around. Nattie felt almost tearful. There was no way he'd go gracefully now. But he didn't, anyway, have that sort of pride, she thought, leaving them for the kitchen to finish the meat sauce. It was down to her to spell out that it was over – and not be wet about it, either.

Shelby appeared in the doorway. 'Dan and Pol are coming, Sam says,' he remarked, 'and a few more. Quite a little party!'

She looked at him nervously, cold inside. Then pulling the pan off the ring, she said, 'We do need to talk, Shelby. Can we go for a drink someplace, catch our breath?' She held hers.

'Sure,' he said staring back, giving nothing away.

The nearest pub was packed. It was awful. Students pushing, gassing, shouting, how could they possibly talk? Shelby's arm was round her waist and his nearness was scary; she didn't want to weaken. 'This is hardly the place,' she said, talking into his ear, 'but I've got to say it. Sorry, but we can't go on. I'm seeing Ahmed now.'

He lifted her hair and kissed her ear in return. 'Since when?'

She shifted stiffly. 'Since I last saw you. You didn't call, your mobile's always off . . . It is very new, but I don't do two-timing. I'm ending it, Shelby. You're hardly around, expecting me always to be waiting . . . You know how much I've cared—'

He lifted her hair again and shouted, 'I can't hear! Let's go talk outside.'

He took out a twenty-pound note and tossed it on to the bar. 'Keep it, Mitch,' he said to the ginger-haired American barman. They'd had a Diet Coke and a beer.

'Thanks, man.'

It was beginning to rain. 'You could hear perfectly well,' she said looking ahead, glad to have got out it was over. It made her feel cleansed, like showering away sand after the beach. 'I'm very sorry, but you do understand? I'm not a thing, like a bed, there for your occasional use—' He'd want to hurt her, she thought; make her pay for it. Beautiful sexy good looks didn't add up to humility and doing the decent thing.

'What about love?' he said, resting his arm on her shoulders in the wet cobbled street. 'You've left that out of account. I don't shout about it, but I do love you, Nattie. I've been so busy with deals – making money, but it's all for you—'

'No, Shelby,' she said bravely, 'that won't wash. Nothing does any more. You're a wonderful lover, but you're not in love with me. Please can we end this as friends?'

They were back in Hawthorn Terrace. Her key was out, she was desperate to be indoors with the protection of the others, with time to get ready for Ahmed. All the heartache, the painful pull of Shelby's sexy irresistibility, was in the past; she felt almost revolted. It was bemusing how meaningless and superficial it had been. In contrast, she thought, to her strangely confident feelings now.

Shelby stopped where they were and gripped her upper arms. 'You'll see what washes,' he said nastily. 'Have your little PC shag. You'll pay for it. I'll see to that – and get you back.' He let go of her, fixing her with his cold eyes. 'Now, which of those two shall I fuck tonight? Perhaps Milly, she's softer. Sam's a bitch.'

'Do what you like,' Nattie muttered, shivering. 'Try not to hurt my friends.'

She wished with all her might he would just get in his fast new Mustang and go, anywhere, as far as his wheels would take him.

'I've got some weed on me,' he said menacingly as they went indoors, his voice granite hard, 'and I'm feeling generous. Your little friend might as well have it good while it's going. It won't be for long.'

No one about, the girls must be changing. The lasagnes were prepared and foil-topped in the kitchen, as well as a huge bowl of salad, a Milly special. There were baguettes, cheddar and Brie, tubs of ice cream in the freezer. Nattie switched on the oven to have it ready. Then hearing Shelby on his mobile, she hurried upstairs.

Millie was just freeing up the bathroom. Nattie bagged it and ran a small bath. She washed quickly, feeling as tight-wound as a ball of wool, desperate to be ready before Ahmed arrived. Shelby could do or say anything. Wrapped in a skimpy towel and clutching her clothes, peering out first to be sure to avoid him, she darted up to her room.

She decided on a black mini and jade scoop-neck T-shirt. Lips glossed, hair loose, she felt more prepared, but couldn't unravel much even then. Was Ahmed late? She'd left her watch in the bathroom. Where was he? His last text had said, about eight.

Picking up her watch Nattie saw it was half-past, and she could hear Milly's tinkly laughter downstairs. A knot of misery formed as she went on down.

Shelby was with Milly on the sofa and had hold of her hand. 'He's reading my palm,' she laughed.

Nattie smiled back opaquely. 'He'll get it wrong, he can't see into the future.'

'Touché,' Shelby said with a hard stare. 'Want a drink, a smoke?'

She shook her head and was making for the kitchen when the doorbell rang. Nattie spun round like a shot-at gazelle, desperate to beat Shelby to the door.

It was Dan and Pol, but she could see Ahmed was further up the street and waved to him. Pulse racing, she pressed the pair of third-year students to go on ahead indoors.

She met Ahmed partway, clear of the house. 'Hi!' she smiled. 'Sorry about my call – it's cool with you, now, though? Shelby is still here. I've told him it's over—'

Ahmed was in a white shirt and his brown leather jacket, and looking at her in a way that brought quivers like a comb being drawn over her skin. He took her hand. 'Can you just keep on smiling like that?' His hand was fondling hers with an urgency she shared.

If only they could go somewhere, Nattie thought, cut and run. Why didn't he kiss her while they had the chance? But then she'd heard his outburst on the phone, his true feelings coming through, but he couldn't really know hers. He wouldn't want to push it too much, she thought. It felt strange having that slight advantage.

'We'd better go in, I suppose!' He squeezed her hand harder. They shared a look then Ahmed let go of her hand, she opened the door and they went in.

Nattie introduced him and was surprised how polished he was, how easy with people. But she'd only really seen him alone and he was ex-BBC and a reporter on a national newspaper after all. No, she thought, it was his warmth of personality showing through.

He produced some bars of Kendal Mint Cake from an inside pocket saying it was hardly an offering, but Dan got all excited and started asking after the Lakes. Ahmed was understandably reticent, just muttering about being there for work.

He turned to Shelby and said pleasantly, 'I believe you met my flatmate the other day, Jake Wright. He's a friend of Jane Morris.'

'Oh yes, the long-faced lugubrious architect, Eton and Oxford. Plays it the other way, doesn't he?' Shelby's face was a mask. Nattie wholly hated him at that moment. The implication – that being gay was the only possible reason Jake could want to share with Ahmed – was disgusting.

Ahmed handled it. 'Jake's not gay – but anyway, would you hold that or his school against him?'

Shelby grinned coldly. 'Many things, not those. Champagne – or are you too religious?' Ahmed was struggling to control powerful distaste, Nattie thought.

Sam, though, sharp and sappy as ever, was enjoying the tension like mad.

'We've been picking up the vibes all week, Ahmed,' she said. 'Couldn't wait to see what the fuss was about. You're good, better than I expected, a cool dude.'

'The Sam seal of approval,' Shelby said cuttingly. 'What an accolade.'

There were more arrivals, which was as well. Dan and Pol were looking confused, Milly, awkward. Nattie went to the kitchen to put in the lasagnes, feeling a bag of raw nerves.

'Can I help?' Her heart leaped as Ahmed came in the kitchen. 'Peel veg or anything?'

She was squatting down to the old gas oven and banged the door shut. As he gave her a hand up she shook her head mutely.

'Can I kiss you then?' Nattie nodded. The music, Katy Perry, the chat, it all sounded so close. The kiss felt stolen, like being a pair of adulterers. Her lips trembled as they separated, still holding hands.

'When the cat's away . . . Two little mice, how sweet!' ' She started and saw Shelby leaning lackadaisically against the doorframe. Had he been there long?

Nattie felt desperate, dreading a scene. Ahmed was rigid. Milly came beside Shelby then, probably sensitive to the situation. 'Okay to open a couple more bottles, Shelby?' she asked. He was average height, but Milly was small and had to gaze up.

'That's what they're there for, darling,' he said, encompassing her soft plump shoulders. He kissed her ear and her skin became suffused with an embarrassed blush.

Shelby's lush black hair was gleaming; he was a beautiful, newly hateful man.

The food went down well, bottles of wine disappeared fast; the room was smoky, everyone loosened up. People were lounging on cushions on the floor, couples leaning against each other, the music reaching into hearts and minds like a flow of blood.

Ahmed wasn't drinking much, but he did look longingly at a

cigarette. Nattie lit one and drew on it, then put it in his mouth; he lit another from it and put that in hers.

She was enjoying the music. Muse, Sparklehorse had been playing; now it was Keane. 'Great sound,' Ahmed said, 'with Tom Chaplin's high voice, and when you think it's a guitar-free band.'

'Surely it's got a guitar?' Pol said in surprise. 'I never knew that. How cool!'

'Ahmed knows it all,' Shelby said. 'He's omniscient.' He started rolling a spliff. 'Want some of this, anyone? Go on, Ahmed, be my guest.'

Others took him up on the offer, Nattie and Ahmed didn't.

Shelby was concentrating on Milly, getting her malleably stoned. Sam needed no urging. Her angular limbs were wrapped round a giant of a rugby player and, without unravelling them, she said drunkenly, 'Thought we were going on to Klute – well, are we or aren't we?'

It was a good club, one of Durham's best. 'Cool idea,' Nattie threw in with no intention of going, intensely relieved when guests slowly began making a move.

People hunted down coats and scarves, couples drifted off. 'Not coming, Nattie?' Shelby inquired sarcastically. He and Milly were by the door, the only ones left.

'Not just now, we're doing the washing-up.' She smiled at Ahmed.

Milly tugged on Shelby's arm and went ahead outside. It was a tense moment. 'Night,' Nattie said, staring steadily, thinking how little he could touch her now.

Shelby met her eyes. 'You haven't seen the last of me, girl,' he said and wandered out.

Why hadn't he left in bitter pique right after the pub? What went on inside the Shelby machine? How could his pride stand it? There was nothing about him resembling love, his heart didn't know the word. Staying and causing her maximum discomfort, Nattie thought, was entertainment; the glazed bored look in his long-lashed blue eyes had masked pleasure as well as his cold calculating fury at being dumped.

Going towards the door he had muttered something to Ahmed. Now she asked anxiously, 'What did he say?'

'Oh, only that he'd do me and settle the score.' Ahmed was leaning against the closed door as if to bar untimely returns. His eyes were warm. 'I can watch my back.'

'I'm sure Shelby will want to get even,' Nattie said.

'Then I'll just have to keep a jump ahead.' Ahmed left the door, kissed her lips and started to clear glasses. 'Come on, you said we're doing the washing-up!'

He got going at the sink and she picked up a tea-towel, but they were quickly distracted. Ahmed dried his hands and came close. 'I couldn't believe there was a chance of being alone with you tonight, I'd expected death by a thousand glances between you and Shelby – proof of where I stood!'

'It wasn't easy, ending it,' she mumbled as he kissed her mouth. She lost herself then. There was nothing shy or cautious about his passionate searching tongue, his pressed body; she felt grafted on like a plant.

Ahmed pulled away, smoothing her hair, looking alarmed. 'I'm sorry – I shouldn't have got so carried away. I've been so insanely impatient and resenting . . . everyone around.' He touched her lips. 'I keep expecting to hear the door even now!'

Nattie felt sick with dread too, tense as anything while they were kissing. 'We can go up to my room and be private,' she said encouragingly. 'It's up the top.'

She wanted more of his loving, his firm body, the flow of energy reaching her.

'I didn't mean, I wasn't hinting—' Ahmed took her face in his hands, his own almost comically anxious. 'I really wasn't,' he said. 'You mustn't feel you need offer that. We could go for a drive, talk in the car—'

She led him by the hand towards the stairs. 'It's not much of an offer actually,' she said, grinning, 'as you'll see. It's the loft room and there's hardly space to stand up!'

He collected his jacket from a chair and gave her back his hand.

Inside her bedroom she closed the door and slid home a small squeaky bolt. She had visions of Shelby returning early with Milly and showing his face at the door.

They stood looking at each other. Nattie sensed Ahmed's reticence, as though he felt that to be in her room was taking advantage. It was different from any past experience of men she'd had.

He took hold of her wrists and brought her closer. 'At the *Post* party I could only take in your face, couldn't take my eyes off it. Later, at home,' he grinned, 'I imagined the rest, the feel of you – and when we had tea I was craving the slightest touch. It put me in a strange daze, being so close to you all afternoon.'

'I loved you reading those lines of poetry.' She stroked his face, smoothed his eyebrows and brushed over his mouth with her fingers, sliding them in then and feeling electric shivers as his tongue explored them. Shivers that ran the length of her body: her desire was swelling and growing like lapping water finding its force. She felt passionate need of this man whom she hardly knew, very confident and sure.

He lifted her hand away and held it against his cheek, but she took it back and began to undo his shirt, sliding in her arms, finding smooth firm skin: the dell of his backbone, its dipping groove. 'Will you undress me?' she said, feeling impelled to lead him on.

Ahmed studied her steadily. 'Are you really sure? It's been upsetting for you, with Shelby. I'd hate you to do anything you'd wish you hadn't in the morning. And it will make everything different. I'm falling for you and I couldn't walk away or leave you alone.'

'I know my own mind,' Nattie said impatiently, 'and I have feelings too. I chose to end it with Shelby tonight, remember? I knew just what I was doing and why.' She leaned to kiss his mouth, all the more sure, and felt with satisfaction, the weakening of his restraint.

'Stand still then,' he said, breaking away. With his eyes on hers, he let his hands follow the lines of her body. Still fixed on her, he lifted away her T-shirt and reached for her bra clasp; his eyes didn't stray. Nor did they as he unzipped her skirt and helped it slip to the floor. She stepped out of it, took off her pants and tights herself using him as a prop, pushing all her clothes clear of them with an impatient foot.

He laid his cheek on her stomach, her thighs. Standing up again, he stared at her breasts and held them, his hands closing round. Nattie knew she had good tits, firm and full, and felt no shyness. Ahmed drew his fingers up to the nipples and held on as he kissed her hungrily before dropping his head to her breasts.

He held her close, hard to his body, his cheek pressed. 'I think I must have died on a Cumbrian hillside, I'm somewhere very high.' Crushed against him, sensing his straining hunger for her, she heard the tenderness in his voice and felt overcome.

'Do what you want, anything that feels instinctive,' she said, having never taken the lead before. Her first experience had been terrible, near rape and the pressure of it beyond her will. Nattie had felt frightened she might never feel the confident trust she did now. She wanted Ahmed's hands on her body, his passionate discovering, and to give her all, however he chose to take it.

The bed was single and small; they dropped down on to the rug on the floor. He rolled her over and explored her back, her buttocks, every nook and hidden corner of her body; he was sensitive to her needs. She wanted him deep within and told him so. 'I want to be joined to you, I need you in me.'

He propped up on an arm. 'I'd be in your life as well, making demands, more and more of them – feeling you're all mine—'

'And you don't think I'd feel the same?' Nattie unpropped his arm and wrapped her limbs round him. 'It cuts both ways, belonging, haven't you thought about that?'

'Would it be awful to have a cigarette? There's a packet and matches on my table.'

'You're no good,' Ahmed said, lighting two and getting back into bed. 'I've been trying so hard to give up.'

'Me, too, but it is sort of the moment. Tell me what happened this afternoon.'

'I had to walk for hours, so I've got a whole lot of blisters! And this man I was seeing smokes non-stop, that was an extra strain.'

'That's dodging the question.' She stroked his smooth chest, thinking how unhealthily white her limbs looked. 'You think he's a terrorist, don't you? Why?'

'I shouldn't involve you. These aren't nice people.'

'I'm not exactly going to meet them,' Nattie said, feeling sure he wanted at heart to talk about it. 'What has he said or done to make you suspect him?'

She was glad that Ahmed felt free to unburden himself, although steadily more horrified as he described the secretiveness, the threats, the shockingly ominous plotting. Ahmed was at pains to say it could all be bravado, but it didn't seem like that to her. 'What now?' she asked in a small voice. 'You've told William about it? Is he going to run this Fahad's scare story, do you think – has he said so?'

'That's the terrible thing. It's a disaster; I can't bear it.' Whatever the 'thing' was, Ahmed made it sound so dramatic that she sat up and bumped her head.

'He wants to see me. I've got to drive to London, I'll have to leave in a few hours.' He kissed the bump, fondled her hair. 'Tomorrow is wiped out and I've been thinking of nothing else all week. But when the editor shouts, you jump – and it is, well, serious. He wanted me to come tonight. I managed to get him to let me have till morning – then you rang and said what you did about Shelby. It was a double whammy!'

Nattie felt bitterly anticlimactic at the thought of him going, Sunday snatched away, being left alone feeling flat and miserable. The lingering afterglow of intensely passionate lovemaking drained away fast. There was even the chance, she thought with a shiver, of Shelby still being around and making life hell.

The most simple, obvious solution suddenly came to her. 'It's not a disaster. I could come with you,' she said, excited at the thought. 'I can share the driving if you like. I've got my licence. I want to be with you,' she said shyly, in need of being reassured that he wanted it, too.

Ahmed looked at her, his face a picture of amazement – then it fell a mile. 'What if your stepfather sent me straight back to Leeds or off doing something? I couldn't leave you stranded.'

'Don't be mad, I'd have a day at home in London. I'll go there anyway while you're seeing William. Mum might come up from Hampshire with him, and Tom should be around too, which'll be nice. I can always get the train back to Durham.'

'Who's Tom?'

'William's son – he lives in the basement flat. He was at the *Post* party, talking to that art critic the whole time.'

Ahmed leaned out of bed and strained to reach for his jacket. 'I've brought you this book,' he said, feeling in a pocket. 'It's just a token.'

As she turned the pages he said, 'It will have to be a very early start, about five. Can you manage that? I'll need to grab my bag from the B&B as we go.'

'I'll set the alarm. Can you write in this now?'

She loved the slim volume on Wordsworth and Coleridge and couldn't care less about morning timings.

He reached into his jacket, found a pen and inscribed it. 'For Nattie – with all the love in my heart.' Then he lay back and took her into his arms.

'You must be exhausted,' she whispered, getting settled, but there was no answer; he was deeply, instantly, unshakably asleep. She hoped the alarm would wake them.

CHAPTER 11

'I never thought,' Ahmed said, glancing at Nattie, his hand straying from the wheel to press against a glorious breast, 'I'd be on the road this morning feeling like I could swing from treetops and take on the world.' Taking on Fahad was another matter, he thought, his stomach curdling.

'You were hard enough to wake, I was shaking you for hours!'

'That's exaggerating.' He brushed back Nattie's long silky-fine hair, needing to see more of her, feeling overcome with every sort of emotion. He couldn't let the fear get to him. It was fear of failure, bombs, of Fahad finding him out – fear of losing Nattie.

'Shall we stop for breakfast soon, at the next services?' She smiled.

He was hungry, in need of coffee. She was so eye-catchingly beautiful, though. 'We shouldn't really be seen together,' he said diffidently. 'People call up newspapers trying to make a few bucks; it's a story, you see, you and me. And anything appearing would blow a great hole in my cover with these extremists – I am supposed to hate all Westerners, even ones as heavenly-looking as you.'

It was hard to think of them as terrorists, although Fahad was one he felt sure. But when Ahmed thought about the others, gentle

prayer-minded Khalid, law-flouting Iqbal with his spiky little beard –
even Yazid who always managed to set his teeth on edge – it seemed
almost beyond belief to think of them as potential fanatical killers.

'Sure, but no one knows who I am,' Nattie persisted. 'Mum's had
this big obsession with never letting the press get near – and she still
has, you'd think I was ten! That's why I'm not on Facebook or anything. She was even edgy about me coming to the *Post* party.'

'She had a point there, as it turns out.'

Standing in a queue with Nattie at the service station, clutching
brown plastic trays, he was feeling both pride and anxiety as she
leaned into him, whispering, laughing, leaving not the slightest
doubt about their relationship. It was ingrained to be reserved with
girls in public and especially risky as things were; he felt nervous.

They loaded the trays with juice, eggs, toast and coffee and cast
round for a table. There was one by the window that seemed unobtrusive, looking out on to the exit route. Early sunlight was flooding
in.

Ahmed disposed of left-behind dirty cartons and sat opposite
Nattie. He shot anxious glances at the nearest people who could all
do with going on diets. There was a hulking elephant of a man reading the *News of the World*, two women bulging out over straps and
waistbands; a spotty Asian in a suit, too, could lose a few pounds.

Ahmed reached out with his legs under the table, to capture
Nattie's. The light was glaringly bright in that place with its plastic
wipe-top tables. She'd had little or no sleep yet still looked unbelievable. She was like a mirage that had miraculously remained, he
thought; his legs were wrapped round the limbs of a living miracle.

Sipping coffee he wondered if Osborne would talk to MI5.
Probably. Running that story about the tankers would cause national

panic, of course. Osborne might think twice about using it – whatever MI5 had to say or advised.

'I suppose William will tell Mum about your Fahad meeting,' Nattie remarked, her mind working along the same lines. 'He never lets on about things usually; it drives her mad especially when he's about to expose some MP or other, but this is different, isn't it? I mean, it's too serious to keep her in the dark.'

She was whispering, but Ahmed still looked round instinctively. 'He probably will tell her,' he agreed. 'I think it is very serious. I'm sure Fahad doesn't trust me enough to tell me about a real terrorist attack, but it could just be a kind of double bluff, I suppose.' Nattie looked at him in alarm. 'I do hope, if your stepfather tells MI5 or anyone, that they don't dismiss it. I'm sure Fahad is a dangerous fanatic.'

He felt guilty talking in those terms and squeezed her hand under the table. 'More coffee?' He smiled. 'I'll get it.' He went to stand in a short queue. It was hard to shake off a powerful gut instinct – it was as visceral as his loathing of Shelby – that Fahad was plotting an attack. His ruthlessness had gleamed bright, he knew what he was doing; Ahmed sensed he was up against a serious operator.

His nerves felt chilled, icicle shivers down his spine, but he had to carry on snooping and play-acting, however little hope there might be of thwarting an evil plan.

He was at the front of the queue. Glancing Nattie's way, he saw a man in low-slung builder's jeans set down a carton on their table and take his place. Nattie indicated his plate, pointed at the buffet queue, then looked firmly away. The fucker was giving her an obvious come-on, Ahmed realized. He threw down some change, grabbed the coffees, and ran.

Nattie got up with obvious relief, seeing him coming. 'I tried to keep your seat, there were plenty of others,' she emphasized, wanting it to be heard.

'I got the coffees to go,' Ahmed said, handing one over to have a free arm to hurry her away. He was keen to be off anyway.

The arsehole was lounging back, staring at Nattie with a repulsive leer.

'Fancy a bit of the brown then, do we?' he drawled from his sedentary position. 'Stupid girl. I could give it you – a shag you wouldn't likely forget.'

'Fuck off,' Ahmed hissed, although conditioned not to make trouble. He saw Nattie swing out with her bag in a way to ensure it made contact with the scumbag's carton of tea. It toppled slowly, almost in slow motion, before showering its entire hot contents squarely all over the man's crotch.

'Oh, sorry,' she called back brightly, as Ahmed yanked her away. 'Don't be mad at me,' she whispered, as a stream of language followed after them that would have made a Glaswegian junkie blush. 'He did ask for it.'

'That wasn't funny,' Ahmed panted, rushing her out to the car. 'Let's have no more hair-raising improvised vigilantism, please.'

He kept careful watch in the mirror, but no huge articulated lorry giving off blue fumes came chasing after them down the motorway.

Scum like that, he thought, had a lot to answer for. It was the ugly amoral face of Britain. Kids in the inner cities, the likes of God-fearing Khalid, were exposed to a daily diet of Islamophobia: foul-mouthed taunts from the drinking, shagging thuggery. It turned Muslim communities even tighter in on themselves. And then the

Islamist extremists like Fahad came along, persuasively distorting their faith and calling for armed jihad.

They were on the outskirts of London, coming in on a dual-carriageway lined with uniform semis; the gardens, too, struggled to be individual. Nattie rang her mother. Ahmed listened attentively to the call, worried about how much she might tell her, yet anxious that he shouldn't interfere.

'I'm almost home in London, Mum – got a lift with a friend . . . You're on the way too? That's great. Why so early on a Sunday? . . . Oh, I see. William doesn't go in very often – still it does mean I get to see you!' She was being wonderfully disingenuous, Ahmed thought. 'I'll be there first,' Nattie said, turning while speaking to give him a smile. 'Oh, and Mum,' she gave another quick glance. 'I broke it off with Shelby last night . . . Yes, I knew you'd say that, I could have written the script! See you in a mo, then. Love you.'

Nattie clicked off and gave a huge beam. 'You're not late! William's an hour away at least. He can't have told her anything yet, she sounded hacked off he was going into the office. Can you just drop me home? You'll call after the meeting?

'I'm not going to say anything to Mum about us yet,' Nattie went on. 'She's so neurotic, she'll only think you'll want to dig around and write things, and if she hears about the meeting with Fahad she might start making a twitchy fuss.'

'It is probably best,' he agreed lightly, feeling heartfelt relief, sure her mother would make a lot more trouble than that. Relaxing enough for a tease, he flicked a glance. 'But you are very trusting . . . I'll be digging around all right, turning up your innermost secret roots. I need to get to know you, right below ground.'

They were going over Westminster Bridge. Ahmed had been surprised to discover her home was in Kennington. He'd imagined the Home Secretary living at some fancy address in Westminster or the West End. 'We live very close,' he said. 'My flat's only a few streets away.'

'Will you go there after seeing William? I could come round—'

'I can't expect you to come to a seedy Brixton flat,' he said, only half joking.

'Didn't you say it was great and you really loved it? Must get your ducks in line!'

He stopped short of the house, thinking of policemen around, and kissed her, finding it hard to let go. He felt an acute pang as Nattie ran down the pavement and in through the gate on that still-bright morning, a sense of his beautiful mirage vanishing just like any other and life reverting to a loveless norm.

Driving slowly away he saw her chatting to a policeman in the front garden – who seemed to look over her shoulder and notice the crawling car.

Ahmed felt seized with overwhelming physical need of her. He foresaw all the complications. Would the Osborne meeting tie him up for the day? Nattie had to come to Brixton, he had to see her later, he thought desperately – before things got tougher and harder and he was back in Leeds.

There was plenty going on at the office with Monday's paper. Ahmed caught up with a few mates and made sure he was seen around. He called Nattie and afterwards sat at his desk trying to think what Fahad could really be planning to do.

Osborne summoned him to his office. There was no small talk.

Spreading his fingers wide on his thighs his editor said, 'I want you to take me through everything exactly as before. I'm going to record it, we can't have any blurred lines.' Ahmed imagined the tape being played back at MI5.

Even well into his stride he couldn't entirely forget the machine. He explained again how he'd made contact then described his walk in the Fells in as graphic detail as possible. The rushing river and beautiful views, boggy shade, the climbing trails that had become dank and shadowy by the time Fahad got to the point.

Getting on to the meat, the story Fahad wanted placed, Ahmed feared it might sound like melodramatic guff. He ploughed on, though, finally reaching the hijacking of petrol tankers to put to lethal use and the dark hints about crashing private planes.

He said he had no way of communicating with Fahad and thought it unlikely the others had either, even Yazid. It was possible he might never hear from Fahad again, but he'd be keeping his hooks into his contacts in Leeds. He spoke of Cumbria-based Haroon who'd seemed a sociable easy-going enigma, and wondered aloud, given the Fell walk, about a Cumbrian cell.

Osborne had asked occasional clarifying questions and been watchful, rocking on his tipped-back chair. But he snorted at that. 'It's about the least ethnic part of the country, hardly likely to be littered with cells.' The tape was whirring, Ahmed felt as if he was accused of being a double agent and there was a lie detector ticking away.

The spooks might dismiss it all as posturing, suspect him of being in league with Fahad's lot, simply a petty little mixer and out to make trouble. It was deflating to think of not being trusted. He felt sure he wasn't being taken for a ride. Fahad was no low-level activist, he'd stake his life on it. Something was going on and Ahmed felt in his bones that it was deadly serious.

His editor was tapping his fingers together. He reached forward to turn off the machine. 'Okay, Ahmed,' he said. 'Write up whatever you think this Fahad, probably not his real name, wants splashed in *The Post*. Whether I do, in fact, decide to give him the oxygen of publicity will depend . . .'

On MI5 or the Home Secretary's reaction, Ahmed thought. Osborne was known round the paper to have had a few run-ins with the spooks, dealings that were short on affability. His relations with them, apparently, were never that smooth.

'Stay in London tonight.' Ahmed wanted to leap up and hug him. 'Keep your phone on. Then you'd better get straight back to Leeds.'

He sat forward with an abrasive glare. 'You've taken this on, remember, and I want results. It matters. Terrorism is the greatest threat we face. I think you're on to something; others may not, they could even question your fucking loyalty. Don't let that get in the way. You owe this country, Ahmed. It's your fucking country, too.'

Nattie wasn't answering her mobile. Ahmed felt dragged down and his tiredness came out with all the vengeance of a filthy cold. Writing up the Fahad story, he was falling asleep at his desk.

He packed up and left the office, thinking of being back in Leeds, with Nattie in Durham. He'd be obsessed with going to see her, but frequent unexplained disappearances would be noticed. Yazid might pass it on; he was obviously Fahad's local eyes and ears. If they discovered he was seeing the Home Secretary's daughter, he was done for. And he could even be putting Nattie at risk.

He was also anxious about Leena, the student in hiding from her

violent father. It was another reason for re-establishing his Leeds cre-
dentials and being properly back in the groove. Somehow he had to
find the girl before her father, in the two weeks left to him, before
he was expected back at his desk at *The Post*.

Nattie would be in London then too, the university term ended,
Christmas approaching. She'd be taken up with family, away in her
mother's constituency, wrapped up in festive togetherness. He felt an
outsider; he couldn't be in a serious relationship openly with her, not
while he was involved with Fahad – probably never at all.

The afternoon ahead seemed all the more precious, given what
might lie in front of him. Why hadn't Nattie called back? Had
Osborne gone straight home? Was there some problem – her mother
wheedling it out? Prickly pride stopped him from trying Nattie
again; he'd already left one message, long and passionate – she could
at least have checked her phone.

When he returned to his car, parked in a side street close to the
Thames, his spirits matched the sight of the river at low tide. It
was a wasteland of matt-brown oozing turgid mud stuck with up-
ended bottles. Hamburg's mud-wrestlers would appreciate it, he
thought.

He stopped the car at a corner-shop and went in for a sandwich.
Two small black girls were buying sweets and he worried about them
being out alone. Was anyone safe in this country? he thought
morosely. Coming out of the shop the sun had gone in; the clouds
were building, bunching close like herded sheep.

Ahmed tried to think positively. There was blue sky up there, after
all. Biting into a tasteless cheese sandwich he imagined flying off with
Nattie to Rome, Athens, Marrakech, looking at antiquities, churches.
There was so much of life to be lived.

His mobile rang and the world faced the right way. 'I was cooking, chopping veg. Tom had the music up, Mum was gassing.'

'Would they mind if you come out for a bit?' She had to, whether they cared or not.

'I just have to stay for lunch, with all of us here – say in about an hour?'

'I'll have the car at the tube station for three,' he said. It at least gave him time to check out the flat and buy flowers. He was on a high again and punched the air.

Watching for her, Ahmed thought about the years ahead. He rolled down a blind: that wasn't for now. She'd taken the lead in sex without a qualm, there was no hint of uncertainty or shyness. Was that a warning, a signal that she was more casual about relationships and he meant little?

Ahmed saw her then and couldn't help a ridiculous smile spreading over his face. A man was walking alongside and he realized with alarm that they were together, talking, laughing. He stiffened, but as they neared him he worked out it must be Tom Osborne. What the hell was she doing?

She reached him and slipped an arm through his. 'This is Tom,' she said, 'you had to meet him. He's my confidant, you see, safer than any girlfriend, and I had to share it with *someone*!'

'Hiya.' Tom grinned, looking awkward. 'She's been on such a way-out high ... And I was coming to get the tube. It won't go anywhere,' he added, accurately reading, Ahmed thought, his own tense reserve.

'It's cool meeting you – can't we give you a lift someplace? I have a car.'

'Tube's easiest. But perhaps a drink sometime when Nattie's home again?'

'Sure thing.'

Tom wrapped his stepsister in a hug and sprinted off into the station.

Ahmed was quite proud of his bedroom, although Enders Street had looked pretty grotty with spilled chips and chucked lottery tickets in the gutters and the '2' loose again on the front door. The room had little furniture: the small double bed, a single-panel pine wardrobe – painted yellow when he'd spotted it in a stack of junk on the pavement, he'd had it stripped. There was an Ikea chest, a pine chair. Tightened his arm round Nattie, he felt pleased with the simplicity, the freshness of his whitewashed walls.

It was already dark outside, they must have slept on and off. 'Can I ask you something?' he said.

She looked up. 'Anything.' Resting her head back, she added, 'You're sounding serious.'

He stroked her soft fair hair. 'Well, you weren't holding back last night – not that I was either . . . But you were giving yourself, taking me so much on trust and it seemed, well, strange.' He couldn't find the right words and hurried on. 'And then there's something hidden; some past hurt, a shadow that feels almost connected. I'm not making much sense, I know, but I want to lift it away and understand.'

'You're sounding like you think I was an easy lay.' Ahmed could feel the rush of blood to his face, his embarrassment at the half-truth of that. 'I can see it might have seemed like it to you,' she said unfazed, turning to be looking at him full-on, 'but it's not how I am, not at all. The uncanny bit is you linking it to things in the past.'

'How do you mean?'

'It was just a bad first time,' she muttered, sounding flat, almost sullen. 'I'd said no and begged him to stop, but by then he thought he'd won through and wouldn't listen. He just went right on ahead – saying I had to do it sometime and like he was doing me a favour.'

Ahmed felt a deep possessive anger. 'But that's rape! It could have really scarred you.'

'He'd call it me being a cock-tease. I had let it get too far. I was six- teen and he was eighteen, at my school and there was another whole term till he left. It did scar me a bit. It was so hard to know what I felt after that. That's why it's connected with flinging myself at you last night. I really knew and didn't want to hang about.'

'What about the watch-giver, though?' he asked, suddenly tense again. 'You still wear that watch.'

'Oh, Hugo.' Nattie looked up with a smile. 'I'll explain about him sometime, but another day. It's my turn, now.'

'Muslim men are religiously shy about sex,' Ahmed said, kissing her, deciding to divert her from a boring trawl through past girls. 'They have to be covered from waist to knee at all times; nudity is prohibited. The really orthodox shave all over too, everywhere, apart from beards; even moustaches must be trimmed. There are instruc- tions on how to wash bits of the body, with what water.'

'This doesn't sound much like you.'

'I'm not religious. There's an Afghan movie, *Osama*, which makes clear how, with all this privacy, girls could pass off as young boys during the Taliban time in Kabul.'

'So am I meant to assume you've had a very shy girl-free past?'

'Well, there have been one or two—'

'Or three or four?'

'It's hard to be all that shy and private as a reporter on *The*

Post . . . My father comes from Peshawar and out there old Pashtuns dye their hair black and their beards ginger with henna; some wear kohl eyeliner and look like extras from *Pirates of the Caribbean.* Things have moved on a bit, now—'

He heard sounds downstairs. It must be Jake getting back – how had it got so late? They scrambled into their clothes, Nattie telling him he had to be covered from waist to knee. He would never live that down. She looked sheepish, coming downstairs from his room to meet Jake.

Jake was drop-jawed, which was very satisfying.

'What's he got that I haven't?' he asked her, looking even more shell-shocked, hearing that Nattie had brought enough supper for three.

'Oh, I just happened to meet Ahmed first,' she replied with her intoxicating smile.

CHAPTER 12

Victoria snapped shut her red box. It was half-past eleven at night and her concentration had gone. The rest would have to wait.

William was back. Tom was back. They were watching a film on the kitchen television, a mobster movie, littered with bloody killings from what she'd seen.

A miserable sinking feeling was lodged in her chest. William had gone out at six on a Sunday evening, disappeared for over an hour without a word. It was stirring up the dust in the attic, memories of Barney doing the same thing.

William was no Barney, thank God, but it seemed odd; he'd been so in on himself all day. Could it just be work? He'd gone into the office on a Sunday – had she surprised him, coming to London, too? Wouldn't he have simply told her, though, if he'd been going back to the paper again? Was it something personal? They never had any secrets apart from professional ones; they shared bank statements even.

And where was Nattie? That was as bad. She'd shot out of the house with Tom after lunch – he'd only been going to an art exhibition, though, whereas Nattie, Victoria thought, had given every sign of having rather different activities in mind. She'd been ages in the bathroom, changed T-shirts twice, even cooked extra food at lunchtime, quite surreptitiously with private smiles, and piled it into plastic tubs.

There was obviously a new love in her life, but why the secrecy if it was making her quite so alight? Could the food business mean a married man or someone in trouble who wanted to avoid being seen out? There was plenty of scope for worry. Victoria hoped she wouldn't end up wishing Shelby back on the scene.

It was always with her, thudding away like a constant pulse, the fear of Nattie choosing badly and getting hurt again. Nattie had confessed to how much harder it was to know her own feelings ever since that first-time abuse, yet it didn't seem to make her any less trusting. Just extra vulnerable, Victoria thought, taking her red box to the front door to have ready for the morning.

'The film's almost ended,' William called, seeing her in the hall. 'You off on up?'

'Yes, I've had it,' she said, going to the kitchen door. 'Can't take any more in and I'm in a stew about Nattie as well. I hate not knowing if she's coming home.'

'It's not midnight yet,' Tom interjected. 'She'd have called if she's staying away.' His look was gentle and covering-up-for-her, still confident and disarming, hauntingly like his father's. Living in the basement flat Tom was always around. Victoria felt close to him, emotionally connected and maternal even. He was Ursula's son, but had none of her sinewy fight and stubbornness. There were times when Victoria found herself almost thinking of him as her own.

Going upstairs, though, she couldn't have felt more out of things. Tense about Nattie, William, and she had work worries, too. The increasing number of nights when she was woken by Adam, her quietly spoken Permanent Secretary, calling before the alarm, urgently needing warrants for the tapping of yet more phones.

Victoria undressed, cleaned her teeth and glared at her dark-shadowed self in the mirror. Was William losing interest? She felt overworked, over-thin, in desperate need of an indulgent holiday. Constituents asked, sounding awed, how she possibly kept her figure with all the formal lunches and dinners she must have to eat. Little did they know she was lucky to get in a meal at all most days.

You chose this life, she told herself angrily, slipping on a silk dressing gown that felt coolly sensuous against her naked skin, needing the reassurance of William's affections. Home Secretary, Privy Councillor – a few hundred colleagues would change places like a shot.

Peter Barnes, she thought, wanted her out of her job and fast. The Foreign Secretary was as deadly as any snake in the Australian outback; he was going round spitting out venom about *The Post*'s dreadful editor, hinting there were serious security implications. Real risks in having a Home Secretary married to a newspaperman, someone so professionally and commercially interested, he was quick to tell colleagues.

And on top of that he was unsubtly spreading it that she wasn't up to the job and the Prime Minister – who wasn't up to his either, in Peter's opinion – should have known better and never have appointed her.

Maybe it was time to sock it back. Victoria sat at her hand-painted pine dressing table, taking off her make-up, and plotted how to do down a fellow Cabinet minister. It would be the first time in her career.

She knew from her friend Nick Bates all about the Foreign

Secretary's very discreet affair with the Covent Garden opera singer, Lisa Chovia. Nick was a government minister, a colleague, young, unmarried and with his ear to the ground. Victoria wasn't sure if William knew about Peter Barnes's involvement yet. Nick only did because he was a passionate opera buff and had a good friend on Covent Garden's board.

Should she tell William? But doing the dirty over a colleague's little shenanigans, and after her own hugely publicized love affair? There were limits, she thought wryly. The hypocrisy would stick in her windpipe and be impossible to shift.

But Nick Bates had uncovered something else potentially far more incriminating. Nick, who was extremely loyal to the PM and furious about Peter Barnes's disloyalty, had called earlier, sounding very galvanized and juiced up. With their mutual loathing of the Foreign Secretary he had enjoyed sharing his new intelligence and she did think it could turn out extremely damaging.

Nick had an aunt living in Peter Barnes's Hertfordshire constituency who was a district councillor and on the planning committee. She had been in touch, he said, asking for advice and clarification about MPs lobbying on local matters. Barnes had been pushing hard for a smallish housing development to be given the go-ahead. He seemed inappropriately keen, Nick's aunt thought, although there was no apparent personal connection.

'Can we have a drink, Victoria?' Nick said excitedly. 'This is not for over the phone.'

She'd agreed, instinctively sure the Foreign Secretary had gone a step too far. Arrogant, overconfident men like Peter, she thought, who went in for walking on water always forgot how easy it was to sink to the depths.

Sitting in front of her oval dressing-table mirror she spun round when a shadow appeared. William had been on the point of putting his familiar-smelling hands – faintly of soap, very much of maleness – over her eyes; those long-fingered hands that she loved.

'Almost had you,' he laughed. 'You were miles away. What dark thoughts were you into, what mischief? It's time you broke out of your straitjacket.' He was sounding natural and cheerful, reminding her about an early cartoon, 'The Schoolgirl Who Always Did Her Homework', massaging away the strain.

'They were quite black thoughts,' Victoria said, getting up with a grin, 'dirty ones too, although possibly to your advantage—'

'Sounds like I'd better get you to bed fast.'

'Well, there's that, but I was actually more on Peter Barnes just then.'

'Am I about to get my first ever tip-off? You're not simply meaning his affair? We do know all about that.' William grinned. 'You needn't look so surprised – we know it all. It's just getting it past the lawyers.'

'No, not Peter's affair, I couldn't be that hypocritical. And nor could you, surely, in all decency – not after us.'

'"Decency" is hardly a buzzword at *The Post*.'

'Don't sound so proud of it. No, this would be more serious. I'll probably hold back only I'm really so pissed off with all Peter's bitching right now.' She was breaking a personal private rule by bitching herself to William about a colleague.

'Barnes does seem overconcerned with the terrible security threat I pose,' he said, 'and exceptionally bothered by our marriage – I thought you politicians were supposed to uphold the institution? He's even talked to Jim. He must think a word in my political editor's ear will get back and I'll lay off in the paper. Some hope!'

William stepped out of his shoes and sat on the bed taking off his socks. 'Barnes knows I'm hardly going to write myself up as a leaker of highly confidential information, a wheedler of classified secrets out of you in bed. Which,' he said, grinning, 'is where I'm very keen to get you right now, secrets or not.'

Victoria sat on her stool and watched as he finished undressing. 'Peter's at me personally, too,' she said. 'He's saying I can't hack it, that the Prime Minister should reshuffle me as fast as political fortunes can turn, that I'm the wrong woman for the job.'

'Careful, you're giving me ideas for a useful slant—'

'You find quite enough of those already. Can't you keep those hatchet instincts focused on the Foreign Secretary?'

'Do you think I'm a security risk?' William asked provocatively, lifting her up and sliding his arms inside the negligee and round her naked waist.

'You just want your praises sung,' she mumbled as he kissed her. As he raised his head and touched her lips she went on self-consciously, needing to clear the air, 'Although, I did worry slightly, what you might be doing tonight, when you went out. It almost felt like shades of Barney!'

William pulled away, looking disbelieving. So stupid, saying that, knowing how paranoid he was about Barney. She wished he'd loosen up, though. Barney was in a really bad way and deserved a little magnanimous understanding.

'I can't believe you said that. Never put us in the same box – just don't. Okay?' Victoria was silent, there was nothing useful to be said.

William moved about the room, carefully hanging up his trousers. She went to sit on the bed and busied herself setting the alarm, deeply frustrated at how quickly a mood could turn.

He came beside her. 'I thought you could trust me a bit more than that,' he muttered, barely looking at her. 'It seemed better not to tell you and get you wound up and edgy, but I was actually seeing your pal Quentin Clayton tonight. I wanted MI5's reaction to something before deciding whether to go to print.'

'I'm sorry,' she said, feeling it, meeting his eyes as he looked up. 'But seeing the DG on a Sunday night – that's something serious.' She held back with a string of questions, thinking of MI5 and security implications: it was better to let William talk. 'Can you tell me about it?'

He picked up her hand and fingered it. 'Remember the young Muslim reporter you met at the *Post* party, Ahmed? He was very keen to be proactive after the Leicester Square bomb and I sent him up to Leeds to do some investigating. He comes from there, an area like Beeston. He's got in with some extremists, potential terrorists, we think. It took him to Cumbria yesterday. He had a long walk in the Fells with the leader whom Ahmed feels sure, and I'm inclined to agree, is ruthlessly committed.'

There had been 'training camps' in Cumbria, Victoria thought, as the adrenaline ripped through her. She still felt a shuddery under-the-skin sense of shame too, at her petty little suspicions. 'And the reason for the meeting?' she asked cautiously.

'Channelling information. This guy, who calls himself Fahad, obviously thinks a reporter on *The Post* could be useful. He wants a terrorist scare-story, petrol-tanker explosions, fed in. That one's been around a while, in fact. They use the press for propaganda whenever possible, trying to stir things up, let us know they mean business – as if we didn't – and get the authorities pointing the wrong way. I decided this was more serious than usual and Quentin should know.'

William squeezed her hand. 'Ahmed's been working hard, building trust, trying not to seem a mole. This Fahad did hint at a genuine plot – private planes, pilot sympathizers – although I doubt he actually trusts my reporter an inch. He sounds a highly professional operator, possibly working internationally and, Ahmed thinks, is planning some attack.'

'You're not going to print any of this? It would cause completely unnecessary panic, be catastrophic.' William kept silent, but then he would. Surely, though, he'd be more responsible than that?

'How did Quentin respond?' she went on, her mind racing, forgetting about not asking questions. William seemed to trust Ahmed completely, but the Service might be less sure.

'I got the feeling the DG rated it more talk than substance. Those poncey spooks are so dismissive of anything coming from the press.' William's irritation with them showed. 'Quentin's an ungiving fish, isn't he, even at the best of times. Nothing lifts off. I can see why you don't go a bundle on him.'

Victoria went into guarded-politician mode. She'd never voiced a syllable of criticism about the DG, certainly not to William. He might have hinted at it in the paper: a rift between the Home Secretary and MI5's Director General was a juicy angle to play.

'What on earth makes you think there's a cigarette paper of difference between us?' she said in a voice like starch.

Her husband grinned. 'You're as easy to read as a pop-up nursery book – your thoughts are helpfully written on your face like surtitles at the opera.'

She stood up in a sudden cold sweat of nerves, totally focused. Quentin had seen William on a Sunday night and for quite a while.

'Did Quentin indicate taking action? You don't need to answer that, of course,' she added hurriedly.

'I had the feeling, which I sincerely hope was wrong,' William's voice was clinking with ice-cubes, 'that MI5 might decide to tap my excellent reporter's phone.' He got up and faced her. 'I sincerely hope,' he repeated with heavy emphasis, 'that you'll tell them where they get off, and in no uncertain terms. Bugging the press would be an appalling slide: big brother, the beginning of a police state.'

Victoria resisted telling him that only last week she had refused to allow the tapping of a journalist's phone. It hadn't been popular. Home Secretaries were meant to accept the Permanent Secretary's advice.

In that case a drugs cartel had been involved. This time, with a threat to the nation's safety, the ever-present fear of terrorism, she would have no compunction – whatever William's sensitivities about press freedom. She knew Islamist extremists had been infiltrating government departments and the airport, taking jobs on the London Underground. The press must also be a target.

Victoria wondered if Quentin had quietly hidden real concern. Would the police take precautionary measures, issue warnings to petrol stations, tell oil companies to alert drivers? Nothing much else they could do. Were there any loopholes to plug where private planes and their pilots were concerned?

She heaved her shoulders and sighed. William took hold of them and gave her a kiss. 'You can't do anything right now – how about coming to bed?'

Victoria felt a despairing sea-swell of near-weepiness rising inside. The tension and pressures were immense, but it was her panicky concern about Nattie tipping the scales.

William looked sheepish. He knew he'd played his part. 'Tell me what's wrong?'

He was loving and sensitive where his stepdaughter was concerned, and she tried to explain. 'Nattie's obviously fallen for this new man, whoever he is, the light's shining out of her like a lit pumpkin. I know I'm being ridiculous, feeling excluded, but I can't help wondering if it's someone married . . . What do you think?'

'Possibly; feels unlikely. Nattie's playing it close and doesn't want you making complications for whatever reason, but from the look of her I'd say she's itching to shout about it with that amazing glow of hers.' He lifted Victoria's hair from her eyes. 'Can't you just be thankful Nattie's happy? She certainly seems to know her own mind for a change.'

That wasn't much reassurance, the opposite really. 'But it's gone midnight, we haven't a clue where she is. I just want her home.'

'Nattie's a woman, darling. You're overtired, talking like that. Let her be in charge.'

While William finished getting ready for bed, Victoria lay, still listening out for the door. He came to join her, positioning himself comfortably and familiarly. She felt the hardness of him and drew him in, feeling aroused. He whispered, 'Did you really think I was with another woman?'

'Just lost my bearings for a moment.'

'Am I helping you find them?' She was, he thought, relaxing and responding, letting go her cares.

The sound of the front door closing brought them back again and she tensed.

'Not brilliant timing,' William sighed, releasing her. 'Go and see all's well, you'll feel better.'

Victoria slid out of bed and shrugging back on her silk dressing gown, heard soft knuckles on the door. 'I didn't mean to get you up,' Nattie said, looked slightly surprised at her mother opening it so quickly. 'I saw the light was still on under the door . . . Just wanted to check in, Mum.'

'It's fine, darling. You've had a good time? Is it back to Durham tomorrow? Will you be getting another lift? Or do you need money for the train?'

'I'm probably off, not absolutely sure – fine for money, thanks. I'll call. It's been great, a surprise trip to London, seeing you, fantastic!' Nattie was glowing brighter than ever. 'Huggers,' she said, with her arms as wide as her smile.

They had a quick, tight goodnight hug. Victoria tried not to, but couldn't help saying, 'You can't tell me anything – all about this new excitement?'

Nattie's face misted up in a private smile. 'Not just for now, but it is pretty special. 'Night, Mum, only a week or so more of term. It's nearly Christmas.'

Victoria kissed her elated daughter's flushed cheek, closed the door and slipped back into bed. William gave her a peck then turned for sleep. The moment was past.

Lying wakeful in the enveloping blackness, the double-glazed silence, she tried to squirrel out a few kernels of worry. She felt disoriented, blindfolded, spun round. It was clutching at straws, she knew, to think that if Quentin believed Ahmed's information to be really serious she would have been contacted already, to authorise warrants.

The DG was doing nothing urgent; sleeping on it probably – unless the Service had dismissed the whole thing out of hand.

On top of Nattie and the nation's safety, Victoria began brooding about her lost miscarried child. He would have been three. Gates top and bottom of the stairs, toys: a nanny . . . Her yearning for another baby was inexplicable, yet as powerful an instinct as the need for survival. Every period brought well-hidden tears.

They were pricking now. Silent blubbing in the dark, she couldn't have felt more ashamed. Forty-two, Nattie, stepchildren – what about all the barren, childless couples in the world?

William spooned up close and reaching round, touched her wet face. 'It'll happen, don't fret – although God knows we'd be mad, our nights are broken enough already.'

'How could you possibly know? It's pitch black; you looked so asleep.'

'I know my wife. I'd even trust her to go out for an hour without telling me where or why.'

Victoria was in the office early. She looked up from her briefing papers; Tony's head had appeared round the door. 'Sir Adam's here to see you, Minister.'

'Of course.' She smiled at her Permanent Secretary as he came in and drew up a chair. She guessed why he was there and her stomach felt taut.

Adam was in his early fifties, balding, a touch overweight: a highly capable mandarin who, apart from an unexpected passion for surfboarding off the Scillies, clung to convention and form. He cleared his throat, preparing to speak.

'The Service is requesting an urgent warrant, Home Secretary, to intercept calls made by Ahmed Khan, a journalist on *The Post,* and Yazid Hussan, a council worker in Leeds.' Adam hesitated. 'They are aware of the sensitivities regarding Khan,' he went on uncomfortably, 'but fear terrorist action is planned. They are concerned.'

Victoria's taut stomach contracted still more. Normally applications for warrants came in a weekly batch, existing ones needing renewal and new requests with the written reasons attached. Quentin, she thought, had shifted speeds. He'd slept on the meeting with William and decided the threat was urgent and real.

And unlike William, who was so taken with Ahmed, the Director General's view would be coldly rational. She'd assumed Quentin had dismissed a junior reporter's information, imagined a faint sheen of condescension glistening on the DG's brow in the light of his desk lamp.

So what if it had done? Her attitude to Quentin, she told herself angrily, had to change. The quality of evidence alone would have decided him.

She stared back at Adam. 'If that's what the Service fears they must have their authorization,' she said without further thought, and readily acceded to the tapping of Ahmed's phone.

CHAPTER 13

'Well, Ahmed, what's next? I take it you want to carry on ferreting around in Leeds for a couple more weeks?'

His editor's voice was strong, business-like, Monday-morningish. 'Yes, of course, absolutely,' Ahmed said, making a supreme effort to stifle a yawn. The phone had woken him up. Shifting weary legs, he hitched up on an elbow and eyed the clock. God, nearly nine.

'I can't let the contact with Yazid and the others drift,' he said, sitting more upright, feeling sharper. 'I want to try to make them think I've made my mark with Fahad, had the seal of approval. Whether they'll buy that, though, and give—'

Bright sunlight was beating in through the white blinds. 'Shall I come in before getting off to Leeds?' he said, rubbing his eyes. 'Do you need to see me?'

The thought of being back in gritty dead-end Harehills made Ahmed's mind fly to Nattie. He wanted her desperately at that moment, the soft feel of her, her special smell like fresh almonds and flower petals. She could have stayed over, he thought resentfully, and not been so bothered about seeming secretive with her mother.

'No, get straight there, don't hang about,' Osborne snapped. 'And call me immediately if your chum Fahad should make contact. Oh, and I don't intend running anything on petrol tankers by the way. Might weaken your street cred with Fahad, although the Leeds lot may not be in the picture on that one.'

Had there been lack of interest from MI5? But that could have soured up Osborne, hacked him off enough to run the story . . . Had his wife put the dampeners on it? Bomb scares must be the last thing the Home Secretary needed, a political minefield.

So hard to believe she was the mother of the girl he'd fallen in love with; it was the weirdest feeling. He was her daughter's boyfriend, in her life, Nattie talked about her, probably too freely . . . Ahmed thought of watching her on television at the time of the bomb, how impressed he'd been. She'd been warm at *The Post* party, with those wide arresting eyes – although Nattie had been wholly distracting. He felt off balance, tossed up in the air, but determined to defy gravity.

He brought his mind back quickly; Osborne was still hanging on. 'I am worried, actually, whether Fahad will get back in touch,' he said, trying to sound thoughtfully alert. 'He's not going to take the smallest chances with me if he's closing in on something; he's been obsessive enough about covering his tracks.'

His editor made no comment, then barked out, giving Ahmed a startled fright, 'Honour killings – where are you on that?'

'It's tricky and delicate,' he answered defensively, having to switch mental tack fast. 'There's a girl called Leena whose father would have killed her, people say, if she hadn't managed to escape. It's a huge mystery how she did, apparently. She's almost certainly in a refuge, though, and they place the girls at risk as far away as possible; she could be anywhere in the country. I think there might be a friend she makes calls to. I'm pursuing that . . .'

He let his words tail, he was waffling. Osborne wanted results.

Released from the call Ahmed brooded despairingly about ever finding Leena. He did know a girl living locally in Leeds, with whom Leena was thought to have been close. If he could win that friend's confidence . . .

Leena's evidence was vital if her father was ever to be convicted and justice done. The refuge would continue to protect her. Publicity would too. And a few more convictions might act as a deterrent, Ahmed thought grimly, make the police keener to get involved. They turned too much of a blind eye, left Muslim communities too much to their own devices and helpless abused girls to flounder.

It was hard to stop yawning; he could have slept for days, hanging upside-down like a sloth. Had Nattie slept in, too? She'd probably been awake ages, pissed off at no word from him. Ahmed grabbed his mobile again and called.

'Sorry,' he said, smiling down the phone when she couldn't stifle a yawn, 'your stepfather's actually just done it to me . . . He could have neatly woken us both if only you'd slept here. If only.'

'Is it straight back to Leeds?'

'Yes, via Durham if you'll let me drive you.' He still felt anxious about making assumptions, still in a daze about being in her life; almost fearful in a way, at how right it felt.

'Yes, please. Will you come up from Leeds and see me?' she said in her soft turning-on voice. 'I'll need you to. Will it give you problems, all the time it'll take and everything?'

'You're joking. I'll live on the roads.' He thought of Yazid who would be watching his every move, but said, 'What about Sam and Milly, will they mind?'

'Why ever?' Nattie snorted. 'They'll think it's cool. Anyway, my room's my private space. There's not much more of this term – you'll be back in London soon after I am, won't you, back at the paper?'

Would he be? Ahmed felt close to the edge of a precipice with ill-intentioned people creeping up, playing Grandmother's Footsteps.

'What's happening?' Nattie asked sleepily. 'How soon have we got to get going? You could come over . . . Mum's been in the office hours, William too.'

Ahmed thought of the policeman in the garden. And he had to get back. Yazid and co. were his only link to Fahad and every fibre, every nerve in his body was flagging up a need for urgency.

'You still there?' she called down the phone. 'You didn't just drop off again?'

'I was thinking,' he said, feeling infinitely tender, 'it's better if I didn't come to the house right now, with all the security. We need to get going. I'll pick you up from outside the tube station, in twenty minutes? Although we could always nip back here . . . I don't do a bad breakfast.'

'Why did I think you did B&B as well?'

'My hotel's never closed . . . Shit!' he exclaimed, sitting bold upright. 'It's Monday! The fucking car. God, I hope it's not been towed away—' He leaped out of bed, pulling on jeans, his mobile clutched between cheek and shoulder. 'But I did dream last night,' he said breathlessly, dragging on a shirt, 'that you'd moved right in with a cat and cook-books, make-up in the bathroom, and made it your home.'

'I still can't get over no ticket! It's an omen, it shows you bring me fantastic luck.' They were halfway to Durham. Ahmed was feeling full of dread, the thought of two more weeks in his ship's cabin of a bedroom, the confines of home. From his small single-pane window that rattled and rasped, he could see the dominating green dome of the nearby mosque.

He wanted to be back in London, in the Brixton flat with Nattie, making love and plans. It was a beautiful day, crisply sunny: only three weeks now till Christmas, he thought, when he'd lose Nattie to her family. He rested his hand on her thigh, almost giddy with emotional need. So much could happen in the two weeks ahead.

He pressed lightly on her thigh. 'You were going to tell me about the watch-giver Hugo. How about now?'

Nattie flashed him a smile. 'It's complicated, a difficult scene. Mum thinks Hugo's the most amazingly suitable thing on two legs, but she's wrong – as things go.'

'That sounds cryptic. Why is she – as things go? Not that I want her to be right!' Ahmed resented suitability being an issue. 'Tell me all,' he said. 'How did it end? It has, hasn't it?' He glanced at Nattie.

'Well, yes and no.'

That came at him like a cricket ball, a hard knock. Nattie was looking down at her hands and her hair was a curtain over her face; he wanted her to toss it back and show lightness in her eyes. 'What do you mean? You're still seeing him? And why is your mother wrong – as things go?' he repeated sardonically.

'Don't get all hung-up! I do still see him, sure, but only as a friend. He's always been that to me, that's really the problem.'

'You mean you're more than that to him?' Ahmed kept his eyes on the road.

'Well yes, I guess, although only so far. The coke has more of a hold on him these days. That's the problem, his habit, why Mum's wrong. But I do kind of feel in Hugo's debt, you see.' She turned anxiously. 'He was really patient and kind when I was being vile after that bad first time; I can't walk away now, when he's slowly destroying himself. I'm scared he's on to heroin. But it's so difficult to help with all the mood swings. If I'm even like just trying to communicate he backs off thinking it's the sympathy vote, which I suppose it is.'

Ahmed didn't know what to think. He asked, still feeling spiky, 'Who is he if your mother's so keen on him? What does he do?' Someone with a plum stuck in his throat probably, and money, he thought nastily.

'He's Ned Markham's youngest son. You know – Secretary of State at Defra.'

Ahmed knew all about Ned Markham. *The Post* had had it in for him for years for being too patrician and laissez-faire. But Ned must be a wily old bird underneath, Ahmed thought, still to be around. It didn't help him to relax about Hugo.

'Ned was Mum's boss in her first job as Housing Minister,' Nattie went on. 'She thinks he's about to step down from the Cabinet and spend more time with his Staffordshire estates – and that Nick Bates will get his job. She likes Nick, she'd be pleased.'

It was a hot political tip that Ahmed thought briefly about passing on. He grinned at Nattie. 'Does your mother tell you things she wouldn't tell your stepfather? Perhaps you shouldn't be telling me – I do work for him!'

'In that case I should never have talked about Hugo. I mean, the crack and stuff . . . You wouldn't ever write about that, would you?'

She was white-faced, looking so vulnerably uncertain, so completely exquisite that he wanted to swing off the road and devour her. 'I thought you trusted me,' he said.

'Hugo's got the most lovely nature,' Nattie carried on, 'well, before his habit. He plays the sax in a jazz band.'

'Does he have a day job, too?'

'Some management consultancy or other that Mum thinks is a proper, square, intelligent career. But he won't hang on to it the way he's going. I do worry.' She glanced at him. 'It was through Hugo, not at uni, that I actually met Shelby; he was often at Hugo's flat. Shelby isn't one of his lot, though, so I didn't feel like I was getting off with his best friend. It seemed odd, Shelby being around so much. They weren't that close.'

'Was Hugo into coke by then?'

'You mean is that the connection?'

Ahmed hadn't wanted to lay it on. The intelligence about Shelby's dealing had come third hand after all, but his loathing was brim-full, frothing over the sides.

'I'm shit scared Shelby might be there if I go round to Hugo's in the vac,' Nattie said, letting her question about dealing hang fire. 'He's sure to try to get even; he'll be determined. What do you think he'll do?'

It was a question to which Ahmed had given some thought. Publicity about himself and Nattie would be the most harmful, blowing his cover with Fahad, but it was hard to imagine Shelby wanting to admit to being ditched.

Ahmed told her that, mainly to press home the need to keep schtum. There was nothing to worry about, he promised, with a persuasive grin. Nattie looked barely reassured.

Driving on they talked little, the imminent parting making them both subdued. He sighed at the thought of how flat and lonely he would feel.

After a quick late pancake lunch at the Georgian Teahouse, Nattie walked with him to the car. It was hateful leaving her. Ahmed felt

something wild and intense going on inside him; love was a demanding animal.

When he could no longer see Nattie in his driving mirror and he'd
set course for Leeds, he thought about the week ahead, the pressures
and problems besetting his home community. The families he grew
up with were straddling two cultures, living by two codes: revering
one that was almost medieval, with its currency of loyalty and
threats, despising the other as morally degenerate while grabbing
every benefit going.

The extremists amongst them wanted to Islamise the world –
'Allah's law in Allah's land' – yet the Koran accepted religious diver-
sity. Terrorists clothed themselves in intellectual respectability, he
thought; they demonized the enemy, penetrated minds. Did Fahad
with his obvious hatred of the un-believing rest of the world envis-
age the absolute power of Islam as 'the solution', like Hitler?

Ahmed tried to isolate his thoughts, but his need of Nattie clung
on. Hiring a car for the Fahad meeting was one thing, but keeping
it on for nocturnal trips to Durham would be quite another. The car
would be seen, word got round – everybody had extended families,
they knew what went on. Even if he took the train someone's cousin
would be working at the station.

He thought of his father whose minicab hours were six a.m. till
nine or ten at night. What if he borrowed the car then, and had it
back by dawn? Could he win his father round?

A service station came into view. After filling up with petrol,
Ahmed called home with an update on timing. He decided to call
Yazid as well.

It was during working hours, though. Ahmed imagined him in
some airless council office-space with uniform desks, dealing with

the misuse of wheelie bins and dog-fouling of pavements, feeling infinitely superior to his *Kafir* colleagues all the while.

Yazid did answer at least. 'Oh, Ahmed,' he said, in that whiny suspicious voice of his, 'where have you been? Are you back in Leeds?'

'About half an hour off; fucking long slow journey from London.'

'You had a good meeting, Saturday?' Yazid couldn't hide his curiosity. Fahad didn't, obviously, do much downloading. 'You went on from there?'

'Yes – to feed in the story our brother wanted placed. It landed me with a day in the office. We work Sundays on a daily. I tried hard with the story, but they're shitting their pants about using it. The editor's a weak *kafir*, bastard, in the palm of his lying scheming Home Secretary wife. Still, it got the wind up them, all right. They'll be looking the other way – at the relevant time . . .'

There was a silence. Was Yazid gauging how much Fahad might have begun to trust him? 'Want to come round later?' he offered, which seemed quite a good sign. 'I'd quite like some advice about Khalid.'

'You mean he's got cold feet?' That was an educated shot in the dark.

Yazid had been about to click off. 'We'll save it for later, shall we?' he said.

CHAPTER 14

Reaching Harehills Ahmed felt as if he'd been away for at least a week, not two days. He returned the hire car and set off with his overnight bag for home, stopping on the way to buy his mother a bunch of flowers.

His parents' house was on a corner with a side-sliver of garden. His father had cut a double gate into the fencing and, after a great deal of practice, had now perfected the art of squeezing his Vauxhall minicab sideways on into the awkward space.

The car was there, his father at home. Ahmed thought how best to broach the subject of borrowing it overnight – and to explain the hours he'd be keeping. An offer to contribute to the housekeeping should be made, he knew, although it would lead to a vehement lengthy refusal and be wearying.

His mother was dishing up the evening meal, curried beef with eggplant and okra, and glad he was home in time. Food was always on the go, though, there for any member of the family, at whatever time of day. She beamed at the sight of the flowers, dreary chrysanthemums, all Harehills had to offer, and wiping her hands arranged them lovingly in a fake crystal vase.

She was taller than most of her women friends and wore her hair, now iron-grey, drawn back into a tight knot. His mother was growing thinner with age, Ahmed thought, which was etching in lines, but she never stooped, no awkward bent-kneed slouching, trying to match his father's height. He rather admired that and thought, too, that her bright chestnut-brown shalwar kameez with a long pink scarf, a dupata, round her neck suited her. The scarf doubled as headcover if men other than family came to the house.

'I'd really like to help out a bit and contribute to my keep,' he said, over supper.

The tirade started. Both parents set down their knives and forks and glowered. 'This is your home, Ahmed!' his mother exclaimed bristling, ruffled as an angry hen. 'Have you forgotten that? Don't you come giving us all your London talk, treating us as a hotel. You remember where you are.'

'I'll find a way to say thank you,' he smiled.

His father glared across the table. 'I would like to know what's going on, Ahmed, why exactly you're here. You're tense; I don't like it. Why couldn't you have been a doctor or an engineer and put that great brain of yours to use in more productive ways? Writing for a newspaper, what kind of help is that to the world?'

It was a gramophone refrain. 'I am trying to do useful things, Pops. I can't tell you what, but for good reason; please trust me. And I'm after some help . . . I know it's a lot to ask, but can I possibly use the car late at night, a couple of times this week? I'd have it back before six: earlier than that if need be.'

'Six!' his mother screamed. 'You're seeing a woman, I won't have it.'

'Long before six, Mum,' he said earnestly, thinking she could as easily have screamed *sex*. 'It's just that the things I'm involved in mean a lot of travel.'

His father gave him a beady look. It hadn't been an unqualified denial. Although distances possibly reassured him, he could cope with his son having sex as long as it was carried on discreetly far from home. And he couldn't deny his only son, even if he was a newspaper reporter and involved in some secretive unsettling business. *And* one who'd been gently trying for years, probably clumsily, to make clear to his parents that any attempt to produce girls with a view to marriage was doomed.

Ahmed made his excuses as soon as possible after the meal and walked round to the launderette. He rang the bell by the side entrance with more than butterflies in his stomach; a whole army of fluttering creatures was trying to find a way out.

Yazid was alone. He'd changed out of office clothes and was wearing an expensive-looking camel suede jerkin and tight-fitting charcoal jeans. His own jeans having seen better days, Ahmed thought pleasurably for a moment about shopping for clothes with Nattie. It would be too risky, he had to keep sight of what mattered.

Which, he told himself firmly, was to concentrate all his fire on Yazid. He seemed unusually tense, even more so than Ahmed was himself. Standing by as Yazid made tea, he asked conversationally, mainly for a bit of light relief, 'What were you working on when I called?'

'Residents' complaints: they're all moaning about the new refuse scheme.'

Poor complainants. Ahmed imagined Yazid's balls-achingly pompous replies. He was anxious, too, to know the evening's parameters and asked, sipping a welcome cup of tea, 'Anyone else coming? Iqbal? Khalid's tied up tonight, then?'

'Iqbal's gone already, a few last-minute instructions, I think.' Yazid gave a long and studiously colluding look. 'Khalid, though, is a problem . . . Finished your tea?'

'You mean we might take a walk? Ready when you are.'

They set off out into the chill blackness of a winter's night. A small parade of shops was giving off light and Ahmed felt grateful for that. There was litter everywhere, groups of youths gathering; a drunk was slumped against a glass shop-front. They walked in silence past the shops; Yazid was certainly wound-up. The sense of something imminent, a climax building, was rife.

Ahmed thought about Khalid as they strolled, the shadow behind his eyes, the sense of fear he'd detected in the likable well-meaning kid during the previous week. His heart went out to him. Khalid was vulnerable. There was his absolute faith in God, yet he was too unquestioningly believing, easy meat for devious people seeking to use him for their own ends.

Pity about having to miss the match they'd been going to together, but the meeting with Fahad had come up, as well as Nattie's irresistible invitation to supper. Khalid had looked so disappointed. Still thrilled and grateful for the ticket, but Ahmed sensed the kid's urgent need of a sympathetic supportive shoulder and he felt a vital opportunity had been missed.

Khalid had left school at sixteen with three GCSEs and gone to Pakistan for a year to live with his grandmother and study Islam in one of the Madrassas, the religious schools whose agendas were far too anti-Western in Ahmed's view. He'd heard young men returning from them, talking about a Western conspiracy to destroy Islam and the media being part of the cover-up and controlled by Jews.

Ahmed had been trying to find out more in the few minutes he'd managed to be alone with him, gently prodding in the hope of making progress. 'And you did a little training as well while you were out in Pakistan?' he'd suggested, thinking of all the militant organizations out there, the *jihadi tanzeems*. Khalid had looked away.

'I thought it my duty to strive to be *shaheed*,' he mumbled. He had wanted to be a martyr, Ahmed sensed, to die in a suicide struggle, which some people considered to be sanctified. But that didn't mean he still did, that he'd come home to England and become a terrorist. Khalid could have grown out of it. Talking of his duty he hadn't sounded wholly fired up and committed.

Now Ahmed turned to Yazid and asked cautiously, 'You think Khalid's uncomfortable with things?' Trying to appear at least partly in the know was like treading on pavements of broken glass; there was nowhere safe to put his feet.

'He insists on going to dawn prayers which is giving problems,' Yazid said cryptically. Deliberately, Ahmed thought. Yazid was trained not to talk, but couldn't resist making clear his involvement in whatever ghastly plotting was going on.

They had rounded a corner into the yellowish smoky dark of a Harehills backstreet. It was terraced, tall, forbidding and uphill.

'But you've more fundamental worries, haven't you?'

Yazid's face was in profile, but he still managed a look of self-importance. 'Khalid can't quite let go of traditional Islam; it's his father's influence and a particular Imam, a family friend. We can appeal to his faith and talk of the Holy Prophet Muhammad, but he needs to understand the ideology, the concept of global supremacy. Islam has to dominate; we have to use force. Khalid needs to think more politically.'

'Powerful sentiments,' Ahmed said, in tones of awe, although sucking up to Yazid was anathema. 'I'm sure Khalid will follow your lead. He's a good kid.' Too humble and vulnerable to stand up to these bullies trying to manipulate him, he thought.

Yazid turned and glanced, still immensely puffed-up with his own importance, but it was a strained nervous look, too. 'It's as well to be aware,' he said pompously, 'that phones might be bugged. That call you made earlier wasn't good. This is a critical time, a critical moment.'

Why? Was something about to happen? They wandered back to the flat. Yazid was in on himself one minute and glinting-eyed the next, bursting to preen and boast, by the look of him. It seemed pointless to stick around, dangerous; there was little more to be gained and he risked losing the tenuous links so laboriously forged.

Ahmed saw Nattie the next night. They covered a lot of ground in four hours.

Everything, as he drove home from Durham, felt curiously unreal, the isolated drive at four-thirty in the morning, the clear roads, the night winds calmed. His thoughts were testing company, uncomfortably demanding, coming at him too quickly like questions in an oral test. Ahmed felt under pressure and unable to come up with sound answers.

Nattie had asked about his Christmas plans; would they have time together in London, would he have to be at home? Her mother was going to be away in the Hampshire constituency, she said, or with Nattie's grandparents – they could have the empty house . . .

He shelved that tempting notion and thought back over the completely frustrating time he'd had earlier in the day. There had been the unexpected luck of finding a lead to Leena's friend – a many-times-removed cousin his mother had talked about at breakfast – but then had come the anticlimax of hearing that the friend, Safa, was in Birmingham all week on a family visit. However impatient Osborne might be for progress, the Leena story was going to have to wait.

Ahmed turned on the radio in search of some news headlines. A story was just breaking. As he listened, he had to pull in and stop the car.

'. . . Reports are coming in of an attack on an isolated stretch of rail track south of Sellafield . . .' The track had been tampered with, the report went on, and a train carrying a cargo of radioactive waste derailed. Three people were believed dead, two police guards and the driver.

It was feared that a small quantity of the waste had gone missing. A controlled explosion had been carried out to break the lock on one of the containers.

Driving on slowly, listening to repeat bulletins, Ahmed realized that the public was being told the absolute minimum: no description of the type of waste. 'A small quantity' could mean anything. He knew in his sinking heart there was a chance that the attack could be to do with Fahad. It fitted. It was his geographical area, Iqbal had disappeared, Yazid had been on a razor's edge of nerves . . .

Further information was being given. 'An abandoned rigid inflatable boat has been located at sea in the immediate vicinity. It seems possible the escape plan might have failed. Helicopters have arrived at the scene and a comprehensive search of all vehicles in the area is underway . . .'

It was hard to absorb the full horrifying significance of it all. Ahmed couldn't really believe the plot had failed. Were there any drowned bodies? Surely those would have been mentioned?

Fahad could have thought of an abandoned boat to add to the confusion; it was his style, that sort of cunning – he went in for minutely careful attention to detail.

It could be the work of any terrorist cell. There were enough of them. To imagine Fahad's involvement was to jump to enormous conclusions. He was a dangerous extremist, sure, but on the strength of two unnerving meetings and little hard evidence, to assume his fingerprints were all over this attack was irresponsible, Ahmed knew.

And yet . . . He remembered Fahad unable to hide his pride, talking of fine timing, tying up dates, slotting together all the links in the chain. That seemed to fit more with this ambush than the 'real' plot he'd tossed out, about pilot sympathizers and private planes.

Whoever was responsible for this terrifying attack, though, someone now had radioactive waste at his disposal, the means, experts, wherewithal, to do unthinkable harm. It was the nightmare of all time.

CHAPTER 15

It was quarter to five in the morning. Victoria was ready to leave for the office. She was in the kitchen waiting for the car, erupting with impatience. The call had come half an hour earlier, its shrill tone carving into her sleepy half-consciousness, its message grim. She was still feeling disbelieving horror and hypertension.

William had stirred as the phone rang and stayed silent in bed beside her, listening carefully, she knew, and probably hearing all, in the stillness of early morning. Adam, her Permanent Secretary, had quietly delivered the news in his mandarin-smooth tones. Panic calls at dawn were nothing new, dramas and disastrous cock-ups went with the territory. But this . . .

She had turned away and hugged the phone, more acutely aware than ever, at such a moment of high crisis, of the Foreign Secretary's attacks over the security implications of her marriage to a newspaper editor. Barnes was increasing the pressure, whispering slyly about William's nightly access, campaigning in his underhand way, determinedly spreading the word.

Victoria heaved an agitated, apprehensive sigh. She was desperate to be off. The kitchen lights seemed too glaring and enclosing, cocooning her against her will in a vacuum of bright halogen-lit normality. She felt raw, her senses seared and bloodied by Adam's call. A derailed train with a cargo of High Level Radioactive Waste, three people shot dead, a controlled explosion to break the lock of a container, canisters taken – the potential for catastrophe seemed beyond belief.

The phone went again. Adam had been calling regularly, keeping her in the frame. Grabbing the handset and pacing up and down edgily, she muttered, 'No bodies found, just that empty drifting boat?' She looked up as William came into the kitchen.

'No bodies as yet,' Adam confirmed. 'The police say there's a smouldering burned-out pick-up truck on the beach. It was driven into the water up to its wheel-tops and almost certainly used to transport the canisters to the waiting boat. The truck would have been doused with petrol then and set alight, nothing left to chance.

'It's a desolate area,' he carried on. 'The rail track hugs the coast for a two-mile stretch and is almost on the beach at the point where the ambush took place. But the good news is that one of the missing canisters is in the inflatable boat – that's a great relief. And it seems part of the side of the boat is flat so it's possible the other drum has rolled into the sea. I think we can dare to hope the harsh winter conditions got the better of them—'

Victoria felt it was a very hollow straw. Surely any people in the boat would have held on? She had become obsessed with the idea of a decoy, icy with nerves about it. Something seemed too pat about an abandoned drifting craft and no sign of any bodies. The air and sea search had begun almost right away.

There could have been two boats, after all. And wouldn't the terrorists – as she had to assume they were – have found one heavy, lead-lined cumbersome canister of High Level Waste easier to handle and get away with than two?

'The conditions weren't that bad last night,' she said coolly, adding with a kinder understanding of Adam's need to make things better, 'Let's just pray you're right.' She returned the phone to its stand, seeing all the hallmarks of a cunningly calculated ploy, feeling more on edge than ever.

The questions were stacking up in her head, but she had to wait to put them to Luke Andrews, the anti-terrorism police chief, and Quentin Clayton. Both men were on full alert, marshalling their respective forces and operators and ensuring an instant response. They couldn't be with her for a meeting in her office until six-thirty. Victoria was frantic to be there well ahead, frustrated that Rodney wasn't on duty. Charles, one of the other 'tecs who was on his way, hadn't nearly the same sense of urgency and push.

She marvelled at William's sensitive non-interference; it was her own private agony and responsibility. He was keen to be off to his office as well, she thought, watching him standing over the kettle in his shirt-tails, with a teabag ready for her, a large scoop of coffee in the pot for himself. Even the kettle's noisy cheerful rise to boiling grated on her raw nerves and she jumped as he slapped it back on its stand.

He handed over a steaming mug. His freshly shaven face had a drained look, an early-morning pallor. 'Put some sugar in,' he said, 'I don't trust you to eat during the day. You're doing the early media round, I suppose, not the PM?'

'Yep, meeting Quentin and Luke Andrews first. The two main breakfast television shows, a few regionals, the *Today* programme, Radio Five.'

'You'll have to say more than that tight-arsed early bulletin going out.' William had a uniquely emphatic way of speaking, a sort of graphic authority. 'That won't hold the line for long. *A small amount of radioactive waste!* You can't downplay it that much, the media won't buy it – it's like calling the parting of the Red Sea *a small fluke of the weather*.' He was speaking objectively, she thought, not having a go. 'I mean, what is a small amount?' he demanded. 'Two cylinders, three? And what sort of waste – Medium Level, High Level?'

Victoria stared at him wide-eyed over the mug from which she was gratefully sipping. Those were her least difficult questions. She would have much tougher ones coming at her soon. Why hadn't armed police guards fired a shot? Could the quantity of waste missing produce a dirty bomb? What measures, what steps would she be taking to protect the public? Full honest answers to those questions, she thought, even if she could give them, would leave the nation scared witless.

She smiled wanly at William. 'I can tell you a little about the waste,' she said, confident *The Post*'s last edition was put to bed and it wasn't an unfair advantage. 'It was plutonium-contaminated material, High Level Waste effectively, and being transferred up coast for long-term storage. Two canisters were taken, although one's been found in that drifting boat. They're about three-foot tall, lead-lined and heavy, hardly easy to slip into a back pocket and secrete away – and don't start asking supplementaries, love, because I can hear that's the car at last.'

'Good luck,' he said, helping her into her coat, 'with the media and all the bigger questions. I can imagine how hard they'll be.'

William's quick hug was strong on warmth and meant a lot. He might need watching and give her a few problems, but she left with a sense of his arms as life-saving ropes and greeted Charles less impatiently. After that she sat in the back of the car without saying a word all the way to the office.

Tony was in, and one of her other private secretaries. They were speaking softly, almost whispering; it was the hush of the building, the early-hour dark, Victoria thought, and the shocking reason for being there. She discussed the briefing for the Prime Minister with them, wondering if he would hold her responsible in any way.

Could she have foreseen such a disaster – forestalled it even? Transportation of nuclear waste wasn't a Home Office responsibility, but bombs were. She'd been in the job almost five months; were there other checks and steps she could have taken?

The clock moved on, although time seemed suspended, too. She had a bleak sense of déjà vu waiting for Quentin and Luke Andrews, thinking of a similar meeting after the Leicester Square bomb. That one had yielded no leads, no known links, no breakthrough – was this about to follow the same pattern? What incalculable harm could terrorists achieve with a large canister of High Level Waste in their hands?

She looked up. Tony was at the door. 'The Assistant Commissioner is on his way up, Home Secretary,' he said smiling. It was a small momentary smile admittedly – still unexpected and oddly disconcerting. Was Tony imagining exploding dirty bombs and feeling in need of a release? He came into the room, sorting and tidying a bundle of briefing papers. 'And your daughter's just called,' he added, looking up.

Victoria stiffened, instantly flooded with panic. Why ring the main office and not her mobile or the private line? 'She rang the *office*, Tony? What did she want?'

'Nattie was most insistent about not bothering you, but she'd heard the news and was anxious you shouldn't feel there was anything you could have done.'

Her panic turned to amazement. What on earth was Nattie playing at? Tony's face was impassive. 'I told her,' he said neutrally, 'that I couldn't agree with her more.'

'If we can summarize exactly where we are,' Victoria looked from Luke Andrews to Quentin Clayton, 'and how much can be made public knowledge.' She turned more to Andrews. 'You say the air crews' target call is fifteen minutes? Did they meet it?'

He confirmed that. 'They've been searching well over two hours, now,' he said.

'What about the roads?'

He sat up straighter, which gave him a formidable presence; Luke was a man who towered even when leaning back in a chair. 'We had blocks in place almost immediately, every vehicle stopped and thoroughly searched for a radius of thirty miles. That's been extended now. The traffic is beginning to build, but we're coping; it's mainly commercial vans and lorries. There's no road access to the track at that point, only a coastal footpath – and, of course, direct from the beach.'

'I can see the shock and confusion with the train derailed,' Victoria said, 'but how come two armed Civil Nuclear Police officers didn't fire a single shot?'

Andrews shifted, squared his shoulders. 'There was no moon, which I'm sure was part of the plan. The attackers would have had night-vision goggles, and been lying in wait, of course, but the clincher, I'm afraid, Home Secretary, what we've now learned from discarded cartridges, is that they had AK-47s – machine guns.'

He paused, letting that sink in. 'It had to be headshots and at close range,' he said. 'The CNP officers wear ballistic vests; they're well protected. They are equipped with Heckler and Koch MP5s and Glock 17s – that's a submachine gun and a semi-automatic pistol – but even so, with the surprise element and automatic fire power against them, they didn't have a prayer.' Luke looked down; he was talking about the death of police officers, finding it especially hard to take.

'Handguns are easily obtained on the black market in London and Manchester,' he continued. 'It's not so with automatic weapons. AKs are still very rare in UK crime. Unfortunately that's changing now, but it does still point to a very serious operation, possibly with inter-national input. The weapons were hidden in advance, I expect.'

'The Toyota pickup truck would have managed the terrain all right?' Victoria queried. 'I assume it was stolen. None reported miss-ing yet?'

'Bit early. Some poor bugger's still tucked up in happy ignorance. It's a sandy beach, just a few odd rocks. Sandy quite a way inland too, with only a little scrub. All easily managed.'

'No chance of any DNA on the boat or the retrieved canister?' she asked. It was useless anyway if the terrorists were 'clean skins', unknown to the authorities and with no previous convictions.

'They'll have been wearing wetsuits and skin-tight surgical rubber gloves – still unhampered enough to operate guns.' Andrews's lips compressed in a taut line. 'The chance of any DNA is unlikely—' He stopped and studied close-clipped nails.

He was well aware they had no suspect as yet to match up to, Victoria thought. Every vehicle in the area was being searched: how could you hide a metre-high canister and two, three, four people?

She suppressed a sigh. They must still be in the vicinity, surely? She foresaw a hideously awful scenario, no likely cell to pursue, no bodies, no canister: only a paralysing state of uncertainty. The public demanding action, reassurance.

'We're leaving no stone unturned,' Andrews said tritely, reacting to the look in her eyes. 'There's a boat missing from a Seascale yard, it seems, and—'

'But suppose two were taken,' she interrupted quickly, 'one from elsewhere, say further south. Those fast RIBs can really speed, can't they, and in very shallow water – they'd be almost impossible to track using maritime radar, wouldn't they, Luke? And the equivalent journey would take ages on land. You've got the hills of the Lake District, a sparsely populated coast, few roads, none major or direct. Whereas a boat could have got as far as Morecambe Bay and crossed to Carnforth in under an hour.' The two men were staring at her, Tony as well. 'That's forty miles away,' Victoria said. 'They'd have had a head start.' Her conviction that the abandoned boat was deliberate had caused her to do some serious thinking outside the box.

Andrews looked almost grateful when Tony caused a slight diversion by leaving the room. He came back with a laden tray. 'I, um, ordered in some bacon sandwiches.'

All eyes were on her, but the smell alone made it impossible to refuse. 'We'll have them as we go,' she said, smiling round. 'I want to press on.'

Quentin had been listening with his hands clasped, fingers tightly entwined. He unlocked them and accepted a sandwich, tackling it as fastidiously as a girl with just-painted nails. Victoria felt even more on edge. MI5's Director General had seemed distant all through the discussion, within himself, as though the conversation was background music and not intruding much. He was either feeling above it all or had more consuming concerns.

Tony poured coffee and clattered away plates. Quentin wiped his hands, brushed away non-existent crumbs and held her eyes. 'There is a most delicate difficulty, Home Secretary . . .' Her heart sank; how could there be more?

'Let me first reassure you,' Quentin said, 'that a full contingent of field agents is working on the movements of every known cell, looking for any sign of increased activity or possible lead. But it did seem a worthwhile precaution to make a few additional inquiries about the content and security of the waste . . .'

He hesitated. 'You'll know about nuclear reprocessing – the extraction of uranium and plutonium for recycling into new fuel, but of course there's also the highly radioactive waste produced.' Victoria nodded, anxious to get to whatever was the crux.

'Anyone exposed to that cocktail of High Level Waste wouldn't live long,' Quentin declared ominously. 'For just that reason it is reduced to a powder that is then mixed with liquid glass and stored in lead-lined containers, making it safer by far. A glass block isn't easily dispersed into the atmosphere, not much use in bomb making—'

'But you're saying that at the powder stage—?'

He gave Victoria his smooth emotionless gaze, 'I'm very much afraid, Home Secretary, my inquiries this morning led to the discovery that a small amount of HLW held at the Low Level repository was being stored incorrectly, not cast in glass.'

She swallowed. Such an error seemed almost too devastating to contemplate. 'And you're saying that's what was being transported up coast?'

'Yes. Being transferred smartly back to Sellafield to be cast in glass and stored correctly. Whoever planned this attack has taken immense care with the preparation and acquired an extraordinary inside knowledge by whatever means.'

No one said a word. There had obviously been a desperate attempt to keep the disastrous error secret. Not only was the country facing a monumental security risk, now, on top, the government was going to be accused of an appalling cover-up.

Victoria stared at Quentin. She drew in her breath, letting it out slowly as she spoke. 'You, um, managed to find this out between four and six this morning?' She thought of some poor hapless official being jolted out of a deep sleep – who must now be fervently longing for any possible way he or she could pass the buck.

'Yes, I spoke to the relevant official personally,' Quentin said. 'I know nuclear waste and its transportation is the responsibility of your colleague at Energy, Home Secretary,' he assured emolliently, 'but the importance of finding this canister, and the perpetrators, cannot be understated and that falls to us all. In the wrong hands—' Quentin raised his shoulders; he didn't need to spell out what havoc a bomb made from dispersible nuclear waste could wreak.

Victoria turned to Tony. 'I'm about to do this media round. I'll manage to say the absolute minimum, but I don't see how such an appalling lapse can possibly be kept from the public, it would be terribly wrong. Can you speak to Number Ten while I'm gone, Tony? Make sure they're fully in the picture and find out whether the PM wants to do some media himself.'

Luke Andrews looked at his watch. He was desperate to be back on the case and even, she liked to think, keen to spread the search-net wider to take in Carnforth boatyards and the area round about, further down the coast.

He had stood up and was about to go when another thought came to her.

'If, God forbid, we do discover the boat was a decoy and High Level Waste is in terrorist hands, would anyone making a bomb have to die in the process, Luke?'

'You can find NCB suits on the Internet – even on eBay, Home Secretary,' he replied. 'That's Nuclear Chemical Biological; and gas masks, too. But they'd find someone willing to die, anyway, if they had to. Nothing would stand in the way of these people whoever they are. They're ruthlessly bent on destroying this country's whole way of life. We can only hope they'll fall prey to some tiny slip or weakness or underestimation.' Victoria thought of Leicester Square, the suicide bomber. They still had nothing to go on. Had the same brilliant evil minds orchestrated that, too?

She thanked the lofty police chief and Tony saw him out. She was surprised when Quentin didn't leave also. Resisting a look at her watch she rose from her desk as if to anticipate his departure, and came round to the front, saying with a rueful grimace, 'It doesn't come much worse, does it!'

He eyed her calmly, half-smiling in return, but in a slightly un-related way, almost as if he was acting two roles in a play and about to swap parts, change his character. His expression was curiously more human and it sowed fresh seeds of anxiety.

She had a sudden small-girl need of her father to whom she was closest of her parents, he knew her so well. She valued his advice and intelligent objectiveness more than anything and longed, although hopelessly, for a chance to be able to pour everything out to him – to be alone in her cavernous office and making private calls, not facing Quentin with his obvious need of a quiet word.

She wanted to phone William, too; for no reason other than contact. He would understand and respond. And to speak to Nattie and
thank her for her call, although that didn't need privacy, Victoria
thought, it could be done in the car on the way to this dreaded
round of media that she was so late for. She had to get on.

From Quentin's grave patient gaze he seemed to be waiting for her
thoughts to run their course. She stared at him. 'There's something
else?'

'Well, yes, actually. I asked Tony to give us a minute. There is a
small matter I thought best, perhaps, that you knew about. Forgive
me if you're aware of it already.'

'I'm sure I'm not,' Victoria replied, sick with worry that it would
be to do with William.

'I just thought you should know,' Quentin said calmly, 'that
Ahmed Khan, the *Post* reporter for whom we requested a warrant the
other day, is seeing your daughter.'

Victoria had a flashback to the *Post* party, the young man's dumb-
struck awe, Nattie's warm smiles. She'd been very taken with him,
that was obvious, but it had seemed inconsequential at the time: a
party thing, their paths hardly likely to cross again. Nattie had had
Shelby in her life. And she was safely up in Durham.

It was all falling into place. Her exhilarated glow, the new love she
was flatly refusing to talk about. Why, though, would Nattie be so
determined on secrecy?

Victoria thought it through, staring steadily at Quentin all the
while. 'You're telling me this because you think he's mixed up in
something?'

He slid back into Director General mode. 'You may know,
Home Secretary, that *The Post* sent Khan up to Leeds to do some

undercover investigating. We are following up on the information he's provided. But on a call to your daughter a couple of hours ago he—'

'He called her on Monday morning – at dawn!' Victoria felt horrified, weak-kneed, the intimacy suddenly, starkly brought home. She held on to the edge of the desk.

Quentin continued with his usual calm. 'Khan had been with your daughter and just left, I think, and must have heard the news on the first radio bulletin. He seemed concerned his contacts might be implicated in the attack, or so he told her.'

'Could they be?'

'Anything is possible at this stage.'

She wanted to ask if there was any chance of Ahmed's information giving a useful lead, but she latched more on to Quentin's main message, shuddering as its significance rammed home.

'You mean he was actually talking about his contacts, these people he's seeing he thinks are terrorists, discussing them with Nattie – my daughter?'

'We're not entirely sure where Khan stands or how close his links are, that's really the point.'

Victoria took it in. Quentin had told her all he could or was prepared to. He'd done what he thought necessary and right and needed to get back to Thames House.

He was about to leave. She thanked him then had to ask one last question.

'If, just suppose, Khan is conceivably implicated in any way, why on earth would he tell Nattie that he thought his contacts could be involved in this attack?'

'Well, he might possibly if, say, he wanted to underline his innocence. He'd expect it to get back. That's pure conjecture you understand, not on the basis of evidence.'

As soon as Quentin was out of the door she called William on her private line. 'Did you know,' she asked breathlessly, the moment he answered, 'about Ahmed Khan and Nattie?' She bit on her lip, waiting on his reply, clutching the receiver as tightly as if she were gluing it together. Why was he being so slow and hesitating?

'To be honest, it did cross my mind as a remote possibility,' William said finally. 'It hardly seemed worth mentioning, completely irrelevant. But since you've obviously just heard about it from Clayton, that only confirms he's fucking bugging my reporter's phone. It's shameful. How could you have allowed it! Can't you see?'

'For heaven's sake – just think what we're facing!' Victoria was incensed he could be on about that at such a time. 'You said yourself terrorism's the greatest threat we face. And it's extremely relevant that he's seeing Nattie.' William tried to chip in, but she ploughed on. 'No, please hear me out. He's mixing with would-be terrorists, vicious dangerous men. I'm desperately worried. I only want Nattie to be happy and safe – is that so strange?'

'He's certainly making her happy,' William said with infuriating flippancy. 'It's such a wrong-headed, pointless worry,' he went on forcefully. 'Ahmed will look after her, he's an exceptional young man. Think what you've got to deal with right now, don't get needlessly sidetracked. Just keep your head down and keep strong.'

Victoria felt wretched as she ended the call. Ahmed might be exceptional, but if he was mixing with potential killers she didn't want him seeing her daughter. If only there was a way she and Nattie could have a serious talk.

Her phone rang again. 'I hope you're not thinking of having it out with her?'

'No, William,' she said wearily, 'it would be obvious how I knew and that could risk cutting off any intelligence. I can't interfere. Quentin was showing a human side in telling me at all.' She felt humble about the Director General, grateful that he'd obviously trusted her judgement, her ability to see and stay clearly focused on the immediate threat they faced.

'Ahmed's working for you,' William said, 'for all of us. Try to see it like that.'

Was he, though? She couldn't be entirely certain, Victoria thought. Either way he was playing a dangerous game.

If it could somehow be less obvious how she'd found out – a friend's remark perhaps, or some clue Nattie let slip – then she would definitely talk to her. It seemed vital to stop them seeing each other, at least while Khan was doing what he was. Something had to give; she wanted her daughter safe.

CHAPTER 16

'Have I woken you, Nattie? I'm sorry.'

'No, it's okay, Mum.' Nattie hid her frustration, if not her yawn. She had finally gone back to sleep, wakefully excited after Ahmed left, then far too tensely psyched-up once he'd rung with the terrible news.

'They gave you my message?' She enjoyed imagining her mother's surprise before the very reason for calling hit home again with all the shock of a dousing of ice-cold water. 'I hated the way you felt almost to blame over the Leicester Square bomb,' she said, her heart thudding, thinking of Ahmed's similar feelings that had actually got him involved. 'You never unravelled once, but you were a mournful bag of nerves!'

'Did it show that much? Oh dear! It was wonderful of you to call, it meant a lot – what on earth were you doing, awake at that hour and hearing the news?'

'A friend called and told me.' Nattie let a smile escape as she turned snugly on her side with her mobile. She was half-aware that her mother might wonder about that.

'We're just at a studio, love, but I had to say a special thanks!'

Nattie could hear muffled voices and the banging of car doors. 'You will take extra care and be alert? It's a dangerous time.'

'For heaven's sake, Mum! Life's pretty terrific actually, but for all this. I'm willing for the people to be caught. Love you lots – can't wait to be home next week.'

Nattie folded up her mobile, keeping it close in case Ahmed called. He'd insisted he wouldn't, that she needed sleep. He needed it too, and it wouldn't be fair to call him either, which was immensely frustrating since she couldn't feel more awake and itching to talk.

Pulling the duvet round more tightly she settled back on her side with her knees up. She'd been lying that way just before he'd had to leave, with Ahmed pressed up hard behind, his body touching at every point. His arm had been resting in the dip of her waist, his hand trailing her skin, and he'd been whispering a verse of a love poem in her ear, an anonymous one from an anthology he'd found in Kendal.

'Once did I breathe another's breath . . . And in my mistress move . . . Once I was not mine own at all . . . and then I was in love.' The words were with her still.

She was in love, Nattie thought. It felt unique, new, suffusing. Her life was good, she had a loving family, things she wanted to do and achieve, but now, suddenly, only with Ahmed. Life would be one-dimensional without him, a tooth that was all cavity.

The rain was hard as hailstones against her dormer window, the wind rattling at the frame like a desperate man. It hadn't been blowing a gale in the early hours, she thought, when she'd been shivering in the doorway, watching the taillights of Ahmed's car. That must have been about exactly the time of the ambush and no storm had been raging then. She felt chilled to the marrow, wrapped up tight in her duvet cocoon.

There could be more news, she thought. Nattie aimed the remote and the television blared into life. A nuclear techie with a squeaky voice like a tap that needed a new washer was talking about the content and properties of radioactive waste. '. . . It is then stored in glass, impregnated in it, for reasons of safety,' he was saying in his high-pitched tone. 'Lethal as a dispersible powder, it could make a bomb that would kill thousands . . .' So if it was in glass, she thought, perhaps things weren't quite so grim.

She turned down the volume and lay back feeling confused and alone. The rain was lashing, she wanted Ahmed, his take on it all, his comforting loving grins.

He wouldn't be here for another two days, not till Friday. She felt deprived. He feared his Leeds contacts might start noticing, which seemed mad to her; she couldn't imagine them thinking much of it if they saw him out in his father's car. He felt guilty about coming at all, he said, and taking any risks with her safety; it was dangerous and irresponsible.

But it wasn't stopping him, she thought, hunkering deeper down in bed and reliving the last four hours. She felt smothered in passion, haunted by the soft intense thrill of his touch – wetness between her legs, just thinking about it. There was the lingering smell of the sex too, the faintly stale waft reaching her that was so intensely private and theirs. Ahmed made love beautifully, just as it ought to be.

Suppose he was right and Fahad, the man he'd spent four whole hours on a hillside with, had something to do with that attack? Suppose Fahad found out Ahmed was a mole?

She sent a frantic text. 'Please, please, walk away from it all – you not safe.'

He sent one back. 'More reason than ever to stick in there: thousands not safe now.'

He would say that, she thought, as her pulse quickened and fear gnawed like a rat. At least he wasn't asleep . . . She called and said strongly that she wanted him back at *The Post* and in London, far away from the dark malevolent undercover shadows of Leeds. Ahmed cut the call short, but texted straight back saying his mother had walked in – as she had a habit of doing.

It made Nattie think of her own mother and not telling her about Ahmed when she longed to so much. She remembered her 16-year-old resentment at all the quizzing about boyfriends. Her mother had been right to worry then. Nattie flinched, thinking of being virtually raped that first time; the memories stole up constantly like thieving monkeys and grabbed her peace of mind. The scene, the musty sofa-cushions, Seb's urging and forcing, his livid-pink cock, the pain, the breath-denying, subjugating weight of him . . .

Things couldn't be more different now, although the need for secrecy was real. Her mother was Home Secretary, the terrorist threat was dramatic and she knew from William that Ahmed was mixing with dangerous men.

It was bitterly frustrating, though, with Christmas coming and so much time to be spent with the family. There was the usual week at her grandparents', who Nattie knew would like Ahmed. She loved staying at Brook House, her mother was always more relaxed there too, seeing her own parents. If only Ahmed could come for a couple of days.

She imagined him just being around and part of the family. Meeting William's mother, Violet, who'd grown really eccentric, rattling around that rambling old stone house near Stroud, cursing the rabbits in her garden. Ahmed wouldn't mind; he understood those things. William humoured and teased his mother and they all took a lead. Violet quite liked it and held her own, she was a tough old bird underneath.

Divorce gave Christmas a sad dimension, Nattie thought. There was Barney's loneliness, which she hated. He went to stay with his reclusive gin-drinking father in Cornwall – whom she called Grandpops, yet hardly ever saw – and all the piled-up empties didn't bear thinking about. They'd overflow a bottle bank.

She'd told Ahmed about Barney's drinking, but not, as yet, the violence. Loving her father as she did it would have felt almost like splitting and she didn't want Ahmed put off him before they'd even met.

He had talked about violence in Muslim families and told her about Leena, the girl who'd escaped, whose father and brother had threatened to kill her – the story William wanted him to write. 'Your stepfather's seen it all, over the years,' Ahmed said, 'but he seemed stunned about honour killings, completely scandalized.'

'Well, of course he'd be!' She'd felt indignant. How could Ahmed have imagined William was beyond caring?

Yet William was completely unable to show any compassion for her father. In his book, a man who could hit a woman was lower than beneath contempt. There was no hope of any relationship between them. Poor Dad, she thought anxiously. He had to lick the drink; he wasn't safe. How else could he ever hope to sort out his life and have a chance with some nice new woman?

She had a sudden urgent affectionate need to pick up the phone. Barney was an early riser whatever state he was in; he wouldn't mind, she felt sure.

He sounded pleased. 'Hi, angel, lovely to hear you. How's things?'

'Great, Dad, cool – and you?'

'So-so. Not looking forward to the office! I've got a tricky new property client and my head's like a furred kettle. How's that dago fella of yours? Still around?'

'I've ditched him, Dad, done something right for a change. For somebody else actually – I'm in love!'

Her father hadn't really absorbed it, she knew. He was always gentle and adoring, had never raised a hand to her – unlike with her mother – but he was sort of gone. Living from one treble whisky to the next, through litres of wine and brandy, even losing his sexy looks. Nattie thought he was close to the brink. How could she make her mother *see*? No one else could help him; he still loved her – that was the whole trouble.

The sound was down, but by chance or instinct she noticed her mother was on television. Propping herself up in bed, Nattie thought she was being unusually evasive. Was there something she wasn't telling, some new development too strong for the public's stomach?

An opposition spokesperson came on, demanding answers and explanations. Nattie switched off tetchily and dragged herself shivering out of bed. There were only a few hectic days left of term. Good-fun days: lectures, smiles, meals, pubs. Days of waiting and wishing, too – sleepwalking through till Friday.

It was the last Friday of the Christmas term, a night of partying and bops. Nattie had resisted pressure from Milly and Sam, deciding instead to stay home waiting impatiently for Ahmed. She was in a jittery state. He hadn't called since morning, but she imagined he'd be on his way and would ring her very soon.

She couldn't wait for the incredible lift of seeing him walk in. Her desire was coming in waves and needing outlets, her nipples were so hard they were hurting. She thought of all they would say, do, tell each other; the sexual highs, hers, Ahmed's. His coming did it for her too; it was another whole fantastic high, when giving and taking became plaited like strands of wire and shared one current – ultimate need. Love, she thought, was all about having needs beyond no other.

Sam was still around; they were in the kitchen together having a bite before she went out and it felt slightly anti-social to be thinking so obsessively about later. Milly had already gone out.

Nattie was worried about a shadow there, the elephant in the room that was Shelby. She and Milly hadn't mentioned him once. Some obscenely tall red roses had arrived for Milly, the kind you had to cut right down or they got the full brewer's droop in a day, but as far as Nattie could tell she didn't seem to be seeing him.

Yet she knew Shelby of old; he'd come sidling in, hanging around like a bad smell: a milk-spill, a rotten egg, garbage. And it wouldn't be for love of Milly. He didn't go in for plaited wires and sharing, he was more into score settling and revenge.

Nattie looked slantwise at Sam from her side-on seat at the table. 'Is Shelby still seeing anything of Milly?' she asked casually.

Sam shot her a sharp look, raising an eyebrow. 'Dunno. He's called, I think, and sent those gross OTT flowers. I guess Mills is living in hope. But she didn't much enjoy the other night, you know.' Sam gave another glance and reached for the wine; she saw Nattie's glass was still going, refilled hers and went on.

'I'm not saying she was doing you a favour, girl, she's always fancied that piece of shit, but it was all very new, your thing with

Ahmed, and Mills didn't quite know where she was. She should have, you were handling Shelby just fine. It was quite something to see.' Sam grinned. 'Never thought I would.'

'Seeing was the point,' Nattie said, embarrassed. 'My rose-tinted shades had come off about Shelby.'

'Fuck that,' Sam snorted, 'you met Ahmed.' She sighed theatrically. 'The power of love . . .'

Nattie had been trying earlier, while making supper, to get across that she and Ahmed were lying low. He was really meant to be in Leeds following up on a story, better they weren't too . . . *evident*, she'd said. It had felt like telling a doctor about an embarrassing condition, finding the most delicate way.

'You do like Ahmed, don't you?' she ventured. It seemed to follow on and she couldn't help talking about him. And Sam had been slagging off Shelby, after all.

'He's a bit too good to be true – you sure he's on the level?' Sam's eyebrows shot up again. 'Not up to any funny business?'

Nattie's stomach turned. She felt almost angry enough to hit out. Her fists were clenched under the table as she tried to decide if it was a wind-up, a racist remark – or had Sam read too much into the remark that Ahmed was meant to be in Leeds. If Sam was suspicious, though, mightn't she start spreading it around? Nattie glowered then looked away, feeling panicky.

Sam laughed out loud. 'Touchy, aren't we! He's okay, I like him – we had a cool talk on Tuesday when you were dying for me to go to bed. Your trouble,' she said, still cracking up, 'is that you're both so fucking serious. Boringly in love, a right little pair of do-gooders.'

'So you'd rather do-badders like Shelby,' Nattie muttered sourly, still prickling. She appreciated Sam, but never learned not to rise.

'So what's he up to, Ahmed? I do think he's a keeper, by the way. Is it a big story he's on to – you going to spill?'

'Have some more of the hare or dog or whatever,' Nattie said, waving the wine bottle and forcing a grin. She was feeling sore and not pleased at being called boring – even in the context of being in love. Sam's digs always drove home.

Her mobile rang. A Beck CD was playing at full volume in the other room and even over the music the mobile's tone sounded unnaturally shrill and loud. She saw it was Ahmed calling and sensed something had to be wrong, felt it right through to her fingertips. Her heart was hammering.

'Hi!' she said cheerfully, getting up from the table and trying to banish the fears.

No chance of that. Ahmed's breath was coming in shaky judders. 'Are you alone?' He sounded almost in tears.

'I'll get upstairs,' she said, her heart unbearably loud. She gave an awkward half-smile back over her shoulder, although Sam must surely have guessed something was wrong.

Nattie was frantic to know the worst and, the moment she was out of earshot, she asked urgently, 'What's happened? You're not hurt? What's wrong, for God's sake?'

Her hand was clammy clutching the phone. Ahmed's breathing was still uneven.

'Khalid's dead,' he said finally.

'Oh, my God. I'm so sorry. How did it happen?' Ahmed had really cared about Khalid, calling him 'the kid' and sounding almost paternal; he'd felt dreadfully worried, she knew, sure Khalid was under great pressure. 'Where are you?' she asked. 'Somewhere you can talk?'

'Yes, it's okay, I'm sitting in the car outside home. I've been desperate to call you, but it was impossible really, stuck in the police station where I've been for over an hour. I should go in and tell my parents what's happened, but I can't face it yet.'

Ahmed seemed to be unwinding a bit. Nattie went on up to her room.

'I was just leaving and about to call,' he carried on. 'Out of the house at last – it wasn't easy, my mother's not onside about the car – and I had this wonderful sense of release. I crossed to the shops, car keys in hand, for a bottle of water and saw Khalid.

'He'd been keeping well away from Yazid – who's as good as told me, cursing him like no tomorrow, that the kid had backed off, let them down – and I hadn't seen him for a bit. Khalid had the sort of dejected slouch of a gambler who's blown his last buck and there seemed just a chance I might have got him talking.'

'Did you? Did you find anything out?' Nattie couldn't imagine what was coming.

'It was tough, quizzing him without admitting to being a fraud. I tried to make out like I knew why Yazid was hysterical, but I didn't share that. I wanted him to know I held nothing against him and was just anxious to help—'

Ahmed stopped, as though too affected to go on.

'I'm here for you,' Nattie murmured, near to tears herself. 'Don't talk if it's hard.'

'No, I want to – I can to you. Anyway, all the time I was talking, Khalid just stared. His face was blank, like a clean sheet of paper. Then he started muttering about letting everyone down, doing nothing right in this life, failing the brothers, his parents, his God . . . I tried to break in, but he wasn't hearing me; it was as though he'd set his satnav and wouldn't consider altering course.

'He turned into a big through street – I thought, perhaps, to drown me out with the noise of the traffic—' Ahmed was tensing up again; Nattie sensed it. She sat down on the bed and waited.

'But it wasn't that,' Ahmed suddenly went on. 'Khalid didn't seem to care if I yelled my head off. He was walking quite fast, looking back at oncoming vehicles as though wanting to cross – possibly to shake me off – but then, just as a fucking great articulated lorry came pounding along at a crazy speed, he stepped off the kerb.

'There was a terrible screeching of brakes; the sound still haunts me . . . I'd tried to grab him, but he'd shaken free. I saw the blood dripping into the gutter before I could even look out into the road.'

'I can't bear it,' Nattie cried, thinking that Ahmed could have been pulled off the kerb with him.

'Seeing his poor body crushed under those great pairs of wheels—' Ahmed said in the dull flat tones of someone still in shock. He was silent then said, 'On screen, celluloid sort of sanitizes the impact; bodies fly off cars, it's all just part of the action – this was real, a huge speeding supermarket lorry, a young man's pulverized body—'

Nattie sat motionless on the bed. Tears began trailing down her face. She didn't know Khalid, but Ahmed's agony and heartache was transmitting itself and affecting her deeply. Her image was of a kind, gentle twenty-year-old, fresh-faced, twisted by hard-core indoctrinating politics, the good in him pulling him back.

'Are you crying?' Ahmed asked softly. 'You mustn't. I was thinking I couldn't possibly come tonight, but I feel desperate to see you. Would you mind – just to sit with you for a while? It would be very late.'

She needed him in a whole new way. She should tell him not to, it was madness. 'You're shattered,' she said tightly, 'emotionally drained. You can't possibly drive all this way. Your parents would be horrified.'

'I'll say driving will help, get me functioning.'

'You do know there was nothing you or anyone could have done?'

'There was. I should have anticipated it. I'll never forgive myself, ever.'

Nattie couldn't persuade him otherwise, but nor could she have told him not to come. She felt wanted, depended upon. Ahmed was turning to her at a time of most need and nothing could have swelled her heart more.

She went slowly downstairs again and Sam was waiting at the bottom.

'You okay?' she asked. 'Ahmed, too?'

'No, he's had a sadness. A friend of his was run over and killed today when Ahmed was with him.' Nattie felt it only right to explain. 'He's still coming, but much later.'

'You don't look too brilliant,' Sam said. 'I've got just the thing.' She pushed past, went into her room and came back with a small medallion-shaped silver flask. 'My dad gave it me; it's brandy. He called it insurance so I haven't swigged any. Have a slug of the stuff in your tea – and see that lover of yours does, too.'

CHAPTER 17

Ahmed arrived at two in the morning looking an exhausted wreck. Gaunt, stubbly, with none of his usual heat-shimmers of energy lifting off, he could have spent weeks in a dungeon, Nattie thought. He was showing every inch of the strain.

'It's crazy coming all this way,' she admonished, smoothing his brow and touching lips, 'completely mad.' She pulled on his hand. 'Come and sit down at once.'

She led him to the lumpy studenty three-seater sofa against the wall. It was a maroon-corduroy monster. Milly had draped it with an Indian cotton throw and Sam found a couple of near bald mustard-yellow velvet cushions, which she'd acknowledged were gross, but which had stayed.

They sank down on to it. Ahmed sat forward, keeping hold of her hand. 'I need you, Nattie,' he said, squeezing and kneading her fingers, 'don't leave me.'

Nattie smiled. 'I am just about to, but only to get some tea. You sit tight.' He didn't argue; he was knackered, physically incapable.

She boiled the kettle, thinking he must still be in shock. Khalid had been walking beside him one minute, then a second later a mangled mess, his body trodden in by the giant treads of several tons of lorry like a discarded cigarette. She wondered if Ahmed was feeling a loss of hope on top, a sort of overlayer of depression with his only real chance of a lead snuffed out.

Khalid had known what was going on. He'd had a last-minute switch of loyalties and had pulled back from the brink; he might just have been persuaded to open up. Ahmed was obviously struggling too, she thought, with a wretched sense of helplessness at having failed to save a life. There was always Yazid to keep on at. Yazid might yet overreach himself. You never knew.

Ahmed had taken off his jacket; he'd managed that. He took the tea from her with an absent smile and sat drinking it slowly, gazing over the mug in thoughtful silence. She had sweetened it and added a little of Sam's brandy. He didn't seem to notice and Nattie thought it best not to own up, given the driving. He was very in on himself, almost remote.

They sat silently together, sipping tea. Ahmed carefully set down his empty mug on the unevenly tiled coffee table in front of them, the cause of many spills. He shook his head when Nattie offered more, smiling tenderly, then removed the mug from her hands so that he could take them in his. He was giving her such a steady loving look that she shivered, although she suspected his thoughts were elsewhere.

Returning her hands he leaned and touched her face. 'You see, Nattie darling,' he said, as though she'd just been party to some internal conversation of his, 'I can't tell anyone but you that it was deliberate, that Khalid took his own life. Leave aside suicide bombers and martyrdom – which doesn't wash with traditional Muslims anyway – suicide is as taboo as it gets in the Islamic faith. He'd have been desperate to make it look like a ghastly accident; his family couldn't have borne the humiliation, the stranglehold strain of the truth. They'd have been denied the chance, even, to give him a proper funeral with full religious rites.'

Ahmed needed to talk. Words were a poultice, the bandage soaking up the blood.

He went on, 'Khalid was so set on doing it tonight, so focused and geared. The last thing he needed was my turning up. It's no wonder he looked straight through me. I suspect he went ahead anyway, because he trusted me enough. He knew I'd understand and never tell how it really was. Of course I wouldn't, but it does make it hard for me. There'll be an inquest; it's going to sound feeble saying he tripped and fell, that I failed to save him, that it all happened so quickly—'

'His parents must surely have known the unhappy state he was in,' Nattie said. 'Won't they suspect it was suicide anyway?'

'That's irrelevant really. If it's thought to be an accident they can look people in the eye – probably even genuinely manage to delude themselves. Well,' he said bitterly, 'now they've got another prop, my say so. And they can heap blame on my head as well, for not saving him.' Ahmed heaved such a desolate sigh that Nattie's heart felt rent in two.

She brought her fingers to his face, studying it with anxious eyes, needing to touch: brows, mouth, drained cheeks. 'Have you eaten a single thing since lunch?'

'I really can't face food.'

'Then you've absolutely got to have some sleep.' She put her arm round his shoulders, encouraging him to lean sideways and drop into her lap. He laid his head down and she smoothed his hair, exerting gentle pressure with an elbow to keep him still. 'You must sleep or you'll be in no state whatsoever to drive,' she murmured, bending over him. 'I'd refuse to let you go home.'

'This is home,' he mumbled into her crotch. His arm was draped and she felt his hand taking hold of her leg, clasping it firmly below the knee.

It sounded good, hearing him say it, although it seemed depressingly far from reality. Perhaps they could set up in a flat together, Nattie thought hopefully, if and when all the Fahad horrors were behind them. But it wasn't that easy. She couldn't contribute much in the way of rent, not before her degree – and she might not get a job for ages after that.

It was no time for wistful thought. She went on talking softly, lightly smoothing his hair. 'Give into it; sleep will really help. I'll wake you in good time, promise; don't think about that. I'm fine, I can sleep when you've gone. Put your feet up on the sofa,' she whispered, bending low again. 'Curl up.'

Ahmed wasn't hearing. His head was heavy, his hand round her leg loosening. When it hung limp, giving little twitches and jerks, she sat motionless, resisting the urge to stroke his forehead. He really did need sleep before setting off again.

There was the sound of a key in the door. Sam was back. She was quite tanked up, high on whatever, tiptoeing around with an exaggerated finger to her lips, camping it up like acting in a panto. 'Need a glass of water,' she whispered loudly, sneaking towards the kitchen with her bad-wolf, high-stepping footsteps. Coming back, slopping the glass, she flopped down in the armchair opposite Nattie.

Sam stared in a dilated way then leaned across the coffee table.

'You can't sit there like a sphinx all night, you dumbo,' she whispered stagily, before resting her glass precariously on a table tile and rising out of her chair.

'What the fuck are you about?' Nattie hissed, as Sam collected up the velvet cushions at either end of the sofa and squatted with them right beside her. Sam was being impossible, she felt frustrated and irritated as hell.

'You shift up the sofa, keeping his head supported,' Sam said bossily, 'and I'll shove these underneath.' She was waiting, all poised to go. 'Get on with it, girl!'

Nattie felt a run of pins and needles shunting along, and knew they'd have got worse. She still muttered, 'God, you're a bossy fart,' although she felt more conciliatory when Ahmed didn't wake. She sat looking fondly down on his folded-over body – frowning when Sam hitched his legs up on to the sofa. He still didn't wake.

They sat drinking tea in the kitchen. Sam was less hyper, climbing down from her high, and Nattie felt glad of the company.

'Did you have a good time tonight?' she asked. 'Did you pull?'

'There was this moderately fanciable arsehole,' Sam said. 'I went to his place for a bit, but he was too stoned out of his mind, no use at all, so I pissed off back here.'

They talked on. Nattie thought Sam was dying to be quizzy, but instinctively resisting and she felt new respect. She suspected her housemate was actually in need of something more genuine and rewarding in her life than an occasional random tool and longed for her to find it. Her sharp tongue put people off.

Milly hadn't showed. Nattie kept listening out and looking to the door, worrying, imagining some arsing untimely return. It was almost time to wake Ahmed.

'Mills not back?' Sam asked, picking up on the glances. 'Not tucked up in bed?'

'Nope.' Nattie asked tensely, 'Didn't you see her anywhere about?'

'Nope – the missing Milly! Now who do we think she might be with . . .?' Sam grinned. She jerked her head back, towards the sitting room. 'Is Ahmed staying over? Here for breakfast?'

'He's got to go, like in ten minutes.'

Sam stood up and gave a monumental yawn. 'I'm off. Say hi and bye or whatever from me.' She hung on at the door, still yawning. 'Of course, Milly's sure to walk right in and scupper the last lingering loving kiss.'

'Fuck off up to bed, can't you?' Nattie said fondly. She put the kettle on, sighing, grateful to Sam, at least, for going. She made toast, buttered it, brewed fresh tea in an old yellow tin teapot: a present from Tom. Her favourite tray had turned up, too – things had a habit of walking – a round one with a picture of a large ginger cat. She piled it up with teapot and mugs, milk-carton, plate of toast and took it in.

Ahmed was awake, sitting up. 'Some gnome or inside clock told me it was nearly four. You'd tucked me up like a baby.' He was holding out his arms. 'I need a kiss, but I'm sure I must really stink.' He got up to help with the tray. 'God, and breakfast! I'll come again. Must just get washed up.' He was on his feet, making for the bathroom.

'Don't be long or the toast will be vile,' she called. 'And what about my kiss?'

He was soon sitting beside her, kissing her softly and studying her with a tender smile. 'I'll be all right now; I can manage.' Nattie poured the tea and he went on, 'I was awake for that parting shot of

Sam's, by the way. Hope we've got a few Milly-free minutes, though. I need to talk.'

'About?' Nattie asked, remembering that the next week was Ahmed's last in Leeds. He'd said he might come on Monday and she wanted to firm that up.

'About what a difficult week it'll be. The funeral; there'll be a pre-liminary inquest. And I've got the honour killing story to work on, this girl to see, Leena's friend.' Ahmed pressed at the inner corners of his eyes with two fingers, not so much from tiredness, she felt, as from trying to blur the haunting images of the night. 'I'll keep on at Yazid, praying his soggy brain leaks and he spills out some gold dust. Mostly, though, I'll be worrying myself sick about you – the danger you're in because of me.'

'Can't you lay off being so boring about that?'

'It's guilt. I shouldn't come here this last week before you go home. I can't stay away, though, I'm not made of that sort of stuff, but it's shamefully irresponsible.'

'It's not,' Nattie said irritably, pushing the plate of toast at him. 'Have some, for God's sake, it's filthy cold and congealed.' He took a piece, almost sorrowfully, and she felt awful. 'Please still come on Monday, I'd go mad at home in London, waiting till you're back at *The Post*. That's more than a week – or can you make it in time for the weekend in London?' She imagined having his flat to themselves, cosiness, cooking him meals.

'I really do hope so. It's just impossibly hard to make plans.'

She stared at him and suddenly started to cry. She hated herself for it – how selfish could she get? Ahmed put down his toast and folded her into his chest. 'I want to be where you are, always.' He kissed her hair. 'It's desperate, all this. I just wish I knew what MI5 are about; the country's in uproar, they must be pulling out every stop.'

Nattie sat up. 'You've given them very full descriptions,' she said hotly, 'surely they're out there looking. God knows, things couldn't be worse.'

She thought of the shock of the news that the stuff had been wrongly stored, not cast in glass – the complete panic: people avoiding tube travel, tourists and businesspeople avoiding London, cancelling flights and trips.

'At least the papers are aiming their firepower at the poor Energy Minister,' Nattie smiled, relieved. 'It wasn't Mum's responsibility, but that doesn't usually cut much ice with you lot in the media. I'd never go into politics, that's for sure!'

'Pity,' Ahmed said, 'I'd have had some fun hounding you. The Energy Minister does have to take the flak, though, poor bugger. It's no good him saying he didn't *know*. The media can't be bought off with a faceless civil servant. Only a government scalp, a minister's resignation, will do. They're in full cry, it's like running a fox to ground.'

'You seem quite feisty on an hour's sleep. I'd hoped to have you on the ropes.'

'It's the government on the ropes, right now,' Ahmed said regretfully. 'No arrests, no one detained. And the Prime Minister's on a loser, he can't go on swearing black's white, trying to persuade us that the canister could be bouncing along on the seabed – not to mention all the attackers drowned without trace.'

'Is there any chance the canister did go overboard? They do talk of dredging the seafloor.' Nattie knew she was sounding feebly optimistic.

'I'm quite sure that boat was a decoy. Dredging would be a hopeless job, anyway; they'd know the direction and rate of drift, currents, tides, but not where to start from, the point where the boat got into difficulties – in the unlikely event it did.

'I'm certain Khalid was to have had a role in that attack – driving a van, heaving a boat into the sea perhaps, nothing key or technical. He knew things, though. Had I not been with him and seen it happen, I'd have thought someone pushed him under that truck. I don't know if I'm right about him, but I think Fahad's a professional, he wouldn't want anyone around who's cut loose. Perhaps Khalid suspected his time was short and thought he'd save them the trouble,' Ahmed added acidly.

He stood up and put his jacket on; he wrapped his scarf round his neck, apologizing for it, saying she must be sick of the sight of it – time he was back in London, if only for a change of clothes.

They both knew he was late leaving; there was his father's need of the car. 'What about the other guy – what was his name, Iqbal?' Nattie asked at the door.

'Iqbal's vanished. He didn't have a job, no great routine – I don't even know who his family are, which is unheard of in Pakistani terms.' Ahmed smiled. 'I should have done more early snooping, it's one of the many ways I've failed.'

Nattie was in his arms and looked up. 'What balls you do talk.'

'I thought a lot about everything on the way here.' He held her eyes. 'It is likely MI5 has followed up on all the stuff your stepfather will have given them.'

'Can't you call him William!'

'Possibly, give me time. This is deadly serious, Nattie,' he said, tightening his arms round her. 'There really is a powerful risk of a dirty bomb. MI5 will be doing every single thing in their power, desperately aware of what that missing canister means. They're probably searching for Iqbal – probably already tuned into Khalid's accident. And they might think, rather like me, of the possibility that he was pushed.

'And if that is the case, do you see what it means?' Ahmed paused, but he seemed determined to spell it out. 'I'm the only one who saw it happen. The spooks will have a far greater interest in me . . . They could be bugging my phone – probably already bugging Yazid's. I thought it unlikely, at first, that they'd do mine. I'm a reporter, kind of bona fide, so I took a decision anyway just to forget about it and get on with life. I had nothing to hide, I didn't want to feel inhibited.'

'You're trying to tell me they might suspect you of murder?' Nattie stared at him.

'Khalid's accident could worry them. It's all surmise on my part, not good of me saying it, alarming you like this, but it's not something I could easily say on the phone. The one crumb in this is that I really don't think Yazid's rumbled me; he's dead stupid, for all his degree. I live in hope he'll let something slip, but it's a forlorn one.'

'Well, I hope all your thoughts and surmises are less melodramatic, driving back,' Nattie said, being falsely light-hearted, making it obvious how shaken she was. 'And for God's sake take care. After all you've been through, barely an hour's sleep.'

They had a last hug. She stood watching the dark blue Vauxhall that seemed to have an elderly personality, probably by association, until it had rounded the corner and disappeared. She stayed staring down the road. It felt too final, going in and shutting the door, like sitting back when the train's left the station instead of straining out for a last view.

She glanced the other way up the street. Shelby's silver Mustang was just pulling up. He *was* with Milly; it was no joke after all. God, he was sure to be about to come in.

Nattie felt in a rattle of nerves, hollow as a dried seedpod, and she slammed the door shut with her heart turning over. The thought of Shelby and Milly walking in, the fine-tune timing . . . She raced up to her room like a found-out child, just as the front door was clicking open, and shot the bolt home with relief.

Would Shelby be around all weekend? Nattie flung herself down on her bed and cried. It was her fears for Ahmed, terror of the unknown, a deep sense of helplessness; a deeper one still of frustration at the desperate lack of progress – which must be something her mother felt every minute of the waking day.

Then there was the simmering worry of what Shelby might do to get even.

Nattie thought of something else. Her mother must be being briefed daily. If MI5 had suspicions and reservations about Ahmed, as he seemed to think possible, wouldn't she get to hear? He'd be presented in the blackest possible light, someone causing concern who could even have pushed a man under a truck. Her opinion of him would be formed, judgement clouded, before she even knew he was seeing her daughter.

It was sickening, unbearable to think about. Nattie burned to tell how it was from Ahmed's side. But that was too horribly fraught in itself, a whole can of worms. If her mother knew of the relationship she'd get in a lather of panic, professionally and maternally.

More bucketing tears flooded out, Nattie's interior seawall a pile of rubble. MI5 would argue the case against Ahmed far more coherently. Any passionate countering from a biased daughter would be swept away like autumn leaves. Blown away by her mother's pre-conceptions. Brushed to one side, dismissed.

She calmed down. If only there could be a breakthrough. She sent a text for Ahmed to find later, hoping the beep of his phone might help him stay awake at the wheel. Then, thinking she'd heard the front door and the house was Shelby-free, cleansed again, fumigated, she felt able to get to bed. And eventually to sleep: she didn't stir till eleven in the morning when friends came round and there was a noisy racket going on downstairs.

CHAPTER 18

Four days and nothing: Victoria gazed out of the Edwardian bay window at a drab rain-soaked Southampton backstreet. She was in the constituency office doing her Saturday morning 'surgery' and had one last person to see. No canister, no leads, no arrests, it was like speeding at night in fog with no signposts. They were blundering along in the dark and heading for a calamity.

Four days, too, since Quentin's news about Nattie and Ahmed. Victoria felt beside herself with worry, desperate to talk to her daughter. How, though? How could she possibly, plausibly, know about the relationship without planting the idea that it was through phone tapping? And giving such a clue risked inhibiting Ahmed's calls and hindering MI5.

There was a timid knock, the door opening. 'Hello, Mrs . . .' Victoria looked quickly at the list '. . . Higgs.' She smiled, trying to force her mind back. 'Come on in.'

Mrs Higgs's operation had been cancelled yet again, a third time, and the hospital had only told her on the day. The poor woman's daughter had taken a morning off work, Mrs Higgs's cat was delivered to the cattery, the fridge cleared, newspaper cancelled. Victoria

promised to write to the Hospital Trust and agreed it wasn't on –
which it wasn't. Why couldn't things be better run?

'You've got your problems, too,' Mrs Higgs conceded, then compressed her lips and narrowed bright angry eyes. 'I know what I'd like
to do to these effing terrorists . . . But they'll get the kid glove treatment for sure – and I thought we was meant to live in a fair society!'
She was a small bird-like woman, tinted and tidy, bristling with
indignation.

Victoria smiled patiently and saw her to the door. You have to
catch your terrorist first, she thought, find missing High Level Waste,
foil a catastrophic disaster.

'Well, we got through the list.' Jason, her agent, came in beaming.

'Only because you're more skilful at moving them on than the
Queen!'

Jason was pure gold; he collected jumble, soothed warring helpers,
smooth-talked the local press. 'Have a good rest of weekend,' she
called, going out to the reception area where Rodney was waiting,
her sharp-eyed, patient protection officer.

They went down the office's steep run of steps, out into the wet
grey street where he steered her round a puddled pothole and into
the car. They set off for home. She was thinking of dirty bombs, staring out of her rear window at raindrops beading on a strip of
polished car. They glistened like drops of sweat on skin.

William called as she walked in. 'I'm minutes away with two
excited hungry girls,' he announced cheerily. God, lunch, she
thought, wishing she felt half as breezy.

'Just shoving in the shepherds pie.' She was opening the oven door
with her free hand as she spoke, hoping it was properly thawed.

Nattie cooked for the freezer whenever she came, the greatest help she could give. She stocked it with fruit from the garden too, and in a fit of good intentions Victoria found a polybag of sliced apples and made a large speedy crumble with fistfuls of Nattie's frozen sliced apples, dashes of cinnamon and a packet crumble mix. Barney would have been horrified.

The house was soon wallowing in noise, chat, afternoon-plan-making. Jessie, William's younger daughter, now twelve, asked piercingly intelligent questions over lunch and blonde leggy Emma who was only a year older, talked gaily and incessantly about anything and everything. She couldn't decide whether to be a model or a barrister. Julian, she said, thought she could do both, but advised qualifying first. Victoria, the ex-barrister, agreed that sounded wise.

Tom had driven down to see his sisters. He'd be a wonderful help entertaining them, Victoria knew. She had boxfuls of work, a great white heap of it spewing out on to the table, a rolling smothering A4 avalanche of the stuff to be dealt with.

It was squally outdoors and football on television won the day. William's team, Liverpool, were playing. Emma sprinted out to buy teacakes at the village shop. She wanted to toast them on long forks over the fire just like she'd seen Nattie do.

Victoria worked in the kitchen with an eye to the television set in there, but with the sound turned down. She was into football, a keen, even passionate, supporter of her local team, Southampton. They were back in the Premiership and she felt as much partisan pride as any beer-bellied fan. Southampton were playing Liverpool just before Christmas, a home match and in the holiday break. They planned to go, Tom and Nattie too, and see who could yell the loudest.

It took her mind to a meeting with Luke Andrews and the Counterterrorism Unit about the possible cancelling of large-crowd events at such a time of high alert. They had decided against it. You couldn't stop the whole country functioning and have the terrorists thinking they'd won.

She read a report from the Chemical, Biological, Nuclear Resilience team – all the experts in a banging-heads exercise, over detection of radioactive material, protective kit, advances in decontamination. The detail was never made public for fear of its help to terrorists. The emergency responses were being impressively refined, but she could sense a behind-the-scenes frenzy, a terror-stricken awareness of how imminently it could all be put to the test.

Tom appeared in the kitchen. 'Can I bother you?'

'Of course – like some coffee?' Victoria looked up with a smile, feeling a goosepimply twinge of alarm. He seemed uneasy, lifting and bending his foot in an embarrassed trainer-creasing way. She got up to put the kettle on, then took a chair at the kitchen table. 'Come and sit down. I'm well up in problems these days.'

He pulled out another chair and sat with one of his long legs hitched up. He rested his chin on his hugged knee for a second then sat up and gave a cautious grin. 'I had a call from Shelby – God knows how he had my mobile number! He wants to come round and see you when you're back in London tomorrow night. I'm more than happy to say you're busy, tell him to bugger off and get lost. I can easily do that for you.'

Tom got up and took over the coffee-making, glancing back briefly then concentrating on his task. He seemed very keen to stop her seeing Shelby.

Victoria couldn't work out why, but it had to be connected with Nattie. 'Know what he wants?' she asked, tensing up like pulled thread.

Tom didn't answer, too busy pressing down on the plunger. 'Milk?' he said, adding it anyway, knowing her tastes. He brought over the two mugs to the table.

'What's up, Tom? You're unhappy about this, obviously. What is it that's bugging you?'

'It's just, well, I've met Nattie's new friend and he's good, they're cool together. And Shelby's had a decency bypass, after all. He'll only be out to spread shit and turn you off the guy. It just seems unfair to her—'

'Shelby knows this new friend, then?' Victoria felt guarded; it didn't seem to fit.

'They've met. Shelby wouldn't leave after Nattie tried to end it.' Tom seemed as won over by Ahmed as William.

'It's no secret what I think of Shelby,' she said, standing up, 'but I'd better hear what he has to say. It won't influence me, you can be sure.' Tom was still looking less than happy and the penny finally dropped. 'You're not betraying any confidence of Nattie's; don't think that! Shelby was going to get in touch some way or other, he's not lightly put off.'

Tom coloured slightly and his smile was doubtful. They had a hug, then, taking his coffee, he went back to the game next door. Victoria saw the irony. Shelby was actually playing into her hands. He was an amoral shit, obviously going to slag off Ahmed, but this was just the excuse she needed to talk to Nattie with no suspicions of phone tapping. She could say in all honesty she'd heard about Ahmed from Shelby.

Nattie must surely understand. She was so mixed-up about men. She'd had few illusions over Shelby, but still been drawn to him like a powerless pin to a magnet.

Ahmed was different, altogether higher calibre. Victoria had seen his qualities on one brief meeting, but he was in contact with sympathizers or actual terrorists and he could even have divided loyalties. He wasn't someone Nattie should be seeing.

William was returning the girls, Victoria travelling back to London. The warm embrace of family togetherness felt split. The magic of weekend life, teenage laughter, William, Tom, had been sustaining her. Now, arriving home to an empty house, she had no cosy protection, no ballast, no fingers over her eyes. The worry of Nattie was overwhelming, there was fear of the nation suffering a radioactive bomb, and, more immediately, there was Shelby to be faced. Victoria didn't know where to turn. Even if she phoned her father she would be restricted in what she could reveal.

She had a burning urge to call Quentin Clayton. She would normally go through the office – formality mattered with him – but given the crisis, he'd felt she should have his home number. Quentin had shown a rare human side in telling her about Ahmed, although he'd kept even that to the minimum. She felt briefly guilty, picking up the phone to him, then thought to hell with the Sunday night intrusion and went ahead.

He answered on the first ring; he must be chained to his desk at such a desperate time, feeling tested and stretched to the limit.

'I hate to trouble you, Quentin, but you were good enough to tell me about Ahmed Khan seeing my daughter . . . and, well,' she rushed on, 'I just wondered how the transcripts were reading. Do forgive this call,' she added, squirming with awkwardness.

'Don't give it a thought,' he responded urbanely. 'There's actually nothing in any of Khan's calls to his Leeds contacts inconsistent with an excellent performance of trying to ingratiate himself. One thing perturbs us slightly. A member of the cell he's tracking went under a lorry on Friday and was killed. He'd stepped off the kerb for no apparent reason. Khan was with him, walking close beside. He swears the contact tripped, but it does worry us.'

'I know it's taboo in the faith, but could it have been suicide?'

'We think it unlikely – the young man was deeply religious.'

Victoria thanked Quentin and ended the call. She felt her blood grow chilled. How could they truly know where Ahmed's loyalties lay? Was his keenness to find terrorists and redress some balance all a brilliantly cunning sham? Had he infiltrated *The Post* rather than the reverse? He had, after all, rather instantly happened on a sort of copybook Leeds cell . . . He was an impressive young man, but she felt ghostly, icy fingers of fear dancing. She must see Nattie and have it out.

William was soon back and they had a quick bite together. A rushed one, which meant she was able to hide her extreme tension, then William, who had work to do, made himself scarce before Shelby arrived.

Going to the door to receive Nattie's ex-boyfriend, her nails were digging into her palms. Greeting him she saw his eyes slide inter-estedly to her line-up of red boxes in the hall, as though he found glamour in a bit of ministerial clutter.

'Come into the sitting room,' she said briskly, leading the way.

Shelby was all about glamour, she thought, he was shot through with it like the writing in a stick of Blackpool rock. From his Irish blue eyes to the glitter-jet black hair that fell sexily forward in the way of Barney's floppy blond locks. Shelby was no stick of rock, though: he was insubstantial, glitzily substandard.

He made for one of the two sofas, glancing around on the way. He'd been in the room before, and others in the house . . . 'So what can I do for you?' she asked, sitting down opposite, detesting his clever, sickly charm. She tried to look pleasant while avoiding a smile and studiously not offering a drink. 'I'd rather gathered things between you and Nattie had run their natural course.'

'That's true,' he said, pushing at his hair, which instantly fell forward again, 'and also not true. I was deeply upset and still am. They hadn't run their natural course for *me*. I'm sure you'll think this visit is about sour grapes – and in a sense you're right.' Shelby chewed on a finger with penitent eyes and smiled just as contritely. 'But I do care very much about Nattie. I'm seriously worried about the man she's seeing, the position she's in.' He held Victoria's eyes more directly.

She stared back steadily. Shelby's clothes were quite restrained for once, the all-black look jettisoned in favour of jeans, navy-check shirt and a dark red cashmere sweater. She was in jeans too, and uncrossed her legs to sit forward. 'Why are you "seriously worried", Shelby? That's what you're here to tell me?' She tried to sound and look coolly neutral, cooler than she felt.

'Nattie's told you about this new friend of hers?' Shelby asked.

'You're talking about Ahmed Khan? He's on *The Post* – works for my husband.'

She caught a tiny blink of irritated disappointment. Shelby had rightly suspected that Nattie, for one reason or another, had kept it quiet from her mother. It was only a blink. His face immediately resumed its look of intense anxiety; he might have been a personable young lecturer, vicar or employer, someone responsibly concerned.

'Of course, I bitterly minded Khan stepping into my shoes,'

Shelby continued. 'I certainly felt pretty sore, meeting him the other
night. He had come to see Nattie via Cumbria, although I gathered
he's based in Leeds.'

'Yes, I believe he's writing about the area.' She left it there and
smiled in a way to encourage him on. Shelby hadn't lied yet, she
thought.

'Perhaps you'll understand this,' he said with more hair riffling,
'but I took up with another student in Nattie's house – sort of out
of jealousy and a need to be near Nattie. Well, a couple of nights ago,
I was leaving her very late, in my car, and just happened to see Khan
in his. I'm not sure why, curiosity, bitterness, but I had a sudden
strong urge to follow him.'

'Which night was this?' Victoria wanted to pin him down.

'Um,' Shelby smiled at his own hesitation, 'Friday. But to go
on . . . Khan hadn't seen me, I felt sure, and I kept my distance.
When he didn't take the direction of Leeds I'm afraid my curiosity
grew and made me keep going. Then when he suddenly swung up
a side-road, I thought he'd got wind of being followed and I drew in.
I'd planned to turn round, forget it, but he appeared on foot almost
instantly – just as a car swept past and slowed to let him in. It shot
off again. There were three men in it, I think, and at that point I did
give up and set off on the long drive to London.

'It's probably nothing,' Shelby said disingenuously, 'just to do with
his work, but I've brooded on it, with all that's going on—' He met
Victoria's eyes meaningfully.

'Well, you've got it off your chest,' she said briskly, 'and I take it
you've kept details; description of the car and number plate?' He
nodded.

Did he look just a little furtive at that? It was probably all made up, she thought, just the sort of fabricated nastiness he'd go in for. And the girl he was dating might easily have known which nights Nattie was seeing her new friend.

Shelby wasn't the worry. Quentin feeling 'perturbed' about Ahmed certainly was. What kind of evil ruthlessness did it take to push a fellow human being under a great lorry? Could a bright young reporter on *The Post* really have been turned to that extent – become an extremist fanatic, an undercover militant? It was near impossible to believe, but, at such a terrifying time of crisis, could anything be ruled out?

She began to rise and Shelby was instantly on his feet. 'I really appreciate your finding a few minutes for me, Mrs Osborne. I do know how incredibly busy you are.' He was nauseatingly sure of his ability to charm.

She saw him out, having to struggle to be civil then, closing the door, turned her worries to William. It was easy enough to say that Shelby had tried to paint Ahmed as a raving terrorist – probably wise not even to mention the distressing call to Quentin. But she couldn't keep secret from William her plan to go and see Nattie, they didn't have that sort of marriage. He cared about her, she was part of his life and it was important, quite fundamental.

Victoria's work was unending, but it was like sitting exams in a bad dream, her mind wouldn't function. William came to say he was turning in and she soon gave up the struggle.

He was in bed reading the papers, all the first editions, and looked up with a smile.

She blurted it out straight away, unable to hold back. 'I need to go and see Nattie.'

He knew the reason why. And Victoria knew, from the way his face was shadowing, a look she was all too familiar with, that he was about to voice a strongly argued different view. She felt nervous of a row. William could bend the steel in anyone's backbone, his unique blend of belligerent persuasiveness was a force to reckon with, and she could only plead her case as a mother, couldn't tell him about Quentin's alarming disclosure. It would be a breach of security and she knew William would dismiss as crazy any implication that Ahmed could have done such a deed.

'I must go, love,' she said levelly, 'I have to talk it out with Nattie. I dread having an extreme emotional confrontation, which I know it'll be, but I'm sick with worry. Ahmed's contacts are dangerous. He could be followed going to see her, Nattie could even be kidnapped.' She stared at William's disbelieving face. Was it self-doubt, making her shake with nerves? Was it really the right thing to do?

He gathered up his newspapers and thumped them down on the floor. 'I know you're desperately worried, I sympathize, but that last bit was melodramatic twaddle. Home-grown terrorists aren't going to draw attention to themselves with a kidnap! This isn't Iraq or Colombia, Nattie's not worth a few billion. Maybe it's not the most perfect time for them to have got together, but life's like that – think of us.'

'That's ridiculous,' Victoria threw back in frustration. 'And however perfect and wonderful things are for them now, think of their age. They're going to move on. I've got to try to persuade her not to see him – at least for a while. Can't you see? Can't you understand?' She felt the walls closing in: Tom, William, she was alone in this.

'It's wrong to make any assumptions about age,' William argued. 'Nattie's an adult, a young woman with a mind of her own; she may have found her mate for life, we don't know. Only she does. If you really want to see her move straight out of here and into his Brixton flat,' he went on, fixing Victoria with a slightly smug look of the certainty of his convictions, 'then you're going about it in just the right way.' He turned angrily on his side in bed. He was working himself up, but he loved Nattie, he was motivated by genuine feelings.

'And who was it,' he demanded, flinging back to face her again, 'before you make these overquick judgements about Ahmed, who said I'd unfairly prejudged Julian? Well?'

'You can't possibly make that comparison,' she muttered, remembering William's agony and wild accusations when Jessie, his youngest, went missing. He, along with others, had instantly blamed Julian, his ex-wife Ursula's lover – who it turned out had been desperately hunting for the child. Julian had found her and probably saved Jessie's life.

Her lip was trembling, it had a will of its own. Her ingrained stubbornness, though, was swallowing up that small part of her in need of William's guidance like the sea taking a drowning man. 'I have to do what I think is right,' she mumbled, and went into the bathroom to undress.

Victoria had a chance to see Nattie the very next day. She was going north to visit the relatives of the men shot dead in the attack. It was something she'd felt a deep-seated need to do, but privately with no fuss. The trip had been arranged in great secrecy, she was obsessively anxious that the media shouldn't find out; they would only imagine it was all about publicity.

The moment she arrived in the office, still in a state of great emotional turmoil, Victoria told Tony that she needed to see her daughter, for personal reasons, and wanted to make a detour after the visit. He readily agreed and from his expression she suspected he had an inkling of the problem; he knew Quentin had seen her privately.

She was catching a mid-morning plane to Manchester. Her car had gone north the night before, to be there to ferry her around. The need for protection spilled into her private life as well, which bothered her; she minded going to see her daughter in a ministerial car.

There was a minute between two early meetings and she picked up the phone.

'Hi darling, are you just off to a lecture?'

'Should be – you're giving me a wonderful excuse to skip it! Cool hearing you, Mum. How was the weekend? Jessie and Emma good?'

'Very bouncy, they can't wait to see you at Christmas. Darling, I want to come and see you this afternoon. Can you be there for about half four? Will Sam and Milly be out, possibly? I do need to see you alone.' Her heart was beating furiously, how was she going to make Nattie understand? She wasn't answering. Why the long silence?

'But Mum, I'm coming home on Thursday. And you're busier than the Prime Minister! Much as I'd love to see you—'

Victoria explained about visiting the families of the train driver and guards. 'We must have a talk, Nattie.' There was an even longer silence. 'You see, Shelby came to see me last night,' she added in desperation.

'God, I don't believe it!' Nattie exploded. 'He just turned up? Shit, shit. How dare he. You know what a liar and fucking scumbag he is, Mum.'

'Nattie! I've really got to go – you'll be there, though, half-past four?'

'I'll be here,' she muttered, 'and I'll sort Sam and Milly, see they're not around.'

It had been a glorious day, a transformation in the weather. The sun had come out and Durham looked exquisitely beautiful in the early afternoon. Its historic cobbled streets were bathed in a misty pink light, soft as a watercolour wash, and the peninsular heart of the city hummed with students and Christmas shoppers. The cafés had tables outside, even in mid-December.

The drive from Cumbria had taken less time than expected and Victoria had thought of going into the pedestrian centre to buy cakes for tea. Passers-by would inevitably recognize her, stare and come up to have a word, they always did, but the politician in her was used to that. It went with the territory.

Rodney was with her, keeping a close eye. The carefree festive mood of the shoppers seemed in stark contrast to the grief she'd just been exposed to, the misery of families made fatherless in a single violent instant. She felt overwrought. Had not the people crossing the street to meet the Home Secretary been so naturally friendly and curious, Victoria thought she might have dissolved into tears.

She was feeling the terrible imbalance, too; the authorities seemed to have their feet in cement while the plotters were roaming free. And all the while families were grieving and the nation lived with uncertainty and fear.

The thought of having to beg Nattie to make a great sacrifice filled her with dread; then, suddenly, she was consumed by anger. Somehow, by whatever extraordinary fluke of genius or machiavellian cunning, a bunch of terrorists must have dodged all the roadblocks, lorry searches, vans, cars, and could, at that very moment, be holed up in a safe-house somewhere, perfecting a devastatingly lethal radioactive bomb.

Her daughter's love affair paled into insignificance beside that. Nattie had to hear her out, to listen and understand.

CHAPTER 19

Nattie watched through the front window as the car drew up across the street. And the backup one: it was embarrassing.

She was trembling with anger from head to toe. She had poured out her wrath to Ahmed in texts and calls all day. He thought it was for the best that her mother was coming and that things were in the open. She had to know sometime, and surely, he queried, Nattie had hated the secrecy – probably more than she'd ever let on.

That was true. The tremendous urge to spill out her feelings, to rhapsodize and share the ten-times-over thrill had been buzzing away inside her like a trapped bee. But for her mother to have found out from two-faced Shelby – to be forced on to the back foot by that lying toad . . . And on top of the worry about MI5.

She had been on at Ahmed all day about her conviction that Shelby would have told her mother a whole book of inventive lies about him. Ahmed responded dryly that if that was the worst Shelby could do . . . Which was meant to be calming, a positive, cheer-up line, but which conveyed, distressingly, to Nattie that he privately thought it just an opening salvo, a picador's throw, and Shelby could yet come in for the kill. She felt despairing.

Ahmed had just called again. If, after seeing her mother, she felt he shouldn't come that night, he insisted she tell him.

His words were still in her ears. 'It would be unendurable, I'd cease to be, but I'd understand. I'd know the pressures, your duty to your mother – however it feels inside.'

She went ice cold as a fresh thought struck her. Had he been trying to say he'd rather not come? That was nonsense, she knew, she was just wretched with longing. His blood and hers, pulsing together, she thought, sharing veins.

Her mother couldn't march in trying to dictate to her. Nattie felt bitter, standing at the window, seeing her getting out of the car. She couldn't feel more grimly determined and resolved.

She went to the door. 'Hi, Mum.' She forced a thin smile. Seeing the distress in her mother's eyes made Nattie remember the visits to the grieving relatives and she felt a tug of remorse. 'Was it very hard for you today?' she asked with anxious sympathy. 'I'm sure they appreciated you coming.'

'It was wretched, but it's made me feel all the more driven and determined. Somehow we have to find these killers – if they're not drowned – and see justice done.'

Victoria put down a carrier bag and held out her arms. Nattie let herself be hugged, but grudgingly, feeling stiffly unresponsive. She dreaded the battle ahead, the crushing onslaught of heavy moral pressure. Nothing would sway her, nothing whatever.

Her mother was taking off her coat, smiling awkwardly. 'I was just in Silver Street and bought some cakes. They look really delicious – Milly might have to break her diet!'

It was pointless, all this, Nattie thought, her resentful anger ripening. 'I'll put the kettle on,' she mumbled, stumbling off to the kitchen.

She turned at the door with a sudden urge to let out some bottled-up fury or explode. 'How could you have agreed to see Shelby, Mum? You of all people! It's not as if you've got time on your hands right now. You don't even have any for your own family.'

It was a hollow dig, since her mother had just driven across England to see her. She could tell it had caused a stab of hurt. They eyed each other wanly and warily, each taking in the strain and emotion, clear as daylight in the other's eyes.

She put on the kettle. Victoria had come to the kitchen door. Even at forty-three, even washed-out and stressed to hell, she looked lovely, Nattie thought, staring. She had such a wide-eyed delicate face, so pale today, under the fall of brown hair. People didn't comment on her looks much since she'd been Home Secretary, but before that they never used to stop. Nattie thought of how William just stared some-times – which brought her mind straight back to Ahmed.

'I suppose Shelby told you who I'm seeing now?'

'Yes.'

'And all sorts of disgusting gross lies?'

'I'm sure he told lies or embellishments, but it was more about the people he thought your friend Ahmed might be involved with.' Her mother bit her lip and looked past Nattie into the kitchen. 'Make the tea and then we can sit down and talk.'

'What's there to talk about?' Nattie muttered aggressively. She pulled off the stopper on the teabag jar – Milly insisted on airtight jars – and placed two teabags in mugs with childish precision. She was playing for time, thinking how to put her case most forcefully and get in first.

Her cat-picture tray was nowhere; she found a substitute, carefully wiped it clean of rings and, hanging the J-cloth over the arch of the mixer-tap, stayed facing the sink. 'I'm sorry I didn't tell you about Ahmed, Mum.'

She turned with a small smile. 'I hated keeping it from you. I never have with anything since – well, that time. It's just that, with the undercover work he's doing, I sort of thought you'd make a needless fuss. And I suppose, since you're here, I was right—' She made a wry face.

It was suddenly impossible not to talk about him and give off a glow, some reflex-action switch clicking on her interior sparkling lights. 'I'd never have believed it, Mum, how intensely it's possible to feel. I've been bursting to tell you! If he left me I'd be like nothing, just a hollow skin – but then I feel so sure of him, and that's the wonder, trusting and knowing where he's at.'

She was blushing, she could feel it, and busied about making the tea and loading up the tray. Her mother's silent staring was getting to her. Nattie picked up the tray and pushed past her with it, showing all her tension. She took it to the coffee table and sat down.

Her mother joined her on the sofa and after pouring the tea Nattie had another try.

'You talked like this once, Mum, when I was all cut-up and untrusting after Seb, remember? You said how you felt about William, that I'd meet someone in time and have no doubts, that I'd just know. Well, I have. And I do know. I've got no doubts at all. So please don't come telling me it gives you problems, because that's a waste of your time. You don't even know him for a start – you've only met him once.'

Her mother had reached for the carrier she'd brought and was taking out wedges of cake. She unwrapped them with painstaking slowness and arranged them on a plate Nattie had put on the tray. Even the cake business, the fastidious unwrapping, seemed like it was exerting subtle pressure. Nothing would sway her, Nattie thought, feeling shredded to bits. She sensed they were on the verge of a stand-up row.

Those wide eyes of her mother's weren't helping; the strain was becoming extreme. Surely she wouldn't have believed a word Shelby said? He couldn't really have a clue what Ahmed was doing, but he'd obviously taken a calculated guess. There had been talk of Ahmed spending time in Leeds on that first evening, the supper with friends. He had brushed off queries about his work, but Shelby's nose must have sniffed the air and deduced it was investigative reporting.

'I had to agree to see Shelby,' her mother said defensively, with an uncharacteristic hesitancy gathering in that dreadfully agonized stare. 'I thought it would almost certainly be about something concerning you – which, of course, it was. I'd never believe a word he said, and also, having heard from William that Ahmed was in Leeds, I was on knowledgeable ground. Shelby didn't get quite the reaction he'd been hoping for.

'Perhaps I should have guessed about you and Ahmed – you'd certainly got on at the party.' Her mother smiled, but Nattie angrily sensed in that remark regret at not picking up on it and nipping it in the bud.

'William is very impressed with him, by the way,' Victoria went on. 'He'd mentioned him to me once – even before that night of the party. And he has since told me more about Ahmed's Leeds activities. We never let on much about our respective jobs, too many trade secrets and conflicts of interests, but there are things we share – certainly the serious issues. Things as fundamental as terrorism—'

Nattie looked up at that and stared nervously. Her heart was in her throat. She knew what was coming and fervently wanted to try to forestall it.

'So you know about the people Ahmed's in contact with,' she said. 'He thinks there's one key man, Mum, who's terrifyingly ruthless, brilliantly clever and who could even be behind this latest attack. This man isn't kind of obvious, he's very educated and sophisticated and knows how to blend in . . . like with the British scene. Ahmed says he'd fit in anywhere, the perfect cover. I hate to think what he'd do to moles, though . . . So you can see,' Nattie said passionately, straining every fibre to persuade, 'how fantastically brave Ahmed's being. He's not thinking of his own safety one bit.'

'But is he thinking of yours?'

Shit, Nattie thought, she'd walked right into that. 'All the time,' she glared defiantly, 'constantly. That's the whole point of him.' She gave an involuntary smile. 'Ahmed's gentle and thoughtful, he really cares about people.' She thought of Khalid – she kept seeing his crushed body, the images wouldn't go away – but chose another example of Ahmed's caring. 'For instance, Mum, there's a woman downstairs at his London flat. He worries she's ill and isn't telling because of her cats.'

Her mother looked quite startled by the sudden switch to cats. Although from the set of her face she certainly wasn't going to let it reverse any previous thinking.

She fanned out her hands on her black suit skirt, looked at them and then up again. 'Try to understand, Nattie, how worried I feel. These people are absolutely ruthless. Ahmed's coming here, laying a trail to your door . . . Surely, love, if he's the good decent person you say, if he really loves you, he'd honour what I'm asking you to do. I'm begging you, Nattie, pleading. I'm not asking you never to see him again. But just at this desperate time . . . Can't you see how dangerous it is?'

It was out in the open, baldly said, clearly laid out between them like a gauntlet flung down, a moral-blackmail note for filial loyalty. Nattie felt immune, she'd found a hidden stash of steel and felt coldly determined; she had a confident sense of right on her side. It was unreasonable, unfair, it was her life to lead. There was no way she was going to give in.

She stuck out her chin, glad to be able to absolve Ahmed and play a satisfying trump card. 'Sure, he'd honour what you're asking, he actually told me so when I said you were coming. But *I* won't. *I'm* not going to. I don't think you've any right to ask. And all the more so,' she burst out emotionally, her tight control dissolving, 'when I think what he's doing. Just suppose, God forbid, anything happened to him and I'd been deprived being able to see him before—'

Tears sprang into her eyes. Nattie blinked them back furiously. She thought of Ahmed's pain over Khalid's suicide, how he'd driven through the night to lean on her and share his grief. 'Please see it from my side, Mum,' she begged, suddenly loathing having to fight her mother, feeling stretched to breaking point in two ways. 'Ahmed really needs me now.'

She stared, aching to make her mother see his special qualities. 'He needed me last week, Mum – he'd been with one of his contacts who killed himself, right in front of Ahmed's eyes. If you could have seen his agony . . . This person had needed to make it look like an accident for the sake of his family and his faith, and Ahmed will never say what really happened, he would never let him down . . .'

Her shoulders were shaking uncontrollably and her mother moved closer on the sofa to put an arm round her daughter. But Nattie could gauge from its formal cautious hold that her mother was sticking to her stand.

Nattie dried her eyes; she wasn't softening either. She felt nut-hard, resolved. 'I'm not going to stop seeing him. Do you want me to move out from home?'

'That's the last thing I want. Don't say things like that. I can only ask you not to see him – only for a while. You'll be home in days and have your family around, all of us together over Christmas – seeing Grandpa and Grandma . . .'

That did it. The deep sense of injustice Nattie was feeling gushed out like an oil-spurt and swamped her. She stood up with a white stricken face and rummaged furiously in her lunchtime shopping, a pile of carriers and packages still on a chair.

'See this!' She pulled out a tissue-wrapped brown and cream scarf. 'I bought it for Ahmed today. And do you know why? Because I'd really hoped he could come and stay at Brook House with Grandpa and Grandma, who wouldn't think like you, I know they'd really like him. And this scarf was a kind of a joke – to stop him wearing his Leeds United one with you and William around.'

She covered her eyes, shoulders heaving again. She hated rows more than anything and her frustration and hurt at being denied having Ahmed at home, being accepted, part of the family, knew no bounds. Her mother was saying nothing and Nattie kept her head bowed. She hoped Sam and Milly weren't about to turn up; they'd promised to hang loose, at least till after five, and it was ten past, already.

Nattie had a last try at getting through to her mother, an appeal over her own first love. It was prompted by a tiny niggle, a secret worry about how perfect things seemed with Ahmed. Her mother had married very young, but had it felt just as uniquely wonderful? Things had been bad between her parents for so long.

She looked hard at her mother, red-eyed. 'Were you very much in love with Dad at the beginning?'

The question came as a surprise. Her mother paused.

'There was a strong physical pull. Dad swept me off my feet, I suppose, but a corner of me was never absolutely sure. I'd thought it would all be fine, but, well, you know the rest. It is always better not to rush things, Nattie—'

That had the smell of another own goal. Nattie impatiently stuck her hands inside her baggy sweater and wrapped it round them like a muff.

She wasn't giving up. 'But you married him all the same?'

'I was having you! And as I said, I persuaded myself it would be all right and we'd work it out somehow.' Nattie had half known that, had once read a newspaper article with telltale dates, but it had seemed irrelevant and unimportant. Her mother needn't have got married, the world had moved on. The niggle receded; it hadn't been the same for her mother and she felt back on strong ground.

'It's always seemed sadly ironic,' her mother was saying, 'the bad timing. So effortlessly getting pregnant with you – and with Charlie, although I miscarried him – but now, when I long to have William's baby . . .' Victoria smiled sheepishly, and looked at her watch.

Nattie felt secure in her moral advantage. 'There's something I want to get at *you* about now, Mum, just before you go. Maybe this isn't the time, but it's about Dad. He's in such a bad way. You're the only person who can possibly get him even to think about treatment. How would it be with his firm, his clients and stuff? Would the other lawyers cover for him?'

'I don't really know. They might. His boss, Hugh Simmonds, is decent. That might be workable, but whether Dad would ever go along with it is another matter.'

'I mean, Mum, if you can make time to come here and worry about me when I'm on cloud a-hundred-and-nine, can't you find it in you to help Dad?'

There was the hint of a frown; this definitely wasn't what her mother had come for. 'I don't think you're quite appreciating, darling, the naked threat out there: that missing waste. There could be a nuclear explosion. This really isn't the time—'

Nattie boiled up. 'That's what you always say! There'll be more terrorists, times of high alert, escaped prisoners, buggered up computers. You never find time! You could at least talk to him, just try.'

'I will, very soon. I'm so racked with worry, right now, about *you*. You're putting yourself at risk. Everything's so new and wonderful for you, you're seeing love through a glorious gauzy haze of passion . . . Just suppose, though, Nattie – not Ahmed leaving you or anything – but suppose you found out he hadn't told you things as they really were? That there were . . . anomalies. Think how you'd feel. This is such a tense time. Couldn't you just stand back for a few weeks . . . just for me?'

She was getting into her coat and unable, it seemed, to face looking at her daughter. It had been a monstrous thing to say. Nattie could hardly believe it. Her mother didn't trust him – did she really think he was an evil terrorist?

'Well, I guess we'll pass on the stairs, Mum, when I'm back,' she said with glacial sarcasm. 'I'll make sure I see Ahmed elsewhere. I quite understand he won't be welcome at home. I only wish,' she threw out furiously, 'you could trust your daughter's judgement – and your husband's – and show Ahmed a little loyalty. You don't have any faith, you're suspicious enough to think the worst of him and it hurts like hell.'

For all the protestations and assurances that it wasn't so, they both recognised the germ of truth. 'Bye then,' Nattie said. She was unable to yield to the hug she was given and stood like a post. She sensed her mother was close to tears.

When the two sleek cars had glided off she crumbled. Her heart ached. She wanted her mother back, wanted to say she understood, wished things were different.

But her underlying anger remained. It was a matter of loyalty, she thought. Ahmed wanted to redress terrorist wrongs, he felt a connected sense of responsibility. He said this country had given him extraordinary chances, that he owed it to put something back. He was being loyal. Why couldn't her mother show him a little loyalty in return?

What really got to Nattie most was not being able to bring him home. Apart from glowing pride in him, she couldn't bear there to be any sensitivities, for Ahmed to feel he wasn't approved of. Perhaps she could talk to William. She would tell him, Nattie decided, that she wanted to take Ahmed to meet her grandparents, just for the day, ahead of Christmas, and see what he thought.

The idea made her feel better – more able to face Milly who was just coming in the door. 'Yo, Mills! Coast is clear. Mum said to say hello.'

'How'd it go? Did you get it across about your dad?' Nattie had used that excuse to try to explain away the need for time alone with her mother. Milly dumped down a book bag and Christmas shopping and unzipped a sugar-pink anorak. 'You coming out later or waiting in for A? He's around tonight, isn't he?'

'Sure. I'm not sticking in all night, though.' There was a full end-of-term partying scene and Nattie was game for a couple of hours. She was still smarting after Sam had called her boringly in love.

Ahmed was neurotic about Sam and Milly talking, spreading the word about him coming – desperate about their relationship ever reaching the press. 'Be a spook, Nattie darling,' he kept saying, 'play it down. Think of it being picked up by Yazid. I could try saying it was just a bit of sex and he'd be thinking, with the Home Secretary's daughter? My street cred would be dead!'

Nattie couldn't see it getting in the press, yet Ahmed's safety was constantly in her mind. She tried at times to imagine Fahad's physical appearance: saw a no-neck, thick-shouldered look, vengeful glints in hard eyes . . . Sam would never talk. It would be mad to try to drop hints about keeping quiet to Milly, though – sure to get back to Shelby . . . And he would smell a rat. Rats did, it would be rat smelling a rat and ratting.

Nattie's mobile was ringing. 'I'll take it upstairs,' she said grinning, forgetting about not showing her feelings and her fears. She took the stairs two at a time.

'I'm alone now,' she panted, 'missing you madly. I can't wait for later!'

'But she wanted you to stop seeing me? Did she say so?' Ahmed sounded both agitated and resigned, as if prepared for rejection. Nattie felt deflated suddenly, and apprehensive.

'It's what I want that matters,' she muttered. 'I need to see you. All weekend I've been thinking about Khalid, worrying about you.'

'But are you really sure? I'd hate to think you're going against your mother and all that that means.'

'She can't dictate to me, saying she didn't want it just at this time. Well, what's that supposed to mean?'

'How did you leave it?'

'Like, I'll lead my own life and see her around. It's only Mum and her stupid job.' Nattie felt desperate for him not to feel rejected.

Her tears were silent, but he picked up on them. 'Don't cry. I'll be there just as soon as I can.'

CHAPTER 20

Ahmed clicked off his mobile and looked at his watch. Four hours before he could have the car. He felt knotted up, stranded, stuck in no-man's-land with the sense of disaster drawing unstoppably near. It was like watching a great boulder come thundering towards him and feeling glued, helpless in its path.

His wild drive to Durham on Friday was on his mind. Still in shock from the tragedy of Khalid, he'd let out dry despairing howls. There had been cars on the road, even at midnight, people staring in at traffic lights. He couldn't have cared, nothing had seemed to matter or have any point.

Nattie had been there for him: no questions, no demands, just calm loving support. She was the whole wonderful point.

Another glance at his watch. He'd been doing it all afternoon – pacing like a tiger, dreading she might weaken under pressure and give in to her mother. She hadn't, though. She really wanted him to come that night; killing time lying on his bed in his pokey strait-jacket of a room was driving him mad.

Ahmed thought of the emotional cost to her of defying her mother, how painful it must have been. There was nothing girly or

My-Spacey about Nattie, she was a woman with real depth and heart.

He knew the risks involved in seeing her, that he should find some grit and not go. The nagging feelings of guilt were like a dog tugging away at his trouser leg – tenacious, impossible to shake off. Four hours . . .

Her mother hadn't resorted to threats, as his own would have done with his sisters – she had tried pleading and reason. And he couldn't blame her for feeling panic or even take it too personally. He did, though, think it pointed to his not being entirely trusted by MI5, which made him feel deeply, bitterly resentful.

Should he have warned Nattie, on Friday night, about the chance of his mobile being bugged? He certainly shouldn't have said anything to her about MI5 and Khalid; that had been self-pitying, he felt bad about it. A phone-tap had seemed so unlikely at first, but the idea was gaining ground and it carved him up.

Would it have been better to take his worries to MI5 in the first place? Too late now. Osborne gave an impression of trusting him, but then who knew?

Lying on his narrow bed looking up at old arty posters from his university days, Ahmed tried to imagine the kind of life Fahad might lead behind his carefully wiped-out tracks. He could be a respected scientist, a computer expert – possibly even work in a government office in the north. People were full of surprises and hidden secrets, there were stories in the papers every day to prove it.

Apart from a detailed physical description and his idea of connections with Cumbria, he hadn't, Ahmed thought, been able to pass on a useful thing.

Fahad seemed the sort of man who'd think himself cleverer than all those penetrating minds at MI5, who'd delight in keeping them dangling while taking his time – assuming he *had* actually pulled off the train ambush – in perfecting a devastating radioactive bomb. Where the hell was he going to put it? Trying to fathom that out was driving Ahmed demented.

Idling on his bed wasn't helping, he thought, springing up. He went to sit at his laptop and work on an article on Leeds' renaissance. Osborne was expecting regular pieces, time he filed another. He was putting off going round to see Yazid who had phoned from work. Ostensibly to be sociable and ask him over, but really to quiz him, Ahmed suspected, over the preliminary opening of the inquest.

The article wouldn't take long, there was time to go and still be back for the family meal; calling on Yazid couldn't be ducked.

The opening of the inquest was a formality, Ahmed had explained on the phone, simply the identification of the body. It would be different at the next stage, which filled him with dread. Yazid's attitude had been sickening, that revolting bounce in his voice – it was as if Khalid's death was actually more a cause of satisfaction than sorrow. Yazid had shown no hint of regret on that call, despite all his usual caution about bugged mobiles. Ahmed felt shocked, disbelieving: his loathing for Yazid was deeper and blacker than any ancient well.

He set to at his laptop thinking wearily that most people at *The Post* thought he was having time off. Some holiday: cold, claustrophobic and in the back end of Leeds – typical of Osborne, making constant demands.

Ahmed had thought there was an article to be written about the seismic changes in Leeds. Once every adult male in the country had owned a suit, he wrote, but ever since jeans took over, vast local clothing empires like Montague Burton had vanished from the city.

One of their factories, back in those days, had had a canteen to seat ten thousand.

Leeds had more than survived. It had revitalized and transformed itself into a vibrant thriving city. Ahmed could hear his father reminding him grumpily that Harehills wasn't thriving, while still feeling pride.

He grabbed his leather jacket and Leeds United scarf and, avoiding the streets he had walked with Khalid, he hurried round to Yazid's flat. The thought of being civil to that piece of shit; his hands were forming fists. It was a cold mid-December night, misty and murky, wet plastic bags were flying around, filth in the streets.

There was the usual row of glum-faced loners to be seen through the launderette window below the flat. Yazid, though, who came bounding down to get the door, wasn't looking woebegone. He was in jeans and a canary yellow sweater, shrugging on a black anorak. 'Thought we'd go for a coffee,' he said, brisk and businesslike, adding in a furtive whisper, pointing upwards, 'Walls have ears.' Ahmed hoped they did, that MI5 were doing their stuff.

'Sure,' he said noncommittally, flipping his scarf back over his shoulder and falling in step, keeping as reasonably distant as possible.

Yazid lessened the space. 'The inquest proper won't be easy, will it?' He turned, looking inquisitive, a bit anxious too, but still with his nauseatingly obvious satisfaction – almost positive glee – at what had happened.

Ahmed choked back his disgust; the man had known Khalid as a friend. He fixed Yazid with a flat blank stare and had been about to say that no one would believe the poor kid just stepped out into a heavily trafficked road, when he remembered, thankfully just in time, where he was supposed to be coming from.

He did a sharp U-turn. 'I'll just have to keep on saying the little wimp accidentally tripped and fell,' he said, summoning up a sickly colluding grin.

Raising a knowing eyebrow he grinned some more. 'Makes you remember what ants we all are really, a hefty truck comes trundling by and poof, we're gone.' He sighed loudly. 'I think the inquest's going to be after Christmas now, early in the New Year. At least that's putting off the whole fucking farce for a few weeks.'

'Did those *Kafir* police farts give you a hard time, Friday?' Yazid asked. A smidgen of tension was creeping in, as if he needed to establish Ahmed had given nothing away. They had reached the door of an onion-smelling neon-lit café in a street behind the mosque. Yazid seemed to be waiting on his answer before pushing open the misted-up glass entry door.

'I acted pretty cut up,' Ahmed muttered, clinging to his fixed grin. 'The police weren't that interested. They're trash: plodders, form-fillers. I kept on pushing the same line, same as I'll have to do at the inquest.'

That seemed to satisfy Yazid. 'If it's not till the New Year,' he murmured, pausing frustratingly while they went in. He made for the nearest empty Formica table – furthest from the counter and the few onion-loving customers dotted around – and, leaning very close, continued, 'A certain great cloud will have gone up and your two-bit local inquest won't get much of a look in! That's our little secret, of course,' he confided. 'Just wait till you see the scale and genius of it . . . It's why that yellow-bellied little arsehole, Khalid, had the shits up his pants. He bottled out, too fucking gutless.'

Then, having dropped that chilling little bombshell Yazid winked, took off his anorak, yawned and called out to a waitress for two coffees.

He sipped his cautiously when it arrived, looking over the cup with narrowed eyes, though probably more out of curiosity than suspicion from his generally relaxed cocky mood.

'Where did you go late last Friday, after the accident?' he asked, which explained his slight guardedness. 'My cousin, Hussain, saw you in your father's cab.'

Ahmed tried to look as though he was thinking back, searching his mind. 'Oh, that! I just had to get out from under for a bit. First the police, then my parents – they'd kept on in that dirgy way . . . I told my father driving would calm me down.'

He thought how easy it was to act out lies, once you got into the habit, and that it might be wise to anticipate the cousin seeing him again, later on.

'I've wangled the car for tonight as well! I'm on the make – a *Kafir* girl I met on the train back from London last time; no bad looker and tits. She lives in York.'

'Called?'

'Sam Mills,' Ahmed said without a moment's hesitation. 'Hope she's worth it.'

He walked home from the café feeling a need to gag. His skin was crawling. He would rather have spent time face down in a foul-smelling drain. Pounding adrenaline took over then and redirected his mind.

Yazid had just given away a huge piece of intelligence, the clearest sign yet, that a canister of High Level Waste was in terrorist hands. And also that, whatever the catastrophic disaster planned, it seemed not to be absolutely imminent. Ahmed decided to wait to call Osborne till he was on the road to Durham. After all, as Yazid had said, walls had ears.

He'd clearly implicated himself, although it was one man's word against another, and while Yazid had been stupidly cocky, he'd given little away. He was just a recruiter and organizer, small beer, and Fahad had probably passed on few details. Ahmed even remembered him remarking, out on the Fells, that Yazid was little involved.

His first pulse-throbbing thrill at the thought of a breakthrough was fading; he had a lowering sense of having learned all he could. Ahmed seldom felt a failure; he liked to flatter himself he was without arrogance, but neither did he go in for false modesty. He had a good brain and a glass-full view of his own ability to achieve, yet he sensed this time that his talents were letting him down.

Fahad wasn't going to show any more, at least till the moment of action. The only hope was some weird clue suddenly hitting home, some flash of inspiration. He had little faith in MI5 being ahead, convinced as he was that Fahad was a 'clean skin' and impossible to track down – as well as depressingly many steps ahead of them.

Ahmed tried to avoid driving too fast to Durham; he wanted to be with Nattie, not wrangling with the law. He was wildly impatient, but on edge as well. His father had been out in his cab and seen him going into the café with Yazid. He'd made clear his extreme disapproval of the company his son was keeping.

And his mother too, had made difficulties. She'd discovered he was seeing Leena's friend, Safa, the next evening – nothing was safe from cousins and gossip – and though aware of Leena's flight from her violent father, had no reason to think that Ahmed taking out Safa was in any way connected.

She was far more convinced it was a romantic date, which had got her all excited and made her angrily renew her attempts to stop him

shooting off in the car. Whatever his sordid nocturnal plans might
be, she imagined they wouldn't please Safa, whom she saw as marital manna from heaven. Ahmed crossed thumbs that his lie about the
girl on the train didn't get back to his mother, via the infernal
grapevine.

A lay-by was coming into view. He slowed and pulled in, psych-
ing himself up for another out-of-hours call to his editor.

Bringing up the number, he wondered if Osborne had considered
the possibility of his reporter's mobile being bugged. Surely, though,
Nattie's mother would never tell him such things? At least his editor
wouldn't have to pass on anything more to MI5. They'd be listening
in, hearing every word.

'I may decide,' Osborne said thoughtfully, after being filled in, 'to
run a story on this – probably the usual line: "Information obtained
by *The Post* . . ." It seems to indicate clearly that the boat was a decoy
and that the killers have the stuff and are out there, very much alive.
Does that put you in the shit with your contacts?'

Ahmed thought about it. 'Talk of timescale might,' he said, 'give
Yazid a big fat clue.' He spoke of his progress in finding the honour-
killing girl then drove on.

It was a source of wonder to him that Osborne could contemplate
running a story to cause the government – and the Home Secretary
in particular – the most acute embarrassment possible. How could
they sleep comfortably side by side in bed?

His blood was racing as he hit the streets of Durham. He parked
across from the green front door and didn't need to press the bell.
Nattie had seen him and was standing framed in the doorway, smiling. Ahmed stored the sight of her there in his memory bank.

'No one's around,' she said shyly as he came over. She took his hand and led him in, shutting the door behind them on the cold night air.

Inside, he gazed at her for a few seconds before closing his hands round her wrists and pulling her near. She was wearing some light scent that suited her and there was her own very special smell, too. It was soaking in through his pores, releasing every inhibition in his body; he felt all sense of time, place, order, family ceasing to be.

He fell on her then, kissing her ravenously with all the emotional passion that had been spiralling up inside him for days, all his intense overarching desire.

'Your mother doesn't want this,' he mumbled, tearing open the row of front buttons on her skinny sweater. 'I shouldn't be here.'

'She's not going to walk in,' Nattie said, pushing his head to her breasts. 'The others might, though.'

Ahmed looked up. 'I'm still feeling guilty about being here, but you're a beautiful witch, it's all your fault.'

Nattie got him upstairs.

Guilt was right out of it then. He felt outside its boundaries and very sure of her. He had nothing to prove, there was none of the embarrassment of newness, no caution. And Nattie's abandon was sending him crazy as he felt her exploring hands move down his body and her soft sensuous mouth taking hold. He couldn't get enough of her then and it was driving him to the heights, hearing her moans as she came there too. He wanted to live in her incredible body, feed off it, give it his all.

He came down from his pinnacle and was suddenly besieged with feelings of jealous hatred for Shelby. Nattie hadn't loved him, but imagining them together was like a continual steel-capped boot to the groin. Shelby had lost her, though, for all his persuasive powers and he must be burning to find ways for more dirty revenge.

There was Hugo too, who seemed a different sort of threat. He might be in need of help and support, but Ahmed didn't take kindly to the idea of Nattie showering all her wonderful soft caring on a well-heeled druggie. That wasn't, though, a thought he could easily share.

He began feeling calmer. They were lying slotted together – more or less comfortably – in her bunk of a bed crammed into its sloping corner. He longed for a night in a luxury hotel; he wanted to sleep in her arms in a sumptuous downy white bed and begin all over again in the morning. What had he got to offer her? What chance of their future together?

Nattie extracted a hand from under him and brought it up to touch his face. She smoothed his eyebrows and lifted back the hair off his hot damp forehead.

'What are you thinking?' Her wide amber eyes were anxious.

'About being in love with you. I was daring to think beyond Fahad, hoping we ever get there! I have a terrible fear,' he said, telling it even as it was formulating, 'that whatever he's planning might be connected with Christmas in some way, some awful symbolism like blowing up St Paul's Cathedral. God knows how we can second-guess him and sort him. No easy task!'

He brought her up to date on Yazid. 'Every day I feel more certain that Fahad has the High Level Waste. It is in the land of hunches, though. He could be involved in some quite other plot or even just be a saddo line-spinner, someone who likes to make people think he's Mr Big when he isn't. I called your stepfather, William, on the way here, to fill him in, so I'm sure my hunches will reach MI5. It's all I can do.'

Ahmed hoped she'd think of Osborne passing it on, rather than it being overheard. He regretted ever having mentioned the possibility of phone-taps – although it hadn't made her inhibited on their calls. 'I wish I believed MI5 really trusted me,' he went on, feeling in need of sympathy again. 'They'll probably even look for some ulterior motive in this new stuff. It's awful, feeling not trusted, depressing. I hate it.'

That was a mistake. Nattie's eyes misted up.

'It's only Mum's job, nothing personal,' she muttered.

He kissed her, loved her for caring, but suddenly noticed the time.

Tearing into his clothes he told her about meeting Leena's friend, Safa, next evening, how he was hoping for a breakthrough there at least. 'It'll be a tough job persuading her – and that poor wretched girl in hiding – that I'm on the level. It's quite a worry – I may have to get you to vouch for me!'

'And my little worry,' Nattie whispered, looking guilty, 'is the thought of you out with a girl with a pretty name tomorrow night. Of course I do really want you to be helping Leena, obviously.'

'Don't *you* start not trusting me as well.' He grinned. Nattie was putting on a man's T-shirt to come downstairs with him and he kissed her through the fabric while she pulled it on. 'You're as bad as my mother,' he said, as she reappeared. 'What about all these end-of-term bops? Didn't you once say trust cuts both ways?'

It was four in the morning, chilly and silent as they crept downstairs. There had been sounds of Nattie's housemates returning a while back. Ahmed kissed her. 'When do I see you again?' he asked, feeling all the constraints crowding in again, his frustrations and fears.

'There's Wednesday night – but I'm longing for a London weekend. You did say you'd probably got all you could out of Yazid, squeezed him dry. Will Jake be in Oxford? Mum will be off to Hampshire. I could come and stay, cook you nice meals.'

Ahmed had out his car key. 'You wouldn't get near the kitchen,' he brought up her hand, sticking all four of her fingers into his mouth, 'not when I could be eating you.'

He drove away thinking about his job, his future, his parents, what exactly Shelby might still have in mind; it was all connected and all revolved round Nattie.

CHAPTER 21

'Ahmed. It's ten o'clock, haven't you got work to do? I want to know where you were last night. I don't like it. Your father's too soft on you. I said you should never have gone to London, I knew what it would lead to . . .'

The voice came into focus. It wasn't a dream. Ahmed opened one eye. Fucking hell, he was twenty-five in a month. Time he was back in the city of sin. He sat up, rubbing both eyes, and looked over to the door where his mother was peering in cautiously like someone half-expecting to see a burglar – or a girl in his bed.

'Mum, I have tried to explain. I can't talk about anything to do with work. That's the deal with investigative journalism, we can never reveal our sources. I just can't say.' It didn't feel a total lie – Nattie was a deliciously fruitful, wonderful source.

'I'm not asking about sources,' his mother said sharply, coming right into the room. The concept of his private space was completely alien to her. It infuriated him, the way she'd come in whenever she liked, whatever the time of day, whether he was there working or not, and start tidying his things.

He grinned at her encouragingly, feeling fed up and sarcastic. 'Um, didn't you want me to get on and get dressed, Mum?'

She bent to pick up the underpants and shirt he'd unsuccessfully flung at his desk chair a few hours earlier – she had a sort of laundry kleptomania, a compulsive grabbing of clothes to wash – and stood hugging his dirty smalls to her bosom, glaring, warming up to her theme. She wasn't giving way.

'What's it to do with, this "work"? You've been out all night three times now, even last Friday in that upset state, and it's not right, not healthy. Were you at a nightclub or something till five in the morning? I want to know what's going on.'

He resisted snapping at her. They rowed quite enough already, so instead he smiled at her weakly. 'It's the distances I have to travel, Mum. Can we leave it there?' It was a wishful thought, he knew; she would keep on about it all day like a nagging wife in a sitcom.

She was eyeing him balefully, standing her ground – working up to another salvo, no doubt. 'You've got a girlfriend,' she accused bitterly. 'Is that why you're not getting married?' Her expression became more hopeful, almost pleading, and he knew what was coming. 'Safa's a very nice girl,' she said coyly, 'they're a good family—'

Ahmed scowled. 'You don't even know her. And I thought we'd agreed to have no more talk of marriage,' he said with vehemence. He began to feel more despairing than angry and, partly in an attempt to distract her, partly out of guilt that he'd done nothing yet about it, suggested he take them out. 'This is my last week at home, Mum. I'd really like to say thank you and take you and Pops to dinner on Thursday.'

His mother duly ran the gamut of reactions to that heretic invitation, saying first that nowhere locally was any good and anyway she preferred to cook. He looked sad; he'd really wanted the chance to say thank you and wouldn't it make a nice change? She sniffed; well, perhaps, if his father wanted it . . . It was a small triumph, Ahmed thought.

He'd succeeded in distracting her and his mother knew it. Clicking her teeth in irritated defeat, she swished out of the door and pattered impatiently downstairs.

Ahmed checked she'd gone right down then took his mobile back to bed for an indulgent call to Nattie. 'You up? I'm not waking you, am I?'

'I'm kind of up; flopped round the kitchen in my T-shirt, feeling like, well, one big yawn. We've been sitting here drinking oceans of tea – Sam and Mills have just gone. They kept on about me bring-ing you to one of these parties. I told them we're sort of lying low, that Mum's completely paranoid about the press writing me up and that after being mean to her yesterday, I was trying to be nice! Hope that was okay? I had to say something.' Nattie sounded anxious.

She went on. 'Milly tried to imply it was more about your job and you were on to something all very secret. I gave her some crap about journalists always playing it close and just making everyone else fess all their secrets – that kind of stuff.'

'Did she buy it?' he asked, understanding Nattie's anxiety.

'She had to; I wasn't selling any alternative. I was quite abrupt.'

He hoped that hadn't just got Milly more alerted. Had Shelby been feeding her lines? The sooner Nattie was back in London the better, he thought, longing to be there, too. She brought up Safa again, which amused him, and, lingering over ending the call, he told her he was going to spend the day trying to find leads into Iqbal who'd disappeared off the face of the earth. He seemed, unlike

Khalid, to be a paid-up participator, deep into whatever was going on.

Shaving and dressing, Ahmed enjoyed the thought of Nattie sitting around drinking oceans of tea, which was exactly what his mother and her friends did all day. He often had to go out for more milk. And Nattie being on about Safa again, he loved her showing a bit of jealousy. He couldn't help wondering whether MI5 had been listening in and it made him squirm. How would they read a mention of Iqbal sandwiched in between all the yearning passion? Would they assume he'd tossed it in for deliberate good measure?

His mother was at the bottom of the stairs as he came down. She put a finger to her lips. 'Your little nephew Asim's here and he's asleep. He's got a bad cold, not well enough for nursery group. Will you be very quiet?'

Ahmed nodded. 'I'm out of your hair anyway,' he whispered, fast deciding to take his laptop and work in a Starbucks between sleuthing. 'Not back for lunch.'

She eyed him suspiciously then went on. 'The coroner's releasing Khalid's body today. His aunt's come over from Pakistan, the one he stayed with, a sister from the States. I'll be round there later, but you're seeing Safa, you don't need a meal tonight, I know.'

He imagined Khalid's body lying wrapped in a white cloth in the unlived-in front room of his terraced home. Cousins and other relatives would be travelling the country, to pay their respects; the women going to the house, the men only when it was time to take the body to the mosque. Ahmed pictured the imam leading the congregational prayers. The crowd would be immense; everyone who prayed at the mosque would be there, whether they had known poor Khalid or not.

'The funeral will be tomorrow now, won't it, with the winter dark?' he asked, needing to know. It meant a lot to him to be there. She confirmed that, before a loud wail starting up had her darting away to the kitchen.

Ahmed had a hurried bowl of cereal and a flick through *The Post* — his parents might whinge about his job, but they still took the paper. He collected his laptop and recording machine, having a last look round for anything best hidden from his mother, put on his jacket and the new scarf from Nattie that he really liked, and fled the inhibiting unchildproofed house.

The day stretched coldly ahead. There was hardly a soul about: not even the usual watchful Asians in twos or threes. Too cold for loitering, he thought, as the chill penetrated up through his trainers and his breath was as steamy as a dragon's.

His mind was on Khalid. The kid had been trained and indoctrinated to the hilt, yet still couldn't handle whatever the horror planned; it wasn't surprising he'd buckled. He'd gone in desperation to his God, whom Ahmed hoped would look on him kindly. The thought brought a lump to his throat and made his lip quiver; he vowed with emotional determination to fight Fahad all the way.

Iqbal had earned backhanders at the local kebab house and it seemed a good place to start. The guys there might know a morsel or two about him, even let something slip. Ahmed kicked himself constantly for not being more inquisitive in the early days, but too much probing might have reached Fahad, if Yazid was his eyes and ears.

A mid-morning kebab was not an appealing thought. Ahmed decided to read the newspapers over coffee first, text Nattie, think what to say to Safa that night.

The papers were still government bashing, the Energy Minister taking most of the hits. One of the Foreign Secretary's acolytes had an article in *The Post*'s rival paper, *The Courier,* implying as usual that the Prime Minister had lost his grip and should stand aside.

So that Peter Barnes could ride like a shining white knight to the rescue, Ahmed thought sarcastically. Barnes should watch it, cocky complaisant bugger. With all the rumours of an affair zipping round *The Post* he was on wafer-thin ice.

An hour passed in no time. Ahmed left the snug coffee shop tucking his tiny recording machine into his top-pocket, though without much hope. The cold set in at once. His thoughts were random, tangential: recording machines had been going for a hundred years, amazing, really. His feet were icy, why hadn't someone invented heated shoes? Perhaps someone had.

Two Pakistanis ran the kebab house. One was tall and cumbersomely built, a bearded individual with a drooped eyelid that gave him a rather forsaken look. It invited pity – and patience, he was ponderously slow. The other guy was physically more user-friendly; smaller, lean and clean-shaven, but he gave every impression of being on the make. Not to the extent of Iqbal, who had proudly flaunted his lawbreaking. He'd considered it his Islamist duty.

'Hi ya,' Ahmed said. 'A chicken and a lamb, please, and a Coke.'
'To go?'

'No, I've got all day, actually,' he grinned. He paid up front and waited, watching as the big guy ambled to and fro behind the high counter. It wasn't a bar-top. The seating was at a scattering of yellow-topped tables in the small shop that fronted on to the road. Ahmed imagined it as a butcher's or draper's in a previous decade.

He picked his moment, clearing his throat to attract the big man's attention. 'I, um, just wondered – have you got a mobile number for Iqbal, by any chance?'

The other guy moved with speed alongside. 'What's up? You with the Fuzz or what?'

'He's okay, Taqi,' the hulky one assured soothingly, 'he's a brother.'

Taqi's face was guarded. He flicked a glance at the only other customers: an old woman, masticating at length on a baklava, and a couple of girls wearing the hijab and western dress, who were sitting at a far table by the window.

'I am keen to find him,' Ahmed pressed gently. 'I'm after borrowing his car.'

'Well, you can fuck that. Car's in the street, got no tax, the police are on our backs about it.' Ahmed hoped that at least it might be covered in Iqbal's DNA. Wiry Taqi was still giving him doubtful stares. 'Iqbal never had no mobile; he begged calls off customers the whole time, I had to bawl him out. And he left no address, neither – in case you ask.'

'You talk like he's gone for good.' Ahmed smiled. 'Know where?'

Taqi shrugged.

'Said he had a driving job,' his lumbering friend offered.

'But not,' Ahmed said, smiling some more, 'using his own car, obviously. Is it with a haulage firm or something, do you know?'

'What's this all about?' Taqi was glaring. 'You were on that paper, weren't you? Why are you hanging round up here anyway? I don't like it.'

'Just doing boring local-colour stuff,' Ahmed said yawning. 'If I could have borrowed his car I'd have made on expenses, that sort of idea. But if it's not taxed—'

'Here's your food,' the big one said, edging a plate with two long wooden sticks, chips and a bit of lettuce towards him and looking as sympathetic as a hefty black-bearded hulk with a half-closed eye could manage to do.

Ahmed chose a table far from the counter and ate with a folded newspaper beside him. He felt defeated and bleak: Iqbal's ability to leave no trace was sinisterly professional. The two girls in hijabs – whom he hoped weren't close buddies of Yazid – were chatting nearby; they seemed oblivious and he couldn't help listening in.

'Forget the bio-peel and pills. There's this cream out now with stuff from Japanese mushrooms in it, and an extract of bird-droppings, I think – but it costs.'

'There's a serum that's only £13.99.'

It took Ahmed a while to figure out they were talking of skin-whitening products; he thought of girls back at the office, rushing to stick their faces in any ray of sun.

He texted Nattie, 'You into sunbathing?'

'Why?'

'Our holidays.'

'Will U come skiing in Jan?'

'Can't. Harehills boys didn't do. How about Venice, Paris, Rome, Caribbean?'

She texted back that he'd learn fast and reeled off holiday places of her own. He was smiling as he left the kebab house.

It must have been the progression of thought, but he was suddenly shafted by a premonition that he would be in a battle with Fahad and be killed. It was making him feel disconnected and outside himself, as he'd heard could happen if you were cleanly knifed or lost a limb. It was as vivid as the dreams people have that make them change flights, wedding dates.

The sweat sat cold on his skin, his T-shirt under his sport shirt was drenched. He had to keep going and not be deflected; there was nothing else to do. If he got that close, he told himself, he might be on to something worth dying for.

It crossed his mind to go to the mosque and pray, but he went instead to the library and read T. S. Eliot's *The Waste Land*, still finding it hard to understand. Then, feeling a little calmer and more able to contain the fear, he called to check that his mother had left to mourn with Khalid's women-folk and took himself home.

Safa was there before him.

Ahmed had thought of a place to eat on the outskirts of Leeds, a pub turned more family restaurant. It had a lot of brick wall and an irritating internal fountain, the place certainly hadn't employed a quality interior designer, but it seemed appropriate in its way: innocuous, impersonal and, with luck, an unlikely hangout of cousins.

He'd found her family's phone number in his mother's address book and Safa's mother had passed on her daughter's mobile – eagerly, which felt all too familiar. Safa had naturally sounded quite surprised to hear from him; he had asked if she could spare half an hour, saying that he needed a little help.

She was an optician and worked full time, she'd said. Could it be after six-thirty one night?

He'd tentatively suggested a drink or dinner, and she'd chosen to meet over a meal. She had a car, and could come anywhere.

They'd met only once some time ago. On the way to the pub, as his smelly fuggy bus crawled along in choked-up traffic, he'd felt envious of her car and angry with himself for not booking his father's cab. It could have been charged to *The Post*.

'God, I'm sorry! I've kept you waiting. Will you ever forgive me?' Sliding in on the opposite bench, he smiled humbly, feeling as penitent and flustered as could be.

She was in a black trouser suit, as far as he could see at the table, and looked a little older than he remembered, his age or more. Ahmed felt surprised, both at her choosing to make an evening of it and that she was several years older than Leena, whom he knew was hardly out of her teens.

Safa was smiling back warmly. 'You're not late, I'm rudely early – it was easiest to come straight from work. But you'd probably rather have eaten later than this?'

'No, it's perfect. I'm grateful to you for agreeing to meet.' He thought their excessive politeness was more Jane Austen than drab Leeds eatery, but it was hard not to keep going with it. 'Will you have a drink or sooner just order?' He grinned. 'I'm afraid the food here is never going to challenge Jamie Oliver.'

'I'd love a glass of white wine. I shouldn't have more as I've got the car.'

'I'll join you,' Ahmed said, deciding he'd better keep her company, and catching a waiter's eye. He seldom drank, brought up in an alcohol-free home, and he liked to feel in complete control.

'Your family good?' Safa asked. 'My mother wanted to be remembered to yours.'

'I'll tell her. Everyone well with you, too?' Once duty inquiries and a few mutual contacts were disposed of and the wine had arrived, he took the plunge. 'I guess you must be wondering what this is all about,' he said pleasantly, no doubt making clear, with his slight fidgeting, that it wasn't an easy subject to broach.

'Well, a bit. It's nice to see you again anyway, and get out. I live on my own, but my mother always expects me home. She never understands it's why I left!'

They smiled at each other. Safa was both plain and attractive, he thought. She had a long nose that drew the eye too much, yet plenty of tumbling dark hair to offset it and a generous full-lipped mouth. There was probably a man around, but perhaps with some complication. She was giving attention to immaculately manicured nails.

'The trouble is,' he said a little overloudly, causing her head to jerk back up, 'if I start asking questions you'll clunk down a barrier faster than a car-park bar. You know I'm a reporter. And since I'm Muslim too, you might wonder all the more where my loyalties lie.' Did that sound melodramatic? Was he planting ideas?

'I'm sure you're sincere,' Safa responded lightly. 'And you'd said you wanted help, so I assumed you'd be asking questions. Is this Muslim connected then, whatever you want to ask?'

'Yes – in a word. It's about violence and honour killings.'

'Oh.'

She winced. He could see it, feel it, her feminine and protective instincts to the fore – no Muslim ever wanted to go near the subject, certainly not openly with someone they hardly knew. 'I don't want any quotes,' he said hastily, 'it's not about your personal feelings.' He was blowing this, coming at it too abruptly and cack-handedly, not building her trust first.

He looked at her steadily and said it straight, 'I want Leena's father behind bars—'

'And not just her father,' Safa muttered spontaneously, immediately looking away.

'I know you're a friend of Leena's,' Ahmed said. 'I imagine she must have turned to you at some stage, sensing and seeing you had

your freedom and were beyond the subjugation and repression –
obliteration even, if it avoids shame – of women that still unbeliev-
ably carries on. When you think it's in Britain, in this century, God!'

Safa looked at him quite coldly. 'Have I got my freedom? Has any
woman?'

'Yes,' he said, thinking of Nattie and her mother. 'Not that many
Muslim women perhaps, but things will change. They have to.' He
decided to take big chances and went on, 'You're right not entirely
to trust me – as you obviously don't. I'm here trying to persuade you
to put me in touch with her, because my editor wants a story on
honour killings, I can't pretend otherwise. But he cares, he thinks it's
unbelievable it goes on. And Leena may be comparatively safely
hidden, I assume, in a refuge, but that's no way to see justice done.
If she tells her story, is prepared to give evidence against her own
father it will send powerful signals, help others, make the police
intervene with more heart. They're too keen by half to keep well out
of it.'

He stopped, completely stuck suddenly for anything more to say.

She looked down at her nails. He could read the conflicting pulls,
see into her like an X-ray. 'If I persuade her to meet you there'll be
leaks,' Safa said finally. 'Her father and brother will get to her –
they'll know where she is.'

'How? Why should they? I could meet her on neutral ground,
anywhere she chooses. I don't have to know where she's staying,
myself.'

A waiter was hovering. 'Perhaps we'd better order,' Ahmed said,
frustrated at losing the flow at such a moment.

She nodded and stared at the menu in a distracted way then up at
the young black waiter. 'I'll have the cod. No starter.' She handed

him back her menu and said, before Ahmed could ask, 'No more wine, just some still water.'

He ordered a steak since *The Post* was paying and he was in need of something plain and substantial after being curried-out at home.

The moment they were alone Safa argued his last point as though she'd been forming an answer, not thinking of food. 'You'd pick up clues,' she said, 'even be able to follow her. You'd tell a girlfriend, people on your paper. It would get out.'

He knew she was feeling a weight of responsibility and loyalty, and he in turn felt great empathy. 'My girlfriend lives in London and she isn't Muslim,' he smiled. 'I wouldn't write anything Leena doesn't want, you'd have to trust me on that.

'She may, of course, refuse, you may advise her against it – all I'm doing is begging you just to ask her. What she must have been through—' A thought came to him. 'Was it even true, her affair with a married Hindu doctor – not just a rumour going round that became translated as fact?'

'No, it was true. She was nineteen and he had no intention of leaving his wife; Leena was let down by everyone.'

'How did she manage to escape?'

The waiter was back with a large breadbasket. Safa took a seeded roll and smiled at Ahmed across the table. 'That's quite a story. But perhaps it's better she tells it to you herself.'

CHAPTER 22

Victoria stood at the kitchen backdoor, warming her hands on a mug of tea. The door had glass upper panels and she stared out at the small London garden, which was still shrouded in dark at seven-thirty in the morning, just a dim dusky blur.

In summer it was an artistically untamed tangle: scrambling roses and unchecked shrubs, campanula in the paving. There was an old wrought-iron table where they could eat out. It was all William's work; somehow he found the time. He had a natural way with plants, Victoria thought, an instinctive eye for design and form. Perhaps it accounted for Tom's artistic talent. She turned back from the door with a sigh. Summer seemed an eternity away.

William was standing by the kitchen table eating toast. He was keen to be off, she knew; he liked being in early and reading the late editions while things were quiet.

'You're very tense,' he stated, looking over. 'Is it about Nattie coming home?'

Victoria stared back without answering. It was about Nattie and she didn't want another lecture. 'I'll get home as soon as I can tonight,' William went on. 'You'll be stuck voting, won't you, with the pressure on over this Transport Bill? What a gift to the opposition, a national road-pricing scheme! Think you'll get it through?'

Any work-related query or tease of his had the smell of professional probing, yet she thought for once he was only trying to make light, a kindly hand through the bars of her emotional jail.

'The main vote's at seven,' she said, putting her mug on the kitchen table. She kissed his cheek. 'So I shouldn't be that late. And there aren't too many rebels, we'll get it through okay. No story!' She looked down. 'I am a bit uptight about Nattie. Tom says she's due back about six and he'll be here – he might even go and meet her off the train as she'll have all her stuff.' She looked at William and said with pleading honesty, 'Be wonderful if you can get home early enough for supper together.' He didn't usually leave the office till after nine, but she felt badly in need of him there.

He put his arm round her and gave her a hug. 'I'll try. Must go. The car's outside, Dave's waiting. But . . . Let her bring Ahmed home, love! It's what she wants. She can't bear him to feel her family doesn't approve; that's obvious. And he's fine, absolutely on the level. I'd trust him almost more than anyone I know professionally.'

Victoria extracted herself and took a couple of plates to the dishwasher. William had no right to pile on the pressure. He more or less knew MI5 were tapping Ahmed's phone; not that they were 'perturbed' over the death of a man he was with, which was something she couldn't possibly mention. How could she have Ahmed in the house when MI5 had their doubts? However slight the risk, it still wouldn't be right.

She straightened up from the machine. 'I'm sure he's everything you say. I liked him too, when I met him briefly at your party, but I can't let her bring him home. Please don't press me. But there is, um, just something before you go . . . It's Barney. Nattie wants me to try to persuade him to have treatment. She says he's in a terrible way and I might just be able to tip him into agreeing. I could see him on Sunday night. Can you be understanding and not mind? I'd feel cleaner for trying and Nattie has asked—'

William's face had been darkening as she spoke. 'You really think you've got time for this sort of thing?' he demanded with icy sarcasm, reminding her uncomfortably of her own line of defence with Nattie. 'And hasn't it, by any chance, just occurred to you that we've been married three years now and life's moved on. Barney is *not* your responsibility. He never bloody well was. He knocked you about, for God's sake!' he exclaimed angrily, working himself up. 'I'm not having you seeing him alone. There's a case in the paper this very morning, about a woman who went to collect her mail from her old home and her ex-partner knifed her in a drunken rage.' William was being typically unreasonable, Victoria thought, quivering with tension-fuelled frustration.

'That's beneath you,' she muttered, 'a disgraceful slur on Barney. You know him better than that. He's in a bad way and needs our help—'

'And even if your safety wasn't an issue,' William interrupted, paying no attention, 'it would take more than an evening of your time. Persuading him, following up – we're in a national crisis, for God's sake, Cobra meetings, the lot. You're supposed to be a tough Home Secretary, not some woolly-thinking misguided little bleeding-heart social worker.' He looked at his watch then back at her with one of his vintage glowers. Probably out of guilt, she thought crossly.

'I had wondered about going to see him with Nattie,' Victoria

said, feeling pangs of conscience herself. It would open old wounds,
be challenging and thankless, and Barney, given an inch, would take
a mile of her time and concern. She would never really have faced
such an effortful task without an ulterior motive.

She gave a pale smile and owned up to it. 'If Nattie did come with
me, you see, it might just help, things being as they are between us.'

William eyed her as if to say he'd warned her, she had only herself
to blame, but he refrained from voicing his thoughts and instead
came to give her a kiss.

It was on the mouth and with feeling. They clung for a moment
and she realized how much he resented her wanting to help Barney –
even after all this time.

'Love you,' she said, squeezing his hand, taking comfort from his
jealousy.

William put his cheek to hers by way of goodbye. He stopped at
the door. 'Isn't it time you were off, too?'

She looked at the clock. 'God, yes!' Her bag and camel coat were
on a chair in the hall, red box standing by the door. William hung
on and they went out to their respective cars together. The backup
car was there as well, quite a little fleet of them waiting outside with
engines idling, parked up in the busy South London street.

Victoria had ten precious minutes alone before one of her now regular meetings with the anti-terrorism chief, Luke Andrews, and MI5
Director General, Quentin Clayton, which was sure to plunge her
into even blacker despondency. She picked up *The Post*, whose
restrained, original headline called the road-pricing policy 'Barmy as
a Fruitcake: Political Suicide', but her thoughts were on Nattie.

How would things be when she was home? A gaping chasm had

opened up between them on Monday. Victoria treasured their close-ness. After a few early-teenage teething troubles they'd found a rare understanding: nothing was too sensitive, sinful or embarrassing that it couldn't be shared. Except Ahmed. He seemed to be tugging at the cherished mother–daughter bond like a mistress rocking a marriage. She felt the sting of rejection in Nattie's cold refusal to give him up, an aching yearning to be reunited and back in tune.

Her feelings for Ahmed were real, though, they shone out like the proclaiming beam of a lighthouse, there for all to see. And the warmth of Nattie's spontaneous loyalty made it very hard to believe ill of the young man. He was certainly making her happy – as William had strenuously declared.

But just suppose Ahmed had divided loyalties and was involved in some way? Could anything be worse? Nattie would be inconsolable, broken.

Victoria felt plagued with nerves and trepidation about seeing her daughter later, praying William wouldn't get tied up at the office. It was hard to think of her own testing day ahead. Tackling the prob-lem of Barney together might possibly help build bridges, she thought, but it could hardly be brought up the moment Nattie walked in the door. Suppose she refused to go along with it? She might easily, they were hardly on speaking terms, after all.

Tony came in. 'The Director General's here, on his way up.'

'He's first – and early. That's a first in itself, Tony!'

Tony smiled. 'The Assistant Commissioner isn't far behind. And I believe they now know the source of the leaked information.'

'But no one's being held?'

Tony looked uncomfortable. 'I think not. The Assistant Commissioner will fill you in.'

He left her and returned with Quentin, then slipped out again to meet Luke Andrews. Alone with the Director General, Victoria smiled. He couldn't be seeing much of his family these days, she said. And nor could she, he responded smoothly. Neither of them made any reference to Ahmed Khan.

Andrews arrived – along with the coffee trolley. Sylvia, who trundled it round, was cheerful and wore glitter-frame glasses. She saw to their needs with much chat and chinking of government white and gold chinaware, which held them up for a while.

As soon as she'd left Victoria looked at the police chief. 'You've made progress on finding who was the source of the information about the waste, Luke. Can you tell me all you know?'

He rested his coffee cup, squared his sizeable shoulders and got going.

'We were looking for someone who knew all about the scheduling and movement of waste, obviously,' he said. 'We were able to rule out the authorities responsible for the sites, contactors doing related work and civil servants in Whitehall. After that we narrowed the search down to a logistics manager at Sellafield or Drigg. They have everyday access to schedules,' Andrews explained, 'every reason to study them in detail, it's their job. A logistics manager would have known the level of security deployed and the conditioning stage of the waste travelling between sites.

'I believe, incidentally, it was decided not to alter the security levels on the night of the ambush because it might have drawn attention to the fact that it was an irregular transfer, High Level Waste that wasn't cast in glass.

'The canister taken was at the calcified stage – when it looks like coffee granules and is easily dispersed,' Andrews went on, tediously stating the grim known facts.

'You've identified a particular logistics manager, Luke?' Victoria asked, trying to hide the unreasonable streak of impatience he always seemed to encourage in her.

He was not to be hurried. He took a sip of tepid coffee, returning his cup gingerly to its saucer in the itsy way of someone self-conscious about the clink.

'Yes, we know the man. But I would first like to go over the various stages.' Andrews smiled. 'As we're all aware, huge quantities of liquid High Level Waste constantly arrive at Sellafield to be conditioned and stored. Waste begins its conditioning process by being calcified, is then combined with glass beads, known as glass frit – that's the vitrification stage – then heated in a furnace and finally poured into containers as a melt. The containers are welded shut, decontaminated and put into air-cooled store.'

Victoria had to concede it was helpful to be reminded of the process. He hadn't, though, probably out of delicacy, gone into what had brought about the terrible lapse of security. Only a civil servant had known about it, yet the Energy Minister had to take responsibility and it was the government's wretched cross to bear.

The Vitrification Plant being partially shutdown for repairs had been the cause. With quantities of waste continuing to arrive, an alarming backlog had built up and the storage capacity for HLW at the calcified, coffee-granule stage had been exceeded. Someone had taken the hair-raising decision to store the backlog temporarily at Drigg, just down the track. It was on its transfer back that the train had been ambushed.

She was aware that her attention had wandered when Andrews justifiably cleared his throat. 'Our logistics manager would have known that waste was being stored that wasn't cast in glass,' he said, 'that it was High Level Waste at the calcified stage, and, of course, the date and time of its return transfer, all well in advance.'

Victoria looked from him to Quentin, feeling sudden disbelief. 'But whoever leaked this lethal information to a terrorist cell must have been radicalized and dangerous. How is it possible,' she demanded, 'after strenuous security checks at the time of recruitment and, presumably, regular further checks, for such a person to have gone undetected? Surely his leanings would have come to light?'

Quentin took over, smoothing his hands on his thighs and looking slightly patronizing, although now she thought it was more just his habitual mandarin urbanity.

'We do believe this man's radicalization occurred after his original recruitment,' he began, not sounding at all defensive, despite being on thin ground. 'Logistics isn't, after all, a highly skilled job needing top qualifications – and, you must remember, Home Secretary, the information was only uniquely relevant and sensitive because of a crass decision taken, the irregular transfer of waste for temporary storage.'

She refrained from saying 'touché', which would have pointed up the government's abject position, too much an own-goal. Unless the cell was rounded up fast and calamity averted they might soon be due quite a spell in opposition.

'It is an imprecise area to investigate,' Quentin carried on. 'Assume, for instance, the cell this man was in contact with was unknown to the Service. It would be harder to pick up signs, less reason for suspicion about unusual travel or bank transactions.' Victoria could see the difficulties.

She looked back at Andrews. 'But now we know who this person is, surely it must be possible to track him down? What is his name?'

'Hosaam Asani. The trail has gone cold, I'm afraid, Home Secretary. He was one of only two Asians employed. Sociable, well liked, known to be a believer, although a follower of traditional Islam, according to the checks. Beanpole skinny, one of the lads, known to enjoy a beer. He'd had a holiday in Greece booked and left to go on it two days before the attack. Everything seems to have been consummately planned.'

'He wouldn't have needed a visa for an EU country like Greece,' Victoria said slowly. 'But surely, he could have been picked up there?'

'We immediately traced him to Athens through flight records, but he'd had a few days' start. We think it's likely he was taken by boat to a larger ship in the Mediterranean, probably one bound for Karachi, via the Suez Canal – either boarding it as crew or even stowing away.'

Andrews sat more commandingly upright and gave his Home Secretary a sad look. 'Unfortunately a ship's crew quite often manages to slip into a country without the required visa. It depends a bit on the country . . . This man's family was originally from Pakistan; he knew the lie of his homeland, the language . . . I should think he's already been kitted out with a spanking new passport by his minder and given a large pat on the back for services rendered.'

'Does it suggest a Cumbrian-based cell?'

'None we know of,' Quentin chipped in. 'Might you be thinking of Ahmed Khan's supposed meeting in Cumbria with the man he knows as Fahad?'

Victoria hadn't been. She hadn't got that far. 'Not really. However Fahad did, by all accounts, have an intimate knowledge of the Fells.'

'He could have had walking holidays, gained his experience elsewhere. Always assuming he exists, Fahad could actually be any one of several people, although we've discounted most. Or a "clean skin". And we think there may well be overseas involvement; everything about the ambush indicates that, from the AKs to the leaker's holiday escape route.' Quentin paused. 'Khan mentioned one of his contacts being bean-pole skinny, but from Halifax and with a different name.'

'Wouldn't the names have been false, though, if he's not entirely trusted?' MI5's Director General acknowledged that could be so. There was a good deal more that Victoria wanted to ask him about Ahmed's contacts, but it wasn't appropriate; it was MI5's business, not hers. She suppressed a deep sigh and suspected the others of doing the same. To know who passed on that sensitive information with all its potentially dread consequences and yet to be no further on was like finding a lost map to hidden treasure, only to have it whipped out of your fingers, blown on to a bonfire and swallowed up in the flames.

CHAPTER 23

Victoria left the Home Office for the Commons in a great rush. It was almost seven and she couldn't miss the road pricing vote. It was vitally important and going to be tight, getting it through. Not just to see off the press, although not all the media took William's critical line on the policy, but, with a canister of High Level Waste missing, the political ground was shaking under the government's feet. It was no time to be facing a defeat in the Commons.

Rodney knew all about split-second timing and the car flashed round Parliament Square like a circulating rocket. The division bell hadn't even started to ring as she rushed in through the Members' entrance. There was even time to go to her room and call Nattie, to see she was home and all was well.

After their Arctic parting on Monday, she longed for Nattie to have softened and be warmer. The nervous adrenaline was really punching in, as she brought up Nattie's number, but all she got was her voicemail. She left word to say it would be great if they could all have supper together; a chicken was going in the oven the moment she got home. She hoped Teresa, her small smiling Portuguese daily, had prepared the veg, laid the table.

The division bell began clanging and Victoria hurried to join the milling MPs in Members' Lobby. It was a full turnout with such a close vote, everyone jostling and joking, looking smug or anxious. To be in the crush in that lofty Gothic hallway gave a feeling of living history, it was Westminster letting out its genie and casting its spell, a place of decision-taking, oratory, a place where hopes were realized and dashed.

There were statues of past Prime Ministers on their plinths round the Lobby, all looking on with a variety of expressions. Lloyd George, Thatcher, Atlee; Churchill's with its burnished toe. Touching it was supposed to bring luck to a Member about to speak in the Chamber and it had become polished over time to a gleaming pinky-bronze.

The government Whips were eagle-eyed sentinels ushering their MPs into the Aye Lobby, while the opposition Whips busily encouraged any rebels to vote with the Noes. The two voting lobbies ran down either side of the Chamber with tall desks at the end where clerks crossed names off the list as MPs filed out singly. And Whips stood by as well, counting the departing heads. Bound copies of Hansard lined the walls and narrow benches gave MPs somewhere to sit and natter.

Shifting slowly along in the Aye Lobby, Victoria groaned inwardly when Brian Evans leaped up from a bench. Being nobbled by backbenchers was an occupational hazard – a wearisome one when it was Brian, whom William had once described as having the intellect of a Teletubby. He was sure to have some pet loopy notion to put to her or a whinge about immigration.

'Ah, Victoria! I do want a quick word. My constituents, you know, are up in arms about the—'

'Any other time, Brian,' she flashed him her most glowing smile, 'but I'm in a rush to get home and see my daughter – I'm sure you'll understand.'

She hung on for the result of the vote, trying to avoid Brian in the crush of volatile MPs pushing to find room on the benches. The atmosphere was electric; up in the press gallery political commentators were leaning forward, thirsting for blood.

The two pairs of Whips came in and the numbers were given. 'The Ayes have it, the Ayes have it.' The government had won by fourteen, just all right, given their smallish majority of forty. Victoria hoped it wouldn't mean correspondingly miserable luck at home.

She was back home quickly and, going in the gate, feeling desperately apprehensive, she commiserated with the policeman on duty for a moment about the wet blustery night. The garden seemed eerily to add to her tension, with ink-black shadows beyond the pool of porch-light and dripping leaves. The tall camellia bushes looked darkly foreboding, like two prescient guards. Everything was contributing to a spiralling feeling of turmoil within her.

First thing, Victoria thought, as well as getting a grip, was to turn on the oven if the chicken was ever going to cook in time. Would William be held up at the office? Would Nattie have plans? What chance of a family supper together? A little more of one possibly, if Ahmed was still in Leeds.

Tom had said he thought Nattie would be in. He seemed to accept his role as go-between, although Victoria felt a slight drawing back – he was another of Ahmed's fans. She felt desolate, ostracized and ganged-up-on, with no sympathetic ear, no parental shoulder to weep on. Her own parents would take their granddaughter's side, she was sure.

A distressing thought hit home as she shut the front door. Tom's basement flat had its own entrance; he could ask Ahmed round. That would be so humiliating, Nattie slipping down there the whole time; it would be a mockery.

The music was loud, coming up from the basement. *Back to Black* was playing: Amy Winehouse. Tom's booming iPod flipped to an old Beatles song, 'While My Guitar Gently Weeps'. No good weeping, Victoria thought, trying to contain her thudding heart; no tears.

She knocked on the internal door to the basement, which was slightly ajar. 'Hi, both of you,' she called down. 'You there, Nattie darling? Welcome home!'

Nattie came and stood at the bottom of the stairs, but without looking up or holding out her arms. 'Hello, Mum,' she said, her eyes cast slightly to the side.

She was making it impossible for Victoria to go down and have a homecoming hug. 'Wonderful you're home. It's been a long term,' Victoria said desperately, having to compete with the music. 'You okay for supper about nine? William should be back by then.'

'We'll be around,' Nattie mumbled, as though needing to include Tom for protection. She turned and disappeared into the basement dark.

Victoria hurried to the kitchen where she had a surprise. The oven was on, just reaching the right temperature, its light going dim. Nattie must have found the mobile message, known her mother's timing would be tight.

It was unexpected and hope-giving: the chicken was ready prepared in a pot, a half-lemon in its middle, a packet of tarragon beside it. They were a very herby household after years of Barney teaching his daughter his gourmet ways. Victoria smiled inwardly, thinking Nattie must be itching to come and take over. She did love cooking.

She felt absurdly happy, shoving the bird in the oven, setting about making bread sauce, preparing a fruit salad.

Her uplifted feeling was short-lived. William was home in time, Nattie and Tom did shuffle up from the basement and take their places, but the meal was hardly the most riotous or relaxed of family occasions. It felt like the first night of entertaining a sullen unresponsive child on a foreign exchange, everyone struggling. Nattie and Tom murmured together about whether to go to Glastonbury or the V Festival next summer; it felt a deliberate shutting-out exercise.

William looked crumpled and seemed still in the office, as though preoccupied by some big story that needed thought and action. He soon snapped out of it, though, and began making a positive effort and she loved him dearly for it.

'I had a funny time at a "Women in Health" charity lunch today, Nats,' he said, determinedly involving her while including them all. '*The Post* is its main sponsor and I have to show my face, but these events can be uphill going. The chief executive's a round little barrel of a woman, very well meaning. I'd told her last time that a top table was old hat these days and wouldn't it be good to sit at random tables for a change.

'She didn't seem to take offence and the upshot was I found myself sitting between two extremely glamorous young women today, very appropriately healthy-looking.'

'I'm getting quite jealous,' Victoria said, only half joking.

'No, it's relevant,' he grinned. 'You see, one couldn't stop talking about her meticulous plans for her funeral. She wanted an aria from Tosca, a wicker-basket coffin interwoven with ivy, strewn with lilies . . . I told her a wickerwork coffin might leak, which caused her to go a little white.'

'What about the lady on your other side?' Tom prompted.

'Ah! She talked about staring into her fridge for so long, trying to remember what she'd gone for, that its door-open warning buzzer always started up.'

'At least,' Nattie muttered, 'they weren't obsessed with terrorists and bombs.'

It was an insinuating, cutting remark and it clung to the atmosphere like stale cigar smoke; the fallout enveloped them in a cloud. Back to square one, Victoria thought dismally. And it was so childish and un-Nattie-like. She more than anyone, because of Ahmed, knew the incredible grimness and immediacy of the situation. A radioactive bomb could kill thousands in a crowded public place; it could contaminate an area for miles.

'You don't mind being obsessed about funerals?' William inquired dryly, making clear he thought Nattie was out of order.

'I do that business with the fridge,' Tom said brightly, trying overhard to defuse things, 'standing gawping into it in a daze. I wish I had a buzzer on mine!'

Victoria felt grateful for William's loyal support. She started talking about Tony, her private secretary, whom she'd discovered had a passion for potholing. No one paid any attention. Even William couldn't pretend to be interested.

Tom soon peeled off and went back to his basement. Nattie mumbled about being tired and disappeared upstairs.

William made coffee while Victoria tidied things away in heavy silence. He put it ready on the table and came behind her, crossing his arms over her breasts and kissing her hair. 'Come and sit down – we can't have this collapse. I've got things to tell you, anyway.'

'Sorry!' She turned in his arms, looking shamefaced then pulled out a chair and watched as he poured the coffee, trying hard not to appear too dragged down.

He caught her eye. 'How's your best mate, Peter Barnes? Still giving trouble?' William was grinning and even, it could be said, looking rather cocky. He must be about to have yet another go at him, presumably some dig at Peter's petty feuding or arrogant lack of diplomacy. Hardly ideal traits in a Foreign Secretary, Victoria thought sourly – although she knew more now, and far worse. She'd been feeling incensed for the last couple of days, ever since hearing again from her friend, Nick Bates. He'd made new discoveries about Barnes's conduct that had shocked her rigid.

Nick loathed the man almost more than she did and, after the mutual moan they'd had a couple of weeks back – when he'd mentioned his aunt, a councillor in the Foreign Secretary's constituency, having serious concerns – he had promised to keep her posted.

His aunt had been worried about Barnes's overkeen interest in a local planning application. Nick's most recent call had been to say she had reported back on the council's decision. Barnes had got his way, swayed the council, the additional housing had been approved, but Nick had thought to ask the name of the owner of the land who stood to make a great killing.

It seemed far-fetched, but Victoria had wondered if the land could be connected in any way with the Covent Garden opera-singer whom Barnes was discreetly seeing. There was a connection. The land was registered in her married name.

Victoria had felt disgusted. The Foreign Secretary, smoothing the financial path of his feted opera singer girlfriend? It was a shameful abuse of political position and power. And taking such a crass stupid risk . . . To be exposed for having an affair was one thing, probably survivable. 'The man's only human,' people would have said. But had Peter Barnes become so arrogant now, he considered himself impregnable, above normal codes? If they weren't in such a crisis situation, Nick had said, he'd have been tempted to slip it to the press.

Just Peter Barnes's typical luck, she thought tiredly, well aware he was still on her back, bleating about the security risks of her marriage, wanting her sacked, demoted, paying the price for his bad press – all William's clever pin-sticking journalistic jibes. The Foreign Secretary didn't miss a trick.

William was looking on in amusement. 'I've been watching the cogs going round,' he said, 'seeing you thinking it was about time Barnes had his balls chopped into pieces and fried for tea.'

'Those weren't exactly the thoughts in my head.'

'He may just possibly have it coming to him. Your government isn't, I'm afraid, in for the easiest of rides in the next few days.'

'What the hell's that supposed to mean?' Victoria felt her adrenaline flaring up all over again. Had William really found out all about the planning permission? Nick hadn't dropped hints to the press, she felt sure. The picture, with all its frightening implications, was becoming clear.

William couldn't go for the Foreign Secretary's jugular, not at such a time, not with the country in a state of such high alert. It would be battering a government already slumped on the ropes: the worst possible time. He couldn't – surely he wouldn't do that?

He leaned across the table and squeezed her hand. 'You did kind of let on a while back that Barnes might have stepped a bit far out on to the lake. You weren't just on about his affair, not after us – although ours was in a different class, of course.'

His face softened in a quite unconscious way and Victoria almost stopped feeling enraged. 'So, on the strength of that little untipped wink,' William went on, 'I decided it might just be in the national interest if *The Post* did a little gentle investigating.'

'The *national* interest?' Her heart was hammering again. '*Gentle* investigating? I can't believe this. You can't possibly, seriously, be planning to hole Barnes's boat – not now? That's the opposite of the national interest, for God's sake!'

'Look,' William said, in his powerfully persuasive way, 'the opposition are squabbling like ferrets in a sack, no one's seriously going to call for the government's head right now. The security lapse happened on your watch, but people look to you lot as best placed to sort it. Barnes has behaved abominably, a complete dereliction of duty. He's a dishonest arrogant turd and he's got to go. So you lose a senior minister. Just don't lose too many more.'

He was eyeing her and grinning, looking assertive and confident. 'You never did tip me the wink, of course – I'd almost thought, for one brief titillating, exciting moment, you would – but I suspect, from that deep thinking you were just doing, that you've found out a lot more, just like I have. Shall we compare notes?'

'Don't poke fun,' Victoria said angrily, thinking of bombs, Nattie, all the serious, fundamental things on her plate. 'Peter was never really on the hook from me. I'd have chickened out of telling tales. And not just because of the crisis. I'm a useless dirt-disher.' She glared. 'Few politicians are good at it, you know – unlike the press. You're morality-free zones, answerable to no one, carving up good men and women daily.'

'Bad ones are easier,' William said, 'safer, juicier targets. Going for the great and the good occasionally lands us in the shit.'

'Is it all over tomorrow's paper – whatever it is you're going to accuse him of?'

'Not tomorrow, a few ends to tie up yet. I don't advise warning off Barnes, he might think it all comes from you.' William was trying to be helpful – in his way. 'Perhaps you'll just concede, though,' he smiled, 'that whatever else, I've managed to take your mind off Nattie for a few minutes.'

Victoria felt her lip on the wobble; she bit on it hard. Forget Barnes. Nick Bates would think it came from her, that she'd passed it on . . . She relaxed. He was a friend; he knew her well and would believe her if she said she hadn't. But she *had* tipped William the wink, Victoria thought, just by dropping the merest hint in a weak moment, a suggestion there was something . . . It made her feel slightly dirty, but with only herself to blame.

Did William think it was better she had a little warning of a scandal about to break? She'd complained often enough that he never gave her any. Was there anything to be done? Should she warn the Prime Minister? That would implicate her, though, which she could do without. She just had to sit on her hands and do nothing.

'I'm going to knock on Nattie's door,' she said tightly, getting up from the table, 'just to see if she's talkable to. And I am going to mention about Barney, ask if she'll come with—'

William got up too and came close. He held her face. 'You won't go and see him alone? Will you tell me that straight?' His mouth was hard on hers then, without waiting for an answer. It was his way of pressing his case, saying how much he minded. But what would happen if Nattie wouldn't come with her? Having talked of doing it, promised to help Barney, the commitment had been made. She sighed. There were enough dreadful complications in her life; she couldn't face another.

*

Victoria stood outside Nattie's firmly shut door, knuckles hesitating. She knocked. 'Nattie? Are you there? Can I come in, darling?'

'What do you want, Mum?' she called out without coming near the door.

'Just a quick word about Dad – I'd like to tell you what I've decided. I need your help, but I've been getting started, making a few inquiries.'

'Must it be now? I'm on the phone.'

Of course she would be. Victoria felt hollow. It was lonely, being on the outside. She remembered the intensely private stolen moments, long calls she'd had with William from which she'd drawn such strength and felt a hot burn of jealousy. 'I'll come back then,' she called brightly. 'Ten minutes?'

'I might be quite a bit longer.'

Victoria leaned her forehead on the panelled door feeling exhausted suddenly, utterly shattered. She thought of the call being tapped, MI5 wading through all the reams of transcripts, the passionate outpourings of two young people in love. What a waste of time.

'I've got plenty of work,' she called, lifting her head away from the door. 'I'll leave you as long as you like, but I do want to talk about Dad before bed. I'm off early in the morning and really would like to take you through it – it involves you a little, you see.'

Victoria left it at that and went away for a half-hour. Then she knocked again. Nattie took her time coming to the door and opening it. They stood facing each other, both, she suspected, having thoughts not easily shared. She was anxious. William was watching the end of *Question Time*. He'd be up soon.

Taking a breath she fastened sad eyes on her sullen daughter. 'I am going to try to help Dad. You're right, it's the least I can do. There is a problem, though, which is why I need your help, Nats. William doesn't want me seeing Dad alone. It's silly of him, but . . . will you come and be there when I go? It would ease me in with Dad, help in every way.'

Nattie looked cornered. 'I don't know if I can,' she muttered. 'I may not be free.'

'Just an hour on Sunday night, darling, when I'm back from Hampshire. You and Dad could fix the time.'

'I'll be elsewhere on Sunday.' She gave a petulant sigh. 'All right, I'll speak to him.' She stared at her mother, suddenly looking a miserable child whom Victoria ached to fold up in her arms.

Nattie hardened up again. 'It depends on my plans. I'll text or something. And I'd have to meet you there if it works out, I wouldn't be coming from home.'

CHAPTER 24

English winters had changed, Ahmed thought. As well as milder they seemed so much wetter and stormier. It was blowing a gale again, tearing off loose roof tiles, gusting anything that moved down the street. That was one good thing about wheelie bins: fixed lids. The wind was hammering against his ill-fitting window, the rusty old arm-catch grating and rasping on its prong. It was impossible to get to sleep.

Where were the crisp bright winters of his childhood, sparkly frosts and the air so invigoratingly sharp and chill that going indoors had felt like stepping into a sauna?

He could remember waking up one morning as a very small boy and seeing their patch of garden and the neighbour's path and hedge transformed, glittering and pure white. Ahmed had rushed into his parents, very excited. 'It's snowed!'

'That's frost, silly boy,' his father said. 'It's often white like that when it's a hard frost.'

'No, it's snow, just not much of it, like, well, very short hair – like a white crew cut! Frost is more sort of like smashed glass.'

'Always thinking you know best,' his father had grumbled, 'is

going to get you into a lot of trouble. That's frost; understand? And
don't argue.' Ahmed smiled.

He looked at his watch: twenty past two already. It was all Nattie's
fault, that long call, hearing how upset she'd been on her first evening
home. He was feeling burning impatience to be back in London,
eaten up with need of her.

Sending her a last email might help, Ahmed thought, reaching up
to switch on the spotlight whose neck had developed a droop, like
celery; the light shone annoyingly back on to the wall. He turned it
off and began thinking with affection about his mother and her
litany of complaints all through dinner at the restaurant. The spicy
eggplant was too salty, the saffron sweet pilau short on lemon, the
chicken curry short on cashews. She hadn't been slow on fault-find-
ing. But the slagging-off was part of the fun, the bit she enjoyed; it
added to the occasion.

He tried to clear his mind, but it was no good; sleep wouldn't
come. He kept seeing Nattie's sweet smile and thinking of her wonderful smooth silky thighs – his image of them just at his eyeline
when she'd shaken him awake that first early-morning, bending over
him in a neat pair of skimpy black pants. He'd opened his eyes to
those thighs. He ached to be snug inside them and feeling their grip.

Guilt was keeping him awake, too. It came in various degrees,
different shapes and sizes like a child's educational toy: squares, tri-
angles, crescents that had matching slots. He wanted to tidy his own
away and move on.

He regretted his tetchiness with his parents at dinner when the
whole point had been to say thank you. He'd really flown at them
when they brought up Safa again and he could so easily have brushed
it aside. It was a sensitive area; he'd been thinking of a future with

Nattie that wouldn't happen – and the shock to them if it did. And it had further defeated the object, he thought, rushing to his room the minute they got in. A little conciliatory buttering up from a grateful son had been called for, deference and hugs.

Were they feeling a tinge of relief at his leaving next day, much as they loved him? His parents were getting on, set in their ways; they were probably secretly longing to have the house to themselves again.

Then there was the guilt he felt about Nattie's problems with her mother. She bitterly minded not being able to ask him home and obviously worried dreadfully about his likely sensitivities. It would be as easy as a smile to set her straight – he only had to say that her mother was in an invidious position, that he more than understood, and that Nattie should be a sweeter, kinder daughter. It would smooth both their paths.

But he did feel sensitive and resentful. The sudden powerful presentiment he'd had, about dying at Fahad's hand, was playing into it – especially at three in the morning – and making him feel it all the more strongly. Couldn't the authorities fucking trust him one jot, he thought furiously, when he was putting his fucking life on the line?

Would it have been the same if he'd been a Christian Brit working for *The Post* and going undercover on a mission? Ahmed thought not. He wanted Nattie to keep up her wall of reserve, wanted her mother to go on feeling the weight of the emotional blows. At least he had the warmth of Nattie's unquestioning loyalty.

He recalled again his awe and admiration, watching the Home Secretary make that statement, the night of the Leicester Square bomb. Had his awareness of her as a woman been in some weird telepathic anticipation of falling in love with her daughter? And now he was being denied the chance even to exchange a few words. It mattered to him, getting to know Nattie's mother and burying his resentment.

She was wrong not to trust him, but he knew at heart she was right to think Nattie was vulnerable by association. There were risks in them going about together, being seen around Brixton . . . It was asking too much. Beckham had more chance of becoming President of America, he thought, than for him to find the willpower to keep away.

Shouldn't he at least stay in Leeds, chatting up Yazid till Sunday night? The odds on any more hints or clues seemed remote. And the man had no principles or vision: his horizons stretched about as far as the load of a drunk's projected vomit. No, Yazid was the vomit, a stinky mess of the stuff, and Ahmed couldn't wait to be gone.

The compromise, he thought, settling on his side, was to have a Friday evening drink with Yazid before leaving. Nattie would understand if he was back late. They could still have the night in Brixton and, with Jake off to his parents in Oxford, the flat to themselves . . .

A shiver ran through him. It was too perfect. The weekend was sure to be kiboshed in some way, sure as birds sang in back gardens and rivers flowed.

He hoped not with blood. He was thinking of dirty bombs, of his own people trying to impose an extremist political ideology on the world and of his own deep feelings of failure.

'Hi, Yazid, okay day at work?' Ahmed inquired, standing up as the man he'd come to despise approached his table. It was Yazid's choice of café, in Karnac Road off the A58 and painfully close to where Khalid had died. 'Tea? Coffee? Anything to eat?' he asked, as they both sat down.

Yazid was in a shiny-silver padded jacket, which seemed a mistake with his monkish haircut; it gave him the look of an astronaut about to be launched. 'I'll take tea,' he said graciously, arranging the jacket on the back of his chair. 'They should have green téa on the menu,' he remarked, looking round, 'it's all the rage at the university. I am having good success with the students, you know,' he added, looking insufferably pleased with himself. 'There's a lot of interest.'

'Leena was a student there, wasn't she?' Ahmed asked, when a yawning beefy-armed waitress had slopped down two cups of tea. 'She hasn't come back?' He was curious as to how Yazid might react.

'No sign of her.' Yazid lowered his voice. 'I suspect her family's tracked her down and she's on a visit to Pakistan. Her brother hinted at that! We might not be seeing her again—' He winked.

Ahmed itched to land a fist on his nose. He thought it figured, though. Leena's father and brother would have detested the embarrassment of a successful escape, they'd want to put it about that she'd been dispatched out to relatives to be 'disciplined'.

He stared at Yazid and said as neutrally as possible, 'All she did was fall in love – which can happen to any of us! I feel sorry for the girl.'

'I don't. She brought disgrace and dishonour to her family.' Yazid looked bored, he couldn't care less about Leena. 'So,' he said, his eyes flicking round the near-empty café, 'you're off back south again. Why are you going tonight? I thought you didn't work Saturdays. Is it that girl? Isn't that why you've taken your father's car a few times?'

Ahmed knew he'd been seen once, not that he'd been quite so closely monitored. And Yazid was asking questions, he'd remembered about the Saturdays off . . . But then keeping his eyes skinned was the main task Fahad had set for him – all he was thought good for. It was still worrying. Fahad certainly didn't trust him.

'Taking the car caused some upsets at home,' he said lazily. 'Mum went ballistic! She guessed what it was all about. That girl was a great shag for a train pickup, but I'm straight back to London tonight. My boss at work wants me around tomorrow. There's some demonstration; animal rights, I think. Sounds like an eff-awful yawn.'

He grinned. 'Back to the old routine again, fuck it! More tea?' Yazid shook his head. 'Sure?' Ahmed pressed, burning to get away. It seemed worth having one last push. 'I feel privileged to have met Fahad,' he said smarmily. 'What incredible ability and daring! It's felt like being on a film set these last couple of weeks, being in on all the drama and meeting the stars, so to speak. And now I'm back down south! I'll be so impatient for the climax – marking off the days. Is the date set?'

'My lips are sealed,' Yazid said, with an expression of sumptuous smugness.

It was a flat dead end. Ahmed hadn't expected a golden egg, but had wistfully hoped for some little gem he could have taken away to examine all its facets.

He'd learned nothing. Only, he thought morosely, that Fahad was way ahead of him and had almost certainly never trusted him a millimetre. He'd been playing games, flirted with the idea that Ahmed could have his uses, spun the odd yarn to try to gum up the works a bit, but all the while keeping the upper hand.

And Fahad wasn't a man for loose ends; he'd want to pick off a traitor mole, Ahmed felt sure, when he was less preoccupied with whatever horror was planned.

He shivered inwardly and concentrated on Yazid again, giving a little shrug and attempting to give an understanding look about the need for sealed lips.

'Well, guess I'd better be off,' he said, picking up his jacket. 'Dad's taking me to the station.' He managed a smile. 'It's been great, catching up and having some time with the brothers. Might see you at the end of the month? I'm sure to be up with the family in the Christmas break.'

His mobile sounded loudly. Its jazzy ring came as a shock; Ahmed was still unused to the new tone. One of his little nephews had changed it, prodding him and saying endlessly, 'This one, Uncle? This one?'

He felt edgy, fishing hurriedly in his jacket top pocket for the phone. Nattie knew he was with Yazid, she'd only ring in an emergency. Safa possibly? Calling back with Leena's decision? No, it was sure to be about a mobile phone upgrade or some hard-sell cold call.

It was his editor. Ahmed's adrenaline flowed. Osborne must be about to put the boot in and come on strong over Nattie. Shit. He couldn't do that; he had no right . . . Leaving the call to go on to voicemail he stood up abruptly and went to pay for the tea. Yazid had put on his astronaut's padded jacket by the time he came back; he slung on his own jacket feeling the lack of a winter coat and they left the café together. Outside he gave Yazid's shoulder a light parting punch and set off briskly for home. Yazid, thankfully, was going the other way.

With enough distance between them and a noisy wind for extra protection he called Osborne back. 'Sorry I couldn't pick up, I was with Yazid, the council worker.' His mobile was tight to his ear, his pulse speeding like a wound-up toy car. 'Is anything wrong?' he asked.

'I think you should get back to London,' Osborne said strongly. 'Our insider at *The Courier* has tipped us off; they've got a story on you and Nattie in tomorrow's paper. Shelby – whom I'm sure you know all about – has been spouting, the little cunt, saying God knows what to one of their lousy columnists.'

It didn't come much worse. Ahmed felt a rise of bile in his throat, his melodramatic imaginings had just become a lot closer to hard reality. And what about his parents? They'd read about it soon enough. Fuck Shelby, fuck, fuck.

'I was coming back tonight anyway,' he said. 'I'm really sorry to be the cause of all this. If only Nattie could have been spared it, but I suppose it was kind of inevitable that Shelby would try something on. We don't, um, know what he's saying?'

'Well, it won't be a glowing endorsement. You'd better try to drum up some tale for your Leeds chums. Which won't be easy. There'll be a bit of follow-up media too, cameras out for a happy snap – you know how it works. And given the view your Leeds cell might take of all this, I wouldn't advise being seen with Nattie this weekend.'

'Does she know yet?' Ahmed hated the thought of having to break it to her. And the thought of not seeing her . . . The acuteness of his plight was beginning to bite deep.

'I'm about to have a word with her now,' Osborne said. 'Talk it through, figure out what's best. She'll call then, I'm sure. You'll need to watch your back – even tonight. The papers are on sale at main London stations from ten-thirty after all.'

'I'd really appreciate you telling Nattie,' Ahmed said. 'I'll ring Yazid as soon as I'm on the train and try to patch up the gaping holes in my cover.'

'We'll do a story ourselves, for tomorrow's paper,' Osborne commented, as though his mind was running ahead. 'About you meeting at the party, love at first sight, some angle like that – spike *The Courier*'s guns.'

Ahmed wished they would leave well alone. His parents took *The Post*. But it made no difference, he thought wearily. A streetful of neighbours and friends would be round waving the paper before the first kettle of the day had boiled.

'It'll be a short burst of press,' his editor carried on, 'no great legs to the story. But you will need a cool head and sharp eyes in the back of it now. You might have been sniffing out terrorists, but I think the situation's just been reversed.'

Bound for London on a Friday night the train was fairly full. Ahmed had said nothing to his parents about the story. Warning them in advance was too complicated, better to wait for their hysterical call next day.

Why hadn't Nattie called? Surely Osborne must have talked to her by now. Where could they go? How could they meet? He felt almost tearful. Emotional, too, about Osborne's support. Ahmed didn't think he was misreading things, but feeling the trust was genuine made him all the more desperate for some tiny measure of success. He had to have a flash, a flicker of memory, and find a way of seeing into Fahad's mind.

Which meant calling Yazid and trying to spin a yarn, he thought, but how the hell did you prove yourself a good loyal terrorist's friend when the papers were talking up your love affair with the Home Secretary's daughter?

He looked round. The carriage was full and it wasn't an easy call to make at the best of times . . . There was always the john, Ahmed thought, taking his bag with his laptop and pushing along the

carriage. The smell of piss was more dominant than disinfectant and
he was already queasy with nerves; his hands were sweaty, heart thudding. He sat on the pan, took a long breath and finally called.

'Hi, Yazid, you okay to talk a minute? There's something I didn't
come clean about earlier and it's on my mind – especially as it's in
tomorrow's papers. That call in the café was from my boss, actually,
and he's just told me.'

'Oh, yes?' Yazid sounded suspicious. 'Well, let's hear it,' he said
coldly.

'It's about that girl I've been seeing, that shag. Only she's not the
pickup on the train, just hard to explain so I chickened out!'

Complete silence: Ahmed felt panicky. He hurried on. 'I met the
one I've been seeing through the paper, actually – at a party for her
stepfather who's the editor. She's at Durham University. I've been
driving up there—'

'So what's so hard to explain? Is this the fat slob editor you work
with?'

'No, the paper's editor-in-chief; this girl's mother is the Home
Secretary, you see – not that you'd think so, seeing her with all those
Kafir students at Durham, all stoned out of their tiny fucking minds.
I've actually been hoping,' Ahmed said quickly, trying not let Yazid
in again, 'that back in London she'd ask me home. I'd really hoped
for the chance of a good crafty snoop and being able to come up
with something useful for you. But I've fucked up all round! Her
mother's found out she's seeing a Muslim and I'm banned from the
house. And now her ex-fuck has shit-arsed on me and slagged me off
in our rival paper, *The Courier*.'

'And I'm really supposed to believe all this, this Home Secretary
garbage?'

'Well, you'll read about it tomorrow. It'll be there in the paper like a sore thumb.'

'So that explains a lot, I'd say,' Yazid snorted. 'That really takes the piss.'

Between the stink of the stuff all around him and his nerves, Ahmed swallowed back nausea. Cold sweat was pricking on his forehead. 'What are you getting at?' he asked, trying to keep his voice light.

'You're London trash, thinking you know it all the whole time. Too snotty to ask our advice . . . You were that near picking off the fucking Home Secretary? For fuck's sake! And you have to go and blow it? God, what a missed opportunity.' Ahmed could hear the excitable frustration in Yazid's whining, condescending tone.

'I sure have blown it,' he said contritely, knowing that brighter minds would see it very differently, see him for the sham impostor that he was.

Fahad knew any young reporter on a top national paper had to be sharp as a new-blade razor. He'd been suspicious of Ahmed from the start and if he ever needed more cast-iron proof . . . 'You know what happens to brothers we can't trust,' he had threatened, out on that Fells walk. The menacing words were still loud in Ahmed's ears.

A hefty fist on the loo door set up some competition and a megaphone voice yelled angrily, 'What's going on in there? You shitting for fucking Britain or what?'

Ahmed called back humbly that he'd be out in a sec. Yazid was still on the line and he muttered, 'Must go, people waiting. I'm in the lav.' It seemed an entirely suitable place for calling Yazid, he thought, which was probably for the very last time.

He opened the door and slipped smartly past the irate door-basher who swore handsomely in his wake. The jazzy tone of his mobile started up then; Nattie was ringing.

'Just let me get somewhere I can talk,' he said, making for a between-carriage area where there was a square of people-free space. 'Don't go away!' He had never been more in need of her call.

'Your phone's been busy an absolute age. I've been desperate! I can't bear to think how awful this is for you. Shelby must have wheedled a few clues out of Milly, sussed you were doing some kind of undercover work . . . God, he does know how to do maximum damage. And he gets away with it too, which is so unfair. I just wish I could think he had it coming.'

Nattie wasn't, Ahmed thought in astonishment, sounding at all down. Her voice had a real bounce that was baffling. He knew how to do in Shelby all right, he thought – although not in a way she'd want. *The Post* would be very interested to investigate Shelby's drug dealings and his newsworthy clients like her friend, Hugo, the Cabinet Minister's son . . . It was hardly the time, but his urge to hit back was growing.

'I'll be waiting by the barrier,' Nattie carried on, astounding him some more. 'Don't miss me! William's been so terrific, I can't tell you. And Tom. Who on earth were you talking to for so long, by the way?'

'Yazid. Just trying in vain to save my skin! But hold on, darling Nattie – does William know about you coming to the station? He thought we should lie low and avoid more press attention. I really don't think . . .' He let his words trail away, aching to see her much too much and feeling helpless. And the damage was done, after all.

'William knows. We've got it all mapped out for the whole weekend. I can't wait to see you. Must go, I'm at the tube and I don't want your train getting in before I'm even there!'

She couldn't do that, leave him hanging in the air without a clue, Ahmed thought; how could anything be more frustratingly cruel? He went back to his seat feeling alive again – and wanting to stay that way. His morbid sense of defeat was out of the window. No more cold sweats and nausea, a single call from Nattie had made him full of fight and determination, passionately needing to see her again. Ten past ten: was there ever going to be a longer twenty minutes?

CHAPTER 25

Ahmed could see Nattie at the barrier. She had him in her sights too, and waved frantically. He was pushing through a logjam of passengers, trying not to trip over all the wheeled bags or biff any old ladies with his swaying rucksack. The mix of travellers was always hard to fathom – where were they going at ten-thirty at night? His laptop case weighed a ton with the accumulated junk of four weeks out of the office – reference books, articles, notebooks; the sides of the bag were stuffed to bulging.

Closer to the gate he noticed people giving Nattie looks. They always did, although seeing such a huge elated smile on her lovely face, they were following her eyes to see where it was aimed. Ahmed was rigidly tense about *The Courier*. He'd been brought up to avoid shows of emotion, but nothing could have held him back or embarrassed him. He just wanted to reach Nattie and crush the breath out of her.

'And the train was even on time!' she yelled out, beaming. As he reached her and dumped down his bag, her glorious smile shadowed with sudden anxiety. 'Promise you're not too uptight? You mustn't be.'

'Far from it.' He kissed her long and hard; the whole of King's Cross could have drawn up chairs to watch for all he noticed or cared. She tasted so sweet, so wonderful.

'Come on, we need a taxi and there'll be a queue. I can't wait to tell you the plan!' She had an excited gleam in her eyes, pulling urgently on his hand before he could even pick up his bag.

Elated though he felt himself, Ahmed still found her buoyed-up bounciness bemusing. He couldn't think what she'd hatched up with William. 'Tell me what's going on here,' he panted, trying to keep up and hold an arm round her. 'You cut me off mid-call on the train, leave me high and dry with no clues. Where's this taxi taking us, at least?'

'Not far,' Nattie said, with her infectious smile, 'then it's a magical mystery tour.'

Standing in the straggling line for cabs and feeling noticed, aware of people's fidgety stares, Ahmed's feet began to touch the ground more firmly. He looked searchingly up and down the queue as if expecting to see Fahad there, calmly appraising him. He couldn't help a grain of impatience setting in.

'I need to tell the cab where we're going,' he muttered peevishly, wanting to be in charge. 'William thought you shouldn't come to Brixton—'

'I know. Let me sort the taxi,' Nattie smiled, 'and I'll fill you in as we go.'

They were at last at the head of the queue. 'William says it can go on expenses,' she said, as one drew up and they got in

She gave her home address in Kennington. It came as a shock. Sitting back, Ahmed squeezed her hand tight and raised his eyebrows skywards. 'What gives?'

Nattie only smiled. He felt a crushing tension; he couldn't believe her mother had softened that much, it didn't seem in character. They must just be dropping Nattie off, he thought, and her keyed-up mood was all about something next day. He'd blithely assumed they'd have the night together, if not the weekend. Elation had been a glorious suppressor, a snug blanket over his nerves. Now fear was elbowing it out, he could feel it cold on his skin, spreading steadily like an oil slick.

Ahmed looked back at her. 'Don't we get to be alone at all with this plan of yours?' He touched her long gossamer hair. The feeling of hollowness was unbearable; he cupped her face, held her eyes. Her skin was so delicate, he thought, aching with need, it allowed her inner giving self to show through, and that unique golden glow.

She was looking expectant. His fingers went to her hair again, winding it round for a tighter grip. He wanted to pull her close and kiss her, she was waiting for it, eager, but he could only stare.

'What is it?' she asked softly.

'Just . . . stuff.'

She brushed over his lips. 'Tom's lending us his car. We're calling at his flat to collect it.' She lowered her voice, glancing towards the cabbie. 'And we can see *The Courier* and *The Post*, William was going to drop them in. Then we're off! Staying at a hotel near Oxford. And tomorrow—'

Ahmed didn't need to know about tomorrow. His mouth found hers; he devoured her. He told her what a twat he felt. 'I thought we must be delivering you home.'

'I've booked us in at the Bear in Woodstock,' Nattie said. 'It's hardly a hidden-away nook, but it's on the way, we'll be getting there late and they have night porters and stuff. It's pre-paid – William says it's a little early Christmas present.'

'No!' Ahmed's emotions were yo-yoing from one extreme to another, he knew, but he felt quite insulted. 'That really carves me up. We don't go unless I can take you. Sorry, but you're going to have to call and undo that.'

She banged on the glass divide and called to the driver. 'It's right here. The one with the trellis on top of the wall.'

Ahmed paid off the cab. 'I'll call the hotel myself and rebook with my card,' he muttered, hating his own bitterness. But a luxurious night together was too precious and beyond expectation to be a handout; it felt demeaning, anticlimactic. It meant a lot to be the giver and feel ownership. He could handle borrowing Tom's car in the circumstances, though. That was different.

'You're very proud,' Nattie said, tucking an arm awkwardly through his as he handled his luggage. 'And prickly!'

She kissed his cheek, said, 'Hi,' to the policeman in the garden then led Ahmed down some slightly dank, stone basement steps. Leaves were swirling and collecting by the door; the gloomy base-ment stairwell wasn't helping his mood.

His sudden sourness was all about a build-up of tension and nerves; being in the house where he wasn't wanted, whether in Tom's flat or not – about to discover what damage Shelby had done. 'Sorry!' he whispered, squeezing her hand, trying to make amends.

Tom's welcome was warm. 'Hi, both! Come on in. Train good? Coffee? Wine?'

'It's fantastic of you, all this,' Ahmed said effusively, feeling ill at ease.

Nattie was kissing Tom's cheek and obviously feeling the opposite. 'Don't give him wine with the driving,' she laughed. 'Your car, remember! Can we have tea?' It was just what Ahmed felt like. 'Is it bad, the stuff in the papers, Tom?' she asked. 'I can't believe Shelby's talked up being ditched – surely he'd hate people thinking that?'

'He's certainly talked up himself, the shit slime-bag,' Tom said. 'It's a truth-lite piece, but I'm sure that comes across. Your mum won't like it, Nats! Have a look while I put the kettle on. Dad's done you both proud, though – and he gets much bigger readership!'

Tom went into the kitchen. Ahmed dumped his gear and stayed in the small hallway to call the hotel. He prayed there was enough in his account to cover the room-rate. When his card was approved the relief was intense. It mattered to him, being the provider. He followed Nattie into the living room with a feeling of possessive satisfaction.

The whole flat smelled of turps and oils, artist's paraphernalia, and there was a stack of Tom's paintings against the walls. A plain grey sofa had a colourful throw of embroidered squares; it was beautifully stitched and looked quite like the one his parents had, which was made by Afghan refugees in one of the camps round his father's home town of Peshawar.

'That's from Tom's gran,' Nattie said, following his gaze, 'Ursula's mother. His grandfather was a diplomat and I think it comes from Pakistan.'

The Courier and *The Post* were on a makeshift table, just a sheet of solid glass over two giant wicker hampers. Ahmed picked up *The Courier* with a tightening of his gut and soon found the double-page interview piece with Shelby.

It was headlined 'The Cheryl Jones Interview', and the strapline read, 'Home Secretary's Links to Terrorist Suspects'. That was gross, Ahmed thought violently.

Shelby was photographed, looking glamorous in a crisp open-neck shirt, sitting cross-legged, plying his most engaging grin. There was a stunning picture of Nattie, one of her mother looking pained . . . none of himself. *The Post* would have found one, he thought proprietorially, but then it was a far classier and more successful paper.

He began reading, feeling dangerous hatred. 'Shelby Tait, the brilliant young financier son of impresario Marcus Tait, talks about his recent split from the Home Secretary's daughter, Natalia, and his deep concerns over the new man in her life.'

There was a puke-making intro about Shelby's broken heart – how anyone could possibly give him up was beyond Cheryl Jones, it seemed. She really laid it on about his captivating appeal, his financial success '. . . and so delightfully reticent. "I'm more facilitator than financier," he told me charmingly. "I help people do deals . . ."'

Ahmed read that he was a terrible influence in Nattie's life with his dubious activities and highly suspicious contacts. 'Nattie's fellow students have been very concerned: he's been turning up at two in the morning, leaving at four . . .'

Cheryl Jones reported that Shelby had left Durham once, in the small hours, and seen Ahmed having a roadside meeting with three men in another car.

The lying worm, he thought, turning to *The Courier*'s editorial on another page. It was a cause for great alarm, the paper ranted, that a reporter acting so suspiciously should have complete freedom of access to immediate members of the Home Secretary's family. It was a shocking risk at such a time of high alert – hadn't there been enough lapses of security? And shouldn't the Home Secretary be worried too, simply as a mother of a vulnerable teenager?

The paper harped on about wider security issues, her marriage to an unreliable newspaper editor. It was well known that the Foreign

Secretary – a man of impeccable integrity – believed it a very unsatis-
factory state of affairs, however high his regard for his comely colleague.
A graceful departure was called for, in *The Courier's* view. The Prime
Minister should be capable of wielding the knife and she should go.

Nattie had come to read over his shoulder; her nearness was intoxicating. 'Peter Barnes is always bitching and briefing against Mum,'
she said. 'He's such an arsehole.'

Ahmed looked up and kissed her lips. 'I keep in touch,' he said,
'and the word's out at *The Post* that we might be about to do him.
Not before time.'

'God, that would shiver up the government!' Tom said, coming in
with the tea. 'How bad is *The Courier* stuff for you, Ahmed? Does
Dad's piece help at all?'

Ahmed thought of his parents reading it . . . The piece in *The Post*,
a big lead item in the diary column, was all about hitting it off at the
party, love at first sight – there was even a large picture of himself and
Nattie, laughing into each other's eyes. They'd obviously been too
engrossed to notice any camera flashes.

'My family will get a surprise!' he said lightly. 'And though I feel
terrifically proud and it'll usefully spike *The Courier*, I can't honestly
say it's much help in other ways.'

'You mean it blows your cover?' Tom said, getting the message.

'Well, yes. But my baddies are going to twig that whatever. Shelby
knew what he was doing all right!' Ahmed thought how much more
acutely his life was in danger now. He couldn't share that with
anyone, certainly not Nattie; she mustn't start sensing any of his fear.

They were in a four-poster bed in an end-of-corridor room, char-
acterful and beamed, freshly decorated. It was in the hotel's annexe,

to Ahmed's relief. Arriving in the early hours they'd only had to see the night porter for the key.

He felt supremely safe and contented, lying with Nattie in his arms; he licked her shoulder and trailed her arm with light fingers. She shivered deliciously and he felt himself stir. 'How can I have possibly found you?' he murmured.

'Through your job – like most people do.'

'Don't be so prosaic and routine. Can't you join me on a higher plane?'

'I'm very happy with my own level, thank you. How late do they do breakfast – did you look?'

'We're having it in bed. It's sorted. I've done the thing for the door.' He'd been keen to avoid having breakfast with other guests who might look up from their papers and stare; Nattie was eye-catching enough without more national coverage.

And there was the need for privacy for the inevitable call from home, which would shatter his dreams and pierce his eardrums more than any loud cockerels and church bells. He dreaded to think of Nattie overhearing it.

He felt for her hand. 'Tell me more about your grandparents. We don't, I suppose, get to share a room?' He held his breath. Of all the surprises Nattie could have sprung, telling him she wanted him to come and stay with her maternal grandparents had been the greatest. And it was perfect in press-dodging terms. 'Well? Is this to be our only night alone? Put me out of my agony.'

'Gran will have put you in the spare, she's made that way, but they'd expect us to be together, they'd think it weird if we weren't. Your bed's the double so I might come knocking.'

'Why knock,' he murmured, stroking up a breast as she turned on to her back, 'when you'll find an open door.' He was feeling the nipple harden.

'You're exhausting.' Nattie firmly returned his hand. 'You can't be up for it again! You were even sending me texts at three in the morning yesterday.' She reached down and gave him a brief feel, kissed him then faced away. 'You should get some sleep,' she threw back. 'Grandpa's no slouch. He's a match for William, they have cool set-tos at Christmas for hours.'

Ahmed settled on his side with an arm draped over her. The bed felt luxurious, he had her body-warmth, the scent of her petal-soft skin to ward off any Fahad demons. If he was going to die, he thought sleepily, he was having a pretty stunning send-off.

He woke to the sound of a ringing mobile. He was instantly awake and reaching out for Nattie, but felt only an expanse of cold sheet. It caused momentary concern before he heard her in the bathroom. Sitting up, rubbing away sleep, eyeing the clock, he stretched out for his mobile that had finally stopped ringing. Nine-thirty: breakfast was due. No point putting it off, he thought, it had to be done.

He called back. 'Hi, Mum. You just rang.'

'Why didn't you answer, Ahmed? Are you alone – is that flatmate there?'

'I'm not actually at the flat, Mum. I'm, um, sort of on the way to Worcestershire, having a weekend with friends.'

'What friends? Are you driving? Are you with the Home Secretary's daughter?'

'I'm not in a car, I'm just about to have some breakfast . . . actually we're on the way to stay with her grandparents. I'm very sorry about all the press. I know how upsetting it must be for you and Dad. It's a . . . very great pity,' he finished lamely.

'Her grandparents on her father's side?'

'No, the maternal ones.' Only his mother, he thought, could get worked up about the precise blood-side of Nattie's relations.

'You're going to be staying with the Home Secretary's *parents?*' His mother's voice went up a few octaves. She'd been reasonably con-trolled . . . just saving it up.

'Well, yes. With this silly stuff in the papers it seemed best being out of London.'

He tensed as the bathroom door opened a fraction. Nattie's head came round and he shrugged his shoulders in a gesture of smiling helplessness. He dreaded her hearing the stream of hysteria that must be about to gush out of his mobile like an unstoppably flooding water main.

She smiled back and pulled the door closed again. She under-stood. Ahmed tuned into his mother again, feeling more able to mop up, if not stem the flow.

'Nearly four weeks you were with us,' she was saying, 'and you didn't breathe a word! How could you do that? The phone hasn't stopped ringing all morning.'

'I can imagine, Mum,' he said dryly.

'Have you taken enough clean clothes – you've been to the flat, got something smarter than the things you had up here? Can you stop anywhere for a new winter coat? That leather thing's no good. Is she going to be there, too?'

'Of course. Nattie's with me right now, actually, Mum—'

'No, no, the Home Secretary, stupid! Of course the girl's with you, I'm not that dim.'

'Oh, she's far too busy for weekends in the country,' Ahmed said briskly, as the light slowly began to dawn. 'She's got a huge terrorist threat on her hands, after all.'

He'd never in a million years have guessed the snob factor would kick in and his parents would glide over all other considerations. It was depressing in a way; he'd hoped they were above lording it over the neighbours – their boy in with people in high places. He suppressed his resentment at the truth of the matter. Nattie's mother wasn't, in fact, smiling on him.

'Your father wants a word.'

Ahmed changed hands, wiped his sweaty palms. He pictured his father's frown lines covering his forehead, the set stern look on that much-loved face, and girded himself. It was hard to know what to expect.

'Ahmed, tell me straight. Are you working for MI5?'

'If I was, Pops, I couldn't say, but no, I'm just working for my paper – just like I said. Direct to the editor-in-chief,' he added, thinking he might at least get what genuine credit was due.

'But you *haven't* said, that's my point. Is this undercover work? I want to know.'

'Yes, well, not exactly – it was my choice to do something. I was upset about the Leicester Square bomb. It was because the editor took an interest in me that I met Nattie.'

He persuaded his father to leave it at that. He assumed his parents had seen both papers, certainly *The Post* with the love aspect, but they had both rather pointedly left that side of things well alone. Ahmed wondered how far the snob factor would take him. They weren't focusing on marriage, he thought – for the moment.

And nor should he be. That wasn't for now. Would he even last out the year before Fahad got to him? If only he could reach Fahad first, just work it out and get there.

The breakfast turned up and Nattie came out of the bathroom, wrapped in white towelling. 'How was it with the parents? Tricky?'

'They think I'm getting above myself, hobnobbing with the likes of you.'

'No, seriously – you were worried.'

'Tell you in the car.' He held out his arms. 'Come back to bed, breakfast can wait.'

'It'll be stone cold.'

'We can cover it up with the duvet. I'll keep you warm—' He yanked the duvet clear and draped it over the tray where she'd put it on a small round table. Then he was back in bed, holding out his arms.

'Do you always win out?' she mumbled, sweet-smelling and naked. 'Your parents were quite right about getting above yourself. I'm on their side.'

They were on B roads, less battered by high winds than on the motorway. Ahmed was intrigued by Nattie's excited impatience to see her grandparents; she was wriggling like a small child, fidgety as a dog nearing familiar surroundings.

'It means a lot to me, coming here and showing you off,' she explained. 'I've had every Christmas and Easter at Brook House; I'd come here alone by train when I was young with Mum ringing to check. It's my second home. And Grandpa's a dude; he's had a rocky ride with a prison sentence for euthanasia, but everyone stood by him. He's like that.'

'I've read about his trial in your mother's cuttings. Given the age of the woman, her pain, it did seem unfair.' The cuttings on the Home Secretary were voluminous, interviews, profiles; the press had made much of her father's prison record.

'Grandpa's sentence was nearly forty years ago,' Nattie said, 'and nobody's been to prison for euthanasia since.'

Ahmed changed the subject. 'Does your mother know you're bringing me here?' He had put off asking that, but it was on his mind.

'She must, I think. William does, obviously. And Grandpa will have told her for definite, he's very straight. I haven't seen Mum apart from that awful supper when I got back. She went to Hampshire very early in the morning. William stayed to do his Friday *Firing Line* programme – and dropped in the first editions for us to see.'

She eased Ahmed's hand off the wheel and kissed it, eyeing him. 'I want to talk to you about Dad sometime. You've remembered about me going to see him on Sunday night with Mum? I'm dreading it. Not seeing him, just the business of persuading him about treatment for the drink, and all the tensions, mine with Mum, hers with Dad.'

Ahmed had nothing useful to say. 'We'll need to be in London about nine? I'm at work again Monday anyway, and Tom'll want his car. It's really great to drive. I don't know how to thank him – a present doesn't seem nearly enough.'

'Don't be mad. It's quite old, it was Mum's before she was ever a minister. Tom's lucky to have it. William says he'll be broke for life unless he gets more commercially minded. If only he could find a huge great benefactor and stay true to his art.'

They had passed a sign saying Troomley and were in the village centre with a small green on the right. 'It's there, up that lane. The house is very old in the middle, but with a gross Edwardian bay. The garden's Grandpa's great love.'

'So what else did you want to say about your dad?'

'I'll get round to it.' Ahmed sensed it was something difficult for her to put across. She smiled. 'At least we've made it by one – bet you anything, though, Gran still says, "I was just starting to worry".'

Nattie hugged her grandparents while Christie, their spaniel, circled round energetically, wagging his whole body. Ahmed stayed with his head buried in the car, busying himself lifting out their gear. He felt nervous; he was sure to fall short of expectation after Nattie's inevitable build-up.

He eyed her grandfather through the windscreen, seeing a lean, white-haired man wearing an old tweed jacket with patched elbows and a pair of even older baggy dark-green cords. Ahmed imagined them smelling earthy and doggy and thought of his mother's worries about clean clothes. He backed out of the car. Nattie and her grandfather were coming over.

'John Winchwood.'

Ahmed took the outstretched hand. 'It's good to meet you.' He was glad of a warm handshake.

'And I'm Bridget.' Nattie's grandmother, who looked far less challenging, came to John's side. Her hair was iron-grey and drawn back, rather in the style of his own mother's, although Bridget had more of a soft, dimply matronly look about her. Turning to Nattie she said, 'I was just starting to worry, dear. Lunch is all ready, it's that fish pie you like with the smoked haddock and mussels.'

'Told you!' Nattie exclaimed, prodding him, shining-eyed and giggly as a teenybopper. 'I said you'd say that, Gran, about worrying. I've told Ahmed lots and it's cool we could come and you can meet him, because I love him so very much.'

CHAPTER 26

Nattie felt irrationally cross with Ahmed; he was too much on his best behaviour, more like chatting to his head teacher than having lunch with her grandparents in their bright cosy kitchen. It was hardly a massively heavy scene after all. She wanted him to be relaxed and part of the family, showing his natural self.

Did the kitchen seem very scruffy to him? There was the scratched, pitted old Aga and equally pockmarked butler's sink; lino instead of smart fired-earth tiles . . . And Christie's dog basket gave off such a potent smell. Ahmed seemed keen on Christie, though; they were rubbing along fine. And she knew he was okay with cats too, which was just as well, considering Agatha covered every chair in the house with her black hairs.

It was foul weather, battering wind and squally rain. Nattie eyed the garden out of the window. Christmas was only ten days away, she thought, feeling nervous strain over her mother. She knew she was winding herself up with the effort of suppressing it. But if it was all getting to her, how much worse must it be for Ahmed?

Was that it? Was it fear making him seem subdued? The whole

terrifying business of his safety had become blurred in the heat of last night's passion, but it wasn't going away.

'I'd better have a peek at the fire,' her grandfather said with a yawn, stretching as he stood up, looking ready for a quick zizz in his favourite armchair.

'I'll make some coffee and bring it in,' Bridget called as he was leaving. She pottered over to the kettle and looked round with a smile. 'Will you help me do the tree sometime tomorrow, Nats – if Ahmed wouldn't mind?'

'Of course he won't!' Nattie glanced at him and his look as their eyes met made her heart feel kicked around like a football; her nerves vanished, all her energies funnelled into reconnection. 'I'd love to, Gran,' she said. 'Be just like old times.'

She was suddenly glad Ahmed hadn't been laying it on like Shelby would have done. She could imagine how agonized, completely tongue-tied she would be, meeting any of his relations in a similar situation.

Her grandmother had the coffee tray ready. 'Let me take that,' Ahmed said, leaping up. 'Nattie will show me where.'

Holding the door for him, she whispered, 'Don't be so boringly polite!'

'You'd rather I was rivetingly rude?'

She ignored that and directed him into the sitting room. 'You're about to have a glimpse of Agatha,' she said. 'You can't exactly miss her; she's gargantuan, but don't take fright or come over all size-ist and talk diets. We've given up. She used to get stuck in her catflap till Grandpa took pity and had one custom built.'

Ahmed looked round for a place to rest the tray. 'Put it on that stool thing.' Nattie pointed to a footstool in front of the fire, covered in one of Bridget's tapestries. It was her own design and surprisingly modern with bright coloured zigzags and stripes.

Squatting down beside it Nattie squinted round at John in his wingback blue chair. 'I'm putting on another log, Grandpa.' He smiled in a benignly condescending way as if to say she didn't have his touch, but no matter. There seemed little need to crow when her log crackled satisfyingly with quick licking tongues of fresh flame.

She poured the coffee and Ahmed handed it round.

'Is my son-in-law as impossible to work for as I've heard?' John asked impassively, taking his cup.

'He's a Colossus, incredibly demanding. People shiver and quake in the shadows as he strides past. Nattie actually asked me that very same question when we met at his party,' Ahmed went on with a smile, taking the cup she held out and going to an opposite chair. 'It was her opening shot and she said it right in front of him, too! But she did suggest finding a quiet corner where I could answer in private.'

'So she took the initiative then?' John inquired, with a slight twinkle.

'Nattie makes all the running. She's in charge.'

'I have to be,' she said with mock affront, enjoying the attention. 'Ahmed says Muslim men are sexually very shy—'

'Nattie dear,' her grandmother intervened, 'you must be making poor Ahmed very embarrassed. What are you both going to do this afternoon? It's miserable out with that bad-tempered wind driving through the valley.' Bridget sighed. 'It must bear a lot of grudges, we've had trees down everywhere.'

'That's awful, Gran. But we're not short of things to do . . . We might watch the football on telly later. I think Ahmed's struggling team are playing.'

'An unfounded slur . . . I wouldn't mind seeing the game, though; we're playing Man United and our feelings towards them . . . well, think Arctic tundra, icebergs, deep-freeze.'

John gave him an interested look. 'But you did go to Manchester University?'

'Sure, but no contest; loyalties formed as a small boy can be very strong.' Ahmed stretched out his legs and Nattie thought he was at last beginning to unwind.

'My Lancashire friends tell me,' her grandfather said innocently, 'that the only good thing to come out of Yorkshire is the westbound M62 . . .'

'Man U will be glad of that escape route later today,' Ahmed was quick to retort.

'What about other university influences?' John said. 'Were there many pressures, even religious ones? There are a lot of questions I'd like to ask.'

'Can they wait till over supper, Grandpa? I'm dying to show Ahmed round – and the garden, before it's dark.' Nattie stood up, suddenly overwhelmed with a need to be alone with him. She had caught the waves of sexuality humming along their private telegraph wire, as he avoided looking where she sat, hug-kneed on the floor.

'Yes, and I'd better take up the bags,' Ahmed said, sounding deceptively mild.

They went upstairs and into her room first. 'This is me,' she said quite proudly. 'It was Mum's as a child and has still got her dolls, as you can see.'

Ahmed put down the bags. Then he was forcing her head back,

thrusting his tongue hard and far. She felt the pain of his gripping fingers pressing and digging into her arms; then he was pulling at her jeans, knocking dolls, books off the shelves alongside where they were.

The house telephone started ringing downstairs. Nattie tensed, but Ahmed was beyond any shared frisson as he slithered her to the floor and drove in up to the hilt. It was for her grandparents, she thought, clamping her thighs round more tightly and shutting out the shrill rings.

Her grandfather called upstairs. 'You there, Nats?' She was clinging, moving with Ahmed and went rigid. 'It's your mum. She needs to talk – can you pick up the phone?'

'Just coming, Grandpa—'

'Just not.' Ahmed's hot cheated breath fanned her ear.

'What the hell can she want?' Nattie muttered furiously. 'We're hardly even on speaking terms . . . Come with me, I need you, I need moral support.' She regretted saying that instantly, suddenly unnerved about what he might overhear.

Hurrying ahead to take the call in her grandparents' bedroom she was zipping her jeans, hitching at her pants that were halfway up and constraining – breathless as she picked up the phone. 'Yes, Mum? What is it?'

Her breathing was still very uneven; Nattie felt embarrassed to think of her grandfather hearing it – and the coolness to her mother – as he returned the handset.

Ahmed had come to the doorway and she smiled over with a hint of reserve in her eyes. He seemed to understand and kept his distance, giving her space and privacy.

'It's about tomorrow and Dad,' her mother was saying defensively. 'I've heard of an excellent place called "Life Works" and I've spoken to someone there who's given me firm and instructive guidance. He said if Dad agrees to treatment he'd be taking a long journey, but we won't even persuade him to look at train times unless we've really rehearsed what to say. We have to present a united front.'

Nattie's mind was on Ahmed and unfinished business. He was leaning against the doorframe with his head back, listening to her side of things; his chest was still heaving, his hands were clenched. Sensing her eyes on him, he tipped his head round and she felt a knot in her stomach then, a sort of yearning dependency. 'It's about Dad,' she whispered over to him, covering the phone.

Her mother was hanging on, expecting some response. 'Can't we talk nearer the time, Mum? I'm not even sure I'm free to go.'

'Stop being so cold with me, Nattie – I thought you wanted to help him? We have to talk now and I'm trying to tell you why. The man I spoke to was very firm; he said we must keep reminding Dad of the hurt his drinking has caused and make him understand the consequence of *not* having treatment; we have to issue sort of threats – and write it all in a letter too, that we leave with him. And all the time we should keep saying how desperate we are to help and stressing how much we love him.'

'But you never really did, which Dad knew, didn't he? So how can saying that wash?' It felt mean, picking her up about not loving him, but it seemed relevant in the circumstances.

'That's why *you're* so key, Nattie, and the letter we leave has to come from you. He's sure of your love, you're everything to him. And he does know I care and always did, however appallingly he behaved. He leaned on me – after all it's why you think I can help persuade him. The letter has to have some ultimatum in it, something dramatic and terrible that will happen if he doesn't agree to begin treatment.'

'Like what?' Nattie muttered, feeling subdued.

'Like saying however much you love him, you'd have to stop seeing him if he isn't prepared to try, and couldn't be in his life any more. That it's for his own good.'

'But that would be impossibly heartless and cruel. Suppose he doesn't go along with it? I couldn't say all that and then not carry it out.'

'They call it tough love, Nats. You really do have to spell it all out – about overhearing actual sounds of violence, how you hated the rows, the drink on his breath.' Her mother paused. 'You have told him we're coming? That's assuming you're free, of course—'

Nattie bridled at the sarcasm, but couldn't help weakening. 'He knows I plan to look in,' she mumbled, 'and that you're coming by. He wanted to cook us supper, but I said not. He'll be on his own, which is lucky. Old Dick's away this weekend, a wedding or funeral or something.'

'I'll see you there then – about nine-thirty? Can you be a bit earlier than me?'

'Probably,' Nattie said sourly, keeping up her cold front.

She ended the call with a thudding heart. How could she possibly write such a letter? It put her in a complete panic. How could she tell Ahmed that her father used to hit her mother? She had to, there couldn't be any dark secrets. If the letter was left till morning, if she'd told him in the night . . . Might he even help her write it?

Ahmed left the doorway and came close, putting an arm round her. 'Want to tell me?'

Nattie kissed his cheek. 'Later perhaps. Mum's got me feeling all screwed-up just now.'

*

After tea Nattie left the two men watching the football on television and helped her grandmother prepare supper. She made spinach soup, always a surefire hit. It was a recipe of her father's that called for fresh-grated nutmeg and chicken stock, but Bridget always had frozen stock in ice-cube trays and whole nutmegs in store, with a midget grater. They were both foodies and had a companionable cook-in.

Nattie decided to change out of her jeans and she gave her grandmother an impulsive hug on the way. 'Thanks for making Ahmed so at home, Gran.'

'Silly thing! Did you expect us not to? It warms my heart, seeing you so happy. You're more sparkly even than at Christmas as a little girl – when I used to say I should put you on the tree, remember! So you're sure the duck breast and vermicelli thing is fine, dear, for the main?' Her grandmother was more into supper than emotional soppiness. 'I thought we'd have it in the dining room for a change and be a bit special as it's Ahmed's first visit.'

Nattie wished her mother had been there to hear that. It put everything into perspective, she thought, letting her grandmother's words stoke her sense of injustice as she went up to change. She put on a short black dress with black woolly tights and a plaited brown-leather belt that she pulled tight. Ahmed said all the right things as she came back into the sitting room.

Over supper, though, he seemed more into football, rehashing the game with her grandfather. It had ended in a draw.

'Man U won't have gone home happy,' he said cockily. 'They'd have expected to pick off Leeds, no problem!'

'Have you swapped allegiances again now, Nattie?' her grandfather inquired with a broad smile, bringing her in. 'You did desert

Southampton for Liverpool after all, when William came on the scene.'

'Much as I love Ahmed . . . No, Grandpa, I like being up there with the winners and watching Leeds and Southampton struggle on.'

She cleared the soup plates and carried in a huge oval platter piled with vermicelli and bean sprouts. Bridget had tossed them together, topped them with carefully arranged slices of duck breast and drizzled over a little richly coloured soy sauce.

Neither of the men got up to help with the weighty dish; they were still deep in conversation, although the subject was very different.

'I've no axe at all to grind,' her grandfather was saying. 'This is purely as it strikes me, but the Koran does seem to give out very mixed messages. I mean, plenty of wrongs have been done in the name of Christianity, but the New Testament doesn't speak the language of war. Whereas the Koran seems to give extremists their justification and armour for promoting jihad.'

'My traditionalist parents would argue with that,' Ahmed said. 'They'd quote Suras in the Koran that show Islam in a peaceful light.' He thought for a moment. 'Like, for example, '"Repel evil with that which is better" or "Let there be no compulsion in religion. Truth stands out clear from error".'

Nattie looked at her grandfather, who was smiling. 'You might have plucked that one out of the Book of John,' he said. '"And you shall know the truth, and the truth shall make you free". So do your parents think then that the more violent Suras are ambiguous, just twisted by the extremists to suit their fanatical ends? As I say, I've really no axe to grind. It is, though, all very worrying.'

'I'm not religious, I'm pretty ignorant about the Koran to my parents' distress, and I've never really asked their views on that. But I did mug up on the jihad Suras before going to the part of Leeds where I've been for a few weeks, and they could be said to give the political activists ammunition, no question.'

Bridget had been bustling around, seeing to everyone's food. 'Do eat now,' she said beaming. 'And don't be so harassing, John! You go at any subject like a terrier.'

'But it's an important one,' Ahmed chipped in, 'and needs to be aired. The word "jihad" means "to strive or struggle", by the way, which is open to different interpretations – like say the struggle against evil – although it is more generally accepted to mean military struggle. It's often followed by the phrase "*fi sabil Allah*", meaning "in the way of Allah".'

He grimaced. 'There are over a hundred and fifty jihad Suras in the Koran and they're uncompromising. "Fight the leaders of unbelief, Allah will punish them by your hands", and they get progressively more violent. "Fight and kill the disbelievers wherever you find them . . . Fight them till all opposition ends and all submit to Allah".'

'If there are other views, though,' John queried, 'why don't the traditionalists speak out more? Can you help on that? Or am I being too harassing?'

'I suspect they just feel uncomfortable making criticisms of fellow Muslims. But with these warring verses – phrases like "Strike terror into the hearts of the enemy" – and all the denigrating of government, encouraging of conspiracy theories, it's a combustible mix. Politically determined activists only need light a match.'

'So what's to be done, in your view? I'm very interested. What are the underlying causes?'

'If only I knew. Obviously there's the conflict between Israel and Palestine, but even within and between Muslim countries you have opposing sects, hatred, the oppression of one sect by another; in some ways it's like the Catholic and Protestant power struggles of the sixteenth century. The Islamic revolution in Iran was a watershed. When the Ayatollah Khomeini overthrew the Shah in the late seventies it was the first time a religious leader had taken political power and I think it reignited the whole concept of Islamic expansion. And some in the Diaspora are the most militant extremists of all.'

Ahmed caught Nattie's eye, ready to be distracted, but her grandfather was looking expectant and she, too, wanted him to carry on.

'There's really little anyone can do,' he said, 'except go on trying to root out terrorists and hope sanity and moderation win through. There are signs. The hard core organizations have become more fragmented of late, we're told – although al-Qaeda are said to be moving into Palestine, which is a frightening thought.'

'Now, Ahmed, there's fruit and cheese,' Bridget said brightly, 'and these date and treacle cookies Nattie thought you might like – perhaps with some ice cream?'

'They look terrific. You made them, Nattie?' She nodded smiling, then jumped nervously when his mobile beeped with a text coming through. He fished in his pocket. She could read the strain in his apologetic smile.

Nattie watched as he scrolled down. She was relieved when he looked up with warm eyes. 'It's from your stepfather. He's saying Peter Barnes is all over tomorrow's *Dispatch*. It'll be a big story, plenty of legs. Seems the Foreign Secretary is really in for it – which means the government too, I'm afraid.'

She thought about all the pressures on her mother and felt guilty. But Christmas was never far from her thoughts and the guilt evaporated like steam.

Trying to hide the bitterness flooding in again, she said lightly, 'Mum was so fed up when William suddenly had that Sunday paper to oversee as well. She'll be looking daggers at him at breakfast tomorrow over this, I'm sure. If it's in *The Dispatch* it is his doing, after all. She'll be livid with him; this on top of all her other worries – however much she's anti Peter Barnes.'

'What's the substance of this story, Ahmed?' her grandfather asked. 'What's the Foreign Secretary supposed to have done?'

'Seriously dabbled in sleaze, I believe. He's been having an affair with an opera singer and there are intimations of a financial scam. How stupid can you get? And it couldn't come at a worse time for the government.'

'Might Barnes have to resign?' John inquired curiously.

'That's the jackpot question! He'd be a real troublemaker on the backbenches—'

'Poor Prime Minister,' Bridget said. 'Who'd ever want that job?'

John was looking at Ahmed thoughtfully. 'Of course you and Nattie have just had your own bit of press. And from what I gather you've been doing, I suppose it must now make you more exposed, put you in a bit of a spot?'

'I can't pretend it's a very comfortable scene.' Ahmed grinned, but Nattie sensed his tension. 'I won't be going back to Harehills, my part of Leeds, for a while, which isn't easily explained to my parents. I'll have to blame it on Nattie! We're all in a spot, though, the whole country, with that missing canister of High Level Waste.'

It cast a cloud. The dangers were suddenly very highlit and stark. Back in the sitting room after clearing supper, Nattie was subdued. She felt panicky about Ahmed's safety, had yet to explain to him about her father, making her miserable all round.

The fire was down to a glowing ember. Ahmed tried to suppress a yawn, not very hard, probably impatient for them to be alone. Nattie sensed his relief when Bridget took the bait and heaved out of her chair. 'Bedtime for us oldsters,' she declared. 'Come on, John, even the young ones are drooping.'

Her grandfather put the guard in front of the fire, reminded Nattie to turn out lights. Then they were alone, moving closer on the sofa, feeling for each other's hand.

Ahmed reached up to switch off a table lamp. The glimmer of red in the grate was fading, becoming grey, lifeless, crumbling ash, and a sort of creaky stillness descended and settled eerily on the room like ghostly dust. The wind outside was still vigorously rustling and shaking the trees as if they were tambourines. Nattie felt frightened, comforted by Ahmed's warm protective hand, his handsome profile as she glanced up at him. He was deep in thought. She feared for him and what was to become of them.

He turned and kissed her tenderly. 'You've been very quiet since supper.'

'It was that call from Mum. Like I said, it was about how to persuade Dad into treatment, but . . . well, she wants me to leave him with a letter and I'm scared about it.'

'Why – because it's hard to write? Can I help?'

'I badly need you to, but I'd have to tell you things about Dad.'

'Is that a problem? I know I'm a reporter, but I'd hope you could trust me by now.'

Nattie smiled, gave his hand a squeeze, then took hers back. She wished he'd just guess, suss it out. It wouldn't sound so baldly awful, simply confirming something, but having to say it cold . . . She felt sure Ahmed would be disgusted and have no time at all for her father.

'Tell me the problem, darling Nattie. Is it some past misdeed? Has he been had up or bankrupted or something? Isn't it better shared?'

'It's just not very easy – well, to explain to you that my father used to hit my mother. It wasn't like often,' she hurried on, 'and I know he really hated himself for it when he was sober. You won't understand, though, that I can still love him.' She hung her head and twisted her hands in her lap until Ahmed took one back and kissed it. He *was* shocked, she could tell; who wouldn't be?

'There had been a vague rumour at the paper along those lines, I believe,' Ahmed remarked, as though not knowing quite what to say, 'but no one took it seriously. It is hard to believe and understand. And especially why your mother stayed married. They were for a long time, weren't they?'

'Sixteen years.'

'You think it was always the drink?'

'Pretty much. The first I knew was when I overheard him shouting and sounds of her being knocked about . . . I hated him for ages, but Mum didn't and I gradually began to understand why not. It was such a vicious circle – sort of frustration with her for doing better than him and not truly loving him that caused the drinking, and then in turn the violence. She always felt guilty underneath as well, for not having quite the right feelings. But—'

'What is it, darling Nattie? Why does it matter quite so much to you what I think?' He was searching her face for clues.

'It matters dreadfully,' she said, with tears springing. 'He's so sort of helpless and not a mean man; good-looking in a sexy way, or used to be, and bright, too. He just throws it all away through lack of control. I love him and care; and it matters desperately to me that people I love, love each other or try to, at least – well, like Mum does—'

'I'll do more than try,' Ahmed said, taking her into his arms. 'I'll gladly meet him whenever you want. He's your father. And if you get him into treatment I'm sure he'll be a new man. Shall we go up now? Will you stay in my room all night and be close?'

'What you told Grandpa about not going to Leeds has got me even more sick with worry,' Nattie said, as they stood up, feeling one layer of tension lifting and another exposed. 'Promise you won't go there? I don't have to spend Christmas here with Mum. I want to be with you.' Ahmed was trying to look dismissive of her fears and not entirely succeeding. He seemed lost for words. She made a half-hearted attempt at lightening things. 'You need a Rodney now, full protection. Shelby deserves to be banged up and doing hard labour. It's such a cock-eyed shit-awful world.'

'It's a fantastic world,' Ahmed said, 'when I can find you in it and we can be here in this wonderful house together.'

CHAPTER 27

A car was arriving, and it was late. It would be William's Saturday-night delivery of the Sunday newspapers, Victoria thought, listening tensely at her desk in the sitting-room alcove. It looked out to the front and she could hear the murmuring of the driver and the Hampshire police on duty. She heard William's voice then, taking in the papers, the thump as he landed their weight on the slippery oak hall chair – which was so highly polished Janet's pointed beaky face must have frowned back at her in its seat.

She could have seen her face in all the furniture in the house; Janet was a fairy godmother in pale-rimmed glasses, she was their salvation from household stress in the country. If the fire smoked she knew a chimney sweep; she knew a man for the hanging gutter, a wasp-nest guru, a mole catcher. William thought she loved lording it over the police, waggling her mop when they walked in earth on their boots or brought the dogs through the house; Victoria said he was the main attraction, that Janet gazed at him in adoration, brought armfuls of vegetables from her garden and was always quoting from *The Post*.

He came into the room then; he had *The Dispatch* in his hand and a shamefaced look on his face. 'Thought you'd better take a peek—'

She could see the headline; it was hard to miss. 'Foreign Secretary In Sleaze Shock'.

William left the paper by her arm and turned for the door. He stopped and looked back. 'You'll be getting plenty of calls about that tomorrow – if not tonight. You wouldn't like just to come to bed now, and forget it?'

She felt a sudden rush of need and pushing back her chair went to catch him up. 'Give me a hug,' she said, looking up earnestly, her arms stiff at her sides.

He enveloped her snugly, trapping her arms, and studied her with teasing eyes. 'I like this postponement of fury. I'd been expecting a wailing explosion.'

'I'll remember you think it's only postponed,' she grinned. 'You go on up. I've just got to pack away my work.'

William cradled her breasts that he often called 'a perfect handful' and kissed her lightly. 'I'll have a read of the papers in bed, but don't be too long. It's late.'

Victoria settled down again at her desk. She heard his feet on the stairs; the squeak of an upstairs floorboard. The wind outside was violent, lashing furiously at the house, almost lifting it up, yet the room seemed unnaturally still and quiet. How could she be so nervy when there were policemen out in the garden, cameras, equipment, full protection – and William waiting upstairs? She drew strength from him and needed him, but her sense of isolation at that moment was complete.

The Dispatch lay on her desk. It hardly needed reading. She was over her conscience about Peter Barnes. William was like a detective writer's perfect sleuth, a Maigret or Sherlock Holmes: show him the smallest crack and he could always unearth a great cavern.

The Barnes issue was serious. The media would have an orgy of sanctimonious hand-wringing, a whole new bout of government bashing, but to think of the country on high alert was to put Peter Barnes into scale. He was an irritant, a fly, a wasp.

There was going to be an attack. You could smell it in the air like thunder. They were sleepwalking towards it, blindfold, helpless. There were men out there with the wherewithal to make a devastatingly destructive radioactive bomb.

At the back of her mind was the feeling that Ahmed Khan held some sort of key. He seemed convinced his contacts were involved – that was clear from the transcripts, so MI5 said. He was at her parents' home, probably with Nattie in his arms – and her daughter was in love with him. Everything seemed frighteningly connected. Why was it so impossible to know whether Ahmed was genuine or not? Was he desperately concerned and trying to help, or a malignant force who could fool even her own father?

The photographs in *The Dispatch* caught her eye. There was one of Peter Barnes looking as though he'd just smelled a bad egg, one of the singer bearing all before her. '*Curvaceous opera singer, Lisa Chovia, close friend of the Foreign Secretary.*' There was a photograph of the piece of land in question. Would Lisa prove to be Barnes's nemesis? Somehow, Victoria thought, he would claw his way back up.

The story made shoddy reading. Barnes had used his power and influence, the paper said heatedly, to nudge a planning decision the way of his 'close friend' and secure a financial killing for her. Councillors expressed 'surprise' and 'disappointment' that their MP should have departed from a right and proper position of neutrality.

Nick Bates's aunt, as chairman of the planning committee, had discreetly made no comment, but the paper mentioned her relationship to a junior minister. Victoria wondered if colleagues might privately accuse Nick of shopping the Foreign Secretary. It did rather let her off the hook . . .

She read the paper's conclusion. 'This is a sorry tale, a disgrace – although sadly what we have come to expect from our politicians. The Foreign Secretary has indulged in a flagrant abuse of his position of trust and authority. This paper is shocked by the impropriety. Peter Barnes holds one of the great offices of state, he is a standard bearer who represents us abroad. What kind of signal does this send? Haven't we a right to expect more? He has brought shame on his government, on Parliament and on our country. The Foreign Secretary must go.'

The 'full story' was on the inside pages. Victoria sighed and began packing up her work. She locked her red box, turned out the sitting-room lights and went upstairs.

William was in bed with the papers so spread about they formed a kind of coverlet. 'You've been an age! What the fuck have you been doing down there all this time?' He sounded cheerfully good-humoured, far from aggrieved.

'Just having a flip through your lascivious Sunday rag.' Victoria made a small space for herself among the newsprint and sat on the bed. She smiled and leaned to trace over his lips, nervous of bringing up anything that touched on Barney. It was too much on her mind, though, not to need to spill it out. 'What am I to do, love? Nattie was an icebox on the phone, I almost lost my cool, and it's not going to be easy tomorrow night at the best of times . . . How am I going to handle her?'

'And how am I expected to handle your sweet-natured ex-husband back on the scene?' William glared. He knew he was being childish, she thought, looking at him anxiously, wanting him to go on. 'You have to loosen up a whole lot with Nattie,' he said. 'Talk to her, ask her about Ahmed. She's in love, she's longing to pour it out. It might even make you understand why your father's as impressed with him as I am.'

He gathered her up and kissed her, scattering papers and making her ache with desire. 'Come to bed,' he said softly. 'Let's have a few hours of togetherness and try to get through the night without a call. Who knows what's lurking around the corner and about to hit us between the eyes.'

They were back in London. Victoria felt quite glad, for once, getting in the car to go on her difficult mission to Barney, that Charles was on duty. Rodney was too sharp, he would have known she was as knotted-up as a bundle of unkempt fishing nets. He'd have read the Shelby interview, known what the tension was all about – that the whole Foreign Secretary drama was a peripheral dot on the far horizon.

'Have you had time to grab a bite of supper, Charles?' she asked, thinking they'd only been back from Hampshire an hour and that he, the driver and backup car pair must have been waiting outside since then.

He turned round from the front. 'You learn to stoke up on food in this game,' he said with a smile. 'You never need worry about us.'

They set off for the Holland Park flat that Barney had shared with his friend Dick since the break-up. Victoria remembered it from years back, going to supper there with Barney in the days when Dick was still married to June. It was splendid, grand and old-fashioned, a rambling run of high-ceilinged rooms in a stately Victorian villa with a huge spreading plane tree out front.

Dick must be sitting on a goldmine, living there so long, she thought. Holland Park properties were off the Richter scale now. He was such a reactionary old bore, material for Bird and Fortune dinner parties; a lesser soak than Barney, but enough of one to be a bad influence. They had their golf, though, and Dick had been wretchedly lonely without June. Victoria wondered what had happened to her – whether she was still around, having those extended lunches with Barney that Dick could never have known about . . .

They were pulling away from the traffic lights in Notting Hill Gate: almost there. Victoria longed to think Nattie might come home afterwards and there'd be a chance to talk. Her need for a spark of warmth from her daughter was greater than a frozen waif's need to kindle a fire.

They took the turning that curved into an elegant Holland Park crescent and drew up outside Dick's imposing property. 'I shouldn't be too long, Charles, around half an hour,' she said, feeling embarrassment as he dutifully accompanied her right up the steps to the entrance.

She rang the bell. 'That you, Mum?' Nattie queried cautiously before releasing the door. She was there, at least, thank God. That was something.

'Hi, darling.' Victoria hurried up the wide carpeted staircase to the first-floor flat. Barney came to the door. It was hard not to register a feeling of shock, almost revulsion, seeing his more recent deterioration: the lank lifelessness of his blond hair, the pink powdery dryness of his puffy face. He'd had a tendency to fleshiness even in his most glamorous heyday. Now his cheeks looked bloated as whales, the dry-skinned patches as flaky as the bark of a London plane tree.

'This *is* a surprise!' Barney beamed, full of the old bonhomie. 'To what do I owe this great honour? Come on in. Have a glass of vino. Nattie's on the white, but there's a good claret going.' His hands were shaking like an old man's – from nerves as well as drink, Victoria guessed, feeling sadly reminded of his father who lived only for his gin. Barney kissed her awkwardly on the cheek as he ushered her into the hall and pressed on the small of her back with a directing hand.

His hand was a conduit, his clear panic transmitting itself, burning through her cord jacket, her grey cashmere sweater. It was going to be painfully tough going.

'You don't mind me looking in?' She turned with a smile. 'Nattie and I . . . Well, there's something we want to discuss. It's important to us.'

'I didn't think this visit was entirely social,' Barney said sardonically. 'So how's life? *The Dispatch* was bitching away again this morning, I saw. *The Post's* bad enough – pity those minders of yours can't see off the press as well—' He was meaning William, probably, from his bitter tone. 'You'll have a glass of the claret?'

'Yes thanks, be nice.' Victoria looked past him to Nattie who had come to the sitting-room door and was listening to her parents' strained conversation. Her beauty, her golden bloom and fragility brought feelings of awe and fear. The faint black shadows under her eyes were a sign of the stress they were all feeling.

She and her mother sat in opposite brocade armchairs. It left Barney the choice of a third similarly formal chair or the mahogany bergère sofa with its stiff seat-cushions and back and sides in canework. This flat was far removed from his taste, which was light and eclectic, Victoria thought, and he'd been living in it for nearly four years.

'How was it in Hampshire?' Nattie asked stiffly.

'Fine, the usual – the papers weren't great reading with the Peter Barnes stuff!' The calls had been non-stop: the press mixing it, colleagues gloating or in panic, the Prime Minister weakly joking to her that at least the media might forget about being blown up for a short while.

Barney was by the dining table pouring Victoria's wine with his back turned. He would have hated being reminded of weekends in Ferndale and the life he'd enjoyed: golf, growing vegetables, flirting with constituents. He'd wanted to keep on the cottage after they'd divorced and had fought against its sale. Victoria had felt meanly selfish insisting, but had dreaded to think of her ex-husband living in the very same village.

He brought over her wine, drinking deeply from his own glass before setting down hers on the marble coffee table. He chose the chair next to Nattie, which meant he was staring across at Victoria. She felt uncomfortable in his direct gaze, but he fidgeted and soon got up for the bottle to refill Nattie's glass.

Then he filled his own and stood drinking, staring across more combatively. 'You want to read me the riot act. You're going to come over all pompous and ministerial and tell me how much I'll end up costing the NHS.' She could hear old resentments about her job surfacing, his obsessive sense of failure, the feeling that everyone patronized him. He was in an immaculate yellow shirt, although his jeans weren't as crisply just-washed-looking as of old. The shirt looked new, fresh out of its cellophane sleeve and she imagined Barney hunting out all the pins with his shaking fingers. Victoria's heart felt heavy; he'd made the effort for her benefit, she knew.

He came back to his chair and sat down.

'Dad . . . Can we have a little talk?'

His head jerked up and he spun round. 'Ah, that old persuasive tone! I can remember, Nattie my angel, when you used to work on me about going to parties – you thought I was a softer touch than Mum!'

'You certainly were.' Victoria laughed, anxious for Nattie to get on with it. They'd agreed she should make the first overture.

'Dad, please listen. This is serious. It's about how badly you need treatment. You must. It's for your own good. You can have it on medical insurance – it is an illness, you just need a doctor to refer you – and Mum says you're covered through the firm. It's a five-week course. I'm, we're both, really determined about this because we love you and care so much.' Nattie was looking at him with miserable devotion.

She hadn't done brilliantly, Victoria thought, tumbling it all out far too fast. The advice had been to be as unemotional as possible, not to blame or criticize, simply to make clear that not having treatment wasn't an option. It was unthinkable.

Barney was affecting an amused sarcastic look, although he seemed incapable of much bravado. 'You seriously think I can just swan off for five weeks – even suppose I should want to?' He rose and went to the dining table. There were two unopened bottles of claret and pulling the cork on one he kept up his facetious façade.

Victoria couldn't bear to see his rapid decline, the swollen papery look of his skin – it was as though a spiteful witch had cast an ageing spell to deny him a fresh start. He refilled his glass and downed it fast, which seemed to steady him, then filled it again and came back to sit down.

'And how would Hugh like it?' he demanded, picking up the

thread again. 'We've just taken on a hotshot new property client; he's an edgy guy with attitude. You think I can just drop Hugh in it? Let's get real around here. I know I drink a bit, but it's contained, does-n't affect things. I can do my job.'

His voice had developed a whining pleading tone like a cornered small-time crook. He was looking at his ex-wife with hurt eyes. 'You left me,' those eyes said, 'for a hard-as-nails cunt who blackmailed and steam-rollered me – if I'd been a tortoise he'd have ripped off my shell. And you married that man, you couldn't have given a fucking damn.'

Nattie sat forward, looking prim. 'You can't go on making excuses, Dad. You have to find yourself again and face your demons. This is it, really, crunch time.'

'Nattie's right, there can be no postponing,' Victoria said carefully. 'You're ill, Barney. You need help. Hugh will work round it, he's a good man. And he has to by law, actually. You lawyers probably don't even know that, but it's true.'

His senior partner, Hugh Simmonds, was insipidly bourgeois, pro-tocol-driven and with a ghastly opinionated wife – the sort of man to leave your face cracked in a frozen smile. Yet those very qualities kitted him up to do the Right Thing. Hugh had shown strength of character in past tricky situations. Behind the grey-suit exterior lurked a surprisingly stallion-like will. Victoria thought she would talk to him, possibly even persuade him to collude with her and innocently suggest it to Barney himself.

'I've found somewhere near Woking,' she carried on, 'and it has a centre in the West End for evening aftercare. It will be stressful for you, a long gruelling journey to recovery, but this place is in a won-derful setting and you'll be constantly looked-after, guided, medically checked. They'll take away all the strain. You'll feel younger, fit and well again, set up for positive life.'

'What a fine little pompous, patronizing speech,' Barney said with a sneer.

Nattie stood up abruptly. 'Listen, Dad. Mum and I are going now. We've made arrangements, booked you in for right after Christmas. We're leaving all the bumph and you'll see what a really cool place it is.' Victoria took a fat manila envelope out of her bag, laid it on the coffee table and stood up too. 'It has to be this way, Dad—'

Victoria looked at her daughter, feeling immense admiration. Nattie was going to do it, manage the very hardest bit, she had that set look on her sweet face.

'I've got to say something terrible, Dad. I won't be coming here any more, no more of our cosy lunches and cook-ins if you let us down over this. It's all out of love, because of how much we care and desperately want you better, but I mean what I say. You really must understand. I'll never see you again if you won't agree to be treated. I love you to death, but I'd still walk out of that door and out of your life for ever.

'And I've written you a letter.' She fished in the pocket of her jeans and brought out a squashed folded-over envelope. 'I've spelled out all the things that have hurt so very badly over the years. Needless pain and all caused by drink—'

Nattie was forced to stop. Barney had crumpled into a heaving heap, brought his arms up over his ears and started a rhythmic hysterical stamp of his foot, thumping faster and faster as if in fury at the carpet for its muffling of the sound. His knee was shooting up and down and hitting his elbow.

Then he suddenly raised his puffy streaming drunken face and stared at them each in turn. It was a glazed look, blank and wretched, but shielding such thwarted rage and blind frustration that Victoria moved quietly to stand in front of her daughter. She knew when Barney was about to lose control and flip.

He grabbed his heavy crystal, well-drained glass and hurled it viciously at the bottles on the table – some still with wine in them, Nattie's white wine in its cooler, a line-up of empties.

The noise was shattering. An empty bottle torpedoed off the table, shot through the open kitchen door and crashed on to the shiny ceramic tiles. It smashed into a thousand pieces. A full bottle toppling against the others caused them to roll like skittles and hit the floor in ghastly bursting splintering succession. The full bottle splayed out claret like shaken champagne. It might have just hit the side of a ship. There was no carpet directly under the table, but wine was spreading everywhere, seeping into the thick-pile Persian-carpeted sitting area, pinking it up like blood through a bandage.

Nattie started to sob.

Barney was staggering drunkenly to his feet and Victoria felt terrified he might lunge for a jagged piece of glass. She moved to be in his way and tried her best to eyeball him. 'Let's just sit down together a minute. Forget the mess. Let's talk it through—'

He hesitated. She held her breath, but he wasn't properly focused; his bloodshot eyes were seeing nothing. He was engulfed, drowning in a sea of intense consuming self-pity, impatient just to brush her aside. He hadn't heard a word.

Nor did he really know what he was doing, she thought, when he flung out an angry uncontrolled arm and pushed at her. She stumbled back, tripping over the corner of the coffee table and falling against the sofa where her head banged the mahogany frame. She saw stars for a few seconds and could feel her leg throbbing and hurting too, where it had caught the edge of the marble table.

Nattie was instantly at her side. 'Mum, Mum, are you okay?'

Her head had stopped spinning and Victoria quickly righted herself to be sitting – rather gratefully – on the sofa. She looked at Nattie's white tearful face and smiled at her panic. 'I'm fine. It was just a tumble. Not much damage!'

She looked beyond her to Barney then. His face had gone white, the dry pinkness turned to chalk. He'd sunk down on his seat; he was trembling all over. The sweat was pouring. He felt her gaze and tried to avert his eyes.

'We'll have to be off,' she said, although without feeling quite able to spring up in a hurry. Barney was over it, but she needed to get Nattie away. Turning to her she murmured in a low tone, 'Fetch me a sip of water, love.' Nattie hesitated. 'Go on, I'm fine.'

Barney had never managed to say he was sorry in the past, but he was frightened out of his wits, and she thought, looking at him, that he might.

He didn't take the chance. Nattie came back with a glass. Victoria had a few sips then got up and touched Barney's hand. 'We really should go. Read Nattie's letter; it's out of love. Call me. You may not still have my mobile number; here's a card.' He stared at her, still shaking and didn't look where she left it on the chair-arm.

She turned to go, cursing the throbbing egg on the back of her head, thinking that at least it didn't show and William need be none the wiser. A shin bruise could have happened anywhere. Nattie had gone towards the door and was waiting. Victoria came alongside and looked back with a heavy heart. She smiled goodbye to Barney.

'I'll do it,' he called. He had never sounded more humble and contrite.

'Oh, Barney, I'm pleased, so glad. It is the right and only way—'

She felt like crying when Nattie said nothing. She didn't run to his side spontaneously and give him a thrilled hug, didn't exclaim happily that it was exactly what they'd wanted to hear. Nattie was mute, sullen and unyielding.

It was dreadfully sad. He had forfeited all her loving goodwill and just when he needed it most acutely. Victoria gave her a tiny nudge. 'Help him,' she whispered. But Nattie seemed to think that meant all the broken glass; she looked in panic at the chaos and knelt down.

'No, no!' Barney called over desperately. 'That's my mess. You go now—' There was a heart-rending catch in his voice.

Nattie got to her feet again and Victoria murmured under her breath, 'Be sweet to him. Say something positive.'

'Thanks, Dad, for saying you'll do it,' she said dully, hardly glancing at him.

They reached the flat door. Barney had come into the hall, but was hovering and keeping his distance. 'Take care, Nattie, angel,' he said with deeply sorrowful eyes when she looked back briefly. 'Go well, both of you.'

Nattie's own eyes filled with tears. 'Love you, Dad,' she mumbled, but in such an inaudible whisper that Victoria only hoped he had heard.

CHAPTER 28

The heavy door to Barney's flat closed behind them with a solid click. Victoria felt shaky and drained, but an immense sense of release. They had done all they possibly could, now it was up to him.

'Dad'll be all right now,' she said turning to Nattie with a smile. 'And he really will go through with it, I'm sure.' She went to the stairs and moved to be near the handrail. Her legs felt quite weak. 'You won't say anything to William about the drama, though, will you?' She looked at her daughter with pleading eyes.

Nattie was staring, making Victoria worry whether she'd really taken that in. 'Mum, you don't look right,' she said with concern, 'you've gone all pale, you might faint. It's like delayed shock or some wobbly reaction. There's that bench seat down in the hall – shouldn't you just sit for a few minutes before we go?'

Victoria liked hearing her say 'we', and since Charles would hurry out of the car to escort them the moment they appeared at the door, it was about the only chance she could see of being private. 'That's a bit over the top,' she said, being only half-heartedly dismissive. 'It's just been rather a long day, that's all, and Dad – well, it was never going to be easy!'

Nattie compressed her lips. She took hold of her mother's elbow as though helping an old woman to cross the road and propelled her purposefully downstairs and to the seat. It was marble and belonged more outdoors, Victoria thought, wondering if some resident had given up a country place and generously bequeathed it to the flats.

The cool of the marble was soothing in the oppressively over-heated hall; a cumbersome freestanding old radiator close by was belching out heat like a ship's boiler. 'Come and sit with me, love,' she said, 'and tell me you'll be understanding about Dad. You've always loved him, for all his faults, and it was the drink getting a hold – you know that.' Victoria smiled anxiously, grateful when Nattie did sit down.

She sat looking ahead with a grim face, then turned and said passionately, 'It was ghastly, Mum. How could he do that? I couldn't bear seeing him throwing that terrible tantrum like a spoiled bullying child. Pushing you and being violent like he used to – and you just taking it meekly like you used to, as well. I'm sure I'd get in a truly desperate rage if . . . well, anyone I was in a relationship with ever did such things. I'd want to fight back.'

Victoria felt shocked. 'You wouldn't really, Nattie. That would be terrible; there's never anything to be gained. And you know alcoholism's an illness with Dad.'

It was true that she had never once wanted to get back at him. Was it to do with not loving him properly? Guilt? If William was ever to treat her badly she'd feel incredibly distraught and disbelieving, she thought, and probably have the most hysterical showdown.

'I'll get over it,' Nattie muttered, 'in time. I just felt so furious, bitterly let down by Dad. He made me so ashamed of him.'

'But he faced it in the end,' Victoria said. 'He found the strength, which is fantastic, really, when you think of it. Are you coming home now, love?' she asked hesitantly, with her heart in her throat.

'Not right away. Can I have a lift to Chelsea, though? You do go right near.'

'Sure. Where in Chelsea?' Victoria felt slightly surprised. Ahmed didn't live there.

Nattie was rubbing at a thumbnail. She looked up. 'South Street: Hugo's flat. You know Tom loaned us the car this weekend? Ahmed didn't want to return it to the house – for obvious reasons.' She glared. 'So I thought of Hugo's flat for somewhere to meet. I said I'd catch up with them there, have a drink and say hi. But I will be back later if that's okay?'

'Of course. When you're home, there might be time for a chat?' Victoria felt for her daughter's hand, but it stayed in her lap, limp and unresponsive as a dead bird.

'About what, Mum?' she muttered. 'Christmas?'

'Just everything,' Victoria said sadly, knowing that was exactly what they did have to talk about. 'Your feelings – what's very special to you about Ahmed.' She ventured another small smile.

Nattie's face softened unexpectedly. 'Sorry, Mum,' she said, 'I know you've had enough aggro for one night, but I'm just so worried about his safety . . . All that crap in the paper, the publicity about us; it's really serious. God, when you think of the lies that Shelby told *The Courier*. Ahmed will be back at his flat tonight – and without me because of the shitty press. I feel sick to think of people out to get him, Mum. He shares with a cool guy called Jake Wright who's very together so that's a bit of protection, but still . . .'

Nattie was looking wretched and forlorn. As well as ratcheting up the pressure, Victoria felt helpless, unable to say anything practical that would reassure.

She also felt impatient to be home; the urge to be well away from Holland Park and Barney had suddenly welled up like milk to the boil. Her head hurt, her shin was painful... She felt stronger, though, for the moment's closeness to Nattie and squeezed her arm trying to transmit the feeling. 'I'm fine now, darling,' she said, 'keen to be off. And I'm sure you must be too!'

The wind blasted in a handful of leaves as she opened the door and it had begun to rain. Charles leaped out, held a sheltering black umbrella and soon had them settled.

Dropping Nattie off in Chelsea, it felt strange seeing Tom's car – her own old Mini-Cooper – parked tidily in the street. It brought back memories of driving it to Hampshire and tense weekends with Barney when her heart was with William. She ached to think of Barney's misery all through the affair. Victoria thought slightly wist-fully, too, of charming, uncomplicated Hugo who had always adored Nattie. But if she was happy to see him with Ahmed along, clearly there was nothing doing. Parents could never second-guess their chil-dren's lives, all the unpredictable, remarkable turns of fate and the future.

'You look exhausted.' William searched her face. 'I don't like this pallor. Did anything happen with Barney?' He stared at her. 'Nattie was there, I hope – she did show?'

Victoria smiled back at him. 'Women do hate being told they look tired.' She glanced over to the table, obliterated by the morning's first editions, and said lightly, 'Fewer black marks on the sheets, tonight! Nattie was certainly there. We actually got him to agree to treatment, which was a major miracle and all her doing. She didn't flinch from delivering that message; she was like a doctor telling it straight, Margaret Thatcher saying there is no alternative!'

That sounded too flippant, Victoria thought, feeling uncomfortable in his gaze and aware of trying too hard. She went to fill the kettle saying over her shoulder, 'Nattie and I had a little chat as we were leaving too – we've broken the ice. She'll be home later, which is great. I could do with some coffee right now, though; it did take it out of me tonight . . . She's gone to Hugo's, they're handing over the car there so she'll have a lift home with Tom, I expect.'

'But not too late, I hope.' William had followed over and was putting ground coffee in his red Thermos percolator. 'You and Nattie do need to thrash things out about Christmas. I'd like to get it all resolved myself – I don't fancy *The Courier* camped outside your parents' garden gate, getting up our backsides. They'll want to beef up the Shelby scam about your "links with terrorists" and do their damnedest to get a pic of Ahmed anywhere near you. It would be damaging all round; he is my reporter, and it's not a story I want getting legs.'

Victoria certainly didn't want that either. She thought it supremely ironical that *The Courier* should be giving her an out, a way of easing the impasse over Christmas and still avoiding contact with Ahmed – which still seemed necessary while he was under MI5 surveillance. Ahmed would understand *The Courier* problem, which meant Nattie would, too.

William took the coffee to the table and picked up a newspaper. Victoria sneaked two painkillers out of her bag and swallowed them at the sink. She sat down with him and he looked up with a grin. 'Monday's papers are still wall-to-wall Barnes; it'll be that way all

week on and off. They'll be flushing old flames out of the woodwork
to spill more beans – we've found one to do it – oh, and one of your
snotty little backbenchers, Ainsley Morgan, has broken ranks. Who
cares what he thinks, but he's pronounced that the Foreign
Secretary's had his chips and must be for the chop.'

That was bad news for Barnes, she thought. When your own side
turned turtle . . .

Soon there were sounds from the basement, voices: Nattie and
Tom home. It would be harder to talk about Ahmed and Christmas
if Tom were there and for once Victoria hoped he'd stay downstairs.

'Maudie's back from Edinburgh,' William said. 'She's here
tonight.'

Victoria smiled. He could always read her mind. Maudie had been
Nattie's best friend ever since school and had become Tom's burning
love, too. She was giving him a hard time, though – mooning after
a singer-guitarist whom she'd met at the Edinburgh Festival and
making Tom dangerously jealous.

He'd unburdened himself to Victoria, sought her out the weekend
of William's party at *The Post*. Tom had seemed almost as desperate
and possessive as Don José in *Carmen* and she dreaded to think what
he'd do if Maudie broke it off. Tom was a dreamer, an artist, mild
and good-natured, but, Victoria had come to realize, capable of a
brooding intensity of feeling. He was close to his father, but had
turned to his stepmother in emotional need. She sometimes wondered how well William really knew his son.

Sipping her coffee, deep in thought, it gave her a start, looking up
suddenly to see Nattie at the door.

William held the percolator aloft. 'Coffee?'

'Yes, thanks.' Nattie came in and pulled out a chair. She sat down opposite her mother looking distant, preoccupied. Then she started to cry.

'Darling! Whatever is it?' Victoria looked at her in alarm.

'It's so mean,' Nattie said, sniffing, quickly over it. 'I've never felt such bitter hatred for anyone. I can hardly see Ahmed now – I'm not getting at you, Mum, not going there again – this is all about that shit Shelby. He's the arsehole of all time.'

She wiped her eyes, looked shamefaced at her outburst, and wrapped her hands round the mug of coffee William had handed over.

'Ahmed says we have to keep dodging the press,' she carried on, 'that if we're photographed together it gives *The Courier* more chance of building on Shelby's lies, which is bad all round – for you especially, Mum, he says.'

'You do see that, Nattie?' William pressed. '*The Courier*'s "links with terrorists" line is very damaging – and we can't have that pissy little rag doing down one of my best reporters.'

'But I can't even go to his flat,' she wailed.

'No,' William agreed. 'Still, I'm sure you'll get round it somehow. It's short-term, things will soon be resolved.'

Victoria gave him a gimlet-eyed look that said, 'How do you know?' She felt as powerless as a prisoner facing a firing squad and wasn't looking forward to another meeting with Luke Andrews, the anti-terrorism chief, and Quentin Clayton in the morning. It was their last planned meeting before Christmas. She feared they had almost accepted, in a morbidly defeatist fashion, that the genius they were facing, who had eluded the entire combined skills of the police and MI5, was now unstoppable.

Nattie was talking to William in a way to exclude her mother. '. . . And you know, Ahmed insisted on paying for the hotel on

Friday; he swapped it on to his card! Oh, and he thought you might
be interested that he's had a call from Safa to say the honour-killing
girl she's in touch with, Leena, has agreed to see him. Safa's told
Ahmed she'll meet him in Cheltenham – probably where her friend's
in a refuge – and take him to a secret rendezvous place.'

'It'll be a good powerful story if Leena tells it all,' William said.
'What happened, her escape, but Ahmed will have a job getting it
out of her, given he's Muslim, male and a reporter. I doubt she'll find
it easy to trust him.'

Victoria was in deep sympathy with that. She felt like a fought-
over wishbone where trust in Ahmed was concerned; the spooks with
their suspicions were tugging on one side and all the people she loved
pulling hard on the other. She couldn't let herself snap.

'Of course Leena will,' Nattie said hotly, avoiding a glance at her
mother. 'She couldn't not – although he did have a job persuading
Safa to trust him in the first place. Ahmed's obsessed with getting
Leena to say enough to put her father and brother behind bars. When
you think of her life at risk from her own family . . . it's horrific. How
can there be so much terrible violence in the world?'

'Well, Home Secretary, only a couple of days to go – you must be
ready for a bit of R and R!' Luke Andrews smiled. Tony had gone out
to the lift block to meet Quentin.

'Rest and Recreation, Luke? I wouldn't be so sure about relaxation!
You won't have any of that this Christmas, I fear. Your family can't
be too pleased.'

'They're used to it,' he said equably, ramrod erect in his seat. 'They
know we're on full high alert. It's whether we make our skiing holiday in January that's the problem . . .'

He tailed off. Doom had really permeated into Luke's psyche, she knew; the sense of impending catastrophe, a feeling they might all have been snuffed out by then. Coming in, he had indicated they had some positive news to tell her once Quentin was there; it was obviously unconnected.

Victoria went over everything in her head yet again. A second boat had almost certainly been used. There was a boatyard at Carnforth, there would have been time enough, on a dark winter's night, to 'borrow' one for a fatal round trip that had included the murders of three policemen and a train driver, the theft of two canisters of High Level Waste. The abandoned boat had been a clever ploy, encouraging the police to concentrate their vehicle search in an immediate thirty-mile area instead of spreading a wider net. That had given the terrorists a vital head start.

It had been possible to plant a slim hope in the public's mind that the second canister of High Level Waste might yet be languishing on the ocean floor. She knew, though, and Luke knew, Quentin knew, that the chances of that were remote.

'Penny for them, Home Secretary?'

'I was just thinking, Luke, how extraordinarily hard it must have been to make off with a metre-high drum of radioactive waste tucked up under their jumpers. How did they do it!'

He was saved having to answer; Quentin and Tony were coming in. MI5's Director General was elegantly suited and shod; his tie had asymmetrical elliptical spots, pink on blue, and somehow managed to be both discreet and original.

Victoria was in a burgundy wool dress. She was feeling pale, tired out at the beginning of the week. It had left a bad taste, having to lie about the cut and livid bruise on her leg. 'So stupid,' she'd said, 'just caught it on the corner of the coffee table as I sat down.' William thought the worst of Barney, yet he had still believed her. She sighed inwardly and concentrated her mind.

As they settled in for the meeting, she asked the usual questions, 'Any progress? Anything to report?'

Quentin crossed his legs and smiled at her: smoothly, neutrally, mandarin fashion, but it was clear he was quietly elated. 'We successfully disrupted a terrorist plot over the weekend – a cell we've had under surveillance for some time. Luke's chaps uncovered a bomb in the final stages of production in a semi in Hayes, to our great relief. Five suspects being held.'

She made all the right congratulatory noises while thinking if only it had been a radioactive bomb . . .

They were, of course, Quentin assured her, pursuing a number of other leads.

'But no leads, I suppose, on any of Ahmed Khan's contacts?' Victoria asked, with some embarrassment since there obviously weren't any. 'No likely Cumbrian cell?'

'We're keeping a close eye. However there's no one we've come across, and not just in Cumbria, to match up to the presumed ringleader known as Fahad.'

It was as unsettling a meeting as all the others. They confirmed Christmas contingency plans. Goodbyes were said in an atmosphere as thick with gloom as the dense yellow fogs of old; they just couldn't see the way through. Victoria's head felt ready to burst. There was something so ominously and obviously symbolic about Christmas, but with nothing to go on, nothing, they could only sit tight and pray.

CHAPTER 29

It was Ahmed's third day back at work and he was plunged in again, up to his elbows in nervous energy, trying to keep abreast of the tidal wave of activity at *The Post*. Aside from a couple of people saying, 'Good break?' or 'How were the folks?', he might never have left his small patch of desk-space, his screen among many, and just had four life-changing weeks away in Leeds.

He struggled on with doing his expenses, his least favourite job, bleakly wishing he'd submitted them earlier and boosted his flagging bank-balance. It had been an expensive month; the thank-you dinner for his parents, wine to thank Tom for the car, the hotel night he'd have paid anything for.

His mobile beeped. Nattie's texts were a lifeline; they kept him aloft, on a higher plane from the office where the adrenaline of ambition burned like brandy, just as Osborne had described in his speech at *The Post* party, that night of meeting her, of falling in love.

Ahmed read her latest text. 'C-day *and* B-day? You cannot be serious!'

'Not 23rd or C-eve,' he sent back, 'nor even night of 22nd. Much to tell about that!'

'Call in lunch hour and spill?'

'U bet!' He had a smile on his lips, tapping it, then looked up to see Desmond Wallis was passing his desk and had stopped.

Des fixed him with a steady bleary eye before clearly arriving at some great thought. 'Robots,' he announced suddenly, with a splendid wobble of jowls.

'Boss?' Ahmed queried with gentle sarcasm, hoping Des wasn't being personal.

'Humabots they're called – robots with human feelings. Going on show at the Science Museum today. It's a Christmas special with the kiddies in mind. Off you go, keep it light, nice and cuddly, and short, two or three paras at most.'

Hardly scoop territory, Ahmed thought, as he grabbed what he needed and ran. 'Hug a Humabot' was hardly destined to make the front page.

He was delighted to cut loose. Covering a robot event could run into his lunch break, give him the freedom to talk to Nattie and more time to hunt for the pendant Christmas present he'd set his heart on for her, but was failing, as yet, to find.

It was the first time he'd been to the Science Museum. He found it breathtaking: everything from Stephenson's original Rocket locomotive to spacecraft launchers. He saw parents pointing out wonders to children and wistfully imagined himself in the future with a son of his own.

The humabot event was drawing crowds. The robots had round soft-toy faces and were supposed visibly to relax with kindness or shrink and tense up if people showed them anger. Small children seemed keener on shaking their fists and snarling than being gentle and the poor robots' pulses and clenched-fist movements were working overtime. Ahmed wondered if mechanical tiredness might set in.

He filed his copy over coffee in a Starbucks, then set off for the tube station, unsure where to shop for Nattie's present. Passing a small jeweller's shop whose window was filled with unwanted carriage clocks, bangles, small-stone engagement rings, functional watches, he peered in with little optimism.

Then he saw it. In a back corner of the window, displayed on a dark blue velvet backing, glinting and amber gold, the perfect colour to reflect Nattie's shining eyes.

He thought it was beautiful – except for the skinny insignificant gold chain, the kind that tangled too easily and acquired tiny impossible-to-undo knots. The price was hidden; it was probably academic. Definitely worth asking, though.

The door had a security buzzer, which seemed a little excessive, given the limited charms of the main stock. It locked shut once he was in and an elderly peroxide blonde behind the counter eyed him up and down, probably assessing his bank balance with brutal accuracy. She looked ready to replace his watch battery or bring out the tray of mini-stone rings.

'Could I see the topaz in the window, please?'

Her face was dubious, but she opened the window-back and brought it out.

Ahmed glanced at the price tag. 'Can you do anything on that – like I was trade?' He smiled, drawing on his entire charm repertoire, as though she were an available girl he wanted to date. The woman took off £20. He got it to £25. 'Now,' he said with a maximum-effect grin, 'another little request! Have you got a chunkier chain than that one?' He felt he might just be winning; she gave him a coyly wry, raised-eyebrow look and agreed to ferret around.

She was gone quite a while. Ahmed noticed an old man on an upper level watching the shop in her absence. Returning, though, she looked depressingly doubtful. 'There's only this gold watch-chain; sorry, it's all I can find.'

It fitted through the holder-loop and looked so perfect he could have kissed her. 'It's great, fantastic,' he enthused, before adding tensely, 'Can it be a straight swap?'

She gave that thought. 'Go on with you,' she smiled, 'if it means that much!'

It did. Ahmed left the shop £275 lighter, feeling life, while Fahad let him live it, was amazing. He'd scored with the pendant, but now Fahad had to be next on the list. The thought made Ahmed's impatience to see Nattie shift gear and become all the more vital; he wanted her with a force that frightened him. Calling her he had to lean against a steadying wall.

'Tell me you've thought of a way to meet,' she demanded, after he'd showered her with passion. 'You're not really working Christmas and Boxing Day? It's inhuman!'

'It's a reporter's lot. But listen, I'm meeting Safa this Friday, in Cheltenham. I'm hiring a car on expenses and could drive on to wherever. I'm free on the twenty-third and twenty-fourth. A whole weekend – and Friday night! Could Tom give you a lift to anywhere? I'm sure we can dodge *The Courier.*'

There was a silence; his heart plummeted. 'Friday night's fantastic,' Nattie said then, 'but it's the battle-royal football match in Southampton this Saturday, William and Mum's teams. We're going as a family, they'd be hurt if I drop out. And my uncle, that's Mum's brother Robert, and his wife and the four cousins always come on Christmas Eve at lunchtime, so I should see them—'

Ahmed tried to salvage what he could. 'I'll need to write up the honour-killing story, assuming Leena talks. If I did that on Saturday, during the match . . . perhaps afterwards I could drive you to somewhere near your grandparents'.' Christmas Eve was more of a problem, he thought. He'd hoped to drive straight to work early on Christmas Day after a third night together, but now saw it had to be late Sunday. He could call in on Jake and his parents at Oxford, though. His flatmate had been pressing him to come anytime over Christmas and Ahmed loved it there, the way Jake's parents stretched his mind.

'You won't keep me away Saturday night,' Nattie said. 'Tom will drop me off, I'm sure, and I needn't be back on Christmas Eve till just before the cousins leave.'

Ahmed felt the need to bank all the time with her he could. 'Friday night,' he said in a concentrated, overcharged way, 'two days and two nights. I'd better get back to the office and find us a discreet anonymous hotel.'

Safa was driving, but had assumed Ahmed was coming by train and chosen to meet at Cheltenham Station. Since it seemed as good a place as any they'd let it stand. He had a new battery in his recording machine, new notepads, a new set of raw nerves. He was entirely in Safa's hands, as uncertain about how things would pan out as setting out on a blind date. The essential ingredient was somewhere private for Leena to feel uninhibited enough to open up, but even that had been impossible to arrange. He waited in the station car park on edge. Safa was due at one.

Des had been festively good-humoured about Ahmed's day out.

He'd borne the mild indignity of being bypassed – orders on the honour-killing story coming direct from the editor-in-chief – with magnanimous fortitude. Ahmed was beginning to feel genuine affection for the old soak and a new eagerness to please.

Safa was ten minutes late. It was a relief to see her silver Renault Clio turning into the car park. She emerged from it in a belted navy coat and black boots, dark hair tumbling glossily over her shoulders, a few strands catching on the wool. She gave a warm smile.

Ahmed asked after her journey from Leeds and suggested a quick bite of lunch. 'And I need help,' he said, 'whether to book a hotel room, somewhere for Leena to be private? I'm a bit in a fog; I couldn't make plans—'

'Shall we drive in convoy and find a quiet pub,' Safa said, 'somewhere for lunch where you can wait while I go for Leena? We'll sort something out then.'

Ahmed was rueing the lack of a concrete plan when she gave him even more to think about. 'You've acquired quite a bit of notoriety back home, you know.'

'Let me guess . . . The men are hostile, the women less so, more curious about my girlfriend's mum?'

'Not bad. People assume it's short-term, not destined to last . . . Your mother's embellishing it a little – from what I've gathered from mine!'

They found a pub whose car park was almost empty, which seemed surprising on a Friday before Christmas. Good for privacy, no great advertisement for the food.

Inside it had a huge eating area. Simply decorated with dark-green paper placemats and napkins, a few fresh flowers on each table; the seats in the bar area were covered in tartan and a log fire was burning in an attractive grate.

There were a few people in the bar, one or two eating at nearby tables, but, Ahmed thought, it couldn't be bettered for a private talk. 'Drink first?' he asked.

They took a couple of mineral waters and the menu to a bar table.

'I can't understand why it's not busier here,' he said, getting up again to place an order for salmon fishcakes.

The barman, a great lumberjack of a man, picked up on the remark. 'We were booked for an office Christmas party, but the firm's going under and cancelled.'

'That's bad luck,' Ahmed said. He stayed leaning on the bar. 'My friend has to go and meet someone off a train later. Okay by you if I sit over a few cups of coffee till they're back? It may be almost an hour.'

'No sweat,' he said cheerily. 'We don't close our doors.'

The food was soon ready. They went to a far table in the restaurant and agreed the fishcakes were good and the place ideal for talking to Leena. Ahmed soon found himself asking about Safa's private life. She was in a flat on her own. He was curious; he liked her. 'How is it, living alone? Do you cook – have friends round?'

'I do have a fella in my life if that's what you mean.' She smiled. Her lively warmth transformed that long-nosed face, Ahmed decided.

'He's married?'

She looked away. 'Don't probe. I can't forget you're a reporter. My fella's not Hindu like the doctor poor Leena fell for; there are none of those complications.'

'Just the obvious one? I'm not probing, only asking as a friend.'

'Every day I swear I'll find the strength to end it, but then I see him . . . He didn't marry for love, it was arranged – it just hasn't worked out. If my parents knew about him it would carve them up, but they wouldn't resort to violence. Leena's been dealt an un-believably brutal hand,' Safa said, standing up. 'You'll be shocked. I'm on my way to get her now.'

Ahmed had a forty-minute wait. He breathed a sigh of relief when he looked out of the window and saw Safa's Clio turn into the car park with a girl in the passenger seat. He went over to the barman and ordered tea and cakes, thinking they might need a little comfort food.

Leena was a small size eight, a tiny slip of a thing. She was in snug dark-navy jeans and a grey anorak with a lighter fake-fur edging to the collar. He'd assumed she'd be wearing the hijab at the least, given her background.

She had huge startled eyes and her nails were varnished in sixties shocking pink. With her pointy shoes, kitten heels, she looked like any Western girl in her early twenties. It was hard to believe she was stuck in a refuge and in fear of her life.

After the introductions and his thanks to Leena for coming, Ahmed led the way back to the table. 'I've asked for some tea,' he said, helping her off with her anorak. 'Hope that's okay?'

'And something to eat?' she asked, pulling out a chair. 'I get hungry when I'm all nerves.'

She kept her startled round eyes trained as he sat opposite prom-ising cakes and more; her eyes were dark pools, gleaming and deep. 'I'm the one with nerves,' he said. 'I hate to think of you having them too!'

The barman lumbered over with the tea and cakes and eyed them with mild interest. He said, as Ahmed offered his overworked card,

'No sweat – just when you're done.'

Safa was pouring the tea. It was impossibly hard to get started.

'I wondered if you'd bring Natalia along,' Leena said brightly, jerking him almost out of his skin. 'She looked so beautiful in the paper. I'd have loved to meet her.'

He felt his face flare, Leena was throwing him at every turn. 'I'll see you do. I know she'd love to meet you, too. It's just that, well, I thought you'd want—'

'Privacy, secrecy? I've made enough fuss about it, but I have to. The people looking after me say my father's been calling at lots of places. They're worried.'

'But you didn't want those people to tell the police?'

'No. You don't know what it's like. It's my family. And the police would be slow, not that interested – my father would get me just the same.'

Leena sipped tea and studied her shocking-pink nails. 'It's like I'm on borrowed time.'

Ahmed felt tremendous empathy; he shared the feeling. He sensed she was close to tears. 'Wouldn't you have worn the hijab at home?'

She nodded. 'It feels better protection like this. And I've left that life. I can't go back, ever again, can't even see my mum.' The dark pools overflowed.

'I can help,' Ahmed said, 'if you'll only trust me enough. Your father and brother should be behind bars. And the paper can help arrange things for you, help you make a new life, somewhere like Canada, America. Have you any friends abroad?'

'But I'd have to go to court . . . There'd be others in the family after me—'

'You'd be well protected – and the publicity would help. People would think at least twice before trying. And your father and brother wouldn't be given bail.'

Ahmed gave a gentle smile. 'And consider,' he said carefully, 'other girls in your position. Honour killings need to be taken far more seriously, given maximum exposure; you'd be helping them, too. Can you trust me, Leena? Can I start the tape and hear your story? We'll hold it up till everything's in place for your full protection. Even my life's on the line, you see, everyone knows I write for the paper—'

'In that case I can't possibly do it – I don't want you at risk, too.'

God, what a fool . . . 'I'll look after me,' Ahmed said firmly, reaching into his pocket to press 'record'. 'Forget that, I won't have a byline; we're both going to be fine.'

Leena grinned. 'I hope so. I can't keep leaning on Safa . . . She saved my life, you see – and two policemen and a dog.'

He raised his eyebrows in query. 'I'll get to that bit,' Leena went on, 'but I'll start right back. My father beat us as children, to teach us discipline. He kept it up, right into my teens; he'd slap me about if he thought I'd been insolent, my sister, too. Not my brother; he's twenty and the favoured one since he was about twelve. My sister's twenty-two, married just months – not her choice, it was all arranged, but she's not unhappy, I think.'

'And you? Was a marriage being planned that you didn't want?'

Safa poured more tea and Leena sipped it, letting her eyes skim round the lonely-looking laid-up tables. The place was deserted, the barman through in the back.

'I felt I'd rather die than have my parents choose for me. I was in love and they had in mind someone in Pakistan, I'd have had to go there for the wedding, come back with him and not get my degree. I asked to be allowed to make my own decision.'

'That didn't go down well, I suppose?'

'My father knocked me to the floor. My brother kicked me. When they came at me again I begged forgiveness and said I'd do it. I thought I'd run away in Pakistan before coming home. There was a sort of truce for a few days after that, but my brother, Arif, began picking up rumours about Hari and he goaded me, swore to tell my father. "I know what you're about, you slut. You wait till Aba hears", that kind of thing.'

She'd used 'Aba', the formal way a son addressed his father. Ahmed thought of his own easygoing relationship, its difference from the harshness of Leena's home.

'So I was kind of primed for trouble,' she smiled. 'I came home from university one evening and said I wanted to go back out to play chess – I like it and belong to the chess club,' she said, almost as an admission. 'But I only had to look at my father; Arif was standing there beside him . . . He closed the kitchen door and I can't tell you the fear in my belly; my heart was beating so fast I had to keep swallowing, almost like trying to douse it down. My mother was out at friends. Perhaps she knew the mood he was in . . .

'"Chess? You think I was born yesterday?" He banged the table so violently a plate jumped to the floor. "You're going nowhere." He hit me then, many times; I fell against the table all dizzy and he picked me off it to hit me again. It was true, of course,' Leena said honestly, 'I was going to see Hari quickly on the way to the club.

'All the time my father was shaking me, hitting me, going crazy, he was spitting out about dishonour to the family, the disgrace, disgusting rumours about a daughter of his. He should never have agreed to my going to university, I'd be leaving immediately. The blows kept coming, my nose was streaming blood; I couldn't focus . . . If I'd lied, said it was all malicious gossip it would have made no difference.'

She was beginning to cry. Ahmed glanced back, but the barman was still out of sight. Recovering herself she carried on.

'I was almost beyond the pain barrier and my father was hissing about my brother escorting me to Pakistan. He was preventing me seeing Hari, who was waiting where we used to meet . . . My mouth was full of blood, I could only slur out the words . . . I said they never need see me again, it was my life to lead.

'His eyes bulged, he looked at me with such cruel crazed hatred I knew I was going to die. It felt like it couldn't come soon enough, though, with the throbbing in my head, dizziness – the agony of Arif's nails digging deep into my skin; he was holding me up while I was beaten and had pushed up my shalwar kameez sleeves for a tighter grip.

'My father's strong hands came round my neck. Arif let go, since those throttling hands were holding me up, and he picked up a chopping knife on the worktop.'

Ahmed felt quite nauseous.

'I've got a horrible scar from my brother's knife. I wish it would fade. But it is only weeks, I suppose.' Leena tossed back her hair and pulled at the black sweater she was wearing. Ahmed shrank a little at the sight of a livid reddish-brown gash to her shoulder, curling down like a large garden worm. The stitch-marks still showed.

'Safa got it seen to,' Leena said, and they exchanged an inscrutable look. 'Then the doorbell rang,' she continued. 'Arif opened the backdoor and looked up the side alley. "Panda car out front," he muttered, sounding quite nervy. My father loosened his hold and I crumpled to the floor; my legs wouldn't support me. But I could hear, despite all the ringing in my ears. Arif was telling my father he'd been with a few brothers last night. "Some *Gora* trash had a go, Aba," he said. "We had to fight our corner." The bell rang again, more insistently. My father went to get it, saying Arif had better come, too. They thought I was beyond bothering about by that stage!

'Arif had the knife, though, and on his way out he bent down and took that passing slash at my shoulder. The fabric being quite thick and wintry helped a bit.'

Ahmed wondered at her buoyancy, her incredible lack of self-pity. He asked Safa, 'Is this where you come in?'

'Not yet – anyway I had no part. Tell him what you managed to do, Leena.'

'Well, Arif hadn't latched the backdoor, I only had to push on it and crawl out.'

Ahmed was wondering why the hell she hadn't crawled to the policemen, but she'd explained that.

'The need to survive,' she was saying, 'is like, well, like that desperate feeling of being in love; you just can't let go. There's a low brick wall between us and the next house, we're end of terrace. A British family live there and they have a dog, some kind of mongrel. My father's scared of dogs and hates living next to non-Muslims, but I'm friendly with the daughter, Sharon, who's fifteen; I like the family and the dog. I feel embarrassed at how my family ignores them.

'I'd seen the family going out when I came home from uni. There's an old granny who's always at home, though, and the dog, Paxo he's called, was in the garden. I made it to the wall, it's only a few feet, and I was lying on it, feeling faint, bleeding into my clothes, trying not to pass out, talking to Paxo, desperate he shouldn't bark. I could hear the rumble of voices, Arif's whinging; the policemen must have been taking a statement or something.

'I managed to roll off the wall and fall towards the house then crawled on in agony, talking to Paxo, and frantically thinking how to get out of sight. There was a wooden lid to a walled container, near that house's backdoor, the sort where dustbins used to be kept before wheelie bins; if I could just get into that . . . I got the lid up a fraction, but it was chocka, full of cement bags and stuff. There were stairs up beside it, it's sort of half-basement back garden, and I could get on top of it at least. I could hear the police leaving; it was awful. Then I suddenly thought of the wheelie bin. I was almost on a level with it. The lid was quite light to lift, I swung in my wobbly legs, reached up with my good arm and flipped it shut.'

'But the smell, you had no air, you were bleeding!' Ahmed cried out in horror.

'I did keep passing out with the stench,' Leena said. 'I had to lift the lid a fraction whenever I could, but I hardly had the strength. I thanked God Paxo was in the garden! He even seemed to know I needed protecting and went and growled at the wall. Arif and my father must have been peering over. He's not fierce, but he can sound it. They shone a torch, I think. I prayed there wasn't a trail of blood, but it had mostly soaked into my clothes. My head – and my heart – wouldn't stop pounding and the pain in my ribs was excruciating. I had two cracked ribs as it turned out.

'Then I had another bit of luck. My mobile was in the pocket of my shalwar kameez. I lifted the lid, the bag of stinking rubbish under me was smelling unbearably, and got just enough air to be able to speak to Safa. I told her to drive till she saw them looking for me and when they were far enough away, not be afraid of Paxo and help me out.'

'It worked,' Safa said. 'I did just that. I called Hari in advance, he'd been waiting for Leena and he is a doctor, and told him he had an emergency to deal with, a matter of life and death. Paxo barked a bit, but he seemed almost human, almost in on it all! I got Leena away, Hari stitched her up and gave her powerful painkillers. He knew about refuges, too.'

'It gives me the sweetest satisfaction,' Ahmed said, 'imagining Leena's father and brother being so thwarted. They must have been scratching their heads! They'd left you for half-dead and you did a Houdini on them. I should think they had a very tense few days, waiting for another visit from the cops.'

'The cops backed off Arif's brawl, though,' Safa said with frustration. 'Unless someone's fatally knifed they don't much want to know.'

Ahmed reached across the table to squeeze Leena's hand. He went to the bar, switching off his recording machine, and the barman appeared from out the back. He seemed pleased to be profusely thanked.

He stared curiously. 'Aren't you that guy in *The Post*? Just last week with the Home Secretary's daughter – where've they been hiding her, I'd like to know.'

'I do work for the paper,' Ahmed answered coyly, overwhelmed by the speed of his notoriety, the power of the press.

'So it said,' the barman observed dryly. 'She's a stunner, all right.'

'I'll be off now. It was good of you to let us hang out here. We got a lot of work done.'

'No sweat.'

Ahmed caught up with Safa and Leena who were already out in the deserted car park. 'Carry on just as you are,' he advised Leena. 'I can reach you through Safa when the time is right. We're going to tell your story and see justice done. Here's my card. Call me any time, night or day. You've lost a family, I know, but I'm sure the world is going to be your oyster, now, though it's taken some prising out of its shell.'

Ahmed gave her a spontaneous hug and they parted. He set off for Southampton.

He couldn't have explained about Fahad, but even, he thought morbidly, if he wouldn't be around to see Leena's story in print, Osborne would make sure it appeared. He thought of Yazid's implication that a bomb would have gone off by January – which led him to Khalid's inquest that he so dreaded. There was Iqbal to look out for, who could be deployed to do Fahad's dirty work . . .

He shivered and drove on; he was still feeling moved beyond belief by Leena's monumental courage, such a slip of a girl with the big round eyes. But she looked bright and alive, a survivor against all the odds.

His thoughts began travelling like arrows; they homed in on Southampton and the hotel room he had booked. Tom was going to take Nattie there. Not long to wait now. His heart began to sing and he put his foot down.

CHAPTER 30

After trawling round outer Southampton a few times Ahmed was glad to see the sign for the hotel. On the website it had looked utilitarian and drab, anonymous but with an ideal separate annexe. 'You'll hate the place,' he told Nattie with embarrassment. 'It's like you'd see in a sordid adultery scene in an American movie. I feel really bad—'

'For God's sake! Do you think I'll be studying the wallpaper? I'd settle for bedbugs at a push . . . But I'll tell you something quite funny about that hotel when I see you.'

She was already in Hampshire with her mother since they were on better speaking terms. Nattie said her mother looked exhausted with the constituency Christmas load. Tom was coming for the football and happy to ferry Nattie to and fro. Then he was driving on to Somerset for Christmas with his mother, Ursula, his sisters and his stepfather Julian.

Ahmed was intensely relieved at the way things had worked out – apart from losing Nattie to her family on Christmas Eve.

After the match they could set off for Worcestershire where he'd found a charming-looking cottage hotel not too far from her grandparents. The rooms had kitchenettes, all facilities and Nattie would enjoy making house. He hoped she didn't have an obsessive love of laundry like his mother.

The Southampton hotel came first, though, and his heart dropped with a clang, turning up its curling speed-bumped drive, unattractively floodlit and lined with dark dusty rhododendrons. It didn't bode well.

He was just parking when Nattie called. His breath came in short pumped-out puffs like a fire-bellows, imagining something wrong, but she was only giving an ETA. Tom was still an hour away from the house.

That meant an hour and a half. Tom could have left earlier, Ahmed thought resentfully. Nattie was only up the road with her mother – couldn't she thumb a lift with fucking Rodney?

He felt ashamed. It was symptomatic, his nerves were in pieces; he wiped his palms on his jeans, cursing at himself, took out his bag and a carrier of food for supper and walked slowly up to the uninviting hotel.

The reception was carpeted in swirls of orange and brown; the place was a complete style-free zone. A cheery young girl brightened the place up a bit, and he traded warm grins as she swiped his card in the hope of a free extension of time in the room. The blurb had said late checkouts would be charged as an extra night. She confided the hotel was busy with functions, but it was a desert of empty rooms. Sure, he could stay on till six, the cleaning could be done next day.

Ahmed thanked her effusively, and went in search of the annex. He thought the room just about got by: a double bed with a prickly-looking fitted brown bedcover, a desk with Internet access, a basic

bathroom, a midget minibar. He used one of the two tumblers provided as a vase for the bunch of freesias he'd bought while shopping
for supper. A takeaway sushi and some fruit had been the best he
could find.

He unpacked bottles of wine and water. He showered, put on a
clean shirt, a blue-check one Nattie approved of, checked the Leena
tape had recorded properly – although he'd used a backup machine
as well – then watched the news. There'd been a monumental pile-
up on the M1, although miraculously no fatalities. Sixteen cars
involved. All the poor sods trying to get to Christmas destinations,
stuck in the unending tailback, could count themselves lucky,
Ahmed thought. He was tensed for breaking news of a radioactive
explosion every time he turned on a television set.

He tried to use the waiting time productively and enclosed himself in a thought box, a padded cell that allowed no room for
impatient lusting, no indulgent longing. He needed to lock mental
horns with Fahad; somehow he had to work it out.

Fahad would be the one to press any activating button, he felt sure.
Wouldn't he want to watch the annihilating cloud going up, see for
himself the culmination of all his lengthy masterly planning? He
would seek out a safely distant vantage point – but where? And when?

And to what end, Ahmed thought yet again – simply loathing of
the West? To stoke his psychopathic dreams? Did he see himself as
triumphant ruler of Islamist Britain?

Any activating device was bound to be a mobile. He had thought
of acquiring a jammer just in case he was ever near enough to use one
and had begged advice from Gerald on the foreign desk who was a
dome-headed gadget and gismo geek.

Gerald asked no questions. 'You'll pick one up in Tottenham

Court Road, easy enough. It is not against the law to own a jammer, although illegal to disrupt the phone network. The law's an ass!'

'I'll try not to be caught using it.'

Sitting at the desk in his magnolia-painted hotel room Ahmed felt a ridiculous need to check his jacket pocket. The jammer was safely there. He carried on thinking. He had to go by his overwhelming hunch and work on the assumption that Fahad had the High Level Waste and now a bomb.

Fahad was a sophisticated loner who'd kept clear of links to cells, he was a man with enough confident faith in his ability to evade MI5 to have held up launching his devastating attack. Why the delay? Parliament had gone into Recess. There were few people around in Whitehall. St Paul's Cathedral? Security would be incredibly tight everywhere, the country was still on high alert.

If Fahad wanted a view, his ultimate climax, he'd need to be on high ground, able to check the direction of winds . . .

His mobile was ringing; Ahmed hardly heard it as he feverishly fiddled with the focus on his thoughts, like a camera or binoculars, trying to gain perfect revealing clarity.

'You let it ring,' Nattie said. 'Hope it wasn't a bad time? We're almost here.'

'Never a bad time! Can Tom make for the car park? I'll meet you there.' He grabbed the room key, slammed the door and ran.

The air was icy and more still than past days, the stormy winds spent. Ahmed felt the chill through his thin shirt, but his shivers were in anticipation and had nothing to do with the cold.

Tom's car turned in, flashed its lights and parked. They were both out of it as Ahmed reached them, Nattie coming beside him and linking fingers in the dark.

'Hi, how you doing? Sorry about the hold-up.' Tom grinned.

'Great of you to help out,' Ahmed said, leaning into the car for Nattie's things. She seemed to have brought at least a dozen carriers. 'Coming to my luxury suite for a glass of wine?' he offered forlornly, reappearing. 'There's an open bottle at the ready—'

'You're a good actor,' Tom remarked, 'you said that almost as though you meant it! No, I'll get on back and keep Victoria company till Dad turns up.' He smiled at Nattie. 'Rodney says we should leave plenty of time tomorrow, Nats. It's a one-thirty kick-off, you will be ready? She's been cooking, Ahmed, smelling out the car. Enough to keep you going in a bunker for weeks. See you!' Tom kissed Nattie and drove away.

Ahmed led her to the annexe with five of her carriers in each hand. Inside their universally uniform hotel room he dumped them thankfully. 'Welcome to my bunker,' he said gently, touching her face, her long silky-soft beautiful hair. Then he pressed her close and made up for a week of lost time.

The prickly brown bedcover was in a heap on the floor. Nattie swung out of bed and, stepping over it with swan-like grace, made for her clutch of carriers. She squatted naked in front of the fridge in a way that made Ahmed want to start all over and began jettisoning the cans and sorry little spirit miniatures. 'I need room for my stuff,' she announced.

He watched idly from the bed as she restocked the fridge, gazing on as she produced a French loaf, the smelling cheese . . .

'There's enough to last us,' she said with a backward grin. 'But you can stir yourself now, light this candle and lay up the desk for dinner. Your freesias are gorgeous.'

'And you're very bossy,' he said, coming to kiss her. 'Muslim males are used to having it all done for them. You'll be making me do my own washing next.'

'And ironing,' she said.

They pulled the desk out from the wall and used the bed-end as a second seat, sitting opposite each other so that he could look at her. Over the sushi – her food would do Saturday night, she said – he asked what the funny thing was she had to tell him about the hotel. 'There can't be anything! I know the place is a comic turn, but—'

'It's just that Mum insisted on knowing where I'd be – we are in her constituency – and while this wasn't exactly the scene of one of her assignations with William, they were both asked to speak at a festival here once. It was when the press were really out to get them and it gave them a chance to meet!'

It was a coincidence Ahmed enjoyed.

'I want to get heavy now,' he said, pouring more Sauvignon and holding her eyes. 'I'm sure Fahad's about to show his hand and I'm sick with worry about your safety. Will you go through every single thing you're doing in the next days?'

'You think about your own safety. I'm safe as houses, just at Gran and Grandpa's. The only thing I might do is go and see Dad. He's in Cornwall with his father for Christmas. It's a long way . . .' she smiled, 'but Mum says he needs love, and I just feel I should.'

'Couldn't you wait till your dad's back in London?' he urged persuasively, anxious after what Nattie had told him had happened at Barney's flat, convinced she'd have underplayed it. 'I could come with you, then, and meet him if you'd like that—'

'I really would – but I think I'll still go to Cornwall. You'll be at work after all.'

Nattie was preoccupied, up from her chosen seat on the end of the bed, rummaging in a bag and levering out slices of upside-down tart from a container and on to cardboard plates. He told her it looked fantastic and her face lit up.

'I've brought teabags and instant coffee and a kettle in case there wasn't one – packets of cereal, milk, orange juice, croissants for the morning.'

'We could probably have had breakfast in the room,' he grinned.

'I didn't want the waiters, Mum's voters, recognizing me.'

'I've got you a little present,' Ahmed said, feeling shy.

'I have for you as well – but let's have them on Sunday morning and be as Christmassy as possible – although that probably means more to me than to you!'

She leaned on her arms to kiss him across the desk. 'You looked unsettled just then. Was it me talking about Christmas?'

He held on to her arm, pressing his cheek to it, overcome with the intimacy of being so understood. He felt his body stirring again, the blood rushing. He licked her skin, drinking in the warm, peachy scent and trapped a few of the tiny golden hairs on her arm between his teeth. 'No, just . . . needs and thoughts and fears,' he said, 'things to get heavy about.'

'Like any in particular?' She sat down on the end of the bed again, holding his gaze.

'Well, Shelby for one.'

'Oh. He hasn't, surely, done anything else?' Nattie looked down, as though feeling guilty. Ahmed didn't know how to explain his obsessive jealousy. The thought of Shelby making out with her never left him; it was corroding as burning acid. It took hold of his mind whose focus should be solely Fahad.

'I'm sure Shelby's done plenty,' he answered, 'but this time it's me. I want to do him. I've got a sort of backlog of hate to deal with. He blew my cover, which I could have done without, but I'd got as far as I could with the Leeds lot. And Fahad won't be showing his hand again – I like to flatter myself that for a moment on that Fell walk he thought I might be genuinely on side. He does, of course, now know for sure he's got a score to settle and I feel a bit like a lame rabbit with a blocked-up burrow. But what really gets to me, the real reason I want to do Shelby, is thinking of him with you—'

It wasn't serving anything, admitting to vicious retrospective jealousy, Ahmed knew, except to explain his need for revenge.

'Just don't go there,' Nattie was saying. 'I hate myself almost as much as I hate him! How would you do him, though? I'm all for it, but don't really see how.'

'Entrapment.'

'What exactly does that mean? I'm never quite sure—' She looked a little uneasy, certainly more dubious.

'Well, we know he deals, you've seen it with Hugo, but without dropping Hugo right in it, which I know you'd hate to do, it's a very hard thing to prove. The police aren't going to bother. Shelby's small beer – even *The Post*, for all its needle over *The Courier* piece, isn't going to lay out on having him followed. But they are sore, and Shelby's been in enough gossip columns to make him reasonably newsworthy, so I do think William might go along with the idea of entrapment.'

'But how does it work? It's a horrible word.'

'Describes it, though. A reporter, not me obviously, hangs out with people in Shelby's circle – my flatmate Jake, for instance, knows one or two – and at some stage the reporter lets slip he's in the market for a bit of weed, skunk, crack or whatever. Maybe he'll buy some a couple of times, casually chatting Shelby up, getting him bragging – not difficult – and all the while he'll be running a tiny tape in his pocket, recording the lot. The police won't touch anything gained by entrapment, it's no good as evidence for prosecution, but the paper will use it – and that won't be much fun for Shelby. Not the sort of publicity he usually courts. And his clients won't like it one bit. They'd run a mile.'

'What about Shelby's own supplier? Would they get nasty?'

'They'd cut off his supplies, but probably no more than that. They'd turn on him, all right, if he owed them money or shopped them, but he'd know better than to do that. What do you reckon, though? Would you mind if I set up that little scam to get even?'

Ahmed could tell Nattie was uncomfortable. People always were. It was the maggoty underside of his business that caused even those who gobbled up filth, sex and sleaze with their Sunday cornflakes to tut-tut about dirty press tactics over afternoon cups of tea.

She was busying herself, throwing used plates in a rubbish bag.

Then she looked up and answered. 'There's nothing I've wanted more these last weeks than to even the score with that arsehole . . . And I suppose there's really no nice way of getting nasty.'

'It's down to you, darling Nattie,' Ahmed forced himself to say, 'although – and here's the heavy pressure bit – I'm too full of poison for my own good. It's like a really crippling Shelby snake bite and this would be the serum to sort me out.'

Nattie gave him an ironic look. 'Put like that it's not down to me at all!' She sighed. 'I guess I do have to start being less squeamish, more of a toughie like William. I've a strong feeling he did something really shifty with Dad or he'd never have got Mum away; she had such a conscience, Dad could always wear her down. It was best for her, whatever William did. I can't hold it against him. Any more than I'd ever hold this grotty tacky way of doing Shelby against you!'

Ahmed couldn't wait to hustle her to bed after that. He made slow luxurious abandoned love feeling freed-up for the permission to play dirty, and able to sleep sweeter with the woman he loved in his arms.

Tom called the next morning to say he'd wait for Nattie in the car park. Ahmed thought he was too embarrassed to come to the room, that their bunker seemed too private and impregnable a place. He would have felt the same.

At the car seeing Nattie off, they talked football a minute or two. Ahmed said it would better for Leeds United's chances in the Premier League if Liverpool duly romped home. Nattie hung on his arm approvingly at that, she was a Liverpool supporter, but Tom, not that interested in football, just gunning for Victoria's team, insisted Southampton would win.

'Some hope,' Ahmed retorted cheerily. He whispered to Nattie that it would be easy to spot her on telly – no camera could resist a lingering look. Then he waved them away.

His mood was flat with her gone. He felt edgy, bursting with impatience to be off to Worcestershire the moment she returned. It made sense, he thought, to be all packed up and he spent time transferring their various bags and carriers to the car.

There was still some thin sunlight, although the wind was getting up again, a colder wind than of late, one that seemed to blow in a sense of gloomy morbidity. Ahmed attributed it to the hours he had alone ahead of him. He shivered and thought at least the food should be fine, the car would be cold as a fridge.

Back in the room he got going on his laptop – logging on first to check his email before playing back the Leena tape, transcribing it at speed and hearing again her powerful moving account.

He did a solid hour then stood up for a stretch. A cup of tea seemed a good idea; he used the kettle and sachets provided. And the match was about to start. Ahmed tuned into Sky – with good timing as it happened; the cameras were just closing in on the Home Secretary and Osborne and he had a glorious glimpse of Nattie, sitting next to her stepfather. Tom was on Victoria's other side. Battle lines drawn.

A commentator was carefully explaining the divided loyalties of the family to a few million viewers, using the press's overworked phrase about a battle royal. Ahmed felt wistfully out of it and a predictable sense of resentment at the way things were – which inevitably drew his mind back to Fahad.

And then suddenly he knew. He saw it all with starkly illuminated, horrific clarity – saw the scale of the atrocity, the annihilating obliterating force of it, the unimaginable consequences. His skin froze; it recoiled, shrank back on his bones, shuddered and flinched, it was pricking all over as with a thousand needles.

It was all so obvious now. The enormity, the towering iceberg of shock was too much for him. He couldn't handle it and doubled over, hanging his head, swallowing back bile then feeling his body convulsing and about to erupt at both ends.

He only just made it to the tiny cramped bathroom. He was drenched in cold sweat and his nausea was rising again. The stench was awful. Ahmed couldn't function. Somehow he had to – and fast. He turned on the bath taps, cleaned up; splashed cold reviving water on his clammy sickly face.

There had to be a chance. How could he have missed that glaring clue? If only, if only . . . Fahad had said it so casually: an insignificant mention of knowing all about the battle royal and yet it had been the giveaway. There was always one tiny slip, Ahmed thought, to trip up the most brilliant of evil plans.

He called Osborne's mobile. It was the cameras trained on Nattie, on Osborne and her mother, he thought, that had sparked his memory. But if only, if only he'd seen it all before.

They would be right at the epicentre; perhaps that would help it be quick . . . All thirty thousand fans, everyone in that capacity crowd would die, many slowly and in excruciating agony, none of them likely to survive. His mobile was pressed to his ear. Osborne was bound to answer, he must. Surely he'd be listening out, have his phone on vibrate, with the country on high alert?

Osborne was the only hope. He could talk direct to the one person who mattered. Ahmed knew nobody else would believe him. Pointless ringing the police.

The ringing stopped; Osborne's mobile went on to voicemail. Ahmed left the most dramatic panic-account that anyone could have ever committed to an answerphone.

He called Nattie. She wasn't answering either. Oh, God . . .

She mustn't know, mustn't die in fear, he thought, as he begged her on the voicemail to tell William to call. 'It's really urgent.' He added then, as lightly as he could manage, 'And remember I love you completely, by the way . . . beyond death, beyond evil. You're my life, all my blue skies.'

The television was still blaring; the noise of the match, that thirty-thousand-strong roar, seemed at crescendo pitch. There must have been a goal, Ahmed thought, with desperate bitterness – it explained why Osborne and Nattie hadn't heard their phones. For pity's sake! Couldn't Osborne even look at his, check if it had rung?

Ahmed held his head in his hands. Minutes were ticking by . . . Did the woman he loved and everyone else in that packed stadium have to lose their lives because someone had scored a lousy goal?

CHAPTER 31

The mind-blasting roar of thirty thousand hyped-up fans had a sharpening effect; Ahmed thought of them all silenced by a radio-active bomb and knew he had to act. He broke through the sound barrier, was over his sickness and impotent helplessness, back in control. He'd never felt a greater determination in his life.

There could still be time. Fahad had to be somewhere near. He might be savouring the thrill and in no hurry to press the button, Ahmed thought. He might be waiting, content to let the game run on – even into the second half. Or was his finger hovering over his mobile? Was Fahad all poised for his ultimate high?

Surely, surely Osborne must call? Ahmed felt confident he would take it seriously, but could he persuade others to as well? Would anyone else believe it was for real? They were suspicious of him, Ahmed thought, they'd never accept it as fact just on his say-so; they'd think he was mixing it, devious, even a ranting loon-bag. MI5 must deal with enough false alarms.

Surely they'd take no chances? He knew exactly what had to be done. But even if they were persuaded, would the authorities act fast enough? Would it be in time?

Ahmed frantically tried Osborne again on the hotel phone; he cursed when the line was busy – then his own mobile began to ring. He answered breathlessly with his mobile clenched between chin and shoulder to be free to write, take down numbers, anything.

'Some fucking message you left,' Osborne snorted. 'You one hundred-per-cent serious? Not hallucinating – fallen overboard? Hardly brilliant timing for a great Damascus revelation if I may say—'

Ahmed couldn't stand it. 'Don't talk, *please*! There is a bomb, I know it, and it could go off in minutes. Just tell them they've got to cut off all the mobile masts, like now, like this second.'

'I've been trying to get that done . . . Victoria's onto the DG as we speak.'

Tears began streaming down Ahmed's face; he wanted to beg Osborne to get Nattie out of that stadium. Shouldn't he be trying to save his family? Couldn't he see they got out somehow?

'Fahad's succeeded this far,' he said, choking back his tears, 'the bomb will be in there. He'll have got round the dog searches, all the extra checks. The security must be just that bit less tight out of London. Fahad will have worked out a way.'

He was cracking up, his sobbing becoming obvious. 'Isn't there a way of getting out Nattie and Tom? Couldn't they just slip away?'

'Not possible, Ahmed,' his boss said firmly. 'All we can do is sit tight alongside this ticking fucking bomb – assuming you're right of course – watch the game and hope for an equalizing goal. Liverpool need to get going and show their spurs.'

That was courage, Ahmed thought. Osborne was staring an agonizing death in the eye and yet he could take the necessary action, joke, show not the slightest sign. God knew, though, what fear and terror he must really feel inside.

His mobile rang again and he jumped. It was Nattie. 'I know something's up, Mum's been on the phone for an age. You will be super careful, whatever's going on? But that was a wonderful message! What have I done to deserve—'

He broke in. 'I'm full of love, darling Nattie. But I can't tell you what's up, not right now. It's Fahad-connected and I desperately need to shift it. Do anything William says. Keep me close in your heart –'

Ahmed clicked off. He stood stock-still. It was pointless just rushing out the door. Think, think, he told himself, staring at his blacked-out laptop screen.

It jogged his memory. He'd been close to a productive thought, just as Nattie was arriving the night before . . . It had been an idea about Fahad wanting his own vantage point, a place where he could see for himself all the action as he pressed the fatal button. And that he'd need to be on high ground, a safe distance away and somewhere where it was easy to check the direction of the wind.

Google Earth might just give a lead. Ahmed sprang to his laptop, full of agitated hope. He logged on, zooming in on streets and areas as fast as his fingers could move, poring over open land, any location he could find. He looked everywhere beyond a three-mile radius of the Southampton stadium that seemed remotely possible.

There were parks close to the stadium, one right next door to it, another about four hundred yards away. They had to be discounted. Too close and there was also the wind factor. It was cold enough to be easterly, Ahmed thought, although knowing little about it, and both parks were to the west. The wind would carry a cloud of High Level Waste, the lethal fallout, that would envelop both parks – and certainly Fahad.

Ahmed looked further afield, momentarily distracted by another surging roar coming from the television. From the singing and chanting it had to be a Liverpool goal. He let the thought pass his mind that Osborne would rather have forgone that goal than be keeping company with a radioactive bomb.

He concentrated on his screen and the lie of the land. To the immediate east there was an estuary and just beyond it was what looked like a vast boatyard. A railway line bordered the boatyard. Well beyond that was what seemed to be another park, a large one; it looked more like common land and raised; it seemed to have a gentle incline. It was criss-crossed with paths and from the aerial photographs Ahmed wondered if it had once been sand dunes. It was in the right direction, assuming the wind was easterly, and generally far enough away to ensure no fallout should reach it.

It looked just the spot from which to view the scene of an incomprehensible atrocity without being irradiated oneself. Was Fahad there now, watching? Was he preparing to gaze on in orgasmic satisfaction as thirty thousand cheering people lost their lives? They would suffer terribly and their families' pain wouldn't end. And there were all those living within the three-mile radius who faced possible death as well. Did the hotel, the very room he was in, come into that radius?

He shook himself. That was a pointless shameful thought. He was already in his jacket and checking the pockets for his recording machine, the mobile jammer, the car key and room key. Then, with one last look round that only made him think of Nattie and remember that he hadn't given her the present, he went shooting out of the door.

Ahmed had local maps with him provided by the hotel and had made careful note of street names before he left. He found the area in ten minutes – driving the hire car through Southampton's suburbs in a way that had elderly locals shaking their fists – and drew up in a lane bordering the park. He stayed by the car a moment, peering across at a path leading up the hill. Litter was blowing around; it looked a desolate place on a chill wintry December afternoon.

A couple of people were leaving with their dogs, wandering down a path towards him, crossing the road.

Ahmed's gut felt sucked in right to his backbone, his whole body was taut as a drum. But his terror, now that he was at the moment of truth, seemed curiously on hold. If he were right and Fahad was up on the high ground, to go face to face with him was certain to mean being shot or killed some way, and yet he felt completely in control. There was a job to be done. He understood how soldiers could go back into the firing line to rescue a wounded comrade; thoughts of self could just disappear when circumstances compel.

He took the facing path with his eyes darting keenly around. The park had something of the appearance of Primrose Hill, although on a much larger scale and with more trees.

The sky had clouded. It was mid-afternoon and yet there was already a feeling of approaching twilight. Had they turned on the lights at the stadium? He couldn't bring himself to turn and glance. Ahmed carried on up the path; it was climbing, it should lead to Fahad if he was at the highest point. The land had become more open, he was leaving the copse of trees behind and feeling more and more exposed.

There was a figure ahead. Medium height, stockily built. Ahmed stared hard in the hazy light; his mind, his senses, were all as sharp as though he were hanging out from a cliff-face. It was Fahad. He was in a light-coloured zipped-up fleece; easy to spot, standing there confidently, gazing in Ahmed's direction, although out beyond.

Ahmed glanced back over his shoulder, the way Fahad was looking, and saw the lights of the stadium. They showed bright, the daylight really beginning to fade. Nattie was in there . . . His hand went to his pocket to switch on the jammer. Would the thing work? If Fahad shot him, would he find it and turn it off?

Carrying on closer he slipped a thumb into his top pocket to press the record button; Fahad could get rid of that too . . . His gun would have a silencer, but perhaps he'd be in a hurry to get away from a slumped body. There was always hope . . .

'Clever, aren't you?' Fahad sneered, when there was no more than ten yards between them. 'We could have used a sharp mind like yours.'

'Who's "we"? You seemed to work very much alone,' Ahmed said, which received no answer. He was close enough to see Fahad's unfathomable dark eyes scanning anxiously behind him. 'Don't worry,' he went on neutrally, with inward bitterness, 'I've got no entourage. I'm not a trusted agent working for the authorities, there's only me. Just tell me, though – what you can possibly, conceivably, hope to achieve?'

'I expect you're unarmed,' Fahad said, not bothering to answer again. There was that clearly remembered cold gleam of absolute ruthlessness showing in his confident gaze. 'You're a disloyal traitor, but spineless, wrapped up in your pathetic sense of virtue. You're powerless, your imminent death will go unnoticed. Unlike all those *Kafir* bastards you've sold out to – all that crowd down there will go out in style. This will be bigger than 9/11. They're all ants on the path to the grand plan, serving Allah's purpose. Well, does that answer your question?'

The man was crazed. Had he not considered that Ahmed had influential mobile numbers, that masts could be being turned off even now? Were they though? Was it all going to be in vain? He was going to die, Ahmed thought, but couldn't Nattie be saved?

'How did you do it?' he asked, knowing his only hope was to keep Fahad talking. 'Perhaps you'd allow me to die knowing. It was masterly planning – just one tiny slip that finally gave me the steer, your mention of the Home Secretary at football matches, but that only came to me after the start of the game.'

'That wasn't a slip,' Fahad said hostilely. 'It was to test your reaction. You'd half defended that woman. She's Home Secretary, our enemy, attacking cells, banging up the brothers, and yet you couldn't easily say so. I knew then you were a sham.'

Fahad's smile was pure evil; the white of his teeth showed. His hand was flexing in his pocket, closing round a gun? Would he then disable the jammer and bring out his mobile?

'You said "we".' Ahmed repeated his earlier question. 'Was that Yazid and Iqbal? Or outside aid – um, AK suppliers?'

'The money comes from home.'

Ahmed thought of Britain as home; it was his birthplace. He carried on, he had to keep Fahad talking. 'But how could you possibly hide that canister with all the road checks?'

'Clever, wasn't it?' Fahad's feathers were puffed, he was preening like a strutting bird. 'The two inflatable boats did the trick – not for all that long, but long enough. We were forty miles away in Carnforth and had a large industrial caterer's van standing by. It was full of barrels of hydrogenated vegetable oil; the canister fitted inside one of them, a bit more snugly than I'd have liked, but the oil covered it. We were away in no time; the search was going on miles up the coast.'

Ahmed stared. 'And the bomb?' He knew. It would be in a drum of oil . . .

Fahad's face filled with demented pride. 'It's nestling invisibly in thick opaque hydrogenated cooking oil; in the kitchens – a floor below the directors' box. The driver who delivered it knew nothing.'

'Why?'

'Why? What a question! I despise them all, patronizing *Kafir* scum. Amoral, sluttish – you think you'll ever be accepted? I was a brilliant student and even my tutors damned me with faint praise. I'm going to see this country under Islamic rule; it's going to happen. I live for the day.'

'What about the Leicester Square bomb? Did you mastermind that, too?'

'Oh yes. I saw the potential in Kamran Yousuf, just as for a brief moment I imagined it might be there in you. I helped that boy find himself, trained him. The Home Secretary's name was wrongly on an acceptance list, that bomb was for her.

'It's different today. This time I know she's there—' The gun was in his pocket, the smile of anticipation on his face unmasked. He looked transparently, triumphantly evil, as he brought it out.

Ahmed didn't flinch. 'I've known love,' he said, 'such as you never will – just like you'll never—'

A shot rang out, but it came from elsewhere. The blood froze in Ahmed's veins. He saw the triumph slide from Fahad's elated crazed face. His gun-holding arm convulsed, but his finger was still on the trigger and as the gun drooped, with the involuntary jerking motion, it was released.

The pain, the agony, the burning made his upper thigh feel on fire; Ahmed crumpled to the ground. His eyes were squeezed tight, but he saw Fahad scrabbling, trying to reach the gun with his left hand. Ahmed tried to kick it clear with his right foot, but didn't have the strength to edge near enough.

And then they were surrounded; by men in black combats. Marksmen, he thought disbelievingly, with high velocity rifles.

Thoughts flowed through Ahmed's dazed mind like clouds in the sky. They'd known where he was, which hotel . . . Must have had him followed . . . They'd left it a bit late, he thought, smiling through his pain.

He was sliding out of consciousness. Voices were telling him to lie still. An ambulance was on its way.

Nattie must be safe, he thought – everyone at the ground.

'What's the score?' he asked one of the ambulance men drowsily.

'One-one, mate – so far. It's still going on.'

CHAPTER 32

'William, why can't you say what's up? I can't stand this.' Nattie had to whisper loudly over the crowd. 'Mum's been on the phone almost the whole match – they'll be on about her empty place, thinking you've had a great row or something. It's Fahad connected, isn't it?' She looked at William, feeling fear in her heart. 'That's what I got from Ahmed, but he hung up on me in a great state, in a fantastic rush.'

'Quite right. If he's trying to save the world he can't be hanging about.'

Her heart kept on beating fast. 'Don't come all that,' she hissed. 'You're dreadfully on edge, I can tell. You can't deny it. It's something really big, that's obvious, and you owe it to me to say. If Ahmed's gone after Fahad he could be in danger of his life.'

'No more than the rest of us – this is pathetic play by Liverpool, so defensive. *Come on the Reds!*' William's attempt to divert her was transparent. Nattie was in despair.

She sat watching without seeing, chewing on her lip. Her mother was still out in the directors' lounge making calls . . . Did she need a landline? Was it that serious? It was hardly routine Home Office business, on a Saturday and so close to Christmas . . .

Tom was sitting the far side of Victoria's empty seat and feeling it too, Nattie thought, looking knotted-up and nervy. They exchanged a rolled-eye glance. The tension was palpable.

He leaned and spoke urgently to his father, having a go at him as well, she thought.

Nattie tried Ahmed's mobile in desperation, knowing it could be a wrong move. It was dead – surely not out of juice? William was fidgeting, constantly glancing at his watch. He sprang up suddenly, and disappeared out to the lounge. He was only away minutes then, returning to his seat, beckoned her close. He was grinning as if his horse had just romped in. 'There's been a bit of a panic on, but I think, thanks to Ahmed, we're all going to live. Can't say more now, you're just going to have to be patient, Nattie love, and watch the match. Only ten minutes left.'

Victoria came back to her seat and William squeezed her hand covertly, but then held on to it, as though his need of contact was just too great. Nattie had no one's hand to hold on to. She felt demented with fear. If Ahmed had gone after Fahad, anything could have happened to him. Her impatience had reached an intolerable peak; she was at screaming point. Three minutes of stoppage time was given and she had to squeeze her eyes tight shut to stop the tears. It was cruel.

Into the last minute her mother began looking round for Rodney. She whispered her thanks to directors, smiled at another local MP. Then suddenly the visiting fans went berserk; Liverpool had scored. It was only a goal, Nattie thought desperately, you'd think it was a gladiator kill. Did they have to cheer for quite so long? She tried Ahmed's mobile again. Not a squeak.

Driving away from St Mary's Stadium she still had to wait. Her mother and William were in the car in front, she and Tom travelling behind with Charles and Mark, the backup detective and driver. It was the first time Nattie had felt grateful for her mother's Home Secretary treatment; they were whisked away in a flash.

She was sitting in the back drumming her fingers. There was sweat on Charles's and Mark's brows, she noticed, and from their shared looks of deliverance and release it was the sweat of relief; they might have just leaped clear of a crocodile's open jaws, she thought.

It was suddenly obvious. Suddenly she knew. William hadn't been joking, saying facetiously more than once that they were all going to live: he'd told her the literal truth.

'There really was a bomb in the stadium, wasn't there, Charles?' she asked innocently.

'Not was – still is! The sooner we put a few miles' distance between us and that place—' Charles meant it; he was white as chalk, his hair sticking to his clammy forehead.

Nattie's thoughts began whirling. After weeks of being warned, Ahmed's determined concentrated focus on it all, the very real threat of a great swathe of annihilation, yet even faced with the terrible reality that had just been averted it still seemed beyond comprehension. Tom, sitting beside her, was silent; she wondered if he was in shock and whether it was about to hit her, too.

Ahmed had been desperate to be one step ahead of Fahad, but had he achieved it? Did anyone know if he was dead or alive; dying, lying in agony? Nattie's fury at William for playing it down and trying to shield her – and Tom – was blind. She couldn't rationalize and simply feel grateful.

They were headed straight for the main police station where her mother hurried in with Rodney. There was a bit of chat between Charles and the police drivers then William came over to their car.

'Shifty up, Mum'll be in there a fair while and we're being given a lift home.'

He spent the brief journey keenly quizzing Mark the driver, asking questions about the finding and dealing with the bomb. Did he *always* have to be thinking about the bloody paper? Nattie felt seething with white-hot anger. 'For God's sake,' she muttered, 'I need to know about Ahmed.'

William put his arm round her. 'He was prepared to die for you,' he whispered. 'That should make you feel better. He's been taken to hospital, shot in the thigh, I think, but Mum's going to call as soon as poss with more info. She knows how you're feeling.'

Arriving home Nattie burst out of the car, desperate for the privacy of indoors. The dark, the heavy twilight, felt malevolent, like the kind of bad dream where running from some terrible evil fate gets you nowhere. It was cold as night too, even at four in the afternoon, and with a bone-chilling wind. 'It's bitter, this easterly wind,' Mark remarked, taking his leave of them. 'Cuts in like a saw.'

The front door clicked solidly closed and William leaned back against it, shutting his eyes a moment, and letting out a long sigh. 'That was tight,' he said, as though he, too, had just escaped some gnashing killer jaws. Straightening up he talked over his shoulder, making his way to the kitchen. 'Mum had urgent calls, a lot to thrash out with MI5. She had to speak to the PM.' Turning on a cheering flood of light he went on, 'She'll want to thank the combat team, phone a few others—'

'I don't want to hear about Mum's fucking calls,' Nattie shouted, in her molten lava of heated fury, following in. She stopped short, absorbing what he'd just said. 'What combat team? Whatever's happened, for God's sake? Can't you just tell us, straight? Do you think we're so lily-livered we can't handle it? I'm frantic to know about Ahmed.' William had been bearing all the strain, she thought suddenly, doing his all. 'Sorry,' she muttered, absorbing how ashen and sapped he looked. 'I know you were only trying to protect us.'

'I couldn't have told you much,' he said, with understanding eyes. 'I didn't know if Ahmed was dead or alive, if the bomb would go off before the mobile masts could be shut down and we'd all be done for . . . I've only just caught up a bit more now – with Mum in the car.'

Tom had followed in, he was beside Nattie, listening and William pulled them both close for an emotional embrace.

She felt more shattered than ever to think what Ahmed had been through. The horror was slowly sinking in. It sapped her resistance and she burst into tears. Angry tears at herself: Ahmed could be sinking fast and she wasn't even at his side.

Her stepfather was there for her. 'We'll have you at the hospital in no time, Nattie,' he said gently. 'I'll take you. I need to see him, too. But Mum's about to tell us more and he'll be in theatre right now, being patched up, I'm sure. The bleeding will need to be sealed, all the dirt and bits of trouser fibres cleaned out . . . Don't look like that! The doctors do know what they're doing.'

Ahmed was in a side room. 'The police requested it,' a nurse said, showing Nattie and William the way; she had a tired, pinched, middle-aged face and looked flustered. The hospital had an understaffed air, just before Christmas. 'You really mustn't stay long. He's lost a lot of blood and will be in considerable pain. Conscious, but not up to visitors.'

'Just tell me he is going to be all right—'

The nurse heard the love and desperation; she slowed in her tracks and looked at Nattie curiously. 'Oh yes, he really should be. It's just that with holes as big as a bullet channel, the body has a nasty habit of thinking you want them kept open. It went in his outer thigh, which is packed with muscles, the best possible place, and straight out the other side. He's very lucky. That bullet could have shattered the bone or spliced a major artery.'

She smiled then and added surprisingly, opening up, 'I used to do a bit of handgun practice; it was quite a hobby of mine. I'd guess it was a Walther PPK made that wound.'

'We can see he's in wonderful hands,' William said silkily.

He had powerful appeal, yet for once it seemed to miss the mark. Nattie thought the hospital might have had a few run-ins with the press. The nurse had recognized him – people did with his television programme – and she looked deeply mistrustful. 'The police,' she said primly, 'have been warning about an invasion of media. I really must ask you not to stay long.'

Ahmed was propped up on stiff white pillows; his eyes looked sunken, his face shaded with dark gaunt hollows. Nattie leaned to kiss him feeling wobbly-kneed. It was a miracle to have found him in the first place and he hadn't been taken away. There was a God. She sat close on the bed and put her cheek to his. It felt cold; he was very weak. His hand found hers, though, which he squeezed so tight her fingers felt crushed.

Sensing his tension, embarrassment at the physical show in front of his boss, Nattie sat back with a smile. She was tuned into Ahmed's shyness at the smallest public display. It was his parents' doing, he'd said, reticence drummed in at an early age.

'You're going to have to get used to being a hero, Ahmed.' William had come closer to stand by Nattie; he was wearing a broad grin. 'It's one thing to save your girlfriend, but her mother, her brother, your boss and thirty thousand football fans as well, that's going some.'

Ahmed looked agonized, on top of his pain. 'I don't want anyone to know, certainly no fuss. There are people who'd think I'd turned traitor . . . It's a loyalty thing. And I should have got there a whole lot sooner anyhow – I feel dreadful.'

'Don't be funny. It has to come out; you can't possibly avoid it. Questions will be asked. Fahad will stand trial, your tape used in evidence – you might wish that crack-shot marksman had polished him off, which would have saved all that, but he didn't.'

'Why not? I could have done without Fahad trying to grab that gun again.' Ahmed gave a wan smile.

'The police must be terrified of potting the wrong guy these days,' William replied. 'Or just showing off their aim! You'll want to be alone with Nattie now, I know. I'll leave you and be off, but we will need to have a proper talk soon.'

'I'm afraid there's the hire car,' Ahmed called, sounding agitated. 'It's still parked near that open land. And my laptop's at the hotel. There's the other hotel I'd booked—'

'The police have picked up the car, the laptop; everything's seen to. Oh, and Tom's looking in, just for a minute; he wants to. He's on his way to his mother's for Christmas, but he'll run you back first, Nats. You can't hang about here, much as you'd love to, or that cross-with-me nurse will be barring you from the door – and I need my hero reporter in good nick and reporting back for work soon.'

Alone with Ahmed at last, Nattie felt more tears trickling out. His eyes held a desperate, hungry look in his drawn, pallid face. So deep with pain, they seemed to reflect the depth of the abyss they had all looked into – and stepped back from just in time.

'Don't, Nattie,' he pleaded, 'I can't stand to see you cry. It's over. When I thought that whole stadium was about to go up in smoke . . . I couldn't cope, I had a collapse and knew all about hell. I couldn't lose you, there'd have been nothing left. But there's everything, now.'

She thought of him walking up to Fahad, quite prepared for his life to be taken and the tears poured. He held her close, but she could feel it causing him extra pain and sat back with a tearful gaze. 'I'll be here first thing in the morning,' she said. 'And you're certainly not having Christmas here alone in this hospital, I'm not leaving your side. It'll be just us, special—'

Ahmed kept softly wiping at her tears with his finger. 'No, you're not doing that; I won't allow it. Come tomorrow, but then I want you with your family and wonderful grandparents for Christmas. My parents will be down from Leeds. I've got things I need to think through. It really is best.' He looked firm and set. She had to give in.

Home from the hospital Nattie felt shaky. Lonely too, and bleak; it was over, as Ahmed had said, but she had an extraordinary grim sense of her life collapsing all around her, of everything going wrong, which was mystifying since in reality it had just been put right.

The full shock of it all was setting in as well, and exhaustion piling on the bleakness. 'I feel really down,' she confided to Tom. 'Scared. Only half the real me – it's weird.'

Tom had put off driving to Somerset till morning, Victoria had refused to let him go that night – not after all they'd just been through, she insisted. Rather brave of her, Nattie thought, since it was keeping him from Ursula, his own mother.

It was hard to worry about Tom for long, struggling with her own low mood, clutched at by fears for Ahmed. And William had just exacerbated those. He'd asked for her help in persuading Ahmed to give the interview for the paper.

Returning from the hospital she'd explained to William about wanting to spend Christmas Eve there, but that Ahmed had insisted she was with the family in Worcester on the day.

'It's how to get there,' she said, 'not an easy evening journey from Southampton.'

'You can have my car. I'll be going with Mum. Although in return I want you to warm up Ahmed. He can't get out of doing that big interview; no getting away with being an unsung hero, you can tell him – no chance.'

Nattie had promised to do her best, while feeling wrapped in a cloak of disquiet. William was right, Ahmed's heroic role was going to come out, but remembering his consternation, his fear of the consequences of an interview, she felt torn in two.

What about other terrorists, the terrorist sympathizers? Personal publicity would only angle the spotlight. Did Ahmed have to go about in fear of his life like a man who'd refused to be blackmailed?

Perhaps there was a compromise. Ahmed would have more control, doing an interview. He could put his own slant on things, minimize his role, talk of trying to use persuasion with Fahad, play up the bold daring and success of the police. William wouldn't be happy, but he couldn't get mad when Ahmed had saved his life.

She could hear William in his study on a heated call, probably to his deputy about tomorrow's dramatic paper. He was always on at him and being scathing.

He came looking for her a while later. 'The police have Ahmed's laptop, but I got them to email me his work on the Leena story. I've just been reading it and it's left me reeling. We'll be running that story,' William said, his face looking implacably set. 'Not just yet, best let the dust settle over Ahmed, but Leena's father and brother will be paying the price, you can be sure.' Nattie felt intense relief; she knew what that would mean to Ahmed.

Time was hanging heavy. Victoria had shot off to Chequers to brief the PM and do a host of media interviews – but not before finding time for a private and revealing talk with her daughter.

It had been warm and reuniting. However, Nattie felt even less able to fathom her own bleakness, which in some way seemed connected with Ahmed. She tried, not very successfully, to shut out the irrational feelings of insecurity.

The talk with her mother was on her mind as well. She had started off cautiously. 'I hope you'll understand, Nattie darling, if I try to explain why things had to be as they were. Remember telling me once about one of Ahmed's contacts taking his life in a way to look like an accident?'

'Yes: Khalid. It was the pressure he was under from the terrorists and his devout belief that finally made him leap in front of that truck,' Nattie emphasized. 'Ahmed will never let on about it, of course. He thinks Khalid probably felt a marked man anyway, for deserting the cell, which encouraged him to take that desperate path.'

Her mother had looked moved and saddened. 'Well, I'm afraid his death fired MI5's suspicions about Ahmed,' she continued. 'They knew suicide is taboo in the faith and Ahmed *had* been walking right beside Khalid . . . They were already tapping his phone, given all he'd told William – which I knew, as I do have to sanction all intercepts – although that was more in the hope he'd lead them down new avenues.'

'Where's this going, Mum?'

'Give me a second. It's just that MI5 don't need my say-so to put someone under surveillance, and after Khalid's death they decided to have Ahmed followed.'

'So *that's* how the marksmen could have got there quite so fast!' Nattie exclaimed, grateful to have one mystery solved.

'Exactly. Whatever your views about MI5's caution and lack of trust – which put me in an impossible situation – it did save Ahmed's life.'

'And all of ours, I suppose,' Nattie said, thinking that Ahmed had led them there; he was the real hero.

'No. Ahmed had done that already. He'd called William and left him in no doubt of the seriousness of the risk. And his phone was being tapped, remember; MI5 heard that call. They checked with me and we were able to get the mobile masts switched off pretty quickly.'

Victoria had rushed off after that, leaving Nattie swollen with love and pride, shedding buckets of tears. She soon recovered and decided that since her mother wasn't likely to be back before nine, cooking supper was the most usefully preoccupying thing she could do.

After calling the hospital, though. She was put through to Ahmed; the staff had to, she made enough fuss. He left her in no doubt of his love and Nattie set about the meal in a lifted mood. She smiled. He would have mixed feelings when she told him next morning about being tailed by MI5 . . .

Chicken breasts and leeks cooked in consommé and cream, Nattie decided; something that shouldn't dry out if her mother was late.

Thinking of recipes put her father in mind; she needed to call him since with Ahmed in hospital she wouldn't be going to Cornwall.

She felt braced for a difficult time: anxious he shouldn't take it as a slight and imagine she couldn't face coming, sure he'd be the worse for wear. 'Sorry, Dad, it's just with everything that's happened . . . it might anyway be easier to see you in London.' She tried to explain in more detail, but could tell he really wasn't tuned in.

'Any place, any time, Angel; always love to see you. Means the world to me. I'm still in London actually, driving down to Grandpops tomorrow. It was the office party last night. I threw myself into it since I won't be seeing any of them for a few weeks – I'm off to Mum's place right in the New Year, you'll be pleased to hear – but it did mean I slept in most of today! Who won the Liverpool–Southampton game? You've jumped ship, haven't you, and deserted the home team? Fickle in football – but not, I hope, in love!'

'It was a draw, Dad. It was quite an eventful match.'

Nattie enjoyed her mother's pleasure at coming home pretty wrung out to find a hot meal ready and waiting – along with her comparatively patient family.

The food and wine helped them all to unwind. 'Christmas is looking up,' William said with feeling. 'I thought between you, Nattie, and your mother's neuroses – she's been seeing bomb-shapes in her muesli – it was going to be like one of those sitcom scenes with even the dog in the doldrums.'

'I didn't expect to find a real bomb in the cooking oil! Such thick stuff, the thing absolutely couldn't be seen. We think someone in the kitchens knew to receive it; the barrel was stored inaccessibly and one of the cooks left early saying he felt ill.'

Nattie wondered whether that man could possibly have been Iqbal.

'Might that be why Fahad waited before pressing the button?' Tom asked. 'To give the man time to get away?'

'I shouldn't think he would have cared if the man lived or died. We've discovered a few facts about Fahad.' She might have just propositioned her husband. William was all ears instantly, while trying hard to hide his obsessive interest. Nattie didn't have a newspaper to fill, but she was pretty keen to know, too.

'Too late for you to use any of this tonight, William,' Victoria said with an amused gleam. 'Fahad's real name is Kanwar Hussein. He's an economist, working for Camden Council. Very respectable by all appearances; married, one son. He didn't mix much, according to someone at the council, but had talked of a love of the Lakes. He'd have been impossible to pick up—'

'When I saw Ahmed tonight,' Tom chipped in, 'he said Fahad had talked about the money coming from abroad.'

'I know,' Victoria replied. 'Thanks to Ahmed's recording machine it's all on tape. And Fahad's been talking. Not about that, but he's quite compos mentis with only a wounded arm, thanks to that brilliant marksmanship, and knows we have the tape. He seems to see no point in not bragging. The man Ahmed knew as Haroon, was working at Sellafield, it appears, and was the one who leaked the crucial facts. Fahad has apparently insisted we'll never get him, though, and said he's already working on the next attack.' She sighed. 'It's going to be a long haul, the battle against terrorism, home grown terrorists . . .'

They all fell silent. Nattie was dwelling on the weeks and months ahead; there were people who'd want to see Ahmed eliminated. The threat would always be there. She felt, too, the weight of the world on her exhausted mother's shoulders and, catching her eye, shared a look of understanding love.

Ahmed had a string of visitors during his few days in hospital. It seemed to Nattie they hardly had a minute of quality time alone together.

Safa came, and brought Leena. It was all a bit shy and awkward. Nattie had felt slightly threatened by Safa. It was obvious how much Ahmed liked her, yet she could see now it was as a friend and confidante. One thing the bomb had achieved, Nattie thought, was to shore up her confidence in Ahmed's love. Despite her unsettled sense of something at odds, it felt sandbagged, solidly walled; they were an item, a single indivisible unit.

Even Desmond, the news editor, looked in. 'Just visiting me old mum who's in a nursing home near here,' he explained gruffly. 'Time you were back at your desk, young man. All this laying about won't do.'

CHAPTER 33

Ahmed was soon back at his desk – just a week later. His interview had appeared the day after Boxing Day, along with a photograph taken in hospital. He'd been a difficult interviewee and taken Nattie's advice a stage too far, she decided, making as clear as day his extreme discomfort with the idea of himself as saviour. The police deserved all the credit, he insisted; he'd done nothing, only uselessly tried to persuade a man bent on destruction not to press the button.

William had got his oar in first, however, lavishly praising Ahmed, describing in the paper's thin Christmas Eve and Boxing Day editions the fearless way he'd been prepared to die to save the lives of others.

Nattie had tried to calm Ahmed down over that. Hardly anyone read newspapers over Christmas, she said, but he'd argued miserably that far too many did and he couldn't bear the fuss. He was almost glad to be in hospital, he grumbled, since it made it easier to refuse all other interviews. No television cameras had got near him.

Nattie had slept at home the previous night, the eve of his going back to work, partly out of deference to Jake. She was mooching about the empty house, worrying about Ahmed's condition. It was far too soon for him to be back at his desk.

He called late morning to make plans for that night. 'Jake's out and I want us to have a special evening at the flat. I still have to give you my little present.'

'And me, too! I've had to wait an age with you not wanting it at the hospital.'

'No cooking tonight,' Ahmed said. 'We'll order in.'

Nattie felt uncomfortable; there had been an unusual intensity in his tone. He wanted to talk, she thought. Was he going to propose? He said often enough she was his whole life.

There were flowers in the flat. Narcissi and daffodils, they seemed earlier every year. Ahmed made love to her as soon as she arrived. Gentle love. She suspected it would have been gentle even had the wound in his leg not been painfully far from being healed. He seemed in that sort of mood. And he said beautiful things, whispering lines of a verse he'd quoted very early on in their relationship. 'Once I was not mine own at all . . . and then I was in love . . .'

Afterwards they sat close on the sofa, drank some Sauvignon and ordered in a pizza.

'This is my present for you.' Nattie fished in her handbag and handed it over before the food arrived. 'I've waited long enough to give it!' She watched as he snapped open the small box. 'I hope it's okay.' She felt anxious; it was an off-beam sort of a present. 'It's a gold signet ring, an old one – Grandpa's got one like it. I've had AK put on it, but it doesn't stand out too much, I hope – not so as it's obvious. I don't expect you to wear it, I know it's not the thing or even really retro or what people usually give, but it was just my need to find a sort of present to last, something from me to you, to keep.'

'It's perfect.' Ahmed was crying, she saw. She'd never seen him cry. He smiled then and put it on. She'd had plenty of opportunity to study his hands, secretly comparing them to hers, and felt confident that since it fitted her wedding-ring finger it should be fine on his little one. It seemed to fit perfectly.

He was feeling it, rubbing it, still overcome; the pain was making him emotional, probably, after a long first day. He reached for a wrapped larger box on the side table. 'My present,' he said. 'I wanted something that was you, and seeing this made me think of your eyes. I hope you'll like it. It'll help me, to think of you wearing it.'

She undid the wrapping, took it out and the deep gold stone caught the light. He wouldn't let her speak. He put it round her neck, put his lips to hers then took both her hands in his. 'Nattie darling, I'm going to America. I'm going to work for *The Post*, be on the New York bureau there for the next year or so – no, don't say anything, let me finish.' He put his fingers over her lips.

'I've thought hard about it and I know it's for the best. I've talked to William, it's all being arranged. I'll be just a bit safer there – but that's the very least of it. What I really do know in my heart is that you should have time to breathe. You are only nineteen. I love you too much. If I married you now as I long to, there would be difficulties, believe me. It might not last and I couldn't bear that; it would be the end of all life – and I've been there already, when I thought I'd lose you to a bomb. I couldn't go there again, it would kill me. Far, far better you finish your degree, meet people, have boyfriends, see how—'

'Stop, stop, I'm not listening,' Nattie put her hands tight to her ears.

'Yes, you are. If, after your degree, you felt just the same way—'

She took away her hands and clenched them tight. 'I'll come to New York. I'll find a job there; you couldn't stop me – if you want me to get my degree, you're going about it all the wrong way.' Her heart was beating like a piston; he couldn't do it to her, she couldn't live without him. All that outpouring of love, all the emotional investment, the caring, the trust – and he could believe she'd go off him? It was unreal.

'Prove me wrong, Nattie. I think you should understand that I do want to marry you, otherwise I'd just be taking all I could get; making the most of you, living for now. It's not like that. I know I run the risk that you'll end up with someone else and I'd have a flat loveless life. I'd rather that risk, though, than have it all go wrong on us and life be just as loveless, only with bitterness thrown in.'

'And I run the risk of you being pressured into marrying to please your parents or falling for someone else in all this time you're so determined to be away from me. I don't want to take that risk and I've got nothing to prove. Why shouldn't my wants count just as much as yours?' Nattie glowered at him, before her lip started to tremble and she had to look away.

'Because I'm older and a man . . . And I know what's best for you. So there!' He picked up her chin and turned her face to him. 'Can I kiss you, Nattie?'

As their lips touched and she looked into his eyes she broke down. She shook with the most violent sobs; his arms tight around her couldn't stop them. 'Jake's cross with me too,' he murmured, smoothing her hair, 'you're not the only one. He'll find a friend to take the room, though, I'm sure. Will you stay here tonight? Can we have this next last week together before I go?'

She thought about the pain they would share, living a week together to last more than a year, the agony of waving him away; seeing him disappear beyond the departure gate. She wanted him to have that agony. She wanted Ahmed to regret every second all week, wanted to see him cry again at the airport; she wanted him to board that plane to New York tasting the salt of their mingled tears.

Would she be able to make him change his mind? That seemed unlikely and her shoulders gently heaved.

'There's Hugo,' Ahmed went on, still with his arm round her, his free hand smoothing her hair. 'He needs looking after. I know you want to help him get clean and you're the one person who could. He loves you, that was obvious, glaringly so, the time I met him when we were taking back Tom's car. And you might find, if he'd pulled through and was the old Hugo again, the one you had a relationship with, that there was a reignited spark –'

Nattie flung off Ahmed's arm and sat bolt upright. She moved away to be able to stare him furiously in the eye. The rage in her almost made her want to strike out.

'I don't love Hugo,' she yelled. 'Can't you get that in your thick head once and for all?'

Ahmed stared back challengingly. 'You're warm when you speak of him. You still wear his watch—'

Nattie felt she'd explode. She undid the watchstrap with fumbling fingers and hurled the thing at the wall. 'I've got to tell the time, haven't I?' She kept up her furious gaze, feeling guilty at hanging on to a watch she loved without a care for Ahmed's feelings, yet still trembling with rage. 'Well?' She stuck out her jaw.

The watch had fallen short of the wall. Ahmed got up, retrieved it from the carpet and stood holding it out. The pain from his injury was clear in his face. 'You're right, you do need to tell the time,' he smiled. 'You can't be late for all those lectures. It is still ticking . . .'

Nattie sprang to her feet. She grabbed it from him and strode to one of the sash windows. Resting Hugo's watch on the sill, she wrestled with the catch and needed all her strength to fling it open. She threw out the watch, following its fall, down two floors, to where it landed in the gutter in the street below. Then she turned and said with a look of triumph, 'Well, it's not ticking now. I don't love Hugo and I never will. I love you.'

They were fighting, was that a good sign? She felt calmer. She would prove it from her side, that would be no problem. But what about him?

'I guess you want your freedom,' she said flatly, all the fight draining out of her. The desolation, though, was there to stay.

It was Ahmed's turn to rage. 'How can you say that? It's a vacuum, not freedom – the very opposite. It's a lonely cage.'

'Well, I'm here if you ever want to come home and settle down,' Nattie muttered.

Then they were kissing, clinging, shuffling back to the sofa. 'You're not meant to be standing,' she whispered. 'Who's going to look after you in an alien country? If I was to call would you put the phone down on me?'

Ahmed's tears were streaming while her tears had dried. It took him a time to collect himself, then he said, gulping, wiping apologetically at his eyes, 'I'd never put the phone down on you. Emails would make me feel looked after – and loved . . . I'll be working hard, writing a book. I've got ideas for a television series.'

'I want your dreadful Leeds scarf,' Nattie said. 'It won't mean much to anyone out there. I'll cheer your team on and try to help them survive in the Premier League.'

'Don't get too cocky, we won the other Saturday when I was a bit preoccupied . . .' He picked up her left arm and kissed her naked wrist. 'If we can meet when I finish work tomorrow, will you let me buy you a Swatch watch? It would be no replacement, just . . . something to help you tell the time.'

'I don't want to think about time in our last precious few days. Can you send me one from America? I'd love that. And,' she said, 'I'll send you a calendar so there's no doubt about when the year comes to an end.'

The future was shrouded, banked, shelved; it was biding its time, but there in all its glory, in gay, lively, primary colours waiting to be lived. And for a single scintillating captured moment, Nattie could see it. She could see the way ahead.